Tales of the Occult

ISAAC
ASIMOV
PRESENTS

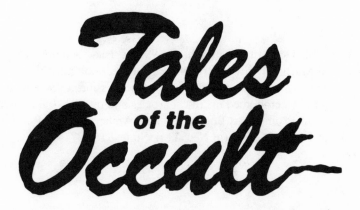

Stories by H. G. Wells, Arthur Conan Doyle, Rudyard Kipling,
Edith Wharton, Edgar Allan Poe, and many others.

EDITED BY
ISAAC ASIMOV, MARTIN H. GREENBERG,
AND CHARLES G. WAUGH

PROMETHEUS BOOKS
700 East Amherst Street, Buffalo, New York 14215

The editors are grateful for Frank D. McSherry's assistance in compiling the lists of additional readings.

Library of Congress Cataloging-in-Publication Data

Tales of the occult / edited by Isaac Asimov, Charles G. Waugh, Martin H. Greenberg.
     p.   cm.
  ISBN 0-87975-506-7
  1. Occultism—Fiction. 2. Fantastic fiction, American.
3. Fantastic fiction, English. I. Asimov, Isaac, 1920-
Waugh, Charles G. III. Greenberg, Martin Harry.
PS648.O33T35   1989
813'.0876'0337—dc19   88-36567
                                    CIP

Table of Contents

Introduction

Isaac Asimov
The Occult

Occult" is from a Latin word meaning "hidden." It is used, in a literal sense, in astronomy. If one astronomical object moves in front of a second, that second object is said to be "occulted" or to undergo an "occultation." Thus the moon can occult the planet Venus, or Venus can occult a star.

In a more familiar sense, however, anything that is hidden from human understanding is considered to be "occult"; and it was customary in the past to suppose that a great many things were so hidden, not only temporarily, but forever. The machinery of the universe about us not only was not understood by human beings but could not be understood by them. Such understanding was the province only of the supernatural knowledge of the gods.

Thus, in the Book of Job, when Job is angered and puzzled over the arbitrary and unfair manner in which evil is inflicted on the just and virtuous, God answers him, finally, not by explaining the reasons for it or by pointing out how matters might seem arbitrary and unjust yet not be so, but only by proclaiming the inborn inability of human beings to understand the occult.

God is quoted as saying: "Where wast thou when I laid the foundations of the earth? . . . Who hath laid the measures thereof, if thou knowest? Or who hath stretched the line upon it? Whereupon are the foundations thereof fastened? or who laid the corner stone thereof? . . . Or who shut up the sea with doors, when it break forth? . . . Hast thou commanded the morning . . . and caused the dayspring to know his place? . . . Hast thou entered into the springs of the sea? or hast thou walked in the search of the depth? . . ."

And so on, and so on, and so on.

So pitiable is my own ignorance that when I first tried to make head or tail of the Book of Job, I grew indignant at God's remarks and thought to myself: But that's no answer. One should enlighten ignorance, not proclaim it triumphantly.

Of course I was young then, but now that I am old I have not changed my mind.

However, back to the occult. There have always been some people who have claimed to understand hidden things, sometimes by revelation from God and sometimes simply by the fact of their own assertions. The occult—things hidden to ordinary observation—also appears in myths and legends.

Now, as a matter of fact, science also deals with the occult in the sense that many of its findings are not accessible to ordinary human beings who make use only of the senses they were born with. No human being, merely by looking at the world about him, listening to it, feeling it, smelling it, tasting it, can possibly know that all matter consists of atoms, that heredity is mediated by DNA molecules, that energy is conserved, that the sun is 93 million miles away, and so on and so on. (The author of the Book of Job might well have had God ask questions about such matters if he himself had had the faintest awareness of the existence of *that* kind of occult.)

The difference between the scientific occult and the nonscientific occult, however, is this. Scientists do their best to explain every step of their findings. No scientific finding is considered valid until it is confirmed by other investigators making use of other instruments in other places, times, and circumstances. Science labors to make as much as possible clear and apparent, and to leave as little as possible hidden and obscure.

Mystics, however, do not attempt to explain, but merely assert. In fact, the last thing they want to do is to explain, since their power rests on the supposed fact that they understand what others cannot; that they have abilities that others do not. In mystery and confusion is their only chance at success.

Oddly enough, it is much easier to believe mystics than it is to believe scientists. Many a person who seriously questions the existence of atoms and who furiously doubts that the speed of light cannot be surpassed accepts UFOs without a murmur and is ready to believe that ghosts exist, that extrasensory perception is a known fact, and so on.

Why is that? Why do people reject the real and fall all over themselves to accept the fake? To me, it seems the answer is that science proclaims the universe to be what it really is, as far as current knowledge will take us. The mystics and charlatans, however, proclaim the universe to be what people want it to be. Given the choice between a cold truth and a desirable lie, which would any person choose who is not totally wedded to rational reality? And what percentage of the human population do you estimate to be totally wedded to rational reality?

Of course if, as a sort of game, we suspend disbelief in the irrational (those of us who have the quirk of rationality), we find that stories about the mystic and occult can often be entertaining. Ghost stories, well told, can be frightening even if you know that ghosts do not exist. Cinderella can touch a deep well of sentiment within us even if we have the notion that fairy godmothers are not to be found. For that matter, we all eagerly believe in happy endings, in the triumph of virtue, in the victory of youth and innocence over age and treachery, and in many other things we find very frequently in fiction and very rarely in real life.

So here we have brought you a wide variety of stories dealing with various forms of the occult, with my brief comments after each.

1

After-Death Experiences

H. G. Wells
Under the Knife

What if I die under it!" The thought recurred again and again as I walked home from Haddon's. It was a purely personal question. I was spared the deep anxieties of a married man, and I knew there were few of my intimate friends but would find my death troublesome chiefly on account of the duty of regret. I was surprised indeed, and perhaps a little humiliated, as I turned the matter over, to think how few could possibly exceed the conventional requirement. Things came before me stripped of glamour, in a clear dry light, during that walk from Haddon's house over Primrose Hill. There were the friends of my youth: I perceived now that our affection was a tradition, which we foregathered rather laboriously to maintain. There were the rivals and helpers of my later career. I suppose I had been cold-blooded or undemonstrative—one perhaps implies the other. It may be that even the capacity for friendship is a question of physique. There had been a time in my own life when I had grieved bitterly enough at the loss of a friend; but as I walked home that afternoon the emotional side of my imagination was dormant. I could not pity myself, nor feel sorry for my friends, nor conceive of them as grieving for me.

I was interested in this deadness of my emotional nature,—no doubt a concomitant of my stagnating physiology; and my thoughts wandered off along the line it suggested. Once before, in my hot youth, I had suffered a sudden loss of blood, and had been within an ace of death. I remembered now that my affections as well as my passions had drained out of me, leaving scarce anything but a tranquil resignation and the faintest dreg of self-pity. It had been weeks before the old ambitions, and tendernesses, and all the complex moral interplay of a man had reasserted themselves. It occurred to me that the real meaning of this numbness might be a gradual slipping away from the pleasure-pain guidance of the animal man. It has been proven, I take it, as thoroughly as anything can be proven in this world, that the higher emotions, the moral feelings, even the subtle tenderness of love, are evolved from the elemental desires and fears of the simple animal: they are the harness in which man's mental freedom goes. And, it may be that, as death overshadows us, as our possibility of acting diminishes, this complex growth of balanced impulse, propensity, and aversion, whose interplay inspired our acts, goes with it. Leaving what?

I was suddenly brought back to reality by an imminent collision with a butcher-boy's tray. I found that I was crossing the bridge over the Regent's Park Canal which runs parallel with the bridge in the Zoölogical Gardens. The boy in blue had been looking over his shoulder at a black barge advancing slowly, towed by a gaunt white horse. In the Gardens a nurse was leading three happy little children over the bridge. The trees were bright green; the spring hopefulness was still unstained by the dusts of summer; the sky in the water was bright and clear, but broken by long waves, by quivering bands of black, as the barge drove through. The breeze was stirring; but it did not stir me as the spring breeze used to do.

Was this dullness of feeling in itself an anticipation? It was curious that I could reason and follow out a network of suggestion as clearly as ever; so, at least, it seemed to me. It was calmness rather than dullness that was coming upon me. Was there any ground for the belief in the presentiment of death? Did a man near to death begin instinctively to withdraw himself from the meshes of matter and sense, even before the cold hand was laid upon his? I felt strangely isolated—isolated without regret—from the life and existence about me. The children playing in the sun and gathering strength and experience for the business of life, the park-keeper gossiping with a nurse-maid, the nursing mother, the young couple intent upon each other as they passed me, the trees by the wayside spreading new pleading leaves to the sunlight, the stir in their branches—I had been part of it all, but I had nearly done with it now.

Some way down the Broad Walk I perceived that I was tired, and that my feet were heavy. It was hot that afternoon, and I turned aside and sat down on one of the green chairs that line the way. In a minute I had dozed into a dream, and the tide of my thoughts washed up a vision of the Resurrection. I was still sitting in the chair, but I thought myself actually dead, withered, tattered, dried, one eye (I saw) pecked out by birds. "Awake!" cried a voice; and incontinently the dust of the path and the mould under the grass became insurgent. I had never before thought of Regent's Park as a cemetery, but now, through the trees, stretching as far as eye could see, I beheld a flat plain of writhing graves and heeling tombstones. There seemed to be some trouble, the rising dead appeared to stifle as they struggled upward, they bled in their struggles, the red flesh was tattered away from the white bones. "Awake!" cried a voice; but I determined I would not rise to such horrors. "Awake!" They would not let me alone. "Wike up!" said an angry voice. A cockney angel! The man who sells the tickets was shaking me, demanding my penny.

I paid my penny, pocketed my ticket, yawned, stretched my legs, and feeling now rather less torpid, got up and walked on towards Langham Place. I speedily lost myself again in a shifting maze of thoughts about death. Going across Marylebone Road into that crescent at the end of Langham Place, I had the narrowest escape from the shaft of a cab, and went on my way with a palpitating heart and a bruised shoulder. It struck me that it would have been curious if my meditations on my death on the morrow had led to my death that day.

But I will not weary you with more of my experiences that day and the next. I knew more and more certainly that I should die under the operation; at times I think I was inclined to pose to myself. The doctors were coming at eleven, and I did not get up. It seemed scarce worthwhile to trouble about washing and dressing, and, though I read my newspapers and the letters that came by the first post, I did not find them very interesting. There was a friendly note from Addison, my old school friend, calling my attention to two discrepancies and a printer's error in my new book; with one from Langridge, venting some vexation over Minton. The rest were business communications. I breakfasted in bed. The glow of pain at my side seemed more massive. I knew it was pain, and yet, if you can understand, I did not find it very painful. I had been awake and hot and thirsty in the night, but in the morning bed felt comfortable. In the night-time I had lain thinking of things that were past; in the morning I dozed over the question of immortality. Haddon came, punctual to the minute, with a neat black bag; and Mowbray soon followed. Their arrival stirred me up a little. I began to take a more personal interest in the proceedings. Haddon moved the little octagonal table close to the bedside, and with his broad black back to me began taking things out of his bag. I heard the light click of steel upon steel. My imagination, I found, was not altogether stagnant. "Will you hurt me much?" I said, in an off-hand tone.

"Not a bit," Haddon answered over his shoulder. "We shall chloroform you. Your heart's as sound as a bell." And, as he spoke, I had a whiff of the pungent sweetness of the anaesthetic.

They stretched me out, with a convenient exposure of my side, and, almost before I realised what was happening, the chloroform was being administered. It stings the nostrils and there is a suffocating sensation, at first. I knew I should die,—that this was the end of consciousness for me. And suddenly I felt that I was not prepared for death; I had a vague sense of a duty overlooked—I knew not what. What was it I had not done?

I could think of nothing more to do, nothing desirable left in life; and yet I had the strangest disinclination to death. And the physical sensation was painfully oppressive. Of course the doctors did not know they were going to kill me. Possibly I struggled. Then I fell motionless, and a great silence, a monstrous silence, and an impenetrable blackness, came upon me.

There must have been an interval of absolute unconsciousness, seconds or minutes. Then, with a chilly, unemotional clearness, I perceived that I was not yet dead. I was still in my body; but all the multitudinous sensations that come sweeping from it to make up the background of consciousness, had gone, leaving me free of it all. No, not free of it all; for as yet something still held me to the poor stark flesh upon the bed, held me, yet not so closely that I did not feel myself external to it, independent of it, straining away from it. I do not think I heard; but I perceived all that was going on, and it was as if I both heard and saw. Haddon was bending over me, Mowbray behind me; the scalpel—it was a large scalpel—was cutting my flesh at the side under the flying ribs. It was interesting to see myself cut like cheese, without a pang, without even a qualm. The interest was much of a quality with that one might feel in a game of chess between strangers. Haddon's face was firm, and his hand steady; but I was surprised to perceive (*how* I know now) that he was feeling the gravest doubt as to his own wisdom in the conduct of the operation.

Mowbray's thoughts, too, I could see. He was thinking that Haddon's manner showed too much of the specialist. New suggestions came up like bubbles through a stream of frothing meditation, and burst one after another in the little bright spot of his consciousness. He could not help noticing and admiring Haddon's swift dexterity, in spite of his envious quality and his disposition to detract. I saw my liver exposed. I was puzzled at my own condition. I did not feel that I was dead, but I was different in some way from my living self. The grey depression that had weighed on me for a year or more, and coloured all my thoughts, was gone. I perceived and thought without any emotional tint at all. I wondered if every one perceived things in this way under chloroform, and forgot it again when he came out of it. It would be inconvenient to look into some heads, and not forget.

Although I did not think that I was dead, I still perceived, quite clearly, that I was soon to die. This brought me back to the consideration of Haddon's proceedings. I looked into his mind, and saw that he was afraid of cutting a branch of the portal vein. My attention was distracted from details by the curious changes going on in his mind. His consciousness was like the quivering little spot of light which is thrown by the mirror of a galvanometer. His thoughts ran under it like a stream, some through the focus bright and distinct, some shadowy in the half-light of the edge. Just now the little glow was steady; but the least movement on Mowbray's part, the slightest sound from outside, even a faint difference in the slow movement of the living flesh he was cutting, set the light-spot shivering and spinning. A new sense-impression came rushing up through the flow of thoughts; and lo! the light-spot jerked away towards it, swifter than a frightened fish. It was wonderful to think that upon that unstable, fitful thing depended all the complex motions of the man, that for the next five minutes, therefore, my life hung upon its movements. And he was growing more and more nervous in his work. It was as if a little picture of a cut vein grew brighter, and struggled to oust from his brain another picture of a cut falling short of the mark. He was afraid: his dread of cutting too little was battling with his dread of cutting too far.

Then, suddenly, like an escape of water from under a lock gate, a great uprush of horrible realisation set all his thoughts swirling, and simultaneously I perceived that the vein was cut. He started back with a hoarse exclamation, and I saw the brown-purple blood gather in a swift bead, and run trickling. He was horrified. He pitched the red-stained scalpel on to the octagonal table; and instantly both doctors flung themselves upon me, making hasty and ill-conceived efforts to remedy the disaster. "Ice," said Mowbray, gasping. But I knew that I was killed, though my body still clung to me.

I will not describe their belated endeavours to save me, though I perceived every detail. My perceptions were sharper and swifter than they had ever been in life; my thoughts rushed through my mind with incredible swiftness, but with perfect definition. I can only compare their crowded clarity to the effects of a reasonable dose of opium. In a moment it would all be over, and I should be free. I knew I was immortal, but what would happen I did not know. Should I drift off presently, like a puff of smoke from a gun, in some kind of half-material body, an attenuated version of my material self? Should I find myself suddenly among the innumerable hosts of the dead, and know the world about me for the phantasmagoria it had always seemed? Should I drift to some spiritualistic *séance,* and there make foolish, incomprehensible attempts to affect a purblind medium? It was a state of unemotional curiosity, of colourless expectation. And then I realised a growing stress upon me, a feeling as though some huge human magnet was drawing me upward out of my body. The stress grew and grew. I seemed an atom, for which monstrous forces were fighting. For one brief, terrible moment sensation came back to me. That feeling of falling headlong which comes in nightmares, that feeling a thousand times intensified, that and a black horror swept across my thoughts in a torrent. Then the two doctors, the naked body with its cut side, the little room, swept away from under me, and vanished as a speck of foam vanishes down an eddy.

I was in mid air. Far below was the West End of London, receding rapidly,—for I seemed to be flying swiftly upward,—and, as it receded, passing westward like a panorama. I could see through the faint haze of smoke the innumerable roofs chimney-set, the narrow roadways stippled with people and conveyances, the little specks of squares, and the church steeples like thorns sticking out of the fabric. But it spun away as the earth rotated on its axis, and in a few seconds (as it seemed) I was over the scattered clumps of town about Ealing, the little Thames a thread of blue to the south, and the Chiltern Hills and the North Downs coming up like the rim of a basin, far away and faint with haze. Up I rushed. And at first I had not the faintest conception what this headlong upward rush could mean.

Every moment the circle of scenery beneath me grew wider and wider, and the details of town and field, of hill and valley, got more and more hazy and pale and indistinct, a luminous grey was mingled more and more with the blue of the hills and the green of the open meadows; and a little patch of cloud, low and far to the west, shone ever more dazzlingly white. Above, as the veil of atmosphere between myself and outer space grew thinner, the sky, which had been a fair springtime blue at first, grew deeper and richer in colour, passing steadily through the intervening shades, until presently it was as dark as the blue sky of midnight, and presently as black as the blackness of a frosty starlight, and at last as black as no blackness I had ever beheld. And first one star, and then many, and at last an innumerable host, broke out upon the sky: more stars than any one has ever seen from the face of the earth. For the blueness of the sky is the light of the sun and stars sifted and spread abroad blindingly; there is diffused light even in the darkest skies of winter, and we do not see their light by day because of the dazzling irradiation of the sun. But now I saw things—I know not how; assuredly with no mortal eyes—and that defect of bedazzlement blinded me no longer. The sun was incredibly strange and wonderful. The body of it was a disc of blinding white light; not yellowish as it seems to those who live upon the earth, but livid white, all streaked with scarlet streaks, and rimmed about with a fringe of writhing tongues of red fire. And, shooting halfway across the heavens from either side of it, and brighter than the Milky Way, were two pinions of silver-white, making it look more like those winged globes I have seen in Egyptian sculpture, than anything else I can remember upon earth. These I knew for the solar corona, though I had never seen anything of it but a picture during the days of my earthly life.

When my attention came back to the earth, again I saw that it had fallen very far away from me. Field and town were long since indistinguishable, and all the varied hues of the country were merging into a uniform bright grey, broken only by the brilliant white of the clouds that lay scattered in flocculent masses over Ireland and the west of England. For now I could see the outlines of the north of France and Ireland, and all this island of Britain, save where Scotland passed over the horizon to the north, or where the coast was blurred or obliterated by cloud. The sea was a dull grey, and darker than the land; and the whole panorama was rotating slowly towards the east.

All this had happened so swiftly that, until I was some thousand miles or so from the earth, I had no thought for myself. But now I perceived I had neither hands nor feet, parts nor organs, and that I felt neither alarm nor pain. All about me, I perceived that the vacancy (for I had already left the air behind) was cold beyond the imagination of man; but it troubled me not. The sun's rays shot through the void, powerless to light or heat until they should strike on matter in their course. I saw things with a serene self-forgetfulness, even as if I were God. And down below there, rushing away from me,—countless miles in a second,—where a little dark spot on the grey marked the position of London, two doctors were struggling to restore life to the poor hacked and outworn shell I had abandoned. I felt then such release, such serenity, as I can compare to no earthly delight I have ever known.

It was only after I had perceived all these things that the meaning of that headlong rush of the earth grew into comprehension. Yet it was so simple, so obvious, that I was amazed at my never anticipating the thing that was happening to me. I had suddenly been cut adrift from matter: all that was material of me was there upon earth, whirling away through space, held to the earth by gravitation, partaking of the earth-inertia, moving in its wreath of epicycles round the sun, and with the sun and the planets on their vast march through space. But the immaterial has no inertia, feels nothing of the pull of matter for matter: where it parts from its garment of flesh there it remains (so far as space concerns it any longer) immovable in space. *I* was not leaving the earth: the earth was leaving *me,* and not only the earth but the whole solar system was streaming past. And about me in space, invisible to me, scattered in the wake of the earth upon its journey, there must be an innumerable multitude of souls, stripped like myself of the material, stripped like myself of the passions of the individual and the generous emotions of the gregarious brute, naked intelligences, things of newborn wonder and thought, marvelling at the strange release that had suddenly come on them!

As I receded faster and faster from the strange white sun in the black heavens, and from the broad and shining earth upon which my being had begun, I seemed to grow, in some incredible manner, vast: vast as regards this world I had left, vast as regards the moments and periods of a human life. Very soon I saw the full circle of the earth, slightly gibbous, like the moon when she nears her full, but very great; and the silvery shape of America was now in the noonday blaze, wherein (as it seemed) little England had been basking but a few minutes ago. At first the earth was large, and shone in the heavens, filling a great part of them; but every moment she grew smaller and more distant. As she shrunk, the broad moon in its third quarter crept into view over the rim of her disc. I looked for the constellations. Only that part of Aries directly behind the sun and the Lion which the earth covered were hidden. I recognised the tortuous, tattered band of the Milky Way, with Vega very bright between sun and earth; and Sirius and Orion shone splendid against the unfathomable blackness in the opposite quarter of the heavens. The Polestar was overhead, and the Great Bear hung over the circle of the earth. And away beneath and beyond the shining corona of the sun were strange groupings of stars I had never seen in my life; notably a dagger-shaped group that I knew for the Southern Cross. All these were no larger than when they had shone on earth; but the little stars that one scarce sees shone now as brightly as the first magnitudes had done, while the larger worlds were points of indescribable glory and colour. Aldebaran was a spot of blood-red fire, and Sirius condensed to one point the light of a world of sapphires. And they shone steadily: they did not scintillate, they were calmly glorious. My impressions had an adamantine hardness and brightness; there was no blurring softness, no atmosphere, nothing but infinite darkness set with the myriads of these acute and brilliant points and specks of light. Presently, when I looked again, the little earth seemed no bigger than the sun, and it dwindled and turned as I looked, until, in a second's space (as it seemed to me), it was halved; and so it went on swiftly dwindling. Far away in the opposite direction a little pinkish pin's head of light, shining steadily, was the planet Mars. I swam motionless in vacancy, and without a trace of terror or astonishment, watched the speck of cosmic dust we call the world fall away from me.

Presently it dawned upon me that my sense of duration had changed: that my mind was moving not faster, but infinitely slower; that between each separate impression there was a period of many days. The moon spun once round the earth as I noted this; and I perceived, clearly, the motion of Mars in his orbit. Moreover it appeared as if the time between thought and thought grew steadily greater, until at last a thousand years was but a moment in my perception.

At first the constellations had shone motionless against the black background of infinite space; but presently it seemed as though the group of stars about Hercules and the Scorpion was contracting, while Orion and Aldebaran and their neighbours were scattering apart. Flashing suddenly out of the darkness, there came a flying multitude of particles of rock, glittering like dust-specks in a sunbeam and encompassed in a faintly luminous haze. They swirled all about me and vanished again in a twinkling far behind. And then I saw that a bright spot of light, that shone a little to one side of my path, was growing very rapidly larger, and perceived that it was the planet Saturn rushing towards me. Larger and larger it grew, swallowing up the heavens behind it, and hiding every moment a fresh multitude of stars. I perceived its flattened whirling body, its disc-like belt, and seven of its little satellites. It grew and grew, till it towered enormous, and then I plunged amid a streaming multitude of clashing stones and dancing dust-particles and gas-eddies, and saw for a moment the mighty triple belt like three concentric arches of moonlight above me, its shadow black on the boiling tumult below. These things happened in one tenth of the time it takes to tell of them. The planet went by like a flash of lightning; for a few seconds it blotted out the sun, and there and then became a mere black, dwindling, winged patch against the light. The earth, the mother mote of my being, I could no longer see.

So with a stately swiftness, in the profoundest silence, the solar system fell from me, as it had been a garment, until the sun was a mere star amid the multitude of stars, with its eddy of planet-specks lost in the confused glittering of the remoter light. I was no longer a denizen of the solar system: I had come to the Outer Universe, I seemed to grasp and comprehend the whole world of matter. Ever more swiftly the stars closed in about the spot where Antares and Vega had vanished in a luminous haze, until that part of the sky had the semblance of a whirling mass of nebulae, and ever before me yawned vaster gaps of vacant blackness, and the stars shone fewer and fewer. It seemed as if I moved towards a point between Orion's belt and sword; and the void about that region opened vaster and vaster every second, an incredible gulf of nothingness into which I was falling. Faster and ever faster the universe rushed by, a hurry of whirling motes at last, speeding silently into the void. Stars, glowing brighter and brighter, with their circling planets catching the light in a ghostly fashion as I neared them, shone out and vanished again into inexistence; faint comets, clusters of meteorites, winking specks of matter, eddying light points whizzed past, some perhaps a hundred millions of miles or so from me at most, few nearer, travelling with unimaginable rapidity, shooting constellations, momentary darts of fire through the black night. More than anything else it was like a dusty draught, sunbeam-lit. Broader and wider and deeper grew the starless space, the vacant Beyond, into which I was being drawn. At last a quarter of the heavens was black and blank, and the whole headlong rush of stellar universe closed in behind me like a veil of light that is gathered together. It drove away from me like a monstrous Jack-o'-lantern driven by the wind. I had come out into the wilderness of space. Even the vacant blackness grew broader, until the hosts of the stars seemed only like a swarm of fiery specks hurrying away from me, inconceivably remote, and the darkness, the nothingness and emptiness, was about me on every side. Soon the little universe of matter, the cage of points in which I had begun to be, was dwindling, now to a whirling disc of luminous glittering, and now to one minute disc of hazy light. In a little while it would shrink to a point, and at last would vanish altogether.

Suddenly feeling came back to me: feeling in the shape of overwhelming terror,—such a dread of those dark vastitudes as no words can describe, a passionate resurgence of sympathy and social desire. Were there other souls, invisible to me as I to them, about me in the blackness? or was I indeed, even as I felt, alone? Had I passed out of being into something that was neither being nor not-being? The covering of the body, the covering of matter had been torn from me, and the hallucinations of companionship and security. Everything was black and silent. I had ceased to be. I was nothing. There was nothing, save only that infinitesimal dot of light that dwindled in the gulf. I strained myself to hear and see, and for a while there was naught but infinite silence, intolerable darkness, horror, and despair.

Then I saw that about the spot of light into which the whole world of matter had shrunk, there was a faint glow. And in a band on either side of that the darkness was not absolute. I watched it for ages, as it seemed to me, and through the long waiting the haze grew imperceptibly more distinct. And then about the band appeared an irregular cloud of the faintest, palest brown. I felt a passionate impatience; but the things grew brighter so slowly that they scarce seemed to change. What was unfolding itself? What was this strange reddish dawn in the interminable night of space?

The cloud's shape was grotesque. It seemed to be looped along its lower side into four projecting masses, and, above, it ended in a straight line. What phantom was it? I felt assured I had seen that figure before; but I could not think what, nor where, nor when it was. Then the realisation rushed upon me. *It was a clenched hand.* I was alone, in space, alone with this huge, shadowy Hand, upon which the whole Universe of Matter lay like an unconsidered speck of dust. It seemed as though I watched it through vast periods of time. On the forefinger glittered a ring; and the universe from which I had come was but a spot of light upon the rings's curvature. And the thing that the Hand gripped had the likeness of a black rod. Through a long eternity I watched the Hand, with the ring and the rod, marvelling and fearing and waiting helplessly on what might follow. It seemed as though nothing could follow: that I should watch forever, seeing only the Hand and the thing it held, and understanding nothing of its import. Was the whole universe but a refracting speck upon some greater Being? Were our worlds but the atoms of another universe, and those again of another, and so on through an endless progression? And what was I? Was I indeed immaterial? A vague persuasion of a body gathering about me came into my suspense. The abysmal darkness about the Hand filled with impalpable suggestions, with uncertain, fluctuating shapes.

Then, suddenly, came a sound, like the sound of a tolling bell: faint, as if infinitely far; muffled, as though heard through thick swathings of darkness,—a deep vibrating resonance with vast gulfs of silence between each stroke. And the Hand appeared to tighten on the rod. And I saw far above the Hand, towards the apex of the darkness, a circle of dim phosphorescence, a ghostly sphere whence these sounds came throbbing; and at the last stroke the Hand vanished, for the hour had come, and

I heard a noise of many waters. But the black rod remained as a great band across the sky. And then a voice, which seemed to run to the uttermost parts of space, spoke, saying: "There will be no more pain."

At that an almost intolerable gladness and radiance rushed in upon me, and I saw the circle shining white and bright, and the rod black and shining, and many other things else distinct and clear. And the circle was the face of the clock, and the rod the rail of my bed. Haddon was standing at the foot, against the rail, with a small pair of scissors on his fingers; and the hands of my clock on the mantel over his shoulder were clasped together over the hour of twelve. Mowbray was washing something in a basin at the octagonal table, and at my side I felt a subdued feeling that could scarce be spoken of as pain.

The operation had not killed me. And I perceived suddenly that the dull melancholy of half a year was lifted from my mind.

Afterword

In past years, books have been published that purport to be serious discussions of experiences during those moments when people under medical treatment experience "clinical death."

Invariably, it would seem, what is experienced is light, warmth, the appearance of benevolent figures, the prefiguration of bliss. In short, there seems to be the beginning of a transition to heaven.

Of course this is purely anecdotal. What we have is what the author of the book says the person in the hospital bed said. It is doubly word of mouth, and there is no objective evidence whatever.

In the second place, since the patient survived to tell the tale, he was not really dead, but in a semi-comatose condition in which he might well experience hallucinations. And what hallucinations would he experience but those he had been taught from childhood—that there are angels and that he would go to heaven when he died?

(Considering the prevalence of human evil, it is strange that I have never come across an out-of-body experience in which an evil figure with horns appears and the "clinically dead" person experiences a great dread.)

What H. G. Wells does, however, is to describe the semi-comatose hallucinations of a person with a scientific view of the universe—a far more interesting tale than those purportedly told by people expecting (or hoping) to go to heaven.

Incidentally, when I went under the knife I experienced no hallucinations whatever, of any kind, perhaps because I am convinced that after death there is nothingness.—I.A.

Additional Reading

Aleister Crowley, "The Testament of Magdalen Blair," in *The Stratagem and Other Stories* (London: Mandrake Press, 1929).

Philip Jose Farmer, "A Bowl Bigger than Earth," in *Down in the Black Gang and Other Stories* (Garden City, N.Y.: Doubleday & Company, Inc., 1971).

H. P. Lovecraft, "The Outsider," in *Best Supernatural Stories of H. P. Lovecraft* (Cleveland, Ohio: World Publishing Co., 1945).

Oliver La Farge, "Haunted Ground," in *Haunted New England,* Charles G. Waugh, Martin H. Greenberg, and Frank D. McSherry, Jr., eds. (Dublin, N.H.: Yankee Books, 1988).

Mark Twain, "Extracts from Captain Stormfield's Visit to Heaven," in *The Mysterious Stranger and Other Stories* (New York: Harper, 1922).

2

Astrology

Rudyard Kipling
The Children of the Zodiac

Though thou love her as thyself,
As a self of purer clay,
Though her parting dim the day,
Stealing grace from all alive,
Heartily know
When half Gods go
The Gods arrive.   EMERSON.

Thousands of years ago, when men were greater than they are to-day, the Children of the Zodiac lived in the world. There were six Children of the Zodiac—the Ram, the Bull, the Lion, the Twins, and the Girl; and they were afraid of the Six Houses which belonged to the Scorpion, the Balance, the Crab, the Fishes, the Goat, and the Waterman. Even when they first stepped down upon the earth and knew that they were immortal Gods, they carried this fear with them; and the fear grew as they became better acquainted with mankind and heard stories of the Six Houses. Men treated the Children as Gods and came to them with prayers and long stories of wrong, while the Children of the Zodiac listened and could not understand.

A mother would fling herself before the feet of the Twins, or the Bull, crying: "My husband was at work in the fields and the Archer shot him and he died; and my son will also be killed by the Archer. Help me!" The Bull would lower his huge head and answer: "What is that to me?"

Or the Twins would smile and continue their play, for they could not understand why the water ran out of people's eyes. At other times a man and a woman would come to Leo or the Girl crying: "We two are newly married and we are very happy. Take these flowers." As they threw the flowers they would make mysterious sounds to show that they were happy, and Leo and the Girl wondered even more than the Twins why people shouted "Ha! ha! ha!" for no cause.

This continued for thousands of years by human reckoning, till on a day, Leo met the Girl walking across the hills and saw that she had changed entirely since he had last seen her. The Girl, looking at Leo, saw that he too had changed altogether. Then they decided that it would be well never to separate again, in case even more startling changes should occur when the one was not at hand to help the other. Leo kissed the Girl and all Earth felt that kiss, and the Girl sat down on a hill and the water ran out of her eyes; and this had never happened before in the memory of the Children of the Zodiac.

As they sat together a man and a woman came by, and the man said to the woman:

"What is the use of wasting flowers on those dull Gods. They will never understand, darling."

The Girl jumped up and put her arms round the woman, crying, "I understand. Give me the flowers and I will give you a kiss."

Leo said beneath his breath to the man: "What was the new name that I hear you give to your woman just now?"

The man answered, "Darling, of course."

"Why, of course," said Leo; "and if of course, what does it mean?"

"It means 'very dear,' and you have only to look at your wife to see why."

"I see," said Leo; "you are quite right"; and when the man and the woman had gone on he called the Girl "darling wife"; and the Girl wept again from sheer happiness.

"I think," she said at last, wiping her eyes, "I think that we two have neglected men and women too much. What did you do with the sacrifices they made to you, Leo?"

"I let them burn," said Leo. "I could not eat them. What did you do with the flowers?"

"I let them wither. I could not wear them, I had so many of my own," said the Girl, "and now I am sorry."

"There is nothing to grieve for," said Leo; "we belong to each other."

As they were talking the years of men's life slipped by unnoticed, and presently the man and the woman came back, both white-headed, the man carrying the woman.

"We have come to the end of things," said the man quietly. "This that was my wife—"

"As I am Leo's wife," said the Girl quickly, her eyes staring.

"—was my wife, has been killed by one of your Houses." The man set down his burden, and laughed.

"Which House?" said Leo angrily, for he hated all the Houses equally.

"You are Gods, you should know," said the man. "We have lived together and loved one another, and I have left a good farm for my son: what have I to complain of except that I still live?"

As he was bending over his wife's body there came a whistling through the air, and he started and tried to run away, crying, "It is the arrow of the Archer. Let me live a little longer—only a little longer!" The arrow struck him and he died. Leo looked at the Girl and she looked at him, and both were puzzled.

"He wished to die," said Leo. "He said that he wished to die, and when Death came he tried to run away. He is a coward."

"No, he is not," said the Girl; "I think I feel what he felt. Leo, we must learn more about this for their sakes."

"For *their* sakes," said Leo, very loudly.

"Because *we* are never going to die," said the Girl and Leo together, still more loudly.

"Now sit you still here, darling wife," said Leo, "while I go to the Houses whom we hate, and learn how to make these men and women live as we do."

"And love as we do?" said the Girl.

"I do not think they need to be taught that," said Leo, and he strode away very angry, with his lion-skin swinging from his shoulder, till he came to the House where the Scorpion lives in the darkness, brandishing his tail over his back.

"Why do you trouble the children of men?" said Leo, with his heart between his teeth.

"Are you so sure that I trouble the children of men alone?" said the Scorpion. "Speak to your brother the Bull, and see what he says."

"I come on behalf of the children of men," said Leo. "I have learned to love as they do, and I wish them to live as I—as we—do."

"Your wish was granted long ago. Speak to the Bull. He is under my special care," said the Scorpion.

Leo dropped back to the earth again, and saw the great star Aldebaran, that is set in the forehead of the Bull, blazing very near to the earth. When he came up to it he saw that his brother the Bull, yoked to a countryman's plough, was toiling through a wet rice-field with his head bent down, and the sweat streaming from his flanks. The countryman was urging him forward with a goad.

"Gore that insolent to death," cried Leo, "and for the sake of our family honour come out of the mire."

"I cannot," said the Bull, "the Scorpion has told me that some day, of which I cannot be sure, he will sting me where my neck is set on my shoulders, and that I shall die bellowing."

"What has that to do with this disgraceful exhibition?" said Leo, standing on the dyke that bounded the wet field.

"Everything. This man could not plough without my help. He thinks that I am a stray bullock."

"But he is a mud-crusted cottar with matted hair," insisted Leo. "We are not meant for his use."

"You may not be; I am. I cannot tell when the Scorpion may choose to sting me to death—perhaps before I have turned this furrow." The Bull flung his bulk into the yoke, and the plough tore through the wet ground behind him, and the countryman goaded him till his flanks were red.

"Do you like this?" Leo called down the dripping furrows.

"No," said the Bull over his shoulder as he lifted his hind legs from the clinging mud and cleared his nostrils.

Leo left him scornfully and passed to another country, where he found his brother the Ram in the centre of a crowd of country people who were hanging wreaths round his neck and feeding him on freshly-plucked green corn.

"This is terrible," said Leo. "Break up that crowd and come away, my brother. Their hands are spoiling your fleece."

"I cannot," said the Ram. "The Archer told me that on some day of which I had no knowledge, he would send a dart through me, and that I should die in very great pain."

"What has that to do with this?" said Leo, but he did not speak as confidently as before.

"Everything in the world," said the Ram. "These people never saw a perfect sheep before. They think that I am a stray, and they will carry me from place to place as a model to all their flocks."

"But they are greasy shepherds, we are not intended to amuse them," said Leo.

"You may not be; I am," said the Ram. "I cannot tell when the Archer may choose to send his arrow at me—perhaps before the people a mile down the road have seen me." The Ram lowered his head that a yokel newly arrived might throw a wreath of wild garlic-leaves over it, and waited patiently while the farmers tugged his fleece.

"Do you like this?" cried Leo over the shoulders of the crowd.

"No," said the Ram, as the dust of the trampling feet made him sneeze, and he snuffed at the fodder piled before him.

Leo turned back intending to retrace his steps to the Houses, but as he was passing down a street he saw two small children, very dusty, rolling outside a cottage door, and playing with a cat. They were the Twins.

"What are you doing here?" said Leo, indignant.

"Playing," said the Twins calmly.

"Cannot you play on the banks of the Milky Way?" said Leo.

"We did," said they, "till the Fishes swam down and told us that some day they would come for us and not hurt us at all and carry us away. So now we are playing at being babies down here. The people like it."

"Do you like it?" said Leo.

"No," said the Twins, "but there are no cats in the Milky Way," and they pulled the cat's tail thoughtfully. A woman came out of the doorway and stood behind them, and Leo saw in her face a look that he had sometimes seen in the Girl's.

"She thinks that we are foundlings," said the Twins, and they trotted indoors to the evening meal.

Then Leo hurried as swiftly as possible to all the Houses one after another; for he could not understand the new trouble that had come to his brethren. He spoke to the Archer, and the Archer assured him that so far as that House was concerned Leo had nothing to fear. The Waterman, the Fishes, and the Goat, gave the same answer. They knew nothing of Leo, and cared less. They were the Houses, and they were busied in killing men.

At last he came to that very dark House where Cancer the Crab lies so still that you might think he was asleep if you did not see the ceaseless play and winnowing motion of the feathery branches round his mouth. That movement never ceases. It is like the eating of a smothered fire into rotten timber in that it is noiseless and without haste.

Leo stood in front of the Crab, and the half darkness allowed him a glimpse of that vast blue-black back, and the motionless eyes. Now and again he thought that he heard some one sobbing, but the noise was very faint.

"Why do you trouble the children of men?" said Leo. There was no answer, and against his will Leo cried, "Why do you trouble us? What have we done that you should trouble us?"

This time Cancer replied, "What do I know or care? You were born into my House, and at the appointed time I shall come for you."

"When is the appointed time?" said Leo, stepping back from the restless movement of the mouth.

"When the full moon fails to call the full tide," said the Crab, "I shall come for the one. When the other has taken the earth by the shoulders, I shall take that other by the throat."

Leo lifted his hand to the apple of his throat, moistened his lips, and recovering himself, said:

"Must I be afraid for two, then?"

"For two," said the Crab, "and as many more as may come after."

"My brother, the Bull, had a better fate," said Leo, sullenly. "He is alone."

A hand covered his mouth before he could finish the sentence, and he found the Girl in his arms. Woman-like, she had not stayed where Leo had left her, but had hastened off at once to know the worst, and passing all the other Houses, had come straight to Cancer.

"That is foolish," said the Girl whispering. "I have been waiting in the dark for long and long before you came. *Then* I was afraid. But now—" She put her head down on his shoulder and sighed a sigh of contentment.

"I am afraid now," said Leo.

"That is on my account," said the Girl. "I know it is, because I am afraid for your sake. Let us go, husband."

They went out of the darkness together and came back to the Earth, Leo very silent, and the Girl striving to cheer him. "My brother's fate is the better one," Leo would repeat from time to time, and at last he said: "Let us each go our own way and live alone till we die. We were born into the House of Cancer, and he will come for us."

"I know; I know. But where shall I go? And where will you sleep in the evening? But let us try. I will stay here. Do you go on?"

Leo took six steps forward very slowly, and three long steps backward very quickly, and the third step set him again at the Girl's side. This time it was she who was begging him to go away and leave her, and he was forced to comfort her all through the night. That night decided them both never to leave each other for an instant, and when they had come to this decision they looked back at the darkness of the House of Cancer high above their heads, and with their arms round each other's necks laughed, "Ha! ha! ha!" exactly as the children of men laughed. And that was the first time in their lives that they had ever laughed.

Next morning they returned to their proper home and saw the flowers and the sacrifices that had been laid before their doors by the villagers of the hills. Leo stamped down the fire with his heel and the Girl flung the flower-wreaths out of sight, shuddering as she did so. When the villagers returned, as of custom, to see what had become of their offerings, they found neither roses nor burned flesh on the altars, but only a man and a woman, with frightened white faces sitting hand in hand on the altar-steps.

"Are you not Virgo?" said a woman to the Girl. "I sent you flowers yesterday."

"Little sister," said the Girl, flushing to her forehead, "do not send any more flowers, for I am only a woman like yourself." The man and the woman went away doubtfully.

"Now, what shall we do?" said Leo.

"We must try to be cheerful, I think," siad the Girl. "We know the very worst that can happen to us, but we do not know the best that love can bring us. We have a great deal to be glad of."

"The certainty of death?" said Leo.

"All the children of men have that certainty also; yet they laughed long before we ever knew how to laugh. We must learn to laugh, Leo. We have laughed once, already."

People who consider themselves Gods, as the Children of the Zodiac did, find it hard to laugh, because the Immortals know nothing worth laughter or tears. Leo rose up with a very heavy heart, and he and the Girl together went to and fro among men; their new fear of death behind them. First they laughed at a naked baby attempting to thrust its fat toes into its foolish pink mouth; next they laughed at a kitten chasing her own tail; and then they laughed at a boy trying to steal a kiss from a girl, and getting his ears boxed. Lastly, they laughed because the wind blew in their faces as they ran down a hill-side together, and broke panting and breathless into a knot of villagers at the bottom. The villagers laughed too at their flying clothes and wind-reddened faces; and in the evening gave them food and invited them to a dance on the grass, where everybody laughed through the mere joy of being able to dance.

That night Leo jumped up from the Girl's side crying: "Every one of those people we met just now will die—'

"So shall we," said the Girl sleepily. "Lie down again, dear." Leo could not see that her face was wet with tears.

But Leo was up and far across the fields, driven forward by the fear of death for himself and for the Girl, who was dearer to him than himself. Presently he came across the Bull drowsing in the moonlight after a hard day's work, and looking through half-shut eyes at the beautiful straight furrows that he had made.

"Ho!" said the Bull. "So you have been told these things too. Which of the Houses holds your death?"

Leo pointed upwards to the dark House of the Crab and groaned. "And he will come for the Girl too," he said.

"Well," said the Bull, "what will you do?"

Leo sat down on the dyke and said that he did not know.

"You cannot pull a plough," said the Bull, with a little touch of contempt. "I can, and that prevents me from thinking of the Scorpion."

Leo was angry, and said nothing till the dawn broke, and the cultivator came to yoke the Bull to his work.

"Sing," said the Bull, as the stiff, muddy ox-bow creaked and strained. "My shoulder is galled. Sing one of the songs that we sang when we thought we were all Gods together."

Leo stepped back into the canebrake, and lifted up his voice in a song of the Children of the Zodiac—the war-whoop of the young Gods who are afraid of nothing. At first he dragged the song along unwillingly, and then the song dragged him, and his voice rolled across the fields, and the Bull stepped to the tune, and the cultivator banged his flanks out of sheer light-heartedness, and the furrows rolled away behind the plough more and more swiftly. Then the Girl came across the fields looking for Leo, and found him singing in the cane. She joined her voice to his, and the cultivator's wife brought her spinning into the open and listened with all her children round her. When it was time for the nooning, Leo and the Girl had sung themselves both thirsty and hungry, but the cultivator and his wife gave them rye bread and milk, and many thanks; and the Bull found occasion to say:

"You have helped me to do a full half field more than I should have done. But the hardest part of the day is to come, brother."

Leo wished to lie down and brood over the words of the Crab. The Girl went away to talk to the cultivator's wife and baby, and the afternoon ploughing began.

"Help us now," said the Bull. "The tides of the day are running down. My legs are very stiff. Sing, if you never sang before."

"To a mud-spattered villager?" said Leo.

"He is under the same doom as ourselves. Are you a coward?" said the Bull.

Leo flushed, and began again with a sore throat and a bad temper. Little by little he dropped away from the songs of the Children and made up a song as he went along; and this was a thing he could never have done had he not met the Crab face to face. He remembered facts concerning cultivators and bullocks and rice-fields that he had not particularly noticed before the interview, and he strung them all together, growing more interested as he sang, and he told the cultivator much more about himself and his work than the cultivator knew. The Bull grunted approval as he toiled down the furrows for the last time that day, and the song ended, leaving the cultivator with a very good opinion of himself in his aching bones. The Girl came out of the hut where she had been keeping the children quiet, and talking woman-talk to the wife, and they all ate the evening meal together.

"Now yours must be a very pleasant life," said the cultivator; "sitting as you do on a dyke all day and singing just what comes into your head. Have you been at it long, you two—gipsies?"

"Ah!" lowed the Bull from his byre. "That's all the thanks you will ever get from men, brother."

"No. We have only just begun it," said the Girl; "but we are going to keep to it as long as we live. Are we not, Leo?"

"Yes," said he; and they went away hand in hand.

"You can sing beautifully, Leo," said she, as a wife will to her husband.

"What were you doing?" said he.

"I was talking to the mother and the babies," she said. "You would not understand the little things that make us women laugh."

"And—and I am to go on with this—this gipsy work?" said Leo.

"Yes, dear; and I will help you."

There is no written record of the life of Leo and of the Girl, so we cannot tell how Leo took to his new employment, which he detested. We are only sure that the Girl loved him when and wherever he sang; even when, after the song was done, she went round with the equivalent of a tambourine and collected the pence for the daily bread. There were times, too, when it was Leo's very hard task to console the Girl for the indignity of horrible praise that people gave him and her—for the silly wagging peacock feathers that they stuck in his cap, and the buttons and pieces of cloth that they sewed on his coat. Woman-like, she could advise and help to the end, but the meanness of the means revolted.

"What does it matter," Leo would say, "so long as the songs make them a little happier?" And they would go down the road and begin again on the old, old refrain—that whatever came or did not come the children of men must not be afraid. It was heavy teaching at first, but in process of years Leo discovered that he could make men laugh and hold them listening to him even when the rain fell. Yet there were people who would sit down and cry softly, though the crowd was yelling with delight, and there were people who maintained that Leo made them do this; and the Girl would talk to them in the pauses of the performance and do her best to comfort them. People would die, too, while Leo was talking and singing and laughing; for the Archer and the Scorpion and the Crab and the other Houses were as busy as ever. Sometimes the crowd broke, and were frightened, and Leo strove to keep them steady by telling them that this was cowardly; and sometimes they mocked at the Houses that were killing them, and Leo explained that this was even more cowardly than running away.

In their wanderings they came across the Bull, or the Ram, or the Twins, but all were too busy to do more than nod to each other across the crowd, and go on with their work. As the years rolled on even that recognition ceased, for the Children of the Zodiac had forgotten that they had ever been Gods working for the sake of men. The star Aldebaran was crusted with caked dirt on the Bull's forehead, the Ram's fleece was dusty and torn, and the Twins were only babies fighting over the cat on the doorstep. It was then that Leo said, "Let us stop singing and making jokes." And it was then that the Girl said, "No." But she did not know why she said "No" so energetically. Leo maintained that it was perversity, till she herself, at the end of a dusty day, made the same suggestion to him, and he said, "Most certainly not!" and they quarrelled miserably between the hedgerows, forgetting the meaning of the stars above them. Other singers and other talkers sprang up in the course of the years, and Leo, forgetting that there could never be too many of these, hated them for dividing the applause of the children of men, which he thought should be all his own. The Girl would grow angry too, and then the songs would be broken, and the jests fall flat for weeks to come, and the children of men would shout: "Go home, you two gipsies. Go home and learn something worth singing!"

After one of these sorrowful, shameful days, the Girl, walking by Leo's side through the fields, saw the full moon coming up over the trees, and she clutched Leo's arm, crying: "The time has come now. Oh, Leo, forgive me!"

"What is it?" said Leo. He was thinking of the other singers.

"My husband!" she answered, and she laid his hand upon her breast, and the breast that he knew so well was hard as stone. Leo groaned, remembering what the Crab has said.

"Surely we were Gods once," he cried.

"Surely we are Gods still," said the Girl. "Do you not remember when you and I went to the House of the Crab and—were not very much afraid? And since then . . . we have forgotten what we were singing for—we sang for the pence, and, oh, we fought for them!—We, who are the Children of the Zodiac!"

"It was my fault," said Leo.

"How can there be any fault of yours that is not mine too?" said the Girl. "My time has come, but you will live longer, and . . ." The look in her eyes said all she could not say.

"Yes, I will remember that we are Gods," said Leo.

It is very hard, even for a Child of the Zodiac who has forgotten his Godhead, to see his wife dying slowly, and to know that he cannot help her. The Girl told Leo in those last months of all that she had said and done among the wives and the babies at the back of the roadside performances, and Leo was astonished that he knew so little of her who had been so much to him. When she was dying she told him never to fight for pence or quarrel with the other singers; and, above all, to go on with his singing immediately after she was dead.

Then she died, and after he had buried her he went down the road to a village that he knew, and the people hoped that he would begin quarrelling with a new singer that had sprung up while he had been away. But Leo called him "my brother." The new singer was newly married— and Leo knew it—and when he had finished singing Leo straightened himself, and sang the "Song of the Girl," which he had made coming down the road. Every man who was married, or hoped to be married, whatever his rank or colour, understood that song—even the bride leaning on the new husband's arm understood it too—and presently when the song ended, and Leo's heart was bursting in him, the men sobbed. "That was a sad tale," they said at last, "now make us laugh." Because Leo had known all the sorrow that a man could know, including the full knowledge of his own fall who had once been a God—he, changing his song quickly, made the people laugh till they could laugh no more. They went away feeling ready for any trouble in reason, and they gave Leo more peacock feathers and pence than he could count. Knowing that pence led to quarrels and that peacock feathers were hateful to the Girl, he put them aside and went away to look for his brothers, to remind them that they too were Gods.

He found the Bull goring the undergrowth in a ditch, for the Scorpion had stung him, and he was dying, not slowly, as the Girl had died, but quickly.

"I know all," the Bull groaned, as Leo came up. "I had forgotten too, but I remember now. Go and look at the fields I ploughed. The furrows are straight. I forgot that I was a God, but I drew the plough perfectly straight, for all that. And you, brother?"

"I am not at the end of the ploughing," said Leo. "Does Death hurt?"

"No; but dying does," said the Bull, and he died. The cultivator who then owned him was much annoyed, for there was a field still unploughed.

It was after this that Leo made the Song of the Bull who had been a God and forgotten the fact, and he sang it in such a manner that half the young men in the world conceived that they too might be Gods without knowing it. A half of that half grew impossibly conceited, and died early. A half of the remainder strove to be Gods and failed, but the other half accomplished four times more work than they would have done under any other delusion.

Later, years later, always wandering up and down, and making the children of men laugh, he found the Twins sitting on the bank of a stream waiting for the Fishes to come and carry them away. They were not in the least afraid, and they told Leo that the woman of the House had a real baby of her own, and that when that baby grew old enough to be mischievous he would find a well-educated cat waiting to have its tail pulled. Then the Fishes came for them, but all that the people saw was two children drowning in a brook; and though their foster-mother was very sorry, she hugged her own real baby to her breast, and was grateful that it was only the foundlings.

Then Leo made the Song of the Twins who had forgotten that they were Gods, and had played in the dust to amuse a foster-mother. That song was sung far and wide among the women. It caused them to laugh and cry and hug their babies closer to their hearts all in one breath; and some of the women who remembered the Girl said: "Surely that is the voice of Virgo. Only she could know so much about ourselves."

After those three songs were made, Leo sang them over and over again, till he was in danger of looking upon them as so many mere words, and the people who listened grew tired, and there came back to Leo the old temptation to stop singing once and for all. But he remembered the Girl's dying words and went on.

One of his listeners interrupted him as he was singing. "Leo," said he, "I have heard you telling us not to be afraid for the past forty years. Can you not sing something new now?"

"No," said Leo; "it is the only song that I am allowed to sing. You must not be afraid of the Houses, even when they kill you."

The man turned to go, wearily, but there came a whistling through the air, and the arrow of the Archer was seen skimming low above the earth pointing to the man's heart. He drew himself up, and stood still waiting till the arrow struck home.

"Are you afraid?" said Leo, bending over him.

"I am a man, not a God," said the man. "I should have run away but for your Songs. My work is done, and I die without making a show of my fear."

"I am very well paid," said Leo to himself. "Now that I see what my songs are doing, I will sing better ones."

He went down the road, collected his little knot of listeners, and began the Song of the Girl. In the middle of his singing he felt the cold touch of the Crab's claw on the apple of his throat. He lifted his hand, choked, and stopped for an instant.

"Sing on, Leo," said the crowd. "The old song runs as well as ever it did."

Leo went on steadily till the end, with the cold fear at his heart. When his song was ended, he felt the grip on his throat tighten. He was old, he had lost the Girl, he knew that he was losing more than half his power to sing, he could scarcely walk to the diminishing crowds that waited for him, and could not see their faces when they stood about him. None the less he cried angrily to the Crab,

"Why have you come for me *now?*"

"You were born under my care. How can I help coming for you?" said the Crab, wearily. Every human being whom the Crab killed had asked that same question.

"But I was just beginning to know what my songs were doing," said Leo.

"Perhaps that is why," said the Crab, and the grip tightened.

"You said you would not come till I had taken the world by the shoulders," gasped Leo, falling back.

"I always keep my word. You have done that three times, with three songs. What more do you desire?"

"Let me live to see the world know it," pleaded Leo. "Let me be sure that my songs—"

"Make men brave?" said the Crab. "Even then there would be one man who was afraid. The Girl was braver then you are. Come."

Leo was standing close to the restless, insatiable mouth. "I forgot," said he, simply. "The Girl was braver. But I am a God too, and I am not afraid."

"What is that to me?" said the Crab.

Then Leo's speech was taken from him, and he lay still and dumb, watching Death till he died.

Leo was the last of the Children of the Zodiac. After his death there sprang up a breed of little mean men, whimpering and flinching and howling because the Houses killed them and theirs, who wished to live forever without any pain. They did not increase their lives, but they increased their own torments miserably, and there were no Children of the Zodiac to guide them, and the greater part of Leo's songs were lost.

Only he had carved on the Girl's tombstone the last verse of the Song of the Girl, which stands at the head of this story.

One of the children of men, coming thousands of years later, rubbed away the lichen, read the lines and applied them to a trouble other than the one Leo meant. Being a man, men believed that he had made the verses himself; but they belong to Leo, the Child of the Zodiac, and teach, as he taught, that what comes or does not come, we must not be afraid.

Afterword

The earliest close observers of the heavens—the Sumerians and the Chinese— were faced with a random distribution of stars of varying brightness. To be able to refer to one star or another it was only natural to imagine them as being interconnected in such a way as to make geometric figures, or even more complex figures similar to the familiar objects known on Earth. These were the "constellations," and stars could then be located as being present in this or that part of a particular constellation.

This was especially true of the band of the sky through which the sun, the moon, and the bright planets traveled. So many of those stars were seen as animals that the band was known as the "zodiac," from Greek words meaning "circle of animals." There were twelve constellations in the zodiac, representing the twelve months of the year, since the sun remained in each constellation for one month in the course of its apparent circuit of the sky.

Naturally, the vivid imagination of human beings invented myths that involved the animals (and people) that were pictured in the zodiac.

This led many people to assume that the constellations represented real objects in the sky, and it is at this level that Kipling tells his story. He uses the objects for symbolic purposes, of course, but modern astrologers do not scruple to lend them a certain reality in working out their nonsensical horoscopes.—I.A.

Additional Reading

L. Adams Beck, "The Horoscope," in *The Openers of the Gate: Stories of the Occult* (New York: Cosmopolitan, 1930).

F. R. Buckley, "Of Prophecy," in *Adventure* May 15, 1932.

Washington Irving, "The Legend of the Arabian Astrologer," in *The Alhambra* (London: Henry Colburn and Richard Bentley, 1832).

O. Henry, "Phoebe," in *Complete Works of O. Henry* (Garden City, N.Y.: Doubleday and Company, Inc., 1953).

E. Hoffmann Price, "The Infidel's Daughter," in *Far Lands Other Days* (Chapel Hill, N.C.: Carcosa, 1975).

3

Clairvoyance

Henry Slesar
The Girl Who Found Things

It was dark by the time Lucas stopped his taxi in the driveway of the Wheeler home and lumbered up the path to the front entrance. He still wore his heavy boots, despite the spring thaw; his mackinaw and knitted cap were reminders of the hard winter that had come and gone.

When Geraldine Wheeler opened the door, wearing her lightweight traveling suit, she shivered at the sight of him. "Come in," she said crisply. "My trunk is inside."

Lucas went through the foyer to the stairway, knowing his way around the house, accustomed to its rich dark textures and somber furnishings; he was Medvale's only taxi driver. He found the heavy black trunk at the foot of the stairs, and hoisted it on his back. "That all the luggage, Miss Wheeler?"

"That's all. I've sent the rest ahead to the ship. Good heavens, Lucas, aren't you *hot* in that outfit?" She opened a drawer and rummaged through it. "I've probably forgotten a million things. Gas, electricity, phone . . . Fireplace! Lucas, would you check it for me, please?"

"Yes, miss," Lucas said. He went into the living room, past the white-shrouded furniture. There were some glowing embers among the blackened stumps, and he snuffed them out with a poker.

A moment later the woman entered, pulling on long silken gloves. "All right," she said breathlessly. "I guess that's all. We can go now."

"Yes, miss," Lucas said.

She turned her back and he came up behind her, still holding the poker. He made a noise, either a sob or a grunt, as he raised the ash-coated iron and struck her squarely in the back of the head. Her knees buckled, and she sank to the carpet in an ungraceful fall. Lucas never doubted that she had died instantly, because he had once killed an ailing shorthorn bull with a blow no greater. He tried to act as calmly now. He put the poker back into the fireplace, purifying it among the hot ashes. Then he went to his victim and examined her wound. It was ugly, but there was no blood.

He picked up the light body without effort and went through the screen door of the kitchen and out into the back yard, straight to the thickly wooded acreage that surrounded the Wheeler estate. When he found an appropriate place for Geraldine Wheeler's grave, he went to the toolshed for a spade and shovel.

It was spring, but the ground was hard. He was stripped of mackinaw and cap when he was finished. For the first time in months, since the icy winter began, Lucas was warm.

† † †

April had lived up to its moist reputation; there was mud on the roads and pools of black water in the driveway. When the big white car came to a halt, its metal skirt was clotted with Medvale's red clay. Rowena, David Wheeler's wife, didn't leave the car, but waited with an impatient frown until her husband helped her out. She put her high heels into the mud, and clucked in vexation.

David smiled, smiled charmingly, forgiving the mud, the rain, and his wife's bad temper. "Come on, it's not so bad," he said. "Only a few steps." He heard the front door open, and saw his Aunt Faith waving to them. "There's the old gypsy now," he said happily. "Now remember what I told you, darling, when she starts talking about spooks and séances, you just keep a straight face."

"I'll try," Rowena said dryly.

There was affectionate collision between David and his aunt at the doorway; he put his arm around her sizable circumference and pressed his patrician nose to her plump cheek.

"David, my handsome boy! I'm so glad to see you!"

"It's wonderful seeing you, Aunt Faith!"

They were inside before David introduced the two women. David and Rowena had been married in Virginia two years ago, but Aunt Faith never stirred beyond the borders of Medvale County.

The old woman gave Rowena a glowing look of inspection. "Oh, my dear, you're beautiful," she said. "David, you beast, how could you keep her all to yourself?"

He laughed, and coats were shed, and they went into the living room together. There, the cheerfulness of the moment was dissipated. A man was standing by the fireplace smoking a cigarette in nervous puffs, and David was reminded of the grim purpose of the reunion.

"Lieutenant Reese," Aunt Faith said, "this is my nephew, David, and his wife."

Reese was a balding man with blurred and melancholy features. He shook David's hands solemnly. "Sorry we have to meet this way," he said. "But then, I always seem to meet people when they're in trouble. Of course, I've known Mrs. Demerest for some time."

"Lieutenant Reese has been a wonderful help with my charity work," Aunt Faith said. "And he's been such a comfort since . . . this awful thing happened."

David looked around the room. "It's been years since I was here. Wonder if I remember where the liquor's kept?"

"I'm afraid there is none," Reese said. "There wasn't any when we came in to search the place some weeks ago, when Miss Wheeler first disappeared."

There was a moment's silence. David broke it with, "Well, I've got a bottle in the car."

"Not now, Mr. Wheeler. As a matter of fact, I'd appreciate it if you and I could have a word alone."

Aunt Faith went to Rowena's side. "I'll tell you what. Why don't you and I go upstairs, and I'll show you your room?"

"That would be fine," Rowena said.

"I can even show you the room where David was born, and his old nursery. Wouldn't you like that?"

"That would be lovely," Rowena said flatly.

When they were alone, Reese said, "How long have you been away from Medvale, Mr. Wheeler?"

"Oh, maybe ten years. I've been back here on visits, of course. Once when my father died, four years ago. As you know, our family's business is down south."

"Yes, I knew. You and your sister—"

"My half sister."

"Yes," Reese said. "You and your half sister, you were the only proprietors of the mill, weren't you?"

"That's right."

"But you did most of the managing, I gather. When your parents died, Miss Wheeler kept the estate, and you went to Virginia to manage the mill. That's how it was, right?"

"That's how it was," David said.

"Successfully, would you say?"

David sat in a wing chair, and stretched his long legs. "Lieutenant, I'm going to save you a great deal of time. Geraldine and I didn't get along. We saw as little of each other as both could arrange, and that was *very* little."

Reese cleared his throat. "Thank you for being frank."

"I can even guess your next question, Lieutenant. You'd like to know when I saw Geraldine last."

"When did you?"

"Three months ago, in Virginia. On her semiannual visit to the mill."

"But you were in Medvale after that, weren't you?"

"Yes. I came up to see Geraldine in March on a matter of some importance. As my aunt probably told you, Geraldine refused to see me at that time."

"What was the purpose of that visit?"

"Purely business. I wanted Geraldine to approve a bank loan I wished to make to purchase new equipment. She was against it, wouldn't even discuss it. So I left and returned to Virginia."

"And you never saw her again?"

"Never," David said. He smiled, smiled engagingly, and got to his feet. "I don't care if you're a teetotaler like my aunt, Lieutenant, I've *got* to have that drink."

He went toward the front hall, but paused at the doorway. "In case you're wondering," he said lightly, "I have no idea where Geraldine is, Lieutenant. No idea at all."

Rowena and Aunt Faith didn't come downstairs until an hour later, after the lieutenant had left. Aunt Faith looked like she had been sleeping; Rowena had changed into a sweater and gray skirt. In the living room they found David, a half-empty bottle of Scotch, and a dying fire.

"Well?" Aunt Faith said. "Was he very bothersome?"

"Not at all," David said. "You look lovely, Rowena."

"I'd like a drink, David."

"Yes, of course." He made one for her, and teased Aunt Faith about her abstinence. She didn't seem to mind. She wanted to talk, about Geraldine.

"I just can't understand it," she said. "Nobody can, not the police, not anybody. She was all set for that Caribbean trip, some of her bags were already on the ship. You remember Lucas, the cab driver? He came out here to pick her up and take her to the station, but she wasn't here. She wasn't anywhere."

"I suppose the police have checked the usual sources?"

"Everything. Hospitals, morgues, everywhere. Lieutenant Reese says almost anything could have happened to her. She might have been robbed and murdered; she might have lost her memory; she might even have—" Aunt Faith blushed. "Well, this I'd *never* believe, but Lieutenant Reese says she might have disappeared deliberately—with some *man*."

Rowena had been at the window, drinking quietly. "I know what happened," she said.

David looked at her sharply.

"She just left. She just walked out of this gloomy old house and this crawly little town. She was sick of living alone. Sick of a whole town waiting for her to get married. She was tired of worrying about looms and loans and debentures. She was sick of being herself. That's how a woman can get."

She reached for the bottle, and David held her wrist. "Don't," he said. "You haven't eaten all day."

"Let me go," Rowena said softly.

He smiled, and let her go.

"I think the lieutenant was right," Rowena said. "I think there was a man, Auntie. Some vulgar type. Maybe a coal digger or a truck driver, somebody without any *charm* at all." She raised her glass in David's direction. "No charm at all."

Aunt Faith stood up, her plump cheeks mottled. "David, I have an idea—about how we can find Geraldine, I mean. I'm certain of it."

"Really?"

"But you're not going to agree with me. You're going to give me that nice smile of yours and you're going to humor me. But whether you approve or not, David, I'm going to ask Iris Lloyd where Geraldine is."

David's eyebrows made an arc. "Ask who?"

"Iris Lloyd," Aunt Faith said firmly. "Now don't tell me you've never heard of that child. There was a story in the papers about her only two months ago, and heavens knows I've mentioned her in my letters a dozen times."

"I remember," Rowena said, coming forward. "She's the one who's . . . psychic or something. Some sort of orphan?"

"Iris is a ward of the state, a resident at the Medvale Home for Girls. I've been vice-chairman of the place for donkey's years, so I know all about it. She's sixteen and amazing, David, absolutely uncanny!"

"I see." He hid an amused smile behind his glass. "And what makes Iris such a phenomenon?"

"She's a seer, David, a genuine clairvoyant. I've told you about this Count Louis Hamon, the one who called himself Cheiro the Great? Of course, he's dead now, he died in 1936, but he was gifted in the same way Iris is. He could just *look* at a person's mark and know the most astounding things—"

"Wait a minute. You really think this foundling can tell us where Geraldine is? Through some kind of séance?"

"She's not a medium. I suppose you could call her a *finder*. She seems to have the ability to *find* things that are lost. People, too,"

"How does she do it, Mrs. Demerest?" Rowena asked.

"I can't say. I'm not sure Iris can either. The gift hasn't made her happy, poor child—such talents rarely do. For a while, it seemed like nothing more than a parlor trick. There was a Sister Theresa at the Home, a rather befuddled old lady who was always misplacing her thimble or what-have-you, and each time Iris was able to find it—even in the unlikeliest places."

David chuckled. "Sometimes kids *hide* things in the unlikeliest places. Couldn't she be some sort of prankster?"

"But there was more," Aunt Faith said gravely. "One day, the Home had a picnic at Crompton Lake. They discovered that an eight-year-old girl named Dorothea was missing. They couldn't find her, until Iris Lloyd began screaming."

"Screaming . . . ?" Rowena said.

"These insights cause her great pain. But she was able to describe the place where they would find Dorothea: a small natural cave, where Dorothea was found only half alive from a bad fall she had taken."

Rowena shivered.

"You were right," David said pleasantly. "I can't agree with you, Auntie. I don't go along with this spirit business; let's leave it up to the police."

Aunt Faith sighed. "I knew you'd feel that way. But I have to do this, David. I've arranged with the Home to have Iris spend some time with us, to become acquainted with the . . . aura of Geraldine that's still in the house."

"Are you serious? You've asked that girl *here?*"

"I knew you wouldn't be pleased. But the police can't find Geraldine, they haven't turned up a clue. Iris can."

"I won't have it," he said tightly. "I'm sorry, Auntie, but the whole thing is ridiculous."

"You can't stop me. I was only hoping that you would cooperate." She looked at Rowena, her eyes softening. "You understand me, my dear. I know you do."

Rowena hesitated, then touched the old woman's hands. "I do, Mrs. Demerest." She looked at David with a curious smile. "And I'd like nothing better than to meet Iris."

† † †

Ivy failed to soften the Medvale Home's cold stone substance and ugly lines. It had been built in an era that equated orphanages with penal institutions, and its effect upon David was depressing.

The head of the institution, Sister Clothilde, entered her office, sat down briskly, and folded her hands. "I don't have to tell you that I'm against this, Mrs. Demerest," she said. "I think it's completely wrong to encourage Iris in these delusions of hers."

Aunt Faith seemed cowed by the woman; her reply was timid. "Delusions, Sister? It's a gift of God."

"If this . . . ability of Iris' has any spiritual origin, I'm afraid it's from quite another place. Not that I admit there *is* a gift."

David turned on his most charming smile, but Sister Clothilde seemed immune to it.

"I'm glad to see I have an ally," he said. "I've been telling my aunt that it's all nonsense—"

Sister Clothilde bristled. "It's true that Iris has done some remarkable things which we're at a loss to explain. But I'm hoping she'll outgrow this—whatever it is, and be just a normal, happy girl. As she is now—"

"Is she very unhappy?" Aunt Faith asked sadly.

"She's undisciplined, you might even say wild. In less than two years, when she's of legal age, we'll be forced to release her from the Home, and we'd very much like to send her away a better person than she is now."

"But you *are* letting us have her, Sister? She can come home with us?"

"Did you think my poor objections carried any weight, Mrs. Demerest?"

A moment later, Iris Lloyd was brought in.

She was a girl in the pony stage, long gawky arms and legs protruding from a smock dress that had been washed out of all color and starched out of all shape. Her stringy hair was either dirty blond or just dirty; David guessed the latter. She had a flatfooted walk, and kept twisting her arms. She kept her eyes lowered as Sister Bertha brought her forward.

"Iris," Sister Clothilde said, "you know Mrs. Demerest. And this is her nephew, Mr. Wheeler."

Iris nodded. Then, in a flash almost too sudden to be observed, her eyes came up and stabbed them with such an intensity of either hostility or malice that David almost made his surprise audible. No one else, however, seemed to have noticed.

"You remember me, Iris," Aunt Faith said. "I've been coming here at least once a year to see all you girls."

"Yes, Mrs. Demerest," Iris whispered.

"The directors have been good enough to let us take you home with us for a while. We need your help, Iris. We want you to see if you can help us find someone who is lost."

"Yes, Mrs. Demerest," she answered serenely. "I'd like to come home with you. I'd like to help you find Miss Wheeler."

"Then you know about my poor niece, Iris?"

Sister Clothilde clucked. "The Secret Service couldn't have secrets here, Mrs. Demerest. You know how girls are."

David cleared his throat, and stood up. "I guess we can get started any time. If Miss Lloyd has her bags ready. . . ."

Iris gave him a quick smile at that, but Sister Clothilde wiped it off with, "Please call her Iris, Mr. Wheeler. Remember that you're still dealing with a child."

When Iris' bags were in the trunk compartment, she climbed between David and his aunt in the front seat, and watched with interest as David turned the key in the ignition.

"Say," she said, "you wouldn't have a cigarette, would you?"

"Why, Iris!" Aunt Faith gasped.

She grinned. "Never mind," she said slightly. "Just never mind." Then she closed her eyes, and began to hum. She hummed to herself all the way to the Wheeler house.

†   †   †

David drove into town that afternoon, carrying a long list of groceries and sundries that Aunt Faith deemed necessary for the care and feeding of a sixteen-year-old girl.

He was coming out of the Medvale Supermarket when he saw Lucas Mitchell's battered black taxicab rolling slowly down the back slope of the parking lot. He frowned and walked quickly to his own car, but as he put the groceries in the rear, he saw Lucas' cab stop beside him.

"Hello, Mr. Wheeler," Lucas said, leaning out the window.

"Hello, Lucas. How's business?"

"Could I talk to you a minute, Mr. Wheeler?"

"No," David said. He went around front and climbed into the driver's seat. He fumbled in his pocket for the key, and the sight of Lucas leaving his cab made it seem much more difficult to find.

"I've got to talk to you, Mr. Wheeler."

"Not here," David said. "Not here and not now, Lucas."

"It's important. I want to ask you something."

"For the love of Mike," David said, gritting his teeth. He found the key at last, and shoved it into the slit on the dashboard. "Get out of the way, Lucas. I can't stop now."

"That girl, Mr. Wheeler. Is it true about the girl?"

"What girl?"

"That Iris Lloyd. She does funny things, that one. I'm afraid of her, Mr. Wheeler. I'm afraid she'll find out what we did."

"Get out of the way!" David shouted. He turned the key, and stomped the accelerator to make the engine roar a threat. Lucas moved away, bewildered, and David backed the car out sharply and drove off.

He got home to find Rowena pacing the living room. Her agitation served to quiet his own. "What's wrong?" he said.

"I wouldn't know for sure. Better ask your aunt."

"Where is she?"

"In her room, lying down. All I know is she went up to see if dear little Iris was awake, and they had some kind of scene. I caught only a few of the words, but I'll tell you one thing, that girl has the vocabulary of a longshoreman."

David grunted. "Well, maybe it'll knock some sense into Aunt Faith. I'll go up to see her, and tell her I'll take that little psychic delinquent back where she came from—"

"I wouldn't bother her now; she's not feeling well."

"Then I'll see the little monster. Where is she?"

"Next door to us, in Geraldine's room."

At the door, he lifted his hand to knock, but the door was flung open before his knuckles touched wood.

Iris looked out, her hair tumbled over one eye. Her mouth went from petulant to sultry, and she put her hands on the shapeless uniform where her hips should be.

"Hello, handsome," she said. "Auntie says you went shopping for me."

"What have you been up to?" He walked in and closed the door. "My aunt isn't a well woman, Iris, and we won't put up with any bad behavior. Now, what happened here?"

She shrugged and walked back to the bed. "Nothing," she said sullenly. "I found a butt in an ash tray and was taking a drag when she walked in. You'd think I was burning the house down the way she yelled."

"I heard you did some fancy yelling yourself. Is that what the Sisters taught you?"

"They didn't teach me anything worthwhile."

Suddenly Iris changed; face, posture, everything. In an astonishing transformation, she was a child again.

"I'm sorry," she whimpered. "I'm awfully sorry, Mr.Wheeler. I didn't mean to do anything wrong."

He stared at her, baffled, not knowing how to take the alteration of personality. Then he realized that the door had opened behind him and that Aunt Faith had entered.

Iris fell on the bed and began to sob, and with four long strides, Aunt Faith crossed the room and put her plump arms around her in maternal sympathy.

"There, there," she crooned, "it's all right, Iris. I know you didn't mean what you said, it's the Gift that makes you this way. And don't worry about what I asked you to do. You take your time about Geraldine, take as long as you like."

"Oh, but I *want* to help!" Iris said fervently. "I really do, Aunt Faith." She stood up, her face animated. "I can *feel* your niece in this house. I can almost hear her—whispering to me—telling me where she is!"

"You can?" Aunt Faith said in awe. "Really and truly?"

"Almost, almost!" Iris said, spinning in an awkward dance. She twirled in front of a closet, and opened the door; there were still half a dozen hangers of clothing inside. "These are *her* clothes. Oh, they're so beautiful! She must have looked beautiful in them!"

David snorted. "Has Iris ever seen a photo of Geraldine?"

The girl took out a gold lamé evening gown and held it in her arms. "Oh, it's so lovely! I can *feel* her in this dress, I can just *feel* her!" She looked at Aunt Faith with wild happiness. "I just know I'm going to be able to help you!"

"Bless you," Aunt Faith said. Her eyes were damp.

Iris was on her best behavior for the rest of the day; her mood extended all the way through dinner. It was an uncomfortable meal for everyone except the girl. She asked to leave the table before coffee was served, and went upstairs.

When the maid cleared the dinner table, they went to the living room, and David said, "Aunt Faith, I think this is a terrible mistake."

"Mistake, David? Explain that."

"This polite act of Iris'. Can't you see it's a pose?"

The woman stiffened. "You're wrong. You don't understand psychic personalities. It wasn't *her* swearing at me, David, it was this demon that possesses her. The same spirit that gives her the gift of insight."

Rowena laughed. "It's probably the spirit of an old sailor, judging from the language. Frankly, Aunt Faith, to me she seems like an ordinary little girl."

"You'll see," Aunt Faith said stubbornly. "You just wait and see how ordinary she is."

As if to prove Aunt Faith's contention, Iris came downstairs twenty minutes later wearing Geraldine Wheeler's gold lamé gown. Her face had been smeared with an overdose of makeup, and her stringy hair clumsily tied in an upsweep that refused to stay up. David and Rowena gawked at the spectacle, but Aunt Faith was only mildly perturbed.

"Iris, dear," she said, "what have you done?"

She minced into the center of the room. She hadn't changed her flat-heeled shoes, and the effect of her attempted gracefulness was almost comic; but David didn't laugh.

"Get upstairs and change," he said tightly. "You've no right to wear my sister's clothes."

Her face fell in disappointment and she looked at Aunt Faith. "Oh, Aunt Faith!" she wailed. "You know what I told you! I *have* to wear your niece's clothes, to feel her . . . aura!"

"Aura, my foot!" David said.

She stared at him, stunned. Then she fell into the wing chair by the fireplace and sobbed. Aunt Faith quickly repeated her ministrations of that afternoon, and chided David.

"You shouldn't have said that!" she said angrily. "The poor girl is trying to help us, David, and you're spoiling it!"

"Sorry," he said wryly. "I guess I'm just not a believer, Aunt Faith."

"You won't even give her a chance!"

Aunt Faith waited until Iris' sobs quieted, her face thoughtful. Then she leaned close to the girl's ear. "Iris, listen to me. You remember those things you did at the Home? The way you found things for Sister Theresa?"

Iris blinked away the remainder of her tears. "Yes."

"Do you think you could do that again, Iris? Right now, for us?"

"I—I don't know. I could try."

"Will you let her try, David?"

"I don't know what you mean."

"I want you to hide something, or name some object you've lost or misplaced, perhaps somewhere in this house."

"This is silly. It's a parlor game—"

"David!"

He frowned. "All right, have it your own way. How do we play this little game of hide-and-seek?"

Rowena said, "David, what about the cat?"

"The cat?"

"You remember. You once told me about a wool kitten you used to have as a child. You said you lost it somewhere in the house when you were five, and you were so unhappy about it that you wouldn't eat for days."

"That's preposterous. That's thirty years ago—"

"All the better," Aunt Faith said. "All the better, David." She turned to the girl. "Do you think you can find it, Iris? Could you find David's cloth kitten?"

"I'm not sure. I'm never sure, Aunt Faith."

"Just try, Iris. We won't blame you if you fail. It might have been thrown out ages ago, but try anyway."

The girl sat up, and put her face in her hands.

"David," Aunt Faith whispered, "put out the light."

David turned off the one table lamp that lit the room. The flames of the fireplace animated their shadows.

"Try, Iris," Aunt Faith encouraged.

The clock on the mantlepiece revealed its loud tick. Then Iris dropped her hands limply into her lap, and she leaned against the high back of the wing chair with a long, troubled sigh.

"It's a trance," Aunt Faith whispered. "You see it, David, you must see it. The girl is in a genuine trance."

"I wouldn't know," David said.

Iris' eyes were closed, and her lips were moving. There were drops of spittle at the corners of her mouth.

"What's she saying?" Rowena said. "I can't hear her."

"Wait! You must wait!" Aunt Faith cautioned.

Iris' voice became audible. "Hot," she said. "Oh, it's so hot . . . so hot . . ." She squirmed in the chair, and her fingers tugged at the neckline of the evening dress. "So hot back here!" she said loudly. "Oh, please! Oh, please! Kitty is hot! Kitty is hot!"

Then Iris screamed, and David jumped to his feet. Rowena came to his side and clutched his arm.

"It's nothing!" David said. "Can't you see it's an act?"

"Hush, please!" Aunt Faith said. "The girl is in pain!"

Iris moaned and thrashed in the chair. There were beads of perspiration on her forehead now, and her squirming, twisting body had all the aspects of a soul in hellfire.

"Hot! Hot!" she shrieked. "Behind the stove! Oh, please, oh please, oh please . . . so hot . . . kitty so hot . . . " Then she sagged in the chair and groaned.

Aunt Faith rushed to her side and picked up the thin wrists. She rubbed them vigorously, and said, "You heard her, David, you heard it for yourself. Can you doubt the girl now?"

"I didn't hear anything. A lot of screams and moans and gibberish about heat. What's it supposed to mean?"

"You *are* a stubborn fool! Why, the kitten's behind the stove, of course, where you probably stuffed it when you were a little brat of a boy!"

Rowena tugged his arm. "We could find out, couldn't we? Is the same stove still in the kitchen?"

"I suppose so. There's some kind of electronic oven, too, but they've never moved the old iron monster, far as I know."

"Let's look, David, please!" Rowena urged.

Iris was coming awake. She blinked and opened her eyes and looked at their watching faces. "Is it there?" she said. "Is it where I said it was? Behind the stove in the kitchen?"

"We haven't looked yet," David said.

"Then look," Aunt Faith commanded.

They looked, Rowena and David, and it was there, a dust-covered cloth kitten, browned and almost destroyed by three decades of heat and decay; but it was there.

David clutched the old plaything in his fist, and his face went white. Rowena looked at him sadly, and thought he was suffering the pangs of nostalgia, but he wasn't. He was suffering from fear.

†   †   †

In the beginning of May the rains vanished and were replaced by a succession of sunlit days. Iris Lloyd began to spend most of her time outdoors, communing with nature or her own cryptic thoughts.

That was where David found her one midweek afternoon, lying on the grass amid a tangle of daisies. She was dissecting one in an ancient ritual.

"Well," David said, "what's the answer?"

She smiled coyly, and threw the disfigured daisy away. "You tell me, Uncle David."

"Cut out the Uncle David stuff." He bent down to pick up the mutilated flower, and plucked off the remaining petals. "Loves me not," he said.

"Who? Your wife?" She smirked at him boldly. "You can't fool me, Uncle David. I know all about it."

He started to turn away, but she caught his ankle. "Don't go away. I want to talk."

He came back and squatted down to her level. "Look, what's the story with you, Iris? You've been here over a week and you haven't done anything about—well, you know what. This is just a great big picnic for you, isn't it?"

"Sure it is," she said. "You think I want to go back to that sticky Home? It's better here." She lay back on the grass. "No uniforms. No six a.m. prayers. None of that junk they call food." She grinned. "And a lot nicer company."

"I suppose I should say thank you."

"There's nothing you can say I don't know already." She tittered. "Did you forget? I'm psychic."

"Is it really true, Iris," he said casually, "or is it some kind of trick? I mean, these things you do."

"I'll show you if it's a trick." She covered her eyes with both hands. "Your wife hates you," she said. "She thinks you're rotten. You weren't even married a year when you started running around with other women. You never even went to the mill, not more'n once or twice a month, that was how *you* ran the business. All *you* knew how to do was spend the money."

David's face had grown progressively paler during her recitation. Now he grabbed her thin forearm. "You little brat! You're not psychic! You're an eavesdropper!"

"Let go of my arm!"

"Your room is right next door. You've been listening!"

"All right!" she squealed. "You think I could help hearing you two arguing?"

He released her wrist. She rubbed it ruefully, and then laughed, deciding it was funny. Suddenly she flung herself at him and kissed him on the mouth, clutching him with her thin, strong fingers.

He pushed her away, amazed. "What do you think you're doing?" he said roughly. "You dumb kid!"

"I'm not a kid!" she said. "I'm almost seventeen!"

"You were sixteen three months ago!"

"I'm a woman!" Iris shrieked. "But you're not even a man!" She struck him a blow on the chest with a balled fist, and it knocked the breath out of him. Then she turned and ran down the hill toward the house.

He returned home through the back of the estate and entered the kitchen. Aunt Faith was giving Hattie some silverware-cleaning instructions at the kitchen table. She looked up and said, "Did you call for a taxi, David?"

"Taxi? No, why should I?"

"I don't know. But Lucas' cab is in the driveway; he said he was waiting for you."

Lucas climbed out of the cab at David's approach. He peeled off the knitted cap and pressed it against his stomach.

"What do you want, Lucas?"

"To talk, Mr. Wheeler, like I said last week."

David climbed into the rear seat. "All right," he said, "drive someplace. We can talk while you're driving."

"Yes, sir."

Lucas didn't speak again until they were out of sight of the estate; then he said, "I did what you told me, Mr. Wheeler, 'zactly like you said. I hit her clean, she didn't hurt a bit, no blood. Just like an old steer she went down, Mr. Wheeler."

"All right," David said harshly. "I don't want to hear about it anymore, Lucas, I'm satisfied. You should be, too. You got your money, now forget about it."

"I picked her up," Lucas said dreamily. "I took her out in the woods, like you said, and I dug deep, deep as I could. The ground was awful hard then, Mr. Wheeler, it was a lot of work. I smoothed it over real good, ain't nobody could guess what was there. Nobody . . . except—"

"Is it that girl? Is that what's bothering you?"

"I heard awful funny things about her, Mr. Wheeler. About her findin' things, findin' that little kid what fell near Crompton Lake. She's got funny eyes. Maybe she can see right into that woman's grave—"

"Stop the car, Lucas!"

Lucas put his heavy foot on the brake.

"Iris Lloyd won't find her," David said, teeth clenched. "Nobody will. You've got to stop worrying about it. The more you worry, the more you'll give yourself away."

"But she's right behind the house, Mr. Wheeler! She's so close, right in the woods."

"You've got to forget it, Lucas, like it never happened. My sister's disappeared, and she's not coming back. As for the girl, let me worry about her."

He clapped Lucas' shoulder in what was meant to be reassurance, but his touch made Lucas stiffen.

"Now take me home," David said.

†   †   †

He worried about Iris for another five days, but she seemed to have forgotten the purpose of her stay completely. She was a house guest, a replacement for the missing Geraldine, and Aunt Faith's patience seemed inexhaustible as she waited for the psychic miracle to happen.

The next Thursday night, in their bedroom, Rowena caught David's eyes in the vanity mirror and started to say something about the mill.

"Shut up," he said pleasantly. "Don't say another word. I've found out that Iris can hear every nasty little quarrel in this room, so let's declare a truce."

"She doesn't have to eavesdrop, does she? Can't she read minds?" She swiveled around to face him. "Well, she's not the only clairvoyant around here. I can read her mind, too."

"Oh?"

"It's easy," Rowena said bitterly. "I can read every wicked thought in her head, every time she looks at you. I'm surprised you haven't noticed."

"She's a child, for heaven's sake."

"She's in love with you."

He snorted, and went to his bed.

"You're her Sir Galahad," she said mockingly. "You're going to rescue her from that evil castle where they're holding her prisoner. Didn't you know that?"

"Go to sleep, Rowena."

"Of course, there's still one minor obstruction to her plans. A small matter of your wife. But then, I've never been much of a hindrance to your romances, have I?"

"I've asked you for a truce," he said.

She laughed. "You're a pacifist, David, that's part of your famous charm. That's why you came up here in March, wasn't it? To make a truce with Geraldine?"

"I came here on business."

"Yes, I know. To keep Geraldine from sending you to prison, wasn't that the business?"

"You don't know anything about it."

"I have eyes, David. Not like Iris Lloyd, but eyes. I know you were taking money from the mill, too much of it. Geraldine knew it, too. How much time did she give you to make up the loss?"

David thought of himself as a man without a temper, but he found one now, and lost it just as quickly. "Not another word, you hear? I don't want to hear another word!"

He lay awake for the next hour, his eyes staring sightlessly into the dark of the room.

He was still awake when he heard the shuffle of feet in the corridor outside. He sat up, listening, and heard the quiet click of a latching door.

He got out of bed and put on his robe and slippers. There was a patch of moonlight on his wife's pillow; Rowena was asleep. He went noiselessly to the door and opened it.

Iris Lloyd, in a nightdress, was walking slowly down the stairway to the ground floor, her blond head rigid on her shoulders, moving with the mechanical grace of the somnambulist.

At the end of the hall, Aunt Faith opened her door and peered out, wide-eyed. "Is that you, David?"

"It's Iris," David said.

Aunt Faith came into the hallway, tying the housecoat around her middle, her hands shaking. David tried to restrain her from following the girl, but his aunt was stubborn.

They paused at the landing. Iris, her eyes open and unblinking, was moving frenetically around the front hall.

"What did I forget?" the girl mumbled. "What did I forget?"

Aunt Faith reached for David's arm.

"You're late," Iris said, facing the front door. "It's time we were going." She whirled and seemed to be looking straight at her spectators without seeing them.

"We have to be going!" she said, almost tearfully."Oh, please get my luggage. I'm so nervous. I'm so afraid . . ."

"It's a trance," Aunt Faith whispered, squeezing his hand. "Oh, David, this may be it!"

"What did I forget?" Iris quavered. "Gas, electricity, phone, fireplace . . . Is the fireplace still lit? *Oh!*" She sobbed suddenly, and put her face in her hands.

David took a step toward her, and Aunt Faith said, "Don't! Don't waken her!"

Now Iris was walking, a phantom in the loose gown, toward the back of the house. She went to the kitchen and opened the screen door.

"She's going outside!" David said. "We can't let her—"

"Leave her alone, David! Please, leave her alone!"

Iris stepped outside into the back yard, following a path of moonlight that trailed into the dark woods.

"Iris!" David shouted. *"Iris!"*

"No!" Aunt Faith cried. "Don't waken her! You mustn't!"

"You want that girl to catch pneumonia?" David said furiously. "Are you crazy? Iris!" he shouted again.

She stopped at the sound of her name, turned, and the eyes went from nothingness to bewilderment. Then, as David's arms enclosed her, she screamed and struck at him. He fought to drag her back to the house, pinning her arms to her side. She was sobbing bitterly by the time he had her indoors.

Aunt Faith fluttered about her with tearful cries. "Oh, how could you do that, David?" she groaned. "You know you shouldn't waken a sleep-walker, you know that!"

"I wasn't going to let that child catch her death of cold! That would be a fine thing to tell the Sisters, wouldn't it, Auntie? That we let their little girl die of pneumonia?"

Iris had quieted, her head still cradled in her arms. Now she looked up and studied their strained faces. "Aunt Faith . . ."

"Are you all right, Iris?"

There was still a remnant of the sleepwalker's distant look in her round eyes. "Yes," she said. "Yes, I'm all right. I think I'm ready now, Aunt Faith. I can do it now."

"Do it now? You mean . . . tell us where Geraldine is?"

"I can try, Aunt Faith."

The old woman straightened up, her manner transformed. "We must call Lieutenant Reese, David. Right now. He'll want to hear anything Iris says."

"Reese? It's after two in the morning!"

"He'll come," Aunt Faith said grimly. "I know he will. I'll telephone him myself; you take Iris to her room."

David helped the girl up the stairs, frowning at the closeness with which she clung to his side. Her manner was meek. She fell on her bed, her eyes closed. Then the eyes opened, and she smiled at him. "You're scared," she said.

He swallowed hard, because it was true. "I'm sending you back," he said hoarsely. "I'm not letting you stay in this house another day. You're more trouble than you're worth, just like Sister Clothilde said."

"Is that the reason, David?"

She began to laugh. Her laughter angered him, and he sat beside her and clamped his hand over her mouth.

"Shut up!" he said. "Shut up, you little fool!"

She stopped laughing. Her eyes, over the fingers of his hand, penetrated his. He put his arm to his side.

Iris leaned toward him. "David," she said sensuously, "I won't give you away. Not if you don't want me to."

"You don't know what you're talking about," he said uncertainly. "You're a fraud."

"Am I? You don't believe that."

She leaned closer still. He grabbed her with brutal suddenness and kissed her mouth. She moved against him, moaning, her thin fingers plucking at the lapel of his robe.

When they parted, he wiped his mouth in disgust and said, "What part of hell did you come from anyway?"

"David," she said dreamily, "you'll take me away from that place, won't you? You won't let me go back there, will you?"

"You're crazy! You know I'm married—"

"That doesn't matter. You can divorce that woman, David. You don't love her anyway, do you?"

The door opened. Rowena, imperious in her nightgown, looked at them with mixed anger and disdain.

"Get out of here!" Iris shrieked. "I don't want you in my room!"

"Rowena—" David turned to her.

His wife said, "I just came in to tell you something, David. You were right about the walls between these rooms."

"I hate you!" Iris shouted. "David hates you, too! Tell her, David. Why don't you tell her?"

"Yes," Rowena said. "Why don't you, David? It's the only thing you haven't done so far."

He looked back and forth between them, the hot-eyed young girl in the heavy flannel nightdress, the cool-eyed woman in silk, waiting to be answered, asking for injury.

"Damn you both!" he muttered. Then he brushed past Rowena and went out.

† † †

Lieutenant Reese still seemed half asleep; the stray hairs on his balding scalp were ruffled, and his clothes had the appearance of having been put on hastily. Rowena, still in nightclothes, sat by the window, apparently disinterested. Aunt Faith was at the fireplace, coaxing the embers into flames.

Iris sat in the wing chair, her hands clasped in her lap, her expression enigmatic.

When the fire started, Aunt Faith said, "We can begin any time. David, would you turn out the lamp?"

David made himself a drink before he dimmed the lights, and then went over to the chair opposite Iris.

Aunt Faith said, "Are you ready, my child?"

Iris, white-lipped, nodded.

David caught her eyes before they shut in the beginning of the trance. They seemed to recognize his unspoken, plaintive question, but they gave no hint of a reply.

Then they were silent. The silence lasted for a hundred ticks of the mantelpiece clock.

Gradually Iris Lloyd began to rock from side to side in the chair, and her lips moved.

"It's starting," Aunt Faith whispered. "It's starting."

Iris began to moan. She made sounds of torment and twisted her young body in an ecstasy of anguish. Her mouth fell open, and she gasped; the spittle frothed at the corners and spilled onto her chin.

"You've got to stop this," David said, his voice shaking. "The girl's having a fit."

Lieutenant Reese looked alarmed. "Mrs. Demerest, don't you think—"

"Please!" Aunt Faith said. "It's only the trance. You've seen it before, David, you know—"

Iris cried out.

Reese stood. "Maybe Mr. Wheeler's right. The girl might do herself some harm, Mrs. Demerest—"

"No, no! You must wait!"

Then Iris screamed, in such a mounting cadence of terror that the glass of the room trembled in sympathetic vibration, and Rowena put her hands over her ears.

"Aunt Faith! Aunt Faith!" Iris shrieked. "I'm here! I'm here, Aunt Faith, come and find me! Help me, Aunt Faith, it's dark! So dark! Oh, won't somebody help me?"

"Where are you?" Aunt Faith cried, the tears flooding her cheeks. "Oh, Geraldine, my poor darling, where are you?"

"Oh, help me! Help, please!" Iris writhed and twisted in the chair. "It's so dark, I'm so afraid! Aunt Faith! Do you hear me? Do you hear me?"

"We hear you! We hear you, darling!" Aunt Faith sobbed. "Tell us where you are! Tell us!"

Iris lifted herself from the chair, screamed again, and fell back in a fit of weeping. A few moments later, the heaving of her breast subsided, and her eyes opened slowly.

David tried to go to her, but Lieutenant Reese intervened. "One moment, Mr. Wheeler."

Reese went to his knees, and put his thumb on the girl's pulse. With his other hand, he widened her right eye and stared at the pupil. "Can you hear me, Iris? Are you all right?"

"Yes, sir, I'm all right."

"Do you know what happened just now?"

"Yes, sir, everything."

"Do you know where Geraldine Wheeler is?"

She looked at the circle of faces, and then paused at David's.

His eyes pleaded.

"Yes," Iris whispered.

"Where is she, Iris?"

Iris' gaze went distant. "Someplace far away. A place with ships. The sun is shining there. I saw hills, and green trees . . . I heard bells ringing in the streets . . ."

Reese turned to the others, to match his own bewilderment with theirs. "A place with ships. Does that mean anything to you?"

There was no reply.

"It's a city," Iris said. "It's far away."

"Across the ocean, Iris? Is that where Geraldine is?"

"No! Not across the ocean. Someplace here, in America, where there are ships. I saw a bay and a bridge and blue water—"

"San Francisco!" Rowena said. "I'm sure she means San Francisco, Lieutenant."

"Iris," Reese said sternly. "You've got to be certain of this, we can't chase all over the country. Was it San Francisco? Is that where you saw Geraldine?"

"Yes!" Iris said. "Now I know. There were trolleys in the streets, funny trolleys going uphill . . . It's San Francisco. She's in San Francisco!"

Reese got to his feet, and scratched the back of his neck. "Well, who knows?" he said. "It's as good a guess as I've heard. Has Geraldine ever been in San Francisco before?"

"Never," Aunt Faith said. "Why would she go there? David?"

"I don't know." David grinned. He went over to Iris and patted her shoulder. "But that's where Iris says she is, and I guess the spirits know what they're talking about. Right, Iris?"

She turned her head aside. "I want to go home," she said. "I want Sister Clothilde . . ." Then she began to cry, softly, like a child.

† † †

It was spring, but the day felt summery. When David and Aunt Faith returned from the Medvale Home for Girls, the old woman looked out of the car window, but the countryside charm failed to enliven her mood.

"Come on, you old gypsy"—David laughed—"your little clairvoyant was a huge success. Now all the police have to do is find Geraldine in San Francisco—if she hasn't taken a boat to the South Seas by now."

"I don't understand it," Aunt Faith said. "It's not like Geraldine to run away without a word. Why did she do it?"

"I don't know," David replied.

Later that day he drove into town. When he saw Lucas standing at the depot beside his black taxi, he pulled up and climbed out, the smile wide on his face. "Hello, Lucas. How's the taxi buisiness?"

"Couldn't be better." Lucas searched his face. "You got any news for me, Mr. Wheeler?"

"Maybe I do. Suppose we step into your office."

He clapped his hand on Lucas' shoulder, and Lucas preceded him into the depot office. He closed the door carefully, and told the cabman to sit down.

"It's all over," David said. "I've just come from the Medvale Home for Girls. We took Iris Lloyd back."

Lucas released a sigh from deep in his burly chest. "Then she didn't know? She didn't know where the—that woman was?"

"She didn't know, Lucas."

The cabman leaned back, and squeezed the palms of his hands together. "Then I did the right thing. I knew it was the right thing, Mr. Wheeler, but I didn't want to tell you."

"Right thing? What do you mean?"

Lucas looked up with glowing eyes, narrowed by what he might have thought was cunning. "I figured that girl could tell if the body was buried right outside the house. But she'd never find it if it was someplace else. Ain't that right? Someplace far away?"

A spasm took David by the throat. He hurled himself at Lucas and grabbed the collar of his wool jacket.

"What are you talking about? What do you mean, someplace else?" Lucas was too frightened to answer. "What did you do?" David shouted.

"I was afraid you'd be sore," Lucas whimpered. "I didn't want to tell you. I went out in the woods one night last week and dug up that woman's body. I put it in that trunk of hers, Mr. Wheeler, and I sent it by train, far away as I could get it. Farthest place I know, Mr. Wheeler. That's why Iris Lloyd couldn't find it. It's too far away now."

"Where? Where, you moron? San Francisco?"

Lucas mumbled his terror, and then nodded his shaggy head.

The baggagemaster listened intently to the questions of the two plain-clothesmen, shrugged when they showed him the photograph of the woman, and then led them to the Unclaimed Baggage room in the rear of the terminal. When he pointed to the trunk that bore the initials G.W., the two men exchanged looks, and then walked slowly toward it. They broke open the lock, and lifted the lid.

Three thousand miles away, Iris Lloyd sat up in the narrow dormitory bed and gasped into the darkness, wondering what strange dream had broken her untroubled sleep.

Afterword

The human senses (and those of any other kind of living thing, of course) operate on rational principles and require appropriate transfers of energy. We see, because certain types of energy-containing photons impinge upon the retina of the eye, inducing certain chemical changes that are reflected in the electrical impulses that travel along the optic nerve and are interpreted as vision in the optical lobes of the brain.

Without the photons there is darkness and we cannot see. If the photons reflected from some particular object strike an opaque barrier, they do not reach our eyes and we cannot see the object. If the photons must cover too long a distance, they spread out and not enough of them reach our eyes to make vision possible.

This severe limitation of vision is bothersome and we lose patience with it, understandably enough. One response is to pretend that we don't need photons; that we (or at least some people) can somehow see in the dark, see through barriers, see at a distance, and so on. This is called "clairvoyance" (French for "clear vision").

Clairvoyance is only one of the many ways in which some people imagine that we can perceive without *the restrictions of the familiar senses. Clairvoyance is a form of "extrasensory perception," that is, "perception outside the senses."*

Needless to say, no definite evidence for any form of clairvoyance has ever been presented.—I.A.

Additional Reading

Truman Capote, "Jug of Silver," in *A Tree of Night and Other Stories* (New York: Random House, 1949).

Violet Hunt, "The Operation," in *Tales of the Uneasy* (London: Heinemann, 1911).

Barry Pain, "Smeath," in *Stories in Grey* (London: T. Werner Laurie, 1911).

Elizabeth Spencer, "The Finder," in *The Stories of Elizabeth Spencer* (Garden City, N.Y.: Doubleday, 1980).

Fleta Campbell Springer, "Legend," in *Harper's Magazine* 149, Nov. 1924.

4

Death Portents

Gertrude Henderson
The Emigrant Banshee

A banshee is not lovely, and her ugliness is in proportion to her aristocracy. The hereditary banshee of the O'Gradys was ancient and honorable, and because of these things she was hideous beyond imagination. All instructed people know, of course, that a banshee is a spirit of doom, who floats in the gloom of night to the windows of the family that is her own, flaps her leathern wings, and wails dismally; and that means to the people within that some one is about to die. And all the good old families, all the blue-bloods, trust everything to her judgment, and never die without her warning, and never do her the discourtesy of living after it.

Her face is always long and gaunt and fearsome. Her hair streams in long, dishevelled red locks across and around her face; her teeth are black and long like tusks, and her arms are long and bony, and as she moves on black, bat-like wings, long, indefinite garments trail out behind her, and she is a sight indescribably dreadful; and in all these marks of a true banshee the banshee of the O'Gradys was a distinguished hideousness.

On the edge of a winter's night she floated above the roof of the O'Gradys' ancestral dwelling, swaying slightly in the draught of the smoke that curled up the chimney from cooking the Mulligan potatoes below, and she talked to the doomful wraith of the Sobbing Child who sat on the end of the ridge-pole, listening. The wraith of the Sobbing Child had flitted and wept up and down the roads and by-ways of the country-side for more than three generations, but she was very young compared with the old, old banshee of the O'Gradys, so she sat respectfully silent and listened, while her tears streamed down her face.

"It's hard times these are we're living in; hard times!" said the banshee. "I've wailed for the O'Gradys these seven generations back, faithful. Never a one of 'em died in all those years that I didn't come and wail before it. Drownings and sickness and hangings and the croup and the gout— they've all been the same to me. I've wailed 'em all off, one after another, and sometimes three in a week in a famine time, and never failed a one of 'em. And there isn't a banshee in Ireland—it's the plain truth I'm telling you, and no vanity—there isn't another in all Ireland has a wail as hideous as that I've done for them right along, that makes their blood all curdle up inside of their hearts, and their eyes stick out, and their knees knock together under them; not another one."

"And the last of the family gone now," sobbed the wraith from the end of the ridge-pole.

"The very last one of them all," said the banshee. "I wailed for him four weeks ago this night, and there he lies now in the churchyard. 'Pa-a-a-trick!' I said at his window, and there it is already on the stone over him, 'Patrick O'Grady, aged eighty-four years, seven months.' And never a child of him left, and not a living O'Grady around!"

"Whatever's to become of you, poor lady!" wept the wraith.

"I don't know! I don't know!" said the banshee dolefully.

"You couldn't take up the Mulligans now, could you?" said the wraith timidly, "seeing they've come to live right in the old place, handy."

"Take up the Mulligans, and me an O'Grady banshee! Folks that nobody knows who they are at all, or where they came from! No, I couldn't take up with the Mulligans," said the banshee. "I never wailed for any but the first families yet, and I never will, whatever comes of it."

The wraith lifted her tear-wet countenance to the moonlight.

"Wasn't there a Danny O'Grady," she said, "only brother to Patrick, who went away to America to make his fortune when he was a slip of a boy, fifty or sixty or seventy years back?"

"Yes, there was," said the banshee, "and more's the pity he went. He ought to have stayed and brought up his children to die and be buried decent at home, and we'd never have come to this trouble. Mulligans!" said she, and looked at the chimney smoke with infinite disdain.

"I was thinking could you go over there to America," said the wraith, and her tears flowed afresh at the daring of her suggestion.

"Me go over there to America?" said the banshee.

"Yes, and find Danny and his children."

"And what'd I do over in America?" said the banshee.

"Wail," said the wraith. "What else?"

"Wraith, dear!" said the banshee, "I never thought of it till this minute before!"

"And him the eldest son," said the wraith.

"And with a houseful of children to bring up, most likely," said the banshee.

"And never a one to give him a bit of a warning," said the wraith.

"I'll go this night," said the banshee. "And I'll never forget you for suggesting it. If there's any one belonging to you that's going to be taken off, I'll be proud to wail for him, and I'll do it the most hideous I know how. I will indeed, no matter who it is—if it isn't a Mulligan. Good-by, then, wraith, dear. I'll be starting."

"Good-by," said the wraith. "Good luck to you."

The travelling of banshees is not the travelling of ordinary people, who wear flesh, nor are their ways of finding out things so crude and slow. When the next evening came, there flitted in the murk around the cottage of the American O'Gradys a shape the like of which had never been seen there before. It drew near the window on soundless leathern wings, and its long, lean, pallid visage looked in and numbered the family with huge, silent satisfaction. Then it flew to the chimney and there rested, and murmured to itself in a voice that was like the sound of winds:

"There's Danny O'Grady himself; an O'Grady, if ever there was one. But getting on, Danny is. He's waited for me. And Danny his son, that's a man grown, and young Danny's wife, and seven children around them. And there's other O'Gradys near by, old Danny's other children and their families. Oh, it's a fine thing I came to America! Sure it's a fine land, it is so!

"Did you hear that now!" said the banshee suddenly, and swept her long, hanging, red locks away from her ear to listen better. Somebody was coughing under the roof, and coughing seriously. The banshee dropped to the window again.

"It's himself," she said. "It's old Danny. Do you see how it shakes him, the creature! Oh, it's needing me he'll be, soon enough, Danny will."

A fresh cough seized the little old gentleman inside, and his family banshee watched him with a kind of rapturous absorption till it passed.

"It's not one instant minute too soon I got here," said she. "That's a mortal bad cough Danny has. It might have carried him off any day in the middle of the night, and him with never a notion he was going till he was laid in his grave. To think of the risk he's had, and me there in the old country all the time and never knowing! It'd maybe make him take to his bed and go off this night out of pure gratitude and comfort if he knew I was here, and it'd all be done decent and home-like, just as if he was back in Ireland.

"I wonder had I better give him his warning this night," she meditated, "or would you wait the night and see by tomorrow will he last a week or so yet?"

For some minutes she watched at the window, muttering to herself at intervals. Finally she let go her hold on the shutter, regretfully. "I'll risk him the night," she said. "But he'll be going soon," and she floated back to the chimney.

The next night and the next she watched him intently. The third day old Danny took to his bed with a fever.

"Now you see what a blessing it is I'm here," said the banshee to herself when she looked in and saw him. "When he's like that is the time an O'Grady wants his own banshee, whatever land he's in. Sure it's the very minute now if ever it will be."

So saying, she clutched at the shutters of his window with her lean, hard fingers, and made ready for a mighty flap of her leathern wings, the prelude to such a wail as had never been heard in America before. It was the first time her voice had been lifted in her new land, and she meant it to be masterly and frightful. She flapped her wings together once, twice, three times, loud and ominously, and paused before the wail. Danny inside pulled the blankets up around his chin.

"There's a shingle loose on the shed roof," said he. "Don't you hear it flap?"

The banshee heard him, but without taking in what he said; she was absorbed in what was about to come. She flung back her head and wailed direfully:

"Da-a-a-nny!"

Then she looked in to see the family struck with the terror she was accustomed to see in recognition of her efforts.

"Do you hear how the wind blows, father?" said young Mrs. Danny, placidly rocking by the fire.

"Yes," said Danny from his bed. "It's a cold night it'll be."

The banshee was amazed. More than that, she was wounded. Nobody had ever offered her such an affront in her whole career, and she had made sacrifices for this family. She stood perfectly still for a moment.

"They aren't used to it," she whispered to herself. "Maybe they didn't just hear."

Again she threw back her head and again the wail rose in long, quavering cadences, "Da-a-a-nny!" She opened her eyes and looked again. Danny lay with eyes half shut, and his breath came evenly. Nothing interrupted the quiet of the room but the little squeak of Mrs. Danny's rockers.

The banshee's long hand trembled on the shutter. She summoned all her powers for one last, nerve-shattering shriek. Out came the third wail, a prolonged, shuddering, frightful, final "Da-a-a-an-ny!" and as she heard the appalling sound of her own voice her heart was proud, and she knew she had never done anything more horrible through all the seven generations. Still, for an instant she hesitated to open her eyes again. When she did look, Danny had lifted himself on an elbow, and Mrs. Danny's rockers were still.

"Did you hear that?" said Danny.

"Yes. I did," said Mrs. Danny.

"Whatever do you think it was?" said Danny. "That's more than the wind and the shingle just."

"Oh," said Mrs. Danny, her face suddenly clearing and her rocker beginning its squeak again, "it's that cat of Mrs. Maloney's next door, the old ugly thing!"

Danny lay back again on his pillow.

"That's what it was," said he.

The banshee flapped heavily to the chimney-top and sat there shivering and miserable, a dishonored banshee. After seven generations of fidelity she had come to America and wailed her uttermost, and not an O'Grady had quivered an eyelash. After a while she began to whimper to herself.

"If he'd seen his grandfather go! Not half such a wail as that, and all the children's eyes as if they'd jump out of their heads! The first wail I gave—'It's the banshee!' he said, and turned over on his back, and folded his arms on his breast as resigned, and never spoke a word afterward. Oh, but he was a fine gentleman! And the beautiful wake they had over him!"

Very late in the night she began again to mutter to herself.

"But it's the warning all the same," she said. "They heard me, anyhow, even if they didn't know who I was. Old Danny'll go. He'll never see another night come. It's the warning."

Very long after that she stirred uneasily and moaned something more to herself.

" 'That cat of Maloneys!' said she, 'The old ugly thing!' "

For a whole week after that night she watched with painful anxiety, but by the end of that time old Danny was better, and before the end of the second one he was up and about again, and heartier than before. It was a cruel blow to the banshee. But it was only the beginning. She brooded over her discomfiture for some weeks. Then she decided to show herself to somebody. It was a thing she seldom condescended to do, but she thought a sight of the terror she had been used to see when she did was a tonic she needed to brace her nerves.

She chose a dark night, with clouds and some wind. A policeman came up the street, and she thought he was Irish by the looks of him. She gestured with her long arms, and shook out her long red locks, and turned her face his way, and crossed the road in front of him. He walked stolidly on. She crossed his path again, and a third time, and a fourth, each time nearer. The last time she chattered her teeth and moaned a little. He stopped. "The poor old body must be out of her wits," he said. "It's a bad night for an old woman like her to be out by herself. Have you lost your way, ma'am?"

The banshee shrunk into the shadow, and again rose heavily to the chimney-top. The policeman looked around. "Where did the woman go so fast?" he said. Then, not finding her, he sauntered along down the block.

"It's the trouble that's wearing me down," she said. "I'm losing all my looks. To think of the hideous thing I used to be, and now he takes me for an old woman! I'd better have stayed at home with the Mulligans."

She had no heart for another effort that night, and all the next night and the next she sat huddled and hidden in a dim chimney-corner, like a wisp of smoke caught there, and revolved her insults within her. In the early dusk of the third evening, while the sky in the west was still pink, she lifted her head suddenly, and through the veil of her red locks resolve looked out of her red-rimmed eyes. She shook out her black wings silently and drifted down from her chimney into the roadside, and, keeping in the uncertain shadows of the trees, went up the road toward the cottage where old Danny's youngest boy lived with his family. It was still almost day, but if it took broad sunlight itself to open people's eyes to her, she was determined now that she must be seen and realized. And that is most significant, for at home in Ireland no self-respecting banshee will go abroad before the night is in its full blackness; and this one, being of unusual aristocracy, had always kept to thick clouds, besides, and utter starlessness, and had a fastidious taste for storm nights, with thunder and lightning.

At some distance from the house small Timmy O'Grady was showing his sister Norah how high he could climb up into a tree and not be scared, and then how recklessly he could swing himself down and not fall. But, fired by her admiration, he ventured too boldly, and fell. It was only from a low limb, and was not serious, but he lay still a minute, feeling how much he was hurt, to make sure whether it was worth while to cry. Norah was sure it was and began lustily, upon which encouragement Timmy drew up his face and opened his mouth for a howl of his own. But before the first sound of it could come, a spectacle caught his eyes that checked it and fastened his mouth open in utter amazement. The banshee, hair streaming, eyes lurid, her garments flying in mad disorder in the wind, was running to and fro in front of him, now wringing her bony fingers, now beating the air with her lean arms, and in the instant he saw her she drew back her wrinkled lips and out from between the black fangs of her teeth came hissing and howling and shrieking such a sound that Norah stopped short in the very middle of a scream and opened her eyes to the size of saucers. "I'm the banshee!" she wailed, "the banshee of the O'Gradys! You're going to d-i-i-e! The banshee of all the O'Gradys! Ti-i-immy! You've fallen out of the top of a tree and broken your neck, and it's truth I'm telling you! Oh, Ti-i-immy!"

"I ain't either," said Timmy indignantly. "I ain't hurt."

The banshee was in too much frenzy of delight at her chance, and at being seen, to notice what he said. She tore at her hair, and "Ti-i-immy! Ti-i-immy!" she wailed on, and "Ti-i-immy! Ti-i-immy!" never noticing that she was far past the third time.

Timmy wriggled to his feet and backed over toward his frozen sister.

"You stop that!" he said stoutly, quaking but valiant.

Norah seized her brother's jacket the moment it was within reach.

"Who's she?" her stiff lips managed to whisper.

"She's just a crazy old woman," said Timmy. "I ain't afraid of her."

The banshee stopped her gesticulations, and her wail died. She noticed that Timmy was on his feet again.

"Timmy," she said wheedlingly, "I'm no old woman at all."

"You go away," said Timmy. "I'll throw stones at you if you scare my sister any more."

"Timmy, jewel," quavered the banshee, but her voice was full of apprehension.

"You run home, Norah," said Timmy. "I'll keep her off."

"I'm your own banshee!" Suddenly rage strengthened her voice again, but she ended in a whimper—"The banshee of the O'Gradys; seven generations!"

"You ain't either!"

"I'm not?"

"No, you ain't."

"And who would I be then?" The tone was feeble and bewildered.

"I don't know; but you ain't a banshee, 'cause there ain't any such thing."

"There ain't?"

"No, there ain't!"

"Who says there ain't?"

"My father says there ain't, 'cause I heard about one in a story, and I asked him."

The banshee's sinking courage made a last desperate rally. "Your father!" she sniffed. "What does your father know! He's no Irishman! He never set foot in it. You ask your grandfather if there ain't any such a thing as a banshee. You ask old Danny. He'll tell you!"

"Ho!" jeered Timmy, now clearly the master, "he says there ain't any, too, and there ain't, neither. You come along with me, Norah."

Her small legs shook, but she obeyed him, and the two children turned and fled down the road toward home, Timmy sending back a glance now and then to see that the crazy one was not venturing to pursue them.

She, poor thing, stood motionless for a long time. At last she crept back to her corner by old Danny's chimney.

Deep in the night she was still there, motionless, silent. Utter stillness surrounded her, and the blackness, without a star. A sound began, and fell, and rose, and tore through the air hideously. She uncovered her head and listened.

"It'll not be another one, will it?" said she. "It's never another one in this cruel bad country, is it?"

A sudden thought stung her, and she shrieked back in a passion. "It's all him that's done it," she raged. "It's that odious cat of the Maloneys, with the black heart of him, and the howls of him every night, so the Maloneys nor the O'Gradys nor Danny nor anybody in America knows a banshee any more when they hear her!"

Like a sudden blast of wind she swept from the chimney to the back fence, and stopped with a clatter of wings beside a dark bunch in the fence corner.

"It's you that's done it," she cried, "you ugly beast, you, with your pitiful, weak little voice, and your wailings any time at all and every time at all, that a new-born baby wouldn't be frightened of, taking the very words out of the mouth of an honest banshee woman that never did you any harm and wailed faithful for her family these seven generations back, and never once out of the time till that black night she set foot in America, and the cruel, ungrateful country that it is!"

The cat turned his head her way, but his glittering green eyes looked far, far beyond her. Then he lifted his voice and howled to heaven. A plan flashed across the banshee's fury. "I'll wail for you," she shrieked, "and then you'll die! I'll—"

Would she? Wail for a cat? A black cat in America, and she the O'Grady banshee for seven generations? Pride lifted in her for one instant, but the full surge of her frenzy swept her past pride, past humiliation, and her wail rose and rent the night. It quavered and broke and sunk, and the voice of the cat rose in its wake and shrieked and fell. Close upon it followed the banshee's wail again, and upon that the cat's. A third time the banshee's rose, and in the very middle frightfulness of it the cat turned his black face to the black arch of the sky and drowned it utterly with a cry of such fiendishness that the banshee shrouded her head with her robes and shrunk into silence. When the last echo of the cat's voice had shivered away, he turned the gleam of his green eyes solemnly one way and then the other, but the fence was empty.

On a summer night, in the midst of a summer storm, the wraith of the Sobbing Child sat on the ridge-pole of the Mulligan house, and her tears dripped with the rain. Suddenly a familiar presence was beside her. She looked up, with her eyes streaming.

"And is it yourself back?" said she. "How are all the O'Gradys?"

"Hush!" said the banshee. "Don't you ever talk O'Gradys to me. They've no breeding. Their family's a mushroom to the Mulligans. The Mulligans are the real old stock. They go back to the beginning. I'm the banshee of the Mulligans, not the O'Gradys!"

There was a long silence.

"What did you think of America, then?" sobbed the Child in a weak voice.

"It's no place for a decent banshee," said the hereditary banshee of the Mulligans, "or a decent wraith either. You take my word, and don't you ever go there as long as you're a sobbing wraith and there's a road left in Ireland."

The Child wept dismally; tears coursed down her furrowed cheeks, and she said no more. The banshee rustled her leathern wings and moaned a little in gloomy and perfect content.

Afterword

A "banshee" is an Irish expression meaning "a woman of the fairies."

It is natural for a family to want to feel important, and it is not given to every family to be important in a worldly sense. However, there is a certain cachet in having supernatural entities interested in your family, however poor it may be. Surely, if they are interested, then a person belongs to a family of worth and honor.

Now death is not an easily understood phenomenon. Some people who are sick or physically hurt may die, while others who seem equally sick or hurt may live. It is not always easy to tell whether such a person will live or die; but, presumably, supernatural spirits with a greater knowledge of the future can tell. A banshee attached to a particular family may wail at a forthcoming death in that family; and while that may be bad news, it carries a melancholy kind of honor with it.

Incidentally, the existence of banshees is easily proved if one is generous in what one accepts as evidence.

The night is full of mysterious sounds made by living creatures, by the wind, by inanimate objects. If someone is lying sick, it is possible to hear a sound every night that can be interpreted as the wail of a banshee. If the person survives, it was not a banshee but something else. If the person dies, it was a banshee, and thus the anecdotal evidence in favor of its existence mounts, to the point where it takes an unfeeling skeptic to doubt it.

Most evidence in favor of mysticisms is of this sort. Never trust anecdotal evidence.—I.A.

Additional Reading

Katherine Fullerton Gerould, "On the Staircase," in *Scribner's Magazine* 54, Dec. 1913.

Thomas Hardy, "The Superstitious Man's Story," in *The Haunted and the Haunters,* Ernest Rhys, ed. (London: Daniel O'Connor, 1921).

John D. MacDonald, "The Straw Witch," in *The End of the Tiger and*

Other Stories (New York: Fawcett, 1962).

Saki (pseud. of H. H. Munro), "The Wolves of Czernogratz," in *The Toys of Peace and Other Papers* (London: John Lane, 1919).

Henry Van Dyke, "Messengers at the Window," in *American Magazine* 74, Oct. 1912

5

Devil Worship

Nathaniel Hawthorne
Young Goodman Brown

Young Goodman Brown came forth at sunset into the street at Salem village; but put his head back, after crossing the threshold, to exchange a parting kiss with his young wife. And Faith, as the wife was aptly named, thrust her own pretty head into the street, letting the wind play with the pink ribbons of her cap while she called to Goodman Brown.

"Dearest heart," whispered she, softly and rather sadly, when her lips were close to his ear, "prithee put off your journey until sunrise and sleep in your own bed to-night. A lone woman is troubled with such dreams and such thoughts that she's afeared of herself sometimes. Pray tarry with me this night, dear husband, of all nights in the year."

"My love and my Faith," replied young Goodman Brown, "of all nights in the year, this one night must I tarry away from thee. My journey, as thou callest it, forth and back again, must needs be done 'twixt now and sunrise. What, my sweet, pretty wife, dost thou doubt me already, and we but three months married?"

"Then God bless you!" said Faith, with the pink ribbons; "and may you find all well when you come back."

"Amen!" cried Goodman Brown. "Say thy prayers, dear Faith, and go to bed at dusk, and no harm will come to thee."

So they parted; and the young man pursued his way until, being about to turn the corner by the meeting-house, he looked back and saw the head of Faith still peeping after him with a melancholy air, in spite of her pink ribbons.

tle Faith!" thought he, for his heart smote him. "What a wretch
e her on such an errand! She talks of dreams, too. Methought
e there was trouble in her face, as if a dream had warned
her what work is to be done to-night. But no, no; it would kill her to
think it. Well, she's a blessed angel on earth; and after this one night I'll
cling to her skirts and follow her to heaven."

With this excellent resolve for the future, Goodman Brown felt himself
justified in making more haste on his present evil purpose. He had taken
a dreary road, darkened by all the gloomiest trees of the forest, which
barely stood aside to let the narrow path creep through, and closed
immediately behind. It was all as lonely as could be; and there is this
peculiarity in such a solitude, that the traveller knows not who may be
concealed by the innumerable trunks and thick boughs overhead; so that
with lonely footsteps he may yet be passing through an unseen multitude.

"There may be a devilish Indian behind every tree," said Goodman
Brown to himself; and he glanced fearfully behind him as he added, "What
if the devil himself should be at my very elbow!"

His head being turned back, he passed a crook of the road, and, looking
forward again, beheld the figure of a man, in a grave and decent attire,
seated at the foot of an old tree. He arose at Goodman Brown's approach
and walked onward side by side with him.

"You are late, Goodman Brown," said he. "The clock of the Old South
was striking as I came through Boston, and that is full fifteen minutes
agone."

"Faith kept me back a while," replied the young man, with a tremor
in his voice, caused by the sudden appearance of his companion, though
not wholly unexpected.

It was now deep dusk in the forest, and deepest in that part of it
where these two were journeying. As nearly as could be discerned, the
second traveller was about fifty years old, apparently in the same rank
of life as Goodman Brown, and bearing a considerable resemblance to
him, though perhaps more in expression than features. Still they might
have been taken for father and son. And yet, though the elder person
was as simply clad as the younger, and as simple in manner too, he had
an indescribable air of one who knew the world, and who would not have
felt abashed at the governor's dinner table or in King William's court, were
it possible that his affairs should call him thither. But the only thing about
him that could be fixed upon as remarkable was his staff, which bore
the likeness of a great black snake, so curiously wrought that it might
almost be seen to twist and wriggle itself like a living serpent. This, of
course, must have been an ocular deception, assisted by the uncertain light.

"Come, Goodman Brown," cried his fellow-traveller, "this is a dull
pace for the beginning of a journey. Take my staff, if you are so soon
weary."

"Friend," said the other, exchanging his slow pace for a full stop, "having kept convenant by meeting thee here, it is my purpose now to return whence I came. I have scruples touching the matter thou wot'st of."

"Sayest thou so?" replied he of the serpent, smiling apart. "Let us walk on, nevertheless, reasoning as we go; and if I convince thee not thou shalt turn back. We are but a little way in the forest yet."

"Too far! too far!" exclaimed the goodman, unconsciously resuming his walk. "My father never went into the woods on such an errand, nor his father before him. We have been a race of honest men and good Christians since the days of the martyrs; and shall I be the first of the name of Brown that ever took this path and kept"—

"Such company, thou wouldst say," observed the elder person, interpreting his pause. "Well said, Goodman Brown! I have been as well acquainted with your family as with ever a one among the Puritans; and that's no trifle to say. I helped your grandfather, the constable, when he lashed the Quaker woman so smartly through the streets of Salem; and it was I that brought your father a pitch-pine knot, kindled at my own hearth, to set fire to an Indian village, in King Philip's war. They were my good friends, both; and many a pleasant walk have we had along this path, and returned merrily after midnight. I would fain be friends with you for their sake."

"If it be as thou sayest," replied Goodman Brown, "I marvel they never spoke of these matters; or, verily, I marvel not, seeing that the least rumor of the sort would have driven them from New England. We are a people of prayer, and good works to boot, and abide no such wickedness."

"Wickedness or not," said the traveller with the twisted staff, "I have a very general acquaintance here in New England. The deacons of many a church have drunk the communion wine with me; the selectmen of divers towns make me their chairman; and a majority of the Great and General Court are firm supporters of my interest. The governor and I, too—But these are state secrets."

"Can this be so?" cried Goodman Brown, with a stare of amazement at his undisturbed companion. "Howbeit, I have nothing to do with the governor and council; they have their own ways, and are no rule for a simple husbandman like me. But, were I to go on with thee, how should I meet the eye of that good old man, our minister, at Salem village? Oh, his voice would make me tremble both Sabbath day and lecture day."

Thus far the elder traveller had listened with due gravity; but now burst into a fit of irresponsible mirth, shaking himself so violently that his snakelike staff actually seemed to wriggle in sympathy.

"Ha! ha! ha!" shouted he again and again; then composing himself, "Well, go on, Goodman Brown, go on; but, prithee, don't kill me with laughing."

"Well, then, to end the matter at once," said Goodman Brown, considerably nettled, "there is my wife, Faith. It would break her dear little heart; and I'd rather break my own."

"Nay, if that be the case," answered the other, "e'en go thy ways, Goodman Brown. I would not for twenty old women like the one hobbling before us that Faith should come to any harm."

As he spoke he pointed his staff at a female figure on the path, in whom Goodman Brown recognized a very pious and exemplary dame, who had taught him his catechism in youth, and was still his moral and spiritual adviser, jointly with the minister and Deacon Gookin.

"A marvel, truly, that Goody Cloyse should be so far in the wilderness at nightfall," said he. "But with your leave, friend, I shall take a cut through the woods until we have left this Christian woman behind. Being a stranger to you, she might ask whom I was consorting with and whither I was going."

"Be it so," said his fellow-traveller. "Betake you to the woods, and let me keep the path."

Accordingly the young man turned aside, but took care to watch his companion, who advanced softly along the road until he had come within a staff's length of the old dame. She, meanwhile, was making the best of her way, with singular speed for so aged a woman, and mumbling some indistinct words—a prayer, doubtless—as she went. The traveller put forth his staff and touched her withered neck with what seemed the serpent's tail.

"The devil!" screamed the pious old lady.

"Then Goody Cloyse knows her old friend?" observed the traveller, confronting her and leaning on his writhing stick.

"Ah, forsooth, and is it your worship indeed?" cried the good dame. "Yea, truly is it, and in the very image of my old gossip, Goodman Brown, the grandfather of the silly fellow that now is. But—would your worship believe it?—my broomstick hath strangely disappeared, stolen, as I suspect, by that unhanged witch, Goody Cory, and that, too, when I was all anointed with the juice of smallage, and cinquefoil, and wolf's bane"—

"Mingled with fine wheat and the fat of a newborn babe," said the shape of old Goodman Brown.

"Ah, your worship knows the recipe," cried the old lady, cackling aloud. "So, as I was saying, being all ready for the meeting, and no horse to ride on, I made up my mind to foot it; for they tell me there is a nice young man to be taken into communion to-night. But now your good worship will lend me your arm, and we shall be there in a twinkling."

"That can hardly be," answered her friend. "I may not spare you my arm, Goody Cloyse; but here is my staff, if you will."

So saying, he threw it down at her feet, where, perhaps, it assumed life, being one of the rods which its owner had formerly lent to the Egyptian magi. Of this fact, however, Goodman Brown could not take cognizance.

He had cast up his eyes in astonishment, and, looking down again, beheld neither Goody Cloyse nor the serpentine staff, but this fellow-traveller alone, who waited for him as calmly as if nothing had happened.

"That old woman taught me my catechism," said the young man; and there was a world of meaning in this simple comment.

They continued to walk onward, while the elder traveller exhorted his companion to make good speed and persevere in the path, discoursing so aptly that his arguments seemed rather to spring up in the bosom of his auditor than to be suggested by himself. As they went, he plucked a branch of maple to serve for a walking stick, and began to strip it of the twigs and little boughs, which were wet with evening dew. The moment his fingers touched them they became strangely withered and dried up as with a week's sunshine. Thus the pair proceeded, at a good free pace, until suddenly, in a gloomy hollow of the road, Goodman Brown sat himself down on the stump of a tree and refused to go any farther.

"Friend," said he, stubbornly, "my mind is made up. Not another step will I budge on this errand. What if a wretched old woman do choose to go to the devil when I thought she was going to heaven; is that any reason why I should quit my dear Faith and go after her?"

"You will think better of this by and by," said his acquaintance, composedly. "Sit here and rest yourself a while; and when you feel like moving again, there is my staff to help you along."

Without more words, he threw his companion the maple stick, and was as speedily out of sight as if he had vanished into the deepening gloom. The young man sat a few moments by the roadside, applauding himself greatly, and thinking with how clear a conscience he should meet the minister in his morning walk, nor shrink from the eye of good old Deacon Gookin. And what calm sleep would be his that very night, which was to have been spent so wickedly, but so purely and sweetly now, in the arms of Faith! Amidst these pleasant and praiseworthy meditations, Goodman Brown heard the tramp of horses along the road, and deemed it advisable to conceal himself within the verge of the forest, conscious of the guilty purpose that had brought him thither, though now so happily turned from it.

On came the hoof tramps and the voices of the riders, two grave old voices, conversing soberly as they drew near. These mingled sounds appeared to pass along the road, within a few yards of the young man's hiding-place; but, owing doubtless to the depth of the gloom at that particular spot, neither the travellers nor their steeds were visible. Though their figures brushed the small boughs by the wayside, it could not be seen that they intercepted, even for a moment, the faint gleam from the strip of bright sky athwart which they must have passed. Goodman Brown alternately crouched and stood on tiptoe, pulling aside the branches and thrusting forth his head as far as he durst without discerning so much as a shadow. It vexed him the more, because he could have sworn, were such a thing possible, that he recognized the voices of the minister and Deacon Gookin, jogging along quietly, as they were wont to do, when bound to some ordination of ecclesiastical council. While yet within hearing, one of the riders stopped to pluck a switch.

"Of the two, reverend sir," said the voice like the deacon's, "I had rather miss an ordination dinner than to-night's meeting. They tell me that some of our company are to be here from Falmouth and beyond, and others from Connecticut and Rhode Island, besides several of the Indian powwows, who, after their fashion, know almost as much deviltry as the best of us. Moreover, there is a goodly young woman to be taken into communion."

"Mightly well, Deacon Gookin!" replied the solemn old tones of the minister. "Spur up, or we shall be late. Nothing can be done, you know, until I get on the ground."

The hoofs clattered again; and the voices, talking so strangely in the empty air, passed on through the forest, where no church had ever been gathered or solitary Christian prayed. Whither, then, could these holy men be journeying so deep into the heathen wilderness? Young Goodman Brown caught hold of a tree for support, being ready to sink down on the ground, faint and overburdened with the heavy sickness of his heart. He looked up to the sky, doubting whether there really was a heaven above him. Yet there was the blue arch, and the stars brightening in it.

"With heaven above and Faith below, I will yet stand firm against the devil!" cried Goodman Brown.

While he still gazed upward into the deep arch of the firmament and had lifted his hands to pray, a cloud, though no wind was stirring, hurried across the zenith and hid the brightening stars. The blue sky was still visible, except directly overhead, where this black mass of cloud was sweeping swiftly northward. Aloft in the air, as if from the depths of the cloud, came a confused and doubtful sound of voices. Once the listener fancied that he could distinguish the accents of towns-people of his own, men and women, both pious and ungodly, many of whom he had met at the communion table, and had seen others rioting at the tavern. The next moment, so indistinct were the sounds, he doubted whether he had heard aught but the murmur of the old forest, whispering without a wind. Then came a stronger swell of those familiar tones, heard daily in the sunshine at Salem village, but never until now from a cloud of night. There was one voice, of a young woman, uttering lamentations, yet with an uncertain sorrow, and entreating for some favor, which, perhaps, it would grieve her to obtain; and all the unseen multitude, both saints and sinners, seemed to encourage her onward.

"Faith!" shouted Goodman Brown, in a voice of agony and desperation; and the echoes of the forest mocked him, crying, "Faith! Faith!" as if bewildered wretches were seeking her all through the wilderness.

The cry of grief, rage, and terror was yet piercing the night, when the unhappy husband held his breath for a response. There was a scream, drowned immediately in a louder murmur of voices, fading into far-off laughter, as the dark cloud swept away, leaving the clear and silent sky above Goodman Brown. But something fluttered lightly down through the air and caught on the branch of a tree. The young man seized it, and beheld a pink ribbon.

"My Faith is gone!" cried he, after one stupefied moment. "There is no good on earth; and sin is but a name. Come, devil; for to thee is this world given."

And, maddened with despair, so that he laughed loud and long, did Goodman Brown grasp his staff and set forth again, at such a rate that he seemed to fly along the forest path rather than to walk or run. The road grew wilder and drearier and more faintly traced, and vanished at length, leaving him in the heart of the dark wilderness still rushing onward with the instinct that guides mortal man to evil. The whole forest was peopled with frightful sounds—the creaking of the trees, the howling of wild beasts, and the yell of Indians; while sometimes the wind tolled like a distant church bell, and sometimes gave a broad roar around the traveller, as if all Nature were laughing him to scorn. But he was himself the chief horror of the scene, and shrank not from its other horrors.

"Ha! ha! ha!" roared Goodman Brown when the wind laughed at him. "Let us hear which will laugh loudest. Think not to frighten me with your deviltry. Come witch, come wizard, come Indian powwow, come devil himself, and here comes Goodman Brown. You may as well fear him as he fear you."

In truth, all through the haunted forest there could be nothing more frightful than the figure of Goodman Brown. On he flew among the black pines, brandishing his staff with frenzied gestures, now giving vent to an inspiration of horrid blasphemy, and now shouting forth such laughter as set all the echoes of the forest laughing like demons around him. The fiend in his own shape is less hideous than when he rages in the breast of man. Thus sped the demoniac on his course, until, quivering among the trees, he saw a red light before him, as when the felled trunks and branches of a clearing have been set on fire, and throw up their lurid blaze against the sky, at the hour of midnight. He paused, in a lull of the tempest that had driven him onward, and heard the swell of what seemed a hymn, rolling solemnly from a distance with the weight of many voices. He knew the tune; it was a familiar one in the choir of the village meeting-house. The verse died heavily away, and was lengthened by a chorus, not of human voices, but of all the sounds of the benighted wilderness pealing in awful harmony together. Goodman Brown cried out, and his cry was lost to his own ear by its unison with the cry of the desert.

In the interval of silence he stole forward until the light glared full upon his eyes. At one extremity of an open space, hemmed in by the dark wall of the forest, arose a rock, bearing some rude, natural resemblance either to an altar or a pulpit, and surrounded by four blazing pines, their tops aflame, their stems untouched, like candles at an evening meeting. The mass of foliage that had overgrown the summit of the rock was all on fire, blazing high into the night and fitfully illuminating the whole field. Each pendent twig and leafy festoon was in a blaze. As the red light arose and fell, a numerous congregation alternately shone forth, then disappeared in shadow, and again grew, as it were, out of the darkness, peopling the heart of the solitary woods at once.

"A grave and dark-clad company," quoth Goodman Brown.

In truth they were such. Among them, quivering to and fro between gloom and splendor, appeared faces that would be seen next day at the council board of the province, and others which, Sabbath after Sabbath, looked devoutly heavenward, and benignantly over the crowded pews, from the holiest pulpits in the land. Some affirm that the lady of the governor was there. At least there were high dames well known to her, and wives of honored husbands, and widows, a great multitude, and ancient maidens, all of excellent repute, and fair young girls, who trembled lest their mothers should espy them. Either the sudden gleams of light flashing over the obscure field bedazzled Goodman Brown, or he recognized a score of the church members of Salem village famous for their especial sanctity. Good old Deacon Gookin had arrived, and waited at the skirts of that venerable saint, his revered pastor. But irreverently consorting with these grave, reputable, and pious people, these elders of the church, these chaste dames and dewy virgins, there were men of dissolute lives and women of spotted fame, wretches given over to all mean and filthy vice, and suspected even of horrid crimes. It was strange to see that the good shrank not from the wicked, nor were the sinners abashed by the saints. Scattered also among their pale-faced enemies were the Indian priests, or powwows, who had often scared their native forest with more hideous incantations than any known to English witchcraft.

"But where is Faith?" thought Goodman Brown; and as hope came into his heart, he trembled.

Another verse of the hymn arose, a slow and mournful strain, such as the pious love, but joined to words which expressed all that our nature can conceive of sin, and darkly hinted at far more. Unfathomable to mere mortals is the lore of fiends. Verse after verse was sung; and still the chorus of the desert swelled between like the deepest tone of a mighty organ; and with the final peal of that dreadful anthem there came a sound, as if the roaring wind, the rushing streams, the howling beasts, and every other voice of the unconcerted wilderness were mingling and according with the voice of guilty man in homage to the prince of all. The four blazing pines threw up a loftier flame, and obscurely discovered shapes and visages of horror on the smoke wreaths above the impious assembly. At the same moment the fire on the rock shot redly forth, and formed a glowing arch above its base, where now appeared a figure. With reverence be it spoken, the figure bore no slight similitude, both in garb and manner, to some grave divine of the New England churches.

"Bring forth the converts!" cried a voice that echoed through the field and rolled into the forest.

At the word, Goodman Brown stepped forth from the shadow of the trees and approached the congregation, with whom he felt a loathful brotherhood by the sympathy of all that was wicked in his heart. He could have well-nigh sworn that the shape of his own dead father beckoned him to advance, looking downward from a smoke wreath, while a woman, with dim features of despair, threw out her hand to warn him back. Was it his mother? But he had no power to retreat one step, nor to resist, even in thought, when the minister and good old Deacon Gookin seized his arms and led him to the blazing rock. Thither came also the slender form of a veiled female, led between Goody Cloyse, that pious teacher of the catechism, and Martha Carrier, who had received the devil's promise to be queen of hell. A rampant hag was she. And there stood the proselytes beneath the canopy of fire.

"Welcome, my children," said the dark figure, "to the communion of your race. Ye have found thus young your nature and your destiny. My children, look behind you!"

They turned; and flashing forth, as it were, in a sheet of flame, the fiend worshippers were seen; the smile of welcome gleamed darkly on every visage.

"There," resumed the sable form, "are all whom ye have reverenced from youth. Ye deemed them holier than yourselves, and shrank from your own sin, contrasting it with their lives of righteousness and prayerful aspirations heavenward. Yet here are they all in my worshipping assembly. This night it shall be granted you to know their secret deeds: how hoary-bearded elders of the church have whispered wanton words to the young maids of their households; how many a woman, eager for widows' weeds, has given her husband a drink at bedtime and let him sleep his last sleep in her bosom; how beardless youths have made haste to inherit their fathers' wealth; and how fair damsels—blush not, sweet ones—have dug little graves in the garden, and bidden to me, the sole guest, to an infant's funeral. By the sympathy of your human hearts for sin ye shall scent out all the places—whether in church, bed-chamber, street, field, or forest—where crime has been committed, and shall exult to behold the whole earth one stain of guilt, one mighty blood spot. Far more than this. It shall be yours to penetrate, in every bosom, the deep mystery of sin, the fountain of all wicked arts, and which inexhaustibly supplies more evil impulses than human power—than my power at its utmost—can make manifest in deeds.

And now, my children, look upon each other."

They did so; and, by the blaze of the hell-kindled torches, the wretched man beheld his Faith, and the wife her husband, trembling before that unhallowed altar.

"Lo, there ye stand, my children," said the figure, in a deep and solemn tone, almost sad with its despairing awfulness, as if his once angelic nature could yet mourn for our miserable race. "Depending upon one another's hearts, ye had still hoped that virtue were not all a dream. Now are ye undeceived. Evil is the nature of mankind. Evil must be your only happiness. Welcome again, my children, to the communion of your race."

"Welcome," repeated the fiend worshippers, in one cry of despair and triumph.

And there they stood, the only pair, as it seemed, who where yet hesitating on the verge of wickedness in this dark world. A basin was hollowed, naturally, in the rock. Did it contain water, reddened by the lurid light? or was it blood? or, perchance, a liquid flame? Herein did the shape of evil dip his hand and prepare to lay the mark of baptism upon their foreheads, that they might be partakers of the mystery of sin, more conscious of the secret guilt of others, both in deed and thought, than they could now be of their own. The husband cast one look at his pale wife, and Faith at him. What polluted wretches would the next glance show them to each other, shuddering alike at what they disclosed and what they saw!

"Faith! Faith!" cried the husband, "look up to heaven, and resist the wicked one."

Whether Faith obeyed he knew not. Hardly had he spoken when he found himself amid calm night and solitude, listening to a roar of the wind which died heavily away through the forest. He staggered against the rock, and felt it chill and damp; while a hanging twig, that had been all on fire, besprinkled his cheek with the coldest dew.

The next morning young Goodman Brown came slowly into the street of Salem village, staring around him like a bewildered man. The good old minister was taking a walk along the graveyard to get an appetite for breakfast and meditate his sermon, and bestowed a blessing, as he passed, on Goodman Brown. He shrank from the venerable saint as if to avoid an anathema. Old Deacon Gookin was at domestic worship, and the holy words of his prayer were heard through the open window. "What God doth the wizard pray to?" quoth Goodman Brown. Goody Cloyse, that excellent old Christian, stood in the early sunshine at her own lattice, catechizing a little girl who had brought her a pint of morning's milk. Goodman Brown snatched away the child as from the grasp of the fiend himself. Turning the corner by the meeting-house, he spied the head of Faith, with the pink ribbons, gazing anxiously forth, and bursting into such joy at sight of him that she skipped along the street and almost kissed her husband before the whole village. But Goodman Brown looked sternly and sadly into her face, and passed on without a greeting.

Had Goodman Brown fallen asleep in the forest and only dreamed a wild dream of a witch-meeting?

Be it so if you will; but, alas! it was a dream of evil omen for young Goodman Brown. A stern, a sad, a darkly meditative, a distrustful, if not a desperate man did he become from the night of that fearful dream. On the Sabbath day, when the congregation were singing a holy psalm, he could not listen because an anthem of sin rushed loudly upon his ear and drowned all the blessed strain. When the minister spoke from the pulpit with power and fervid eloquence, and, with his hand on the open Bible, of the sacred truths of our religion, and of saint-like lives and triumphant deaths, and of future bliss or misery unutterable, then did Goodman Brown turn pale, dreading lest the room should thunder down upon the gray blasphemer and his hearers. Often, awaking suddenly at midnight, he shrank from the bosom of Faith; and at morning or eventide, when the family knelt down at prayer, he scowled and muttered to himself, and gazed sternly at his wife, and turned away. And when he had lived long, and was borne to his grave a hoary corpse, followed by Faith, an aged woman, and children and grandchildren, a goodly procession, besides neighbors not a few, they carved no hopeful verse upon his tombstone, for his dying hour was gloom.

Afterword

The Persians developed a cosmic theory that divided the universe into two principles; one of light and good, the other of darkness and evil. These were equal in power. Human intervention, on one side or the other, might be sufficient to swing the scale either way.

The Jews, under the Persian Empire, absorbed some of this, and Satan became important as the adversary of God (though not equal in power).

Eventually, Jews came to believe that their one God was the sole god of all the universe and that gods worshiped by other people either did not exist or were, in truth, demons. The Christians and Muslims inherited this notion and it therefore became possible to believe that those who did not have your faith did not merely worship other gods but worshiped devils. "False" religions were not seeking good in their own way, but were actively and deliberately worshiping the Devil and the principle of evil.

In medieval and early modern times, people who clung to some old-fashioned ways were viewed as "witches" and devil-worshipers and were hounded fearfully. (Those who saw the "Night on Bald Mountain" sequence in Walt Disney's "Fantasia" were given a picture of literal devil-worship.)

In modern times, there have been those who purported to indulge in actual devil-worship, but I suspect that this was an idle affectation of people who obtained a morbid pleasure in shocking others—about on the level of those who delight in the unnecessary use of vulgarisms at the top of their voices.—I.A.

Additional Reading

Algernon Blackwood, "Secret Worship," in *John Silence: Physician Extraordinary* (London: Eveleigh Nash, 1908).

Robert Bloch, "Sweet Sixteen" (aka: "Spawn of the Dark One"), *Pleasant Dreams* (Sauk City, Wisc.: Arkham House, 1960).

August Derleth, "The Night Train to Lost Valley," in *Yankee Witches,* Charles G. Waugh, Martin H. Greenberg, and Frank D. McSherry, Jr., eds. (Augusta, Me.: Lance Tapley, Publisher, 1988).

Margaret Irwin, "The Earlier Service," in *Madame Fears the Dark: Seven Stories and a Play* (London: Chatto and Windus, 1935).

E. Hoffman Price, "The Stranger from Kurdistan," in *Strange Gateways* (Sauk City, Wisc.: Arkham House, 1967).

6

Doppelgangers

Helen McCloy
Through a Glass, Darkly

In her own mind Mrs. Lightfoot thought of the whole matter as "that unfortunate affair of Faustina Crayle." Characteristically she did not try to find out what had actually happened. She showed little curiosity and no fear. Whether the peculiar gossip about Faustina Crayle was based on malicious lying or hysterical hallucination, its effect was equally damaging to the Brereton School. That was the only thing that mattered to a headmistress as single-minded as Mrs. Lightfoot.

By the end of the week she was comfortably sure she would never hear the name Crayle again. And then, that bright October morning, when she was just settled in the study with her morning mail, Arlene brought her that dreadful visiting card:

> *Dr. Basil Willing*
> *Medical Assistant to the District Attorney*
> *of New York County*

The man, Willing, did not look like her idea of a man who held a political appointment in New York. He entered the room with easy, not ungraceful deliberation. He had the lean figure and sun-browned skin that come from living outdoors. Yet the wide brow and deep-set eyes gave his face a stamp of thoughtfulness. Those eyes were more alert, direct, and disturbing than any she had ever seen.

"Dr. Willing?" Mrs. Lightfoot held his card fastidiously between thumb and forefinger. "This is Massachusetts, not New York. And I fail to see how anything at Brereton can interest the district attorney or his medical assistant."

"That happened to be the only card I had with me," returned Basil. "I rarely use it. The district attorney's office plays only a small part in my working life. I'm a doctor of medicine, specializing in psychiatry. And I've come to see you because Faustina Crayle consulted me. My sister-in-law, Mrs. Paul Willing, employed her as a governess two years ago."

Mrs. Lightfoot could be blunt when necessary. "Just what do you want?"

Basil met this with equal bluntness. "To know why your art teacher, Faustina Crayle, was dismissed after five weeks' employment, without warning or reason given, even though, under her contract, you had to pay her a year's salary for the five weeks."

So Faustina hadn't told him the truth. Or . . . could it be she didn't know the truth herself?

"I've ruled out any defect in teaching method or scholarship, appearance or deportment," Basil was saying. "My sister-in-law would not have employed Miss Crayle if she had any fault so obvious and you wouldn't hesitate to have called such a fault to her attention. What remains? Something libelous that you suspect and can't prove. One of our old friends dipsomania, kleptomania, or nymphomania. Lesbianism is always with us. And now there's communism. Miss Crayle might have concealed any one of these *gaucheries* from my sister-in-law since Miss Crayle did not live with the Paul Willings. She was only in their apartment for a few hours each day."

Mrs. Lightfoot lifted her eyes. "It was none of those things."

Basil saw with surprise that she was genuinely moved. He realized that it was a rare thing for such a woman to feel strong emotion. "What was it, Mrs. Lightfoot? I think you owe it to Miss Crayle to let her know. You've made it almost impossible for her to get another position as a teacher. People talk. And then . . . two curious incidents occurred, just as Miss Crayle was leaving, which she herself cannot explain. She met two pupils on the stairs, girls of thirteen—Barbara Vining and Diana Chase. She said their faces were 'bland as milk' and a pair of light voices fluted demurely: 'Good-bye, Miss Crayle!' But when she had passed them, a sound followed her down the stairwell—a faint, thin giggle, shrill and tiny as the laughter the Japanese attribute to mice. . . . In the lower hall Miss Crayle passed one of the maids. Arlene Murphy. Her behavior was even more extraordinary. She shrank back, with dilated eyes, as if she were afraid of Miss Crayle."

Mrs. Lightfoot was beaten. "I suppose I'll have to tell you."

He studied her face. "Why are you afraid to tell me?"

Her answer startled him. "Because you won't believe me. You'd better hear it from some of the eye-witnesses. We'll start with Arlene." She pressed a bell on the wall beside her.

The maid was as young as the graduating class at Brereton—probably eighteen, at the most twenty. Under a white apron, she wore a gray chambray dress, high-necked, long-sleeved, full-skirted. Mrs. Lightfoot had won the battle for low heels and no cosmetics, but Arlene had carried two other hotly contested points—flesh-colored stockings and no cap.

"Come in and shut the door, Arlene. Will you please repeat to Dr. Willing what you told me about Miss Crayle?"

"Yes, ma'am, but you said not to tell anybody!"

"I'm releasing you from that promise, just this once."

Arlene turned vacant, brown eyes on Basil. Her brows were hairless. This gave her face a singularly naked look. Some glandular deficiency, he suspected. She was breathing through her mouth and that made her look stupid.

"I was upstairs, turning down beds for the night," said Arlene. "When I got through, I started down the backstairs. It was getting dark, but it was still light enough to see the steps. Those backstairs are enclosed, but there's two windows. I saw Miss Crayle coming up the stair, toward me. I thought it was a bit odd for her to be using the backstairs instead of the front. I says: 'Good evening, Miss.' But she didn't answer. She didn't even look at me. She just went on up to the second floor. That was kinda queer 'cause she was always polite to everybody. But even then I didn't think much about it until I went on down into the kitchen and . . ." Arlene paused to swallow. "There was Miss Crayle."

The girl's hands were trembling. Her eyes searched Basil's face for some sign of disbelief. "Honest, sir, she couldn't have got back to the kitchen by way of the upper hall, the front stairs, the dining room, or the pantry. Not in the little time it took me to finish going down the backstairs to the kitchen. She just couldn't, even if she'd run."

"What was Miss Crayle doing in the kitchen?" asked Basil.

"She had some flowers she'd just got in the garden. She was fixing a vase with water at the table by the sink."

"Were the two dressed exactly the same way? The one on the stairs and the one in the kitchen?"

"Like as two peas. Brown felt hat. Bluish gray coat. Covert, I think they call it. No fur, no real style at all. And brown shoes. The kind with no tongues and criss-cross laces they call 'ghillies.' And some old pigskin gloves she always used for gardening."

"Did the hat have a brim?"

"Uh-huh. I mean, yes, sir."

"Did you see Miss Crayle's face on the backstairs?"

"Yes, sir. I didn't look at her particular. No reason why I should. And the hat brim was down over her eyes. But I saw her nose and mouth and chin. I'd swear it was her."

"Did you speak to Miss Crayle in the kitchen?"

"Soon as I got my breath, I says: 'Lord, miss, you give me a turn! I coulda sworn I just passed you on the stair, comin' down.' She smiled and said: 'You musta been mistaken, Arlene. I been in the west garden the last half hour. I only just come into the house and I haven't been upstairs yet.' Well, sir, you know how it is. Something like that happens and you think: 'What the—' I mean: 'Oh, well, I musta been mistaken.' And that's the end of it . . . if nothing more happens. But this time— well, that was just the beginning. In a week or so there was stories going all over the school about Miss Crayle and—"

Mrs. Lightfoot interrupted. "That will do, Arlene. Thank you. And will you please ask Miss Vining and Miss Chase to come to my study immediately?"

"Goethe," said Basil, as the door shut. "The gray suit with gilt edging. Emilie Sagée. And *The Tale of Tod Lapraik*. The *doppelgänger* of the Germans. The *ka* of the Egyptians. The double of English folk lore. You see a figure, solid, three-dimensional, brightly colored, moving and obeying all the laws of optics. Its clothing or posture is vaguely familiar. It turns its head and—you are looking at yourself. A perfect mirror-image of yourself, only—there is no mirror. And that frightens you. For tradition tells you that he who sees his own double must die."

"Only if he sees it face to face," amended Mrs. Lightfoot. "The history of the *doppelgänger* legend is very curious. Lately I've begun to wonder if the atmosphere could act as a mirror under certain conditions, something like a mirage but reflecting only one person . . ."

A light tap fell on the door. Two little girls about thirteen entered the study and curtsied to Basil when Mrs. Lightfoot introduced them as Barbara Vining and Diana Chase.

The drab masculinity of the Brereton uniform merely heightened by contrast the delicate, feminine coloring of Barbara Vining—pink and white skin, silver-gold hair, and eyes the misty blue of star sapphires. The line of her lips was so subtly turned that even in repose they seemed to quiver on the edge of suppressed laughter.

The same uniform brought out all that was plain and dull in Diana Chase: the straight, mouse-colored hair; the pinched, white face; the forlorn mouth. Only the eyes, a clear hazel, showed a sly spark of potential mischief.

They listened gravely as Mrs. Lightfoot explained what she wanted. "Barbara, suppose you tell Dr. Willing what happened. Diana, you may correct Barbara if she makes any mistake."

"Yes, Mrs. Lightfoot." The faint pink in Barbara's cheeks warmed to rose. Obviously she enjoyed being the centre of the stage. "We two were in the writing room on the ground floor. I was writing my brother, Raymond, and Diana was writing her mother. All the other girls were down at the basketball field and most of the teachers. But she was outside the middle window—Miss Crayle. It was a French window, standing open, so I could see her plainly. She'd set her easel up in the middle of the lawn and she was sketching in water colors. She was wearing a blue coat but no hat. It was fun watching the quick, sure way she handled her brush."

"You've forgotten the armchair," put in Diana.

"Armchair? Oh . . ." Barbara turned back to Basil. "There was an armchair in that room with a slip-cover in Delft blue. We called it 'Miss Crayle's chair' because she sat there so often. I rather expected her to come in and sit in that chair when she was through painting and then—it happened." Barbara's voice faded, suddenly shy.

Diana took over. "I looked up and saw Miss Crayle had come in without my hearing her. She was sitting in the blue armchair, her hands loose in her lap, her head resting against the back. She didn't seem to notice me, so I went on writing. After a while, I looked up again. She was still in the armchair. But that time my eyes wandered over to the window and . . ." Diana lost her nerve. "You tell him, Babs."

"Miss Crayle was still sketching outside the window?" suggested Basil.

"I suppose Mrs. Lightfoot told you." Barbara looked at him sharply. "I heard Di gasp, so I looked up and saw her staring at two Miss Crayles— one in the armchair, in the room with us; the other on the lawn, outside the window. The one in the chair was perfectly still. The one outside the window was moving. Only . . ." Barbara's voice wavered. "I told you how quick and sure her motions were? Well, after we saw the figure in the chair, the figure outside the window was—slower. Every movement was sort of languid and weighted. Like a slow-motion picture."

"Made me think of a sleepwalker," added Diana.

"What was the light like?"

"Bright sunlight on the lawn," answered Barbara. "So bright the shades were drawn halfway down inside."

"It was pretty awful," went on Diana. "Sitting there, the two of us, alone in the room with that—that thing in the armchair. And the real Miss Crayle outside painting in that slow, unnatural way. Afterward, I thought of all sorts of things we might have done. Like trying to touch the thing in the chair. Or calling to Miss Crayle from the window and waking her from her—her trance or whatever it was. But at the time— well, I was just too frightened to think or move."

"I sat there and told myself it wasn't happening," said Barbara. "Only it was. I suppose it only lasted a minute or so. It seemed like a hundred years. Then the figure in the chair got up and went into the hall without a sound. The door was standing open and it seemed to melt into the shadows beyond. We sat there about three seconds. Then we ran to the door. There was no one in sight. So we went back to the window but—Miss Crayle had gone. . . ."

When they were alone, Mrs. Lightfoot looked at Basil. "Was a practical woman ever confronted with such a fantastic problem? Six girls have been withdrawn from Brereton already. That's why Miss Crayle had to go."

"But Barbara and Diana are still here. Didn't they write their parents about this?"

"Barbara has no parents—only a brother, a rather lighthearted young man of twenty-six who doesn't take his duties as guardian too seriously. Diana's parents are divorced. The father lives with a second wife in California. The mother is chiefly occupied in nursing her grievances against the father and nagging the courts to increase her alimony. Neither is greatly concerned with Diana. She's been a pupil here since her seventh year. Barbara only came to us this Fall. She's been going to a day school in New York."

Basil studied the intelligent face under the sleek mound of dark hair flecked with gray. "What is your own opinion?"

A hint of defiance crept into Mrs. Lightfoot's voice. "I am a modern woman, Dr. Willing. That means I was born without faith in religion and I have lost faith in science. I don't understand the theories of Messrs. Planck and Einstein, but I grasp enough to realize that the world of matter may be a world of appearances—that even our own bodies are a part of this dance of electrons. What's behind it, we don't know. How does my mind act on my body when I decide to move my arm? Neither psychology nor physiology can tell me. . . .

"By what trick could Faustina Crayle create the illusion of her double? And why? She gained nothing. It cost her a job. She may be an unconscious trickster—an hysteric with impulses to amaze and frighten people, impulses that she can't control because she is not aware of them herself. That might explain why she played such a trick, but not how.

"There is a third possibility. Suppose Faustina Crayle is . . . abnormal in a way that modern science will not acknowledge?"

If Mrs. Lightfoot feared an outburst of that outraged skepticism that is a sure sign of hidden credulity—the fool's fear of being fooled—she had misjudged her man. "Did anyone else see Miss Crayle's double? Besides two girls of thirteen and a maid of nineteen or twenty?"

Mrs. Lightfoot caught the implication. "There was one other witness—middle-aged, sober, reasonably shrewd and observant. Myself."

After a moment, she went on: "I had a dinner engagement outside the school that evening. I came out of my room about six. A pair of sconces are always lighted in the hall at that hour. Each has a hundred-watt bulb under a small shade. Their light extends to the first landing of the front stair. Below that landing the stair was in shadow this particular evening, for Arlene had neglected to turn on the ceiling light in the lower hall. I started down the stair with one hand on the balustrade, moving slowly because my dress had a long, full skirt. As I reached the first landing, someone, one in greater haste, brushed past me without a word of apology and I saw that it was Miss Crayle.

"She didn't actually jostle me, but I felt the drafty displacement of air that you feel when anyone passes closely and swiftly. And her ungloved hand brushed my arm where the skin was bare between my cuff and my glove. That contact was inhumanly cold. I remember thinking: *she must have been outdoors.* . . . I didn't see her face as she passed. But I recognized her back—the brown hat and the blue covert coat, the only outdoor clothes she had except a winter coat still in storage. I was irritated by her rudeness. Manners are important at Brereton. I raised my voice, making it crisp, and peremptory: 'Miss Crayle!'

" 'Yes, Mrs. Lightfoot?'

"Dr. Willing, that answering voice came from the upstairs hall, above me, and I could still see Miss Crayle's back moving into the shadows of the lower hall, below me. I looked up. Faustina Crayle was standing at the head of the stairs, in the full light of the upper hall, wearing the brown hat and blue coat. Her eyes, bright with life and intelligence, looked into mine, and she spoke again: 'You called me, Mrs. Lightfoot?' I looked down. There was nothing in the lower hall then—nothing but shadows. I said: 'I thought you passed me just now on the stair. I didn't know you were just behind me.' She answered: 'That's rather odd. You were going down so slowly and I was in such a hurry to get the evening mail that my first impulse was to slip past you on the stair. But I didn't because I realized how rude that would be.'

"So she'd had the unrealized intention . . . I recalled how often a sleepwalker will carry out an intention previously suppressed in his waking state. Suppose that uncensored, autonomous action of the unconscious mind in sleepwalking could be pushed a little further? Suppose that the unconscious mind could project some form of itself outside the body? Not a material form, but a visible one. Just as mirror-reflections and rainbows are visible and even photographable though materially neither one exists. Or suppose a case of split personality where the secondary personality gathers enough vital energy to project that sort of visible yet immaterial image of itself. . . .

"I assure you it took all the nerve I had to go on down that stair into the darkness and turn on the light in the lower hall. There was no one—except Arlene coming into the drawing room from the dining room. 'Did you meet anyone just now?' I asked her. She shook her head: 'No, ma'am. I haven't seen a soul.' "

"No wonder you didn't dare tell Faustina Crayle why you wished her to leave!" Basil's glance strayed to the lawn outside the window where the autumn breeze tumbled the dead leaves and pounced on them in erratic starts and sallies like an invisible kitten.

"She would have thought me mad. Do you?"

"No. A conformist skepticism is a pretty cheap commodity. He who accepts the incredulities of his time without question is as naïve as he who accepts its credulities." Basil's eyes returned to Mrs. Lightfoot. "You spoke of a drafty sensation when the double passed. Any sound? Swish of air? Rustle of clothing?"

"No sound at all."

"Footfalls?"

"No, but that would be so in any case. The stair carpet is thick and soft."

"Every human body carries some faint odor or combination of odors," mused Basil. "Face powder, lipstick, hair tonic, permanent wave lotion, or shaving lotion. Iodine or some other medicine. The breath odors—food, wine, tobacco. And the clothing odors—mothballs, shoe polish, dry cleaning fluids, Russian leather, or Harris tweed. Finally there are those body odors the soap advertisements worry us about. You are one witness who was close enough to touch the double, however briefly. Did you notice any odor, however faint or fleeting?"

Mrs. Lightfoot shook her head emphatically. "There was no odor, Dr. Willing, unless I missed it."

"I doubt that." He glanced toward a row of flower pots on the window sill. "Only a woman with keen senses would enjoy a fragrance as delicate as rose geranium or lemon verbena."

Mrs. Lightfoot smiled. "I even use lemon verbena on my handkerchief. My one really gaudy vice, but a French firm puts out an essence of *verveine* I cannot resist. It's supposed to be an after-shaving lotion for men, so I'm probably the only woman in the world who uses it."

"Did Miss Crayle use any perfume habitually?"

"Lavender. She always used it on her hair."

"No hint of lavender about the double?"

"No." Mrs. Lightfoot's smile became ironic. "You wouldn't expect a reflection in a mirror to have an odor, would you?"

Basil picked up his hat and driving gloves. "Why did this double of Miss Crayle appear only at Brereton? Didn't Miss Crayle teach at another school last year? A place in Virginia called Maidstone?"

Mrs. Lightfoot looked at him grimly. "I hadn't meant to tell you. Molly Maidstone is a friend of mine and I got the truth out of her a few days ago, under pledge of secrecy, but . . . Miss Crayle left Maidstone last year under precisely the same conditions that she is now leaving Brereton."

† † †

The apartment house stood between Lexington Avenue and the river. Basil passed through a door flanked by copper tubs planted with ivy to a self-service elevator and pressed the button marked Penthouse. In a vestibule on the top floor he lifted a knocker and chimes rang. The young woman who opened the door was tall for her sex, but slenderly fashioned with frail wrists and ankles, tapering hands and narrow, high-arched feet. Her hair was a pale tan, almost a biscuit color, so fine and soft that it had no shape or sleekness, but floated about her small head in a thistledown halo, stirring gently with each movement she made. The long face was sallow and earnest, the lips thin, the nose prominent and rather sharp. She led the way to a terrace. The sun had just set. Beyond the parapet the peaks and valleys of the mountainous city shimmered insubstantially in a silver haze.

Basil offered cigarettes. She shook her head impatiently. He lit one for himself. "Miss Crayle, do you know the German legend of the *dopplegänger?*"

Tears gathered in the cloudy blue eyes. She covered her face with her hands. "Dr. Willing, what am I going to do?"

"Then you do know. Why didn't you tell me before you sent me to Mrs. Lightfoot?"

"Would you have believed me? I don't know anything . . . except what people said about me at Maidstone." Her hands dropped. She turned toward him, apparently unconscious of reddened eyelids. "Now I suppose it's happened again at Brereton. Mrs. Lightfoot wouldn't tell me, but I thought she might tell you—a psychiatrist, working with the district attorney in New York. . . ."

Basil told her all he had learned at Brereton. "Is that the sort of thing that happened at Maidstone?"

He caught a hint of lavender as Faustina dabbed at her eyes with a handkerchief. "Pretty much. Maidstone is quite like Brereton. Only in Virginia instead of Massachusetts. The girls don't wear uniforms but it's strict in other ways. No male visitors except Sunday and so on. After I'd been there a week I knew I was being watched and talked about. Other teachers refused my little invitations for tea or shopping. Even the servants waited on me grudgingly. I took it for hostility. Now I believe it was fear. In my fourth week I got a note from Miss Maidstone. Dismissal with a check for a year's service. I took the note to her study. She was quite emotional about the whole thing. She even wrote me a letter of recommendation. That got me the job at Brereton afterward. You see, though she had to keep it secret because of her school, Miss Maidstone has dabbled in psychic research. She took books out of a locked cupboard and read to me about other 'doubles' that had been reported to various research societies in Europe. She didn't suspect me of fraud. For that very reason she would not keep me at Maidstone."

"Do you believe in this yourself?"

Faustina smiled bitterly. "I know I'm not a fraud. You don't know that, of course. But I do. And I can't see how or why anyone else should play such a trick on me. What remains? When you've lost your job twice because of a thing, you don't think it's just imagination. . . . I'm like Madame du Deffand. I don't believe in it, but I'm afraid of it."

"Of what?"

"Of this . . . thing. Suppose I were to see it myself? I've had just one glimpse, on the front stair at Brereton. All I saw was the back of a figure, dressed in clothes like mine, brushing past Mrs. Lightfoot. That could be anyone who looked like me and wore similar clothes. Even if I were to see a face resembling mine, at a distance, in a dim light—that could be illusion or trickery, a face resembling mine by chance or made up deliberately to look like mine. But if I should suddenly come upon a face close at hand, in a clear light, and recognize it as my own face in every small detail—I believe I should die. Because that couldn't be faked."

"How often was the double seen at Maidstone?"

"Three times. On the front lawn while I was asleep upstairs. On an upstairs sleeping porch while I was teaching a class in a downstairs room. And once it passed an open door while I stood inside the door with another teacher."

Basil crushed the stub of his cigarette in an ashtray. "Miss Crayle, is there anyone who has reason to hate you? Or who would benefit by your death?"

"No one I know of. I have no family. My mother died when I was six and I don't remember my father."

"Any property?"

"A small cottage at Seabright on the Jersey coast, left to me by my mother. And some jewelry. Just trinkets, I suppose, for my mother was not a wealthy woman. Mr. Watkins, the lawyer, is going to have it appraised for me."

"Who gets the jewelry and the cottage when you die?"

"I'm leaving the cottage to a school friend. I'm not supposed to inherit the jewelry until my thirtieth birthday."

"What becomes of the jewelry if you die before then?"

"I really don't recall." The colorless brows knitted. "There was something in the will about that."

"Better give me the name and address of your lawyer . . . Septimus Watkins? He manages half the big trust funds in New York." Basil rose to go. "Are you staying here long?"

"I'm leaving this evening. The friends who live here will be back tonight. They just lent me the place for this weekend. I need rest. And privacy. So I thought I'd go down to the cottage at Seabright."

"Don't." Basil looked up sharply. "Go to a hotel. The biggest, brightest, noisiest hotel you can find. And let me know where you are as soon as you are settled. . . ."

†   †   †

When Basil arrived, Septimus Watkins was just leaving his office. He laid hat and gloves and silver-topped malacca stick back on his desk and sat down without removing his topcoat. While Basil was talking, Watkins' bleak glance traveled toward the window view of Old Trinity, dark and dwarfish among higher buildings. "The whole business sounds like adolescent humor to me."

"Who inherits the jewelry if Miss Crayle dies before thirty?"

"Dr. Willing, I know your reputation. I believe you'll be discreet. So I'll tell you as much as I can. For that is the quickest way to disabuse your mind of the preposterous idea that anything threatens Miss Crayle. That unfortunate girl, Faustina, is illegitimate." Watkins' small, close smile seemed to savor the lubricities of the past, safely sterilized by time. "Did you ever hear of Rosa Diamond? She was the daughter of a man who wrote hymns and lived in Philadelphia. She had red hair. In the nineties she ran away from home—first New York, then Paris. There she became a star of the *demimonde*—one of those fabulous courtesans Balzac describes in such rich detail. A provincial American girl, she learned from her lovers to speak and write perfect French, to understand music and art and letters. It's hard to make your generation understand such hetaerae. Only Paris and Athens in certain periods have produced them."

"Wasn't she co-respondent in a divorce case of the 1900's?"

"In 1912. A corporation lawyer of New York wanted a divorce without accusing his wife. Rosa Diamond was so notorious that he had only to go to Paris and be seen once, driving in the Bois with her in an open carriage, to obtain his divorce. That single drive was considered adequate proof of adultery. It was said that he paid Rosa Diamond a thousand dollars and that they parted at her door without his even kissing her fingertips. But they met again and . . . Faustina Crayle is their daughter. Rosa knew her trade. She was to have been simply a convenience. Instead she altered the whole course of his life. He fell in love with her. . . ."

Again came the little smile of reminiscent salacity. "He brought her back to America. He gave her a town house in Manhattan and a seaside cottage in New Jersey at Seabright. But he didn't marry her. Such men didn't marry such women in those days."

"And that is the origin of that meagre, bloodless girl!" Basil thought of the flat chest, the narrow flanks. "Does she know?"

"I've tried to keep it from her, as her parents wished. Several times she has asked me if she were illegitimate. I lied, but I'm afraid she didn't believe me. . . . It was in 1918, when Rosa was forty-three, that she gave birth to Faustina. The father already had a legitimate heir by his divorced wife. He was in his fifties then and knew he had not long to live—a heart condition which Faustina has inherited. He wanted to provide for the little girl without unpleasant publicity which might affect her future. To avoid mentioning Rosa or Faustina in his will, he gave Rosa a collection of handsome jewels which had belonged to his mother. There was another fund to put Faustina through school, but the jewels—sold at a fair price, with the proceeds invested judiciously—would give her a tidy income for life—say, ten thousand a year in 1918 and even more today. The value of Faustina's jewels has appreciated in the last thirty years, while, unhappily, the crash of 1929 wiped out the fortune left to the legitimate heir. That young man shot himself, leaving two minor heirs, legitimate grandchildren of Faustina's father, who have less money than she today."

"But if Faustina dies before the age of thirty, the jewels revert to these children of her natural half-brother?"

"There was some bad feeling when the grandfather gave family jewels to Rosa Diamond and she developed a sense of guilt about it. According to her will, Faustina inherits the jewels at thirty but if Faustina dies before thirty, I, as executor, must dispose of the jewels according to instructions in a sealed envelope desposited with me, which can be opened only after Faustina's death and in the presence of a probate judge. Rosa herself told me this envelope contains instructions to give the jewels to the legitimate heirs. The sealed envelope was a device she contrived so that her will could be read to Faustina without Faustina learning the name of her natural half-brother or suspecting their relationship. That name I cannot reveal, even to you, Dr. Willing. It would betray a trust to revive such an old, unhappy scandal."

"Do the legitimate heirs know about Rosa's will and the sealed instructions?"

"Naturally. The family knew from the beginning what had become of their jewels. When they asked me if there was any legal way to recover the jewels, I convinced them there was not, by explaining exactly what disposition Rosa had made of them."

"Did you mention Faustina Crayle by name?"

"I believe I did. Why not?"

Wearily, Basil rose to take his leave. "Tell me one more thing: has either of these legitimate heirs any connection with the Maidstone School? Or Brereton?"

"I must decline to answer that."

†   †   †

It was full night when Basil reached the narrow brownstone house on lower Park Avenue where he had lived so many years. Before the war he had regarded it as a poor substitute for his father's home in Baltimore. Now, after years overseas, this was his home and always would be. He loved the river of cars flowing uptown at office-closing time, the soft bloom of curtained lamplight in the low, old-fashioned houses on either side of the wide street, the glitter of the Grand Central building against velvety blue darkness, the whisper of tires, the ring of heels and the nip of frost in the air which announced winter and a new season of gaiety.

Juniper met him in the vestibule. "Some folks waitin' in the library."

Basil went up a flight of stairs to the long, white-paneled "library" that was also living-room and study. Juniper had drawn wine-colored curtains and lighted lamps. At the sound of Basil's step a young man turned swiftly toward the door. The lamplight found golden highlights in the ash-blond hair, cut close to his small head. "Dr. Willing? Forgive this intrusion, but the matter is urgent. I am Raymond Vining, Barbara's brother. It was Mrs. Lightfoot who suggested that we should see you. This is Dr. Willing— Mrs. Chase, Diana's mother. And my *fiancée,* Miss Aitchison."

The women were shadows beyond the lamplight. Basil pressed the chandelier switch. Mrs. Chase had kept the tilted nose, chubby cheeks, and rounded chin of youth, but there were deep lines scored on either side of the mouth. The bright, reddish brown hair was as patently artificial as the tomato-red of her lips. She was dressed with ostentation—dark mink, black velvet, and diamonds. Miss Aitchison was a ripe beauty of eighteen or twenty with splendid dark eyes, golden skin, and fruity, red lips, set off by a neat brown suit and a vivid scarf of burnt orange. Basil paused as he caught the ghost of a familiar fragrance—lemon verbena. But he could not tell which of the three had brought it into the room.

"Do you think I should withdraw Diana from the school?" demanded Mrs. Chase.

"I can't advise you about that." Basil realized she was the sort of woman who tries to unload any responsibility on the nearest man.

"At least you can tell us what has been happening there!"

"All sorts of odd things happen at schools," drawled Miss Aitchison insolently, her legs crossed, a cigarette smoking in one gloved hand.

Basil seized the opening. "You went to Brereton?"

"No, I'm Maidstone and—"

Raymond Vining interrupted. "Dr. Willing, just what did happen? Was it hysteria? Or fraud?"

Basil turned to look at Vining. He had Barbara's fresh pink and white skin, and her eyes, the misty blue of star sapphires. He had her lips— the line so subtly turned that even in repose it seemed to quiver on the edge of laughter. He had the attenuated face and figure Victorian novelists called "aristocratic." Basil had seen the same traits too often in the families of farmers and factory workers to accept the odd biological belief that the human bone structure can be altered in a few generations by property and leisure.

"Was Miss Crayle an agent?" went on Vining. "Or a victim?"

Basil took a book from his shelves. "Here is something that is supposed to have happened in Livonia in 1845. It's been published in various versions by Robert Dale Owen, by Aksakoff, by Flammarion." He began to read aloud. It was almost the same story as Faustina's. Only the girl's school was at Volmar, fifty-eight miles from Riga, and the girl was a French teacher from Dijon, Emilie Sagée, fair, gentle, aged thirty-two. Two identical figures were seen simultaneously by an embroidery class of forty-two girls—

one appearing for several minutes in a chair in the classroom while the other could be seen gathering flowers in the garden outside the window. As long as the appearance remained in the chair, the girl outside moved "slowly and heavily like a person overcome with fatigue." There were other appearances, even more curious, until finally all but twelve of the forty-three girls were withdrawn by their parents and Mademoiselle Sagée was dismissed. She wept and cried: "This is the nineteenth time since my sixteenth year that I have lost a position because of this!" From that moment, when she walked out of the Neuwelcke School, she vanished from history. What became of her, no one knows. But in 1895 Flammarion looked at the birth records in Dijon for 1813—the year of Mademoiselle Sagée's birth if she were thirty-two in 1845. There was no Sagée. But on January 13, 1813, an infant girl named Octavie Saget was born and, of course, Saget is pronounced precisely the same as Sagée in French. In the record after the name appeared the significant word: *illegitimate*.

"There is one striking point about all this," concluded Basil. "The exact parallel between the two cases. In some details the Crayle case is a plagiarism of the Sagée case."

"Except for the illegitimacy," murmured Vining.

"So what?" said Miss Aitchison rudely.

"Someone who wishes to injure Miss Crayle has read the story of Mademoiselle Sagée and adapted it to that purpose. But that isn't the worst. According to tradition, she who sees her own double must die. Miss Crayle lives in fear of seeing the figure herself. This haunting by a double is a constant threat of death to her—psychologically on the same plane as threatening, anonymous letters. It could end in insanity, suicide—even murder."

"How could anyone fake the thing?" cried Vining. "Mirrors?"

"Not when Miss Crayle was painting on the lawn and the double was sitting in an armchair inside the house."

"Alice . . ." Vining turned to Miss Aitchison. "I'm going to take Barbara out of that school. Wouldn't you?"

"I suppose so." Miss Aitchison looked bored.

"You're right!" Mrs. Chase would always join the majority with enthusiasm. "I'm going to take Diana away the first thing tomorrow. . . ."

†   †   †

After dinner Basil called Assistant Chief Inspector Foyle at his Flatbush home. "Nothing we can do tonight," said Foyle, when Basil had outlined facts and conjectures. "You told her to go to a big hotel. Couldn't be any hocus-pocus there. Tomorrow I'll see this Watkins character at his office. If I busted in on his home tonight, it would be twice as difficult. . . ."

†   †   †

It was six forty-five A.M. when the telephone rang beside the bed. "Dr. Willing?" Mrs. Lightfoot's voice roused him. "I'm sorry to disturb you, but a policeman just called me from New Jersey. Faustina Crayle is dead."

† † †

Basil met an early train from Massachusetts at Grand Central and took Mrs. Lightfoot to breakfast in the station. Then he drove her to Centre Street.

"After you phoned this morning I got what dope I could from the New Jersey State Police," said Foyle to Basil. "No evidence of suicide— let alone murder. Not even accident. Just natural death from heart failure. You told me yourself Watkins said her heart was weak."

"I wonder how many people he told . . ." muttered Basil.

"She didn't go to a hotel," added Foyle. "Her friends at the penthouse say Miss Crayle got a phone call that changed her mind about that. She went down to this seaside cottage she'd inherited. Her body could have lain there for weeks if the caretaker hadn't happened to pass the house around three A.M., coming home from a covered-dish supper at the church there. She saw a light and notified the state police. They found the front door ajar, Miss Crayle's key still in the lock outside, and her key-ring dangling. Just one light inside—a lamp in the hall. There's a couple of little parlors to the right of the hall with a pair of transparent glass doors between. Miss Crayle was lying prone in the middle of the first parlor, her head toward the glass doors, still wearing hat, coat and gloves, her purse and dressing-case beside her. Nothing in the room disarranged. No money taken. The Jersey cops found a taxi-driver who drove her from the station to the cottage and left her there around eleven fifty. The doctor says she must have been dead by midnight at the latest.

"It's plain what happened. She unlocked the door and left it ajar with her key in the lock while she stepped inside to switch on a few lights. What every woman does when she enters an empty house alone at night. Before she got any farther than the first parlor, her heart just stopped."

"Did you check alibis?" asked Basil.

"Oh, sure. Mrs. Chase was with a supper party from eleven P.M. to three thirty A.M. Miss Aitchison and Vining were at the Crane Club. Bartender remembers their coming in together at ten P.M. and leaving together at one thirty A.M."

"Anything else?"

"Well . . ." Foyle hesitated. "It's pretty silly. You know how superstitious hayseeds are. One of the yokels down at this place, Seabright, declares he passed Faustina Crayle walking along a backroad at three thirty A.M. He didn't know it when he testified, but that was after the cops had found her dead body. . . ."

† † †

In the car Basil glanced at Mrs. Lightfoot. "I'm going to Seabright."

"May I go with you? I'm beginning to feel responsible for Miss Crayle. If I hadn't turned her out so summarily. . . ."

Miss Crayle's cottage was three miles beyond the village, between pinewoods and sea—white clap-boarding with shutters and door of grayish green. Though the road was unfrequented, Russian olive, bayberry, and scrub pine had been cultivated to mask the windows. A ragged lawn sloped up to the crest of a dune covered with poverty grass. There was no one in sight but the front door was unlatched. "Would police be so careless?" murmured Basil.

Mrs. Lightfoot followed him inside reluctantly. "Dr. Willing, could a . . . a double survive the death of the personality that projected it? Even for a few hours?"

He wasn't listening. He was looking at the hall—white woodwork, white wallpaper flecked with green. A lamp stood on a telephone table in the curve of the stair. Basil examined the bulb—one-hundred watts. The only light in the hall. It would illuminate the hall itself brilliantly, but the light would be low, ceiling and upper wall remaining in shadow. Some radiance would spill through the wide archway into the parlor on the right but it would still be low, and the second parlor, beyond the transparent glass doors, would be lost in shadows. Basil stepped into the first parlor. He pressed a light switch beside the archway. No light came. The bulbs in the ceiling fixture looked smoky. Probably dead.

The second parlor could be reached only by way of the first. The two were almost exactly alike. Each had white woodwork and a bay window at the far end with frilly, white curtains and green upholstered seat. Each had a rug of faded-rose color, slipcovers splashed with roses the same shade, and leaves of faded green. Only close inspection showed a difference in such details as the color of ashtrays and the arrangement of chairs.

"Monotonous," said Basil. "Two rooms in the same colors."

"It would be worse if they were decorated in contrasting colors," retorted Mrs. Lightfoot. "That would make both rooms look smaller by dividing them. Just as a woman in contrasting blouse and skirt looks shorter than a woman in a dress all one color. This way the eye travels from one room to the other without a break and you get the effect of one long room even with the glass doors closed."

"Why doors at all? Why not one big room?"

Mrs. Lightfoot glanced about her. "There's no radiator. Probably no furnace in a summer cottage like this. But with the glass doors closed, this first parlor is small enough to be heated by a portable stove, electric or oil."

Basil walked down the room to the glass doors. "What do you make of these marks?" They were minute scratches on the wooden frames that separated each small transparent glass pane from the others.

"It's hard to paint the wooden frames without smearing the glass," suggested Mrs. Lightfoot. "Amateur painters often cut a piece of cardboard the same size as the pane and fit it inside the frame over the glass while they're painting. Afterward you have to pry out the cardboard. This painter seems to have used a needle."

"It wasn't a painter. The scratches were made after the paint was dry and—"

"What's that?" exclaimed Mrs. Lightfoot. "It sounds like footfalls upstairs!"

"It is," agreed Basil calmly. "I've been listening to them for some time."

The footfalls were coming downstairs. There was no attempt at stealth. The heels rang clear and unafraid on each step. Then came a sudden pause. Basil visualized a figure arrested in motion by sight of the front door, which he had left wide open. The footfalls resumed with a certain caution. In the hall archway appeared the large, formidable figure of Septimus Watkins.

"Dr. Willing!" Surprise seemed to master indignation. "I trust you've learned enough from the local police to accept as I do their statement that Miss Crayle's death was perfectly natural. As I mentioned yesterday, her heart—" His voice wavered, stopped. All three listened to the sound of other footfalls—younger, fleeting—running down the stairs.

"So you didn't come alone?" Basil moved toward the arch. The footfalls ceased as abruptly as they had begun. Basil was the first to speak. "I'm glad Alice Aitchison told me she went to Maidstone."

Raymond Vining moved forward. With him came a faint scent of lemon verbena. "What has that to do with . . . ?"

"Your murdering your grandfather's illegitimate daughter, Faustina Crayle? Everything."

"Don't say a word, Ray!" called Watkins. "I'll get you the best criminal lawyer money can buy!"

Basil spoke as if thinking aloud. "Alice Aitchison must have known or guessed the truth. Enough to charge her as accessory? Probably, since, as your wife, she would share the money you got from the sale of Faustina's jewels when you received them. And Barbara? She's only thirteen, but she's intelligent. She may have guessed—"

"No!" Vining shouted. "Alice didn't know and neither did Barbara! You can charge me but you can't charge them! I won't let you!"

"Why, that's a confession!" gasped Mrs. Lightfoot.

† † †

Not until the drive back to New York did Basil have a chance to give her the details: "I suspected Vining the moment I saw his close family resemblance to Faustina, his grandfather's daughter. He was the only person involved who was physically able to impersonate her double, even under favorable conditions. Both Vining and Faustina had the attenuated 'aristocratic' figure—narrow flanks, finely cut wrists and ankles, tapering hands, slender, high-arched feet. In woman's dress, his figure would look like hers. And in a dim light at a fair distance his face could pass for hers. Both had the 'aristocratic' small head and long, oval face, the prominent nose and thin lips. Both were the ash-blond type, with cloudy blue eyes like star sapphires. Rachel face powder would make Vining's fresh pink skin as sallow as Faustina's. He was actor enough to subdue the mocking expression of his lips to Faustina's look of wistful seriousness. Especially when his face was shaded by a wide hatbrim.

"He discovered the resemblance when Alice Aitchison was at Maidstone a year ago. He wanted to break the strict rule against male visitors on any day but Sunday. He was in love and he wanted to visit her at any time of day or night he pleased. So he used a trick as old as pagan Rome. Remember how the intrusion of young Clodius, dressed as a woman, at a ceremony deigned for women only, caused Caesar to divorce the wife that wasn't above suspicion? Like Clodius, Vining was young, slight, beardless. He could pass as one girl among many girls if he wore a girl's clothing and kept at a distance from others in a dim light. But he didn't pass as one girl among many. He was mistaken for a particular girl— one of the young teachers, Faustina Crayle. Miss Maidstone kept her books on psychic research under lock and key, but they were there. Trust some of the girls to get hold of the key and read about the *doppelgänger* myth. Stories of a mysterious 'double' began to crystallize around Faustina. Alice Aitchison would report the fact to Vining with great glee for she would have noticed his resemblance to Faustina and she would realize how the stories had started. But Vining himself would know why that resemblance existed. Thanks to Watkins, he knew all there was to know about his grandfather's natural daughter and he was in a position to recognize that rather unusual name—Faustina Crayle. He made a point of seeing Faustina for himself. He saw how strong the family resemblance was though the difference in sex, and therefore in dress, made it unapparent to the casual observer. All this gave him the idea for a unique method of murder that would not leave any mark on Faustina's body or even require his presence at the moment of her death.

"When she went to Brereton, he sent his little sister Barbara to the same school as an unconsious spy, reporting to him quite innocently all that went on outside the school. The front and back stairs and the French windows at Brereton made it fairly easy for him to slip in and out of the building, especially when most people who saw him at a distance mistook him for Faustina who had a right to be there. For his more startling effects he chose his witnesses carefully—a stupid, suggestible young servant and two flighty little girls of thirteen, one his own sister who wouldn't give him away if she ever guessed the truth. I think this meeting with you on the stair was accident. You were too shrewd an observer for him to seek you deliberately. But there were bound to be some accidents. He made the best of that one, slipping though the drawing room and out a French window, just before Arlene came in from the dining room. He let his hand brush your arm purposely because he knew his hand was icy cold—he had just come in from outside—and he knew that coldness would be almost as effective as the filmy, unreal texture of the Sagée double's touch which he couldn't imitate. At Brereton he appeared in a coat and hat copied exactly from Faustina's and reproduced one striking incident from the case of Emilie Sagée—slow motions during the appearance of her double. Presumably he did this by drugging something Faustina ate or drank, timed to affect her the moment he appeared as her double.

"No wonder Faustina herself came to believe in the double and fear it. That was how he killed her—with her own fear. He knew the plan of the Seabright cottage—it had belonged to his grandfather. He knew about the two parlors which were the same size and shape, with bay windows facing each other at opposite ends, and the pair of glass doors between the two rooms. Watkins could tell him they were still decorated in the same colors. The rest was simple. He went down to Seabright in Faustina's absence. He obtained mirrors the same size and shape as the panes of glass in the pair of doors and fitted a mirror over each pane, inside the wooden frame. He put dead bulbs in the ceiling fixture of the first parlor. That was all. Except the telephone call to Faustina last night. He would introduce himself as one of the mysterious family she had wondered about for so long and make an appointment to meet her at her own house that same night. He could tell her things about Watkins and her mother that would make his identification convincing. Then he went off to the Crane Club with Alice Aitchison to establish an alibi.

"At eleven fifty Faustina let herself into the dark, empty cottage with a latchkey, leaving it in the door while she snapped on the hall light. It was chance that she stepped into the parlor next. But she was bound to enter it sooner or later that evening and when she did—only one thing could happen. She would press the ceiling switch beside the hall archway. No light would come on since the bulbs were dead. A movement would draw her eyes to the pair of doors, now mirrored. Whose movement? Her own, reflected there. *But she wouldn't know it was a reflection!* She would believe with absolute conviction that there was transparent glass in those doors and that she was looking *through* it. There was nothing to tell her in that first, swift glance that she was looking at the first parlor reflected in a mirror, instead of the second parlor viewed through glass—remember, both rooms were alike in shape and color and the low, irregular light from the single lamp in the hall was deceptive by the time it reached the mirrors in the pair of doors.

"You see what happened? *Faustina's own reflection killed her!* She had a weak heart. For over a year her mind had been subjected to intensive psychological preparation for belief in the *doppelgänger*. As she said: *when you've lost your job twice because of a thing, you don't think it's just imagination.* She toppled face down, frightened to death by the oldest, the simplest of all illusions—her own reflection. She lay dead of terror when there was nothing to terrify anyone—merely a mirror imaging the prone body of a dead girl.

"Vining had to remove the mirrors before the body was found. He went down to Seabright to do that after he'd given Faustina ample time to die. He wore woman's dress for the last time. He might not have been seen at all. As it happened he was seen and mistaken once again for Faustina. When the police checked the time and found 'Faustina' had been 'seen' after she was dead, only one thing could happen. The story of Faustina's double became the story of Faustina's ghost and the police would write the whole thing off as village superstition.

"As Faustina's double, Vining tricked the eye adroitly. No doubt he wore rubber-soled shoes to trick the ear as well, for the double never made a sound. His cold hand even tricked your sense of touch. But there was one grosser, more primordial sense he didn't trick—smell."

"But the double had no odor at all!" objected Mrs. Lightfoot.

"That's the point. Every human body has some odor. Yet you said the double had none. Did that mean it really was inhuman? Or was there some condition that would make one body seem odorless to another? There is just one such condition: when two bodies have the same odor—for example, when they are both using the same perfume. A nonsmoker kissing a smoker is keenly aware of nicotine fumes. Two smokers kissing will each believe the other has a clean breath because neither detects the odor.

"You used lemon verbena. So I knew, after my first talk with you, that *Faustina's double was someone who also used lemon verbena.* Any other odor would have been noticed—except your own. Faustina herself used lavender water. You told me so and I noticed it when I was with her. So the double couldn't be Faustina herself. That narrowed my search considerably. I wanted someone who looked like Faustina, someone who used lemon verbena, someone who had connections with both Maidstone and Brereton, someone who had a motive for injuring or destroying Faustina. Vining alone met all those conditions. When I entered my own library last night I caught a hint of lemon verbena. I wasn't sure which of the three was using it—Mrs. Chase, Miss Aitchison, or Vining. But Vining was the most likely since he was the only man among them and you had told me it was a man's lotion. Today, the moment he came downstairs, I noticed it again. I suppose lemon verbena was such an ingrained habit with him that he forgot to suppress it when he was impersonating the double."

"You've solved the mystery of Faustina Crayle," said Mrs. Lightfoot. "But what about the mystery of Emilie Sagée?"

Basil slowed for a sharp curve, then accelerated. "That is a mystery that we must always see through a glass, darkly. . . ."

Afterword

"Doppelganger" is from German words meaning "double-walker." That is, a person who walks his way through life looking exactly like you, so that he is your "double."

Presumably, since a spirit is incorporeal it can take on any corporeal shape, just as you, when in the nude, can dress in any choice of clothing. A spirit may, therefore, choose to take on a body that is exactly like yours.

This can be for a variety of reasons. It can, conceivably, be done out of kindliness, so that a spirit might take your place and do an arduous task, or accept punishment, while you escape this unpleasantness.

However, human beings are perfectly aware that evil is for some reason more widespread than good or is, at least, more noticeable. Therefore, there is the definite fear that a doppelganger is up to no good; that he, or she, will get you into trouble. (There are, of course, lookalikes in real life, and one always hears tales of people being accused of crimes and sometimes of being punished for misdeeds actually performed by lookalikes.)

If a person really believes in the existence of doppelgangers (malevolent spirits assuming your shape, and not just casual lookalikes) there is a certain added uncertainty to life. It is easy to understand the feeling that if you actually meet a doppelganger face to face, you will die.

Naturally, there has never been evidence that doppelgangers exist, and in McCloy's story a rationalist explanation is used.—I.A.

Additional Reading

John Kenrick Bangs, "Carleton Barker, First and Second," in *Ghosts I Have Met and Some Others* (New York: Harper, 1898).

Henry James, "The Jolly Corner," in *The Ghostly Tales of Henry James*, Ron Edel, ed. (New Brunswick, N.J.: Rutgers University Press, 1948).

John Metcalfe, "The Double Admiral," in *The Smoking Leg* (London: Jarrolds, 1925).

Edgar Allan Poe, "William Wilson," in *The Complete Tales and Poems of Edgar Allan Poe* (New York: Modern Library, 1938).

J. H. Rosne Aine, "The Immortal Curse" (aka: "The Supernatural Assassin"), in *The Best French Short Stories of 1923-24*, Richard Eaton, ed. (Boston: Small, Maynard & Co. Pub., 1924).

7

Dumb Supper

Kris Neville
Dumb Supper

Why shucks, everybody *knows* black is the color of death. If you see something black coming at you in your dreams, you may just as well give up, 'cause you ain't long for *this* world.")

Rosalynn twisted in her chair and picked at a bit of lint on her wool skirt as she looked at the speaker.

("You should have seen the dress Nellie bought over in Joplin; the *cutest* thing.")

Rosalynn extended her legs and looked down at them.

("They say it cost fifty dollars. My!")

Rosalynn hooked her toe under the rocker of the chair before her and set it in motion.

"Oh! Don't do that, dear," Marsha said. "A chair that's empty rocked, its owner will with ills be stocked."

Rosalynn looked up. "I'm sorry," she said.

("Of course it may be a little too low for her, you know. She doesn't have the *figure*.")

Jean Towers came over and sat down by Rosalynn. "Don't mind Marsha. She's just superstitious."

"I didn't mind," Rosalynn said.

"I guess you think we're unfriendly?"

"No," said Rosalynn.

("And they say they're gonna get married next month. And about time, too, if you ask me.")

"I don't think you're unfriendly. I'll just need a little time to get to know you, and then I'll be all right."

("Well, I certainly wish Jude would hurry up and ask me.")

"Amy told me your family just moved in last week."

"Yes," Rosalynn said. "From California. Fresno."

"What do you think of Carthage?"

"Oh," Rosalynn said, "it's—I mean, I think I'll like it. I mean, I'm *sure* I'll like it."

"Sure you will."

"It's just that now—at first, I mean—everybody is talking about people I don't know and places I—"

("And me too!" someone said, and it sent some of the girls off into peals of laughter.)

Jean Towers smiled sympathetically. "You'll get caught up in the swing of things."

"Uh-huh. Ah—could you tell me—" But Jean Towers had left her side.

("And I said to him, 'If you think for a minute that—' ")

Rosalynn picked at the lint again. This was a new town and this was her first party and she wanted—oh, so very bad—to make a good impression: or they maybe wouldn't ask her again. And it was really her place, she knew, to be friendly.

("You girls better have a dumb supper.")

"What would you think of a dumb supper, Rosalynn?" Jean Towers asked.

Rosalynn said, "A dumb supper? Why—I guess, I mean—sure: if you girls want to. I think I'd like something like that."

"Do you have dumb suppers, ever, where you come from?" Amy asked.

Rosalynn said, "It's a game, isn't it?"

"Not exactly—well, I guess you might say it was a game, too: sort of."

"Then I guess we have something like it back in Fresno," Rosalynn said and laughed. For the first time she was included in the general conversation and she was happy. "Why don't you tell me just what it is and then I'll tell you if we had anything like it."

"Well," Jean Towers said, "it's a kind of a legend. Nobody believes in it any more. Except some of the peckerwood people back in the hills. And maybe one or two of the old timers, like Uncle Alvin down on the river bottom." She made a deprecating little gesture. "Course there *are* stories . . . ."

'Maybe you ought to tell her the one Grandma Wilson's always telling."

"I don't know—well—Would you like to listen to it, Rosalynn?"

Rosalynn said, "Yes."

"It all happened in the Rush family. (They're—the Rushes, that is—

they're all over this section now; there's a lot of them around Pierce City, and the Roberts of Webb City are first cousins—but this was a long time ago, maybe a hundred years, when they'd just moved in from Kentucky.) There was a girl in the family, young, name of Sarah. A pretty little thing, friendly, the way Grandma Wilson tells it."

Rosalynn stared down at her shoe tops, wishing she were pretty, trying to believe what her mother told her, "It's not what you look like, honey, that's important; it's the kind of a person you are," and remembering, too, how she looked to herself in the mirror, wondering where she could find a husband for a face like that.

Jean Towers said: "One night at a party—a party like this, I imagine, when the old people were gone—somebody suggested that they have a dumb supper; just like you do suggest things, half joking, half serious: that way. Sarah thought it was a good idea (they used to do things like that back in Kentucky), and she wasn't afraid at all."

Sarah had been a friendly girl; Rosalynn wondered how people got to be that way; how they learned to say the right things and do the right things and make people like them.

"Of course, you understand, a dumb supper isn't really a *supper*. It's just a halfway supper. Nobody eats anything—and there isn't anything to eat, except two little pieces of corn bread."

Rosalynn wondered why she always was half frightened by people; why she had to screw her courage down tight even to come to a party like this. She really wanted to like people and have them like her. And after all, everyone here was friendly—and they'd wanted her to come: or Amy wouldn't have asked her. They were nice enough, too, a little different from the girls back home, but nice in their way, and she'd stop feeling like an outsider in a little while.

"Well, Sarah began to fix for the dumb supper. Now, fixing for a dumb supper has to be done in a special way."

At first Rosalynn through they had resented her—maybe because her clothes were nicer than theirs, or maybe because her father had a better job than their fathers, or maybe because she lived in the big house out on South Main, or maybe because she didn't have an accent like they had and talked faster. But now, with them gathered around her, listening, she saw that they really didn't hate her and it had only been in her imagination all along.

"Everything has to be done *backwards*. Everything, like mixing the batter, striking the match, even walking. Everything opposite from usual."

Maybe she was afraid of people because she thought they all wanted to hurt her. (In her second year of high school, she could still remember burningly what she had heard her best friend say.) Her father had explained it all: "You see, people aren't really as bad as you think; they may be thoughtless, but they're very seldom cruel—Most people aren't like your friend Betty. They'd rather be friendly than unfriendly, if you'll only give them the chance."

"Sarah cooked her corn bread, doing everything backwards, the way it's supposed to be done. And then she set out the plates. Two of them. One for herself and one for her husband."

Rosalynn was going to be a different girl. She was going to make all kinds of new friends (like Jean and Amy and Marsha—the superstitious one.) And she would have the best times talking to them, and parties at her big house—and maybe dates (for she wasn't *that* ugly: only she always seemed to scare the few boys off because she was so timid: but it would be different this time). Then maybe—

"You see, if you do everything just right, according to the story, at least, when you set down at your plate with the backward corn bread on it, your husband will come in (not *really*, I mean, but like a ghost) and set down at *his* plate so you can see his face and that way you get to find out who your husband is going to be."

"Oh," said Rosalynn, resolving to listen more carefully, for if she wanted to make friends, she must remember not to feel sorry for herself, but to be very polite and listen very closely whether or not she was interested.

"At each plate Sarah put down a knife. (They had funny knives in those days with bone handles: and the one she put at her husband's plate had a big, star-shaped chip knocked off of it.)

"By this time the wind was coming up in the North (as it always does at a dumb supper), and you could hear it moan in the trees. It was very quiet in the house, for you mustn't talk—not anyone—at a dumb supper."

"Sarah put a piece of corn bread on each plate and then she sat down, as calm as anything, to wait.

"Everybody was holding their breath, and you could hear the wind blowing louder and louder."

Rosalynn shivered; she really didn't want to hear the rest of the story.

"And then—bang!—the front door flew open and slammed back against the wall, hard, making the house shake. And the wind blew in and made the candles flicker. (This was long ago, before electricity.)

"And just as the candles went out, a figure all in white came rushing in to set down beside Sarah."

Jean Towers paused, and Rosalynn could hear her own heart beating in the stillness.

"When the candle was lit again, the figure was gone. And the knife that had lain by its plate was gone too."

"Is—is that all?" Rosalynn asked.

"No. No, that's just the first part. You see, she really got to see its face. (Or so she said.)"

"Well, sometime after that, maybe a year or two, a stranger came to town; name was Hall. Young man, handsome, good worker, although a quiet sort, not given to talking too much. When Sarah saw him, she knew that was the man who was going to be her husband, for his face was the face of the figure in white.

"She married him and they went to live in a little cabin on her father's property.

"Things went along fine for a year, for he was a good farmer and a sober, loving husband. But one day—

"Well, her father went down to see them, and when he got up to the top of the ridge (the cabin was down in a valley, like), he could see that there wasn't any sign of smoke in the chimney; which wasn't right, for it was a chilly autumn day. The cabin was still, as if there wasn't anyone around. (You know, sometimes you can tell when you see a house that there isn't anybody at home.) Well, he knew immediately that there was something wrong. So he hurried down.

"And what do you think he found in the cabin? . . . Sarah. Lying on the floor. She was lying there with her eyes closed and a knife sticking out between her breasts.

"She wasn't dead, though (but it was just a lucky thing that her father came along when he did or she would have been). And she didn't die, either. But it was quite a while before she could get up and around (the doctors didn't know as much in those days).

"Finally, she told everybody what had happened.

"That morning, when her father found her lying there in the cabin almost dead, she had told her husband (for the first time) about how she had seen his face there at the dumb supper.

"At first he didn't say anything at all—just sort of stared at her. Then he got up and went to a little box he always kept—he wore the key around his neck and wouldn't let anyone see what was in it—and opened it. He took out a knife that was there on a velvet cushion.

"And he turned back to Sarah."

"So you're the witch that sent me through that night of hell!" he screamed, and then he plunged the knife into her.

"It was the knife with the star-shaped chip out of the bone handle."

"And she never saw her husband again."

Rosalynn swallowed. "That—that was—awful," she said.

Marsha laughed thinly.

"You mean that you actually still have dumb suppers?" Rosalynn asked.

"Well," Jean Towers said, "not very often. Oh, maybe once in a while. I mean there's nothing *in* it. Though some of the peckerwoods would say it was witchcraft. Just for a laugh, you know. We don't *believe* it. But it does give you a funny, creepy feeling."

"I think we ought to have one," Amy said. "Then Rosalynn can see— the kind of games we play."

"Yes, let's."

"Let's even let Rosalynn cook it."

"How about it, Rosalynn?"

Rosalynn said: "All right, I mean, if you want to. But let somebody else cook it, why not? I—I'm afraid I never learned how to cook—not even corn bread."

"If *that's* all. We can show you how that's done."

"Well," Rosalynn said slowly, "I'll do it if somebody will too." She turned to Marsha. "You?"

"I wouldn't do it for the *world,*" Marsha said.

"Be still!" Jean told her. And then to Rosalynn: "She doesn't believe anything would happen of course. She—she just doesn't believe in taking chances. All of us here have cooked dumb suppers before."

"Yes," said Marsha. "We have."

"Well, how about you Amy?"

"Me? It's—more fun if only one person cooks the supper."

"Oh . . . I mean, I guess, if you really *want* me to, of course . . ." Rosalynn realized vaguely that it was probably just an ordinary prank they were in on: trying to scare her. Maybe like an initiation stunt. And if she wanted them to be her friends she'd have to go through with it. And not show that she was scared.

"All right," she said, "I'll do it."

Before, it seemed a million times, Rosalynn had wished she wasn't so easy to frighten; even when she was little her parents had to stay in the room until she was asleep; and now and then, still, she would turn on the light at night (which took all her courage) just to be sure nothing was there.

She told herself something that usually worked; she told herself: "They will all be laughing about it next week, and then I can tell them how scared I was and they won't mind at all."

She looked at the wall clock.

There was no help there. Mr. and Mrs. Pierce, Amy's parents, wouldn't get back from Carthage until midnight.

The house was a farm house; four miles out of town. And Rosalynn had no way to leave, even if she wanted to, for she was depending on the Pierces to take her home when they came back.

"Come on," Jean said.

They went into the kitchen where Amy got the proper ingredients: there were three little cups of them, already set out; Rosalynn knew, then, that they had prepared for this.

"Flour," Amy said, pointing. "Corn meal. Baking powder." She drew a glass of water from the tap. "Mix the stuff all together and add the water until it's doughy."

"Salt?" Rosalynn asked.

"I thought you said you didn't know how to make corn bread."

"I—I don't: I just thought it ought to have salt in it—I mean, most things ought to have salt in them."

"Not *this* corn bread, Rosalynn. There isn't supposed to be any salt in *it*."

"Oh! I—see."

"Now. How would you mix these things together?"

"I'd—I'd put the baking powder and the corn meal in the flour and—shake them up, I guess. And then I'd add the water."

"Good. Now listen: Put the flour, the corn meal and the baking powder in the water. Then stir them up. Backwards, you see. And if you usually stir clockwise, be sure to stir counter clockwise this time. And walk backwards. And strike the match for the oven away from you if you usually strike it towards you. Everything backwards."

"All right, I will, Amy. Don't worry."

Amy went on explaining all the details and Rosalynn listened, trying to remember, trying to play the game, so they would ask her to parties all the time.

It was only a silly superstition, and, contemplating the whole thing in the brightly lit kitchen of a farm house, she began to decide it was really nothing to be afraid of . . . Just a silly, childish prank, that's all.

"You're ready, then?"

"Yes, I guess so."

"All right, now. Remember this: no matter what happens: don't talk. None of us can talk. That's the most important thing of all. None of us can talk until it's all over."

"I won't say a word," Rosalynn said.

"Okay. Then you're ready?"

"Yes . . . Only first—I mean, I know it sounds silly, but look—You don't really believe anything's going to happen—I mean, my husband come, or anything like that?"

Amy looked levelly at her; she paused a moment before answering.

"No," she said.

"No more talking," Jean Towers said.

And there was silence.

Rosalynn did everything the way she had been told; everything, that is, but about striking the match. She always struck the match toward herself; and this time, in the spirit of a little girl crossing her fingers before telling one of the little fibs little girls tell, she struck the match in the usual way.

After the corn bread was in the oven, she walked backwards into the living room and sat down to wait for the ten minutes before it came time to set the table.

The other girls, silently as ghosts, had arranged themselves around the room; their eyes were upon her and she felt uncomfortable—like the first time she—well, she had felt everybody watching her then, too. It was something like that. As if they were waiting for something to give.

She thought Jean Towers' face was tense, and Marsha's eyes were—but she was letting her imagination run away with her.

Absolute silence. But for the clock.

She began to feel the vague, uneasy fingers of fear again.

The strangest thing was: None of the girls giggled. They were very still, waiting. They were—serious.

She heard the monotonous tick-tock, tick-tock of the clock.

There was the picture of the Indian, looking hopelessly into the chasm, there on the wall. Drooping spear.

(Tick-tock)

There were the goldfish, over in the corner. Slowly circling.

(Tick-tock)

There was—

Her heart leaped toward her throat.

The clock had stopped!

Rosalynn choked back a scream and her nails dug into her palms.

Slowly she relaxed. Only a clock had stopped, and clocks often stop: every minute, day and night, somewhere in the world, a clock stops.

Maybe the girls had arranged for that too; although it was a little difficult to imagine how they—

She looked at first one and then the other; and tension began to mount within her again. Their eyes were bright and they seemed to be leaned forward, tense, watching her.

Her father had said. "People aren't really as bad as you think: they're very seldom cruel." She tried to believe that.

It was time to begin setting the table. She had to fight with herself to stand; the eyes shifted upward with her.

Even if they hated her, she wasn't going to quit . . . to show she was afraid . . . not now.

(But they would all laugh about it tomorrow.)

She began to walk backward toward the kitchen. Hair along her neck bristled.

Silence.

She began the slow, awkward process of setting the table for herself and for a guest.

And then from far away! She tried to close her ears to it.

The second plate clattered loudly on the table.

She felt tears form, and her nose wrinkled and tingled. She could not scream.

She could only move toward the drawer, take two knives.

The expression on their faces: And she knew now. They *did* hate her: each of them. They were straining, listening, holding their breaths to hear it, and it grew louder!

They hated her: maybe because her father had a better job than their fathers, or maybe because she didn't have an accent and talked faster. *But they hated her!*

Rosalynn forgot about them. She was at the table again, and her movements were forced from her. She wanted to run and scream and cry.

She put the second knife before the second plate. (It had a good, stainless steel handle.)

Wind in winter! Wind from the North, moaning in the trees: wind in winter in Southern Missouri.

("It always comes up at a dumb supper," Jean Towers had said.)

. . . Mr. Pierce had said, that evening, that it was going to be a hard winter. But wind in winter? . . .

Marsha's eyes were glassy, and her breath came short.

Screaming wind, tearing at the house, gripping it, shaking it. In winter?

She took out the corn bread, using a pot holder to keep from burning her hands. She cut it into two pieces. The corn bread was soggy: she should have baked it longer.

She put the large piece on *his* plate.

She felt herself sitting down. There was nothing else she could do: she tried to fight but her muscles were caught in a clammy vice.

There was terror in her mind, overflowing it.

(The three goldfish, in the living room, were still circling slowly.)

The icy wind seemed all around her—caressing her, *kissing* her, muttering, muttering, like an obscene lover.

Weak. She was weak. Her skin crawled.

Something—from Outside.

Outside what?

Just Outside. That's all—Outside of—everything.

The girl-faces, now: blank, wide-eyed, drained. Waiting, waiting.

She tried to move her lips and the wind stopped them with a frozen kiss.

And the wind was everywhere; a laughing, insane fury; a cold, musty breath.

Frozen. Everything was frozen. Time stood still. Waiting for her husband to come.

He came.

She looked up from her plate and saw him.

A shadowy figure, unreal, tenuous, flowing into the room. Flowing toward her.

Her heart beat, beat, beat.

He was going to sit down beside her—her bridegroom!

Wind, evil wind.

The lights faded, growing weaker and weaker. And the white wrapped figure, settling into the chair prepared for it. It turned its head and stared full into Rosalynn's face.

She found that she could scream now; her voice was shrill, and it went on and on and on in the darkness. . . .

†   †   †

Finally the lights came back on.

The girls were circled tightly around her, their faces tense.

"What did he look like?" Marsha asked.

"He—he—it had no face; it wasn't my husband. It was—only—only blackness: awful black, blacker than the blackest night. . . ." She was sobbing.

"There, there, now," Jean Towers said, "you musn't cry. Take my handkerchief. It's nothing to cry about."

"No," said Marsha, "you musn't cry."

Suddenly the girls were bustling around her, wonderfully sweet and nice, drying her eyes, saying soft words to her, leaning over backwards to be helpful.

Rosalynn was shaking. "Let me alone," she begged. "*Please* let me alone. You *hate* me. I know you do."

"Shucks, no, we don't either," Marsha said.

For a long moment the words seemed to echo in her mind; and then they began to call up new echoes.

Slowly she came to remember it—an overheard scrap of conversation. She knew the meaning of black, and why they were being so nice to her. For Marsha had said, "Black is the color of Death."

And she knew, too, who was ultimately to be her only true friend and bridegroom.

Afterword

Through most of history, women have been able to find fulfillment only through their husbands. There have been cases of women who made their mark in society on an equal basis with men (one can think of Cleopatra, Boadicea, and Eleanor of Aquitaine) but these have been exceptional.

In general, the unmarried woman has simply been an unwelcome charge on her family. She has been an "old maid" and a figure of fun who is usually portrayed as an embittered and acidulous woman (and well she might be, considering that her social position is nil and that she can usually get along only as an object of charity, or in such an unregarded occupation as that of a chaperone or governess).

Under such circumstances, young women, as they progressed through their teens, would become increasingly aware that somehow they must attract

the attention of some young man—one who, it is devoutly to be hoped,
had some property or form of livelihood, and who was reasonably handsome
and kind-hearted. But if all this failed, then some young man—or old man,
for that matter, because any husband was better than no husband.

Naturally, a wide variety of superstitious observances grew up that
would ensure marriage (even today bridesmaids try to grab the bridal
bouquet), or that would, better yet, give someone some indication of who
the husband would be.

This can lend itself to horror, as Neville's story shows, and it is fortunate
we live in a time and place in which women may wish to be married
but need not be condemned to it.—I.A.

Additional Reading

Paul Green, "Supper for the Dead," in *Salvation on a String and Other
Tales of the South* (New York: Harper, 1946).

Blanche Bane Kuder, "From What Strange Land," in *A Century of Horror
Stories,* Dennis Wheatley, ed. (London: Hutchinson, 1935).

Charles R. Maturin, "Leixlip Castle," in *The Grimoire and Other
Supernatural Stories,* Montague Summers, ed. (London: Fortune Press,
1936).

Manly Wade Wellman, "Dumb Supper," in *Who Fears the Devil* (Sauk
City, Wisc.: Arkham House, 1963).

8

Evil Eye

Edgar Allan Poe
The Tell-Tale Heart

True!—nervous—very, very dreadfully nervous I had been and am; but why *will* you say that I am mad? The disease had sharpened my senses—not destroyed—not dulled them. Above all was the sense of hearing acute. I heard all things in the heaven and in the earth. I heard many things in hell. How, then, am I mad? Hearken! and observe how healthily—how calmly I can tell you the whole story.

It is impossible to say how first the idea entered my brain; but once conceived, it haunted me day and night. Object there was none. Passion there was none. I loved the old man. He had never wronged me. He had never given me insult. For his gold I had no desire. I think it was his eye! yes, it was this! One of his eyes resembled that of a vulture—a pale blue eye, with a film over it. Whenever it fell upon me, my blood ran cold; and so by degrees—very gradually—I made up my mind to take the life of the old man, and thus rid myself of the eye for ever.

Now this is the point. You fancy me mad. Madmen know nothing. But you should have seen *me*. You should have seen how wisely I proceeded—with what caution—with what foresight—with what dissimulation I went to work! I was never kinder to the old man than during the whole week before I killed him. And every night, about midnight, I turned the latch of his door and opened it—oh, so gently! And then, when I had made an opening sufficient for my head, I put in a dark lantern, all closed, closed, so that no light shone out, and then I thrust in my head. Oh, you would have laughed to see how cunningly I thrust it in! I moved it slowly—

very, very slowly, so that I might not disturb the old man's sleep. It took me an hour to place my whole head within the opening so far that I could see him as he lay upon his bed. Ha!—would a madman have been so wise as this? And then, when my head was well in the room, I undid the lantern cautiously—oh, so cautiously—cautiously (for the hinges creaked)—I undid it just so much that a single thin ray fell upon the vulture eye. And this I did for seven long nights—every night just at midnight—but I found the eye always closed; and so it was impossible to do the work; for it was not the old man who vexed me, but his Evil Eye. And every morning, when the day broke, I went boldly into the chamber, and spoke courageously to him, calling him by name in a hearty tone, and inquiring how he had passed the night. So you see he would have been a very profound old man, indeed, to suspect that every night, just at twelve, I looked in upon him while he slept.

Upon the eighth night I was more than usually cautious in opening the door. A watch's minute hand moves more quickly than did mine. Never before that night had I *felt* the extent of my own powers—of my sagacity. I could scarcely contain my feelings of triumph. To think that there I was, opening the door, little by little, and he not even to dream of my secret deeds or thoughts. I fairly chuckled at the idea; and perhaps he heard me; for he moved on the bed suddenly, as if startled. Now you may think that I drew back—but no. His room was as black as pitch with the thick darkness (for the shutters were close fastened, through fear of robbers), and so I knew that he could not see the opening of the door, and I kept pushing it on steadily, steadily.

I had my head in, and was about to open the lantern, when my thumb slipped upon the tin fastening, and the old man sprang up in the bed, crying out—"Who's there?"

I kept quite still and said nothing. For a whole hour I did not move a muscle, and in the meantime I did not hear him lie down. He was still sitting up in the bed listening;—just as I have done, night after night, hearkening to the death watches in the wall.

Presently I heard a slight groan, and I knew it was the groan of mortal terror. It was not a groan of pain or of grief—oh, no!—it was the low stifled sound that arises from the bottom of the soul when overcharged with awe. I knew the sound well. Many a night, just at midnight, when all the world slept, it has welled up from my own bosom, deepening, with its dreadful echo, the terrors that distracted me. I say I knew it well. I knew what the old man felt, and pitied him, although I chuckled at heart. I knew that he had been lying awake ever since the first slight noise, when he had turned in the bed. His fears had been ever since growing upon him. He had been trying to fancy them causeless, but could not. He had been saying to himself—"It is nothing but the wind in the chimney—it is only a mouse crossing the floor," or "it is merely a cricket which has made a single chirp." Yes, he has been trying to comfort himself with these suppositions; but he had found all in vain. *All in vain;* because Death, in approaching him, had stalked with his black shadow before him, and enveloped the victim. And it was the mournful influence of the unperceived shadow that caused him to feel—although he neither saw nor heard—to *feel* the presence of my head within the room.

When I had waited a long time, very patiently, without hearing him lie down, I resolved to open a little—a very, very little crevice in the lantern. So I opened it—you cannot imagine how stealthily, stealthily—until, at length, a single dim ray, like the thread of the spider, shot from out the crevice and full upon the vulture eye.

It was open—wide, wide open—and I grew furious as I gazed upon it. I saw it with perfect distinctness—all a dull blue, with a hideous veil over it that chilled the very marrow in my bones; but I could see nothing else of the old man's face or person: for I had directed the ray as if by instinct, precisely upon the damned spot.

And now have I not told you that what you mistake for madness is but over-acuteness of the senses?—now, I say, there came to my ears a low, dull, quick sound, such as a watch makes when enveloped in cotton. I knew *that* sound well too. It was the beating of the old man's heart. It increased my fury, as the beating of a drum stimulates the soldier into courage.

But even yet I refrained and kept still. I scarely breathed. I held the lantern motionless. I tried how steadily I could maintain the ray upon the eye. Meantime the hellish tattoo of the heart increased. It grew quicker and quicker, and louder and louder every instant. The old man's terror *must* have been extreme! It grew louder, I say, louder every moment!— do you mark me well? I have told you that I am nervous: so I am. And now at the dead hour of the night, amid the dreadful silence of that old house, so strange a noise as this excited me to uncontrollable terror. Yet, for some minutes longer I refrained and stood still. But the beating grew louder, louder! I thought the heart must burst. And now a new anxiety seized me—the sound would be heard by a neighbor! The old man's hour had come! With a loud yell, I threw open the lantern and leaped into the room. He shrieked once—once only. In an instant I dragged him to the floor, and pulled the heavy bed over him. I then smiled gaily, to find the deed so far done. But, for many minutes, the heart beat on with a muffled sound. This, however, did not vex me; it would not be heard through the wall. At length it ceased. The old man was dead. I removed the bed and examined the corpse. Yes, he was stone, stone dead. I placed my hand upon the heart and held it there many minutes. There was no pulsation. He was stone dead. His eye would trouble me no more.

If still you think me mad, you will think so no longer when I describe the wise precautions I took for the concealment of the body. The night waned, and I worked hastily, but in silence. First of all I dismembered the corpse. I cut off the head and the arms and the legs.

I then took up three planks from the flooring of the chamber, and deposited all between the scantlings. I then replaced the boards so cleverly, so cunningly, that no human eye—not even *his*—could have detected any thing wrong. There was nothing to wash out—no stain of any kind—no blood-spot whatever. I had been too wary for that. A tub had caught all—ha! ha!

When I had made an end of these labors, it was four o'clock—still dark as midnight. As the bell sounded the hour, there came a knocking at the street door. I went down to open it with a light heart,—for what had I *now* to fear? There entered three men, who introduced themselves, with perfect suavity, as officers of the police. A shriek had been heard by a neighbor during the night; suspicion of foul play had been aroused; information had been lodged at the police office, and they (the officers) had been deputed to search the premises.

I smiled,—for *what* had I to fear? I bade the gentlemen welcome. The shriek, I said, was my own in a dream. The old man, I mentioned, was absent in the country. I took my visitors all over the house. I bade them search—search *well*. I led them, at length, to *his* chamber. I showed them his treasures, secure, undisturbed. In the enthusiasm of my confidence, I brought chairs into the room, and desired them *here* to rest from their fatigues, while I myself, in the wild audacity of my perfect triumph, placed my own seat upon the very spot beneath which reposed the corpse of the victim.

The officers were satisfied. My *manner* had convinced them. I was singularly at ease. They sat, and while I answered cheerily, they chatted familiar things. But, ere long, I felt myself getting pale and wished them gone. My head ached, and I fancied a ringing in my ears: but still they sat and still chatted. The ringing became more distinct:—it continued and became more distinct: I talked more freely to get rid of the feeling: but it continued and gained definitiveness—until, at length, I found that the noise was *not* within my ears.

No doubt I now grew *very* pale;—but I talked more fluently, and with a heightened voice. Yet the sound increased—and what could I do? It was *a low, dull, quick sound—much such a sound as a watch makes when enveloped in cotton.* I gasped for breath—and yet the officers heard it not. I talked more quickly—more vehemently; but the noise steadily increased. I arose and argued about trifles, in a high key and with violent gesticulations, but the noise steadily increased. Why *would* they not be gone? I paced the floor to and fro with heavy strides, as if excited to fury by the observation of the men—But the noise steadily increased. Oh God! what *could* I do? I foamed—I raved—I swore! I swung the chair upon which I had been sitting, and grated it upon the boards, but the noise arose over all and continually increased. It grew louder—louder—

louder! And still the men chatted pleasantly, and smiled. Was it possible they heard not? Almighty God!—no, no! They heard!—they suspected!—they *knew!*—they were making a mockery of my horror!—this I thought, and this I think. But any thing was better than this agony! Any thing was more tolerable than this derision! I could bear those hypocritical smiles no longer! I felt that I must scream or die!—and now—again!—hark! louder! louder! louder! *louder!*—

"Villains!" I shrieked, "dissemble no more! I admit the deed!—tear up the planks!—here, here!—it is the beating of his hideous heart!"

Afterword

"If looks could kill" is the familiar expression we use to indicate that someone has looked at someone else with hatred.

Well, why not? It is easy to imagine that someone who has learned how to make use of the power of some malevolent spirit can cast spells and make certain mystic motions that can bring harm to an enemy.

But why not etherealize? Why bother to go through unnecessary words and motions? Why not simply concentrate the wish *to do harm. That would be much better, since not only would it save you time and trouble, but it wouldn't give you away. If someone catches you mumbling or making odd movements, he may, in a fit of fury, kill you before you kill him. If you simply* think *evil at him, you will catch him unaware.*

It is hard to think evil without glaring and frowning, however. In reverse, to wear a look that seems full of anger and hatred betokens evil thoughts toward anyone to whom the look is directed.

Hence people find themselves watching out for harmful looks of hatred, especially in a face that is unpleasant even in repose—as, for instance, when a face is ugly or deformed. In that case, any glance looks unpleasant, and such a person may be said to have an "evil eye."

I remember when I was young my friends and I were always clenching our fists and extending the first and fourth fingers while shouting, "Horns." That was a representation of the devil, I eventually found out, and was used to ward off evil eyes by an opposing devil, so that we could win whatever game we were playing.—I.A.

Additional Reading

Leonid Andreyev, "Lazarus," in *Famous Modern Ghost Stories,* Dorothy Scarborough, ed. (New York: Putnam, 1921).

William Hemmingway, "O'Tunnaigh and the Evil," in *Munsey's Magazine* 94, June 1928.

Richard Sale, "The Medusa of 49th Street," in *Detective Fiction Weekly* 135, Mar. 30, 1940.

George Ethelbert Walsh, "The Glass Eye," in *Black Cat,* June 15, 1910.

Edith Wharton, "The Eyes," in *Ghosts* (New York: Appleton-Century, 1937).

9

Exorcism

Edward Bulwer-Lytton
The House and the Brain

A friend of mine, who is a man of letters and a philosopher, said to me one day, as if between jest and earnest, "Fancy! since we last met, I have discovered a haunted house in the midst of London."

"Really haunted?—and by what? ghosts?"

"Well, I can't answer that question: all I know is that—six weeks ago my wife and I were in search of a furnished apartment. Passing a quiet street, we saw on the window of one of the houses a bill, 'Apartments Furnished.' The situation suited us; we entered the house—liked the rooms—engaged them by the week—and left them the third day. No power on earth could have reconciled my wife to stay longer; and I don't wonder at it."

"What did you see?"

"Excuse me—I have no desire to be ridiculed as a superstitious dreamer—nor, on the other hand, could I ask you to accept on my affirmation what you would hold to be incredible without the evidence of your own senses. Let me only say this, it was not so much what we saw or heard (in which you might fairly suppose that we were the dupes of our own excited fancy, or the victims of imposture in others) that drove us away, as it was an undefinable terror which seized both of us whenever we passed by the door of a certain unfurnished room, in which we neither saw nor heard anything. And the strangest marvel of all was, that for once in my life I agreed with my wife, silly woman though she be—and allowed, after the third night, that it was impossible to stay a fourth in that house.

Accordingly, on the fourth morning I summoned the woman who kept the house and attended on us, and told her that the rooms did not quite suit us, and we would not stay out our week. She said, dryly, 'I know why: you have stayed longer than any other lodger. Few ever stayed a second night; none before you a third. But I take it they have been very kind to you.'

" 'They—who?' I asked, affecting to smile.

" 'Why, they who haunt the house, whoever they are. I don't mind them; I remember them many years ago, when I lived in this house, not as a servant; but I know they will be the death of me some day. I don't care—I'm old, and must die soon anyhow; and then I shall be with them, and in this house still.' The woman spoke with so dreary a calmness, that really it was a sort of awe that prevented my conversing with her further. I paid for my week, and too happy were my wife and I to get off so cheaply."

"You excite my curiosity," said I; "nothing I should like better than to sleep in a haunted house. Pray give me the address of the one which you left so ignominiously."

My friend gave me the address; and when we parted, I walked straight toward the house thus indicated.

It is situated on the north side of Oxford Street (in a dull but respectable thoroughfare). I found the house shut up—no bill at the window, and no response to my knock. As I was turning away, a beer-boy, collecting pewter pots at the neighboring areas, said to me, "Do you want anyone at that house, sir?"

"Yes, I heard it was to be let."

"Let!—why, the woman who kept it is dead—had been dead these three weeks, and no one can be found to stay there, though Mr. J—— offered ever so much. He offered Mother, who chars for him, £1 a week just to open and shut the windows, and she would not."

"Would not! and why?"

"The house is haunted: and the old woman who kept it was found dead in her bed, with her eyes wide open. They say the devil strangled her."

"Pooh!—you speak of Mr. J——. Is he the owner of the house?"

"Yes."

"Where does he live?"

"In G—— Street. No. —."

"What is he—in any business?"

"No, sir—nothing particular; a single gentleman."

I gave the pot-boy the gratuity earned by his liberal information, and proceeded to Mr. J——, in G—— Street, which was close by the street that boasted the haunted house. I was lucky enough to find Mr. J—— at home, an elderly man, with intelligent countenance and prepossessing manners.

I communicated my name and my business frankly. I said I heard the house was considered to be haunted—that I had a strong desire to examine a house with so equivocal a reputation—that I should be greatly obliged if he would allow me to hire it, though only for a night. I was willing to pay for that privilege whether he might be inclined to ask. "Sir," said Mr. J——, with great courtesy, "the house is at your service, for as short or as long a time as you please. Rent is out of the question—the obligation will be on my side would you be able to discover the cause of the strange phenomena which at present deprives it of all value. I cannot let it, for I cannot even get a servant to keep it in order to answer the door. Unluckily the house is haunted, if I may use that expression, not only by night, but by day; though at night the disturbances are of a more unpleasant and sometimes of a more alarming character. The poor old woman who died in it three weeks ago was a pauper whom I took out of a workhouse, for in her childhood she had been known to some of my family, and had once been in such good circumstances that she had rented that house of my uncle. She was a woman of superior education and strong mind, and was the only person I could ever induce to remain in the house. Indeed, since her death, which was sudden, and the coroner's inquest, which gave it a notoriety in the neighborhood, I have so despaired of finding any person to take charge of the house, much more a tenant, that I would willingly let it rent-free for a year to any one who would pay its rates and taxes."

"How long is it since the house acquired this sinister character?"

"That I can scarcely tell you, but very many years since. The old woman I spoke of said it was haunted when she rented it between thirty and forty years ago. The fact is, that my life has been spent in the East Indies, and in the civil service of the Company. I returned to England last year, on inheriting the fortune of an uncle, among whose possessions was the house in question. I found it shut up and uninhabited. I was told that it was haunted, that no one would inhabit it. I smiled at what seemed to me so idle a story. I spent some money in repairing it—added to its old-fashioned furniture a few modern articles—advertised it, and obtained a lodger for a year. He was a colonel retired on half-pay. He came in with his family, a son and a daughter, and four or five servants: they all left the house the next day; and, although each of them declared that he had seen something different from that which had scared the others, a something still was equally terrible to all. I really could not in conscience sue, nor even blame, the colonel for breach of agreement. Then I put in the old woman I have spoken of, and she was empowered to let the house in apartments. I never had one lodger who stayed more than three days. I do not tell you their stories—to no two lodgers have there been exactly the same phenomena repeated. It is better that you should judge for yourself, than enter the house with an imagination influenced by previous narratives; only be prepared to see and to hear something or other, and take whatever precautions you yourself please."

"Have you never had a curiosity yourself to pass a night in that house?"

"Yes. I passed not a night, but three hours in broad daylight alone in that house. My curiosity is not satisfied but it is quenched. I have no desire to renew the experiment. You cannot complain, you see, sir, that I am not sufficiently candid; and unless your interest be exceedingly eager and your nerves unusually strong, I honestly add, that I advise you not to pass a night in the house."

"My interest *is* exceedingly keen," said I, "and though only a coward will boast of his nerves in situations wholly unfamiliar to him, yet my nerves have been seasoned in such a variety of danger that I have the right to rely on them—even in a haunted house."

Mr. J—— said very little more; he took the keys of the house out of his bureau, gave them to me—and, thanking him cordially for his frankness, and his urbane concession to my wish, I carried off my prize.

Impatient for the experiment, as soon as I reached home, I summoned my confidential servant—a young man of gay spirits, fearless temper, and as free from superstitious prejudices as any one could think of.

"F——," said I, "you remember in Germany how disappointed we were at not finding a ghost in that old castle, which was said to be haunted by a headless apparition? Well, I have heard of a house in London which, I have reason to hope, is decidedly haunted. I mean to sleep there to-night. From what I hear, there is no doubt that something will allow itself to be seen or to be heard—something, perhaps, excessively horrible. Do you think if I take you with me, I may rely on your presence of mind, whatever my happen?"

"Oh, sir! pray trust me," answered F——, grinning with delight.

"Very well; then here are the keys of the house—this is the address. Go now—select for me any bedroom you please; and since the house has not been inhabited for weeks, make up a good fire—air the bed well— see, of course, that there are candles as well as fuel. Take with you my revolver and my dagger—so much for my weapons—arm yourself equally well; and if we are not a match for a dozen ghosts, we shall be but a sorry couple of Englishmen."

I was engaged for the rest of the day on business so urgent that I had not leisure to think much on the nocturnal adventure to which I had plighted my honor. I dined alone, and very late, and while dining, read, as is my habit. I selected one of the volumes of Macaulay's *Essays*. I thought to myself that I would take the book with me; there was so much of the healthfulness in the style, and practical life in the subjects, that it would serve as an antidote against the influence of superstitious fancy.

Accordingly, about half-past nine, I put the book into my pocket, and strolled leisurely toward the haunted house. I took with me a favorite dog—an exceedingly sharp, bold and vigilant bull-terrier—a dog fond of prowling about strange ghostly corners and passages at night in search of rats—a dog of dogs for a ghost.

It was a summer night, but chilly, the sky somewhat gloomy and overcast. Still there was a moon—faint and sickly, but still a moon—and if the clouds permitted, after midnight it would be brighter.

I reached the house, knocked, and my servant opened with a cheerful smile.

"All right, sir, and very comfortable."

"Oh!" said I, rather disappointed; "have you not seen nor heard anything remarkable?"

"Well, sir, I must own I have heard something queer."

"What—what?"

"The sound of feet pattering behind me; and once or twice small noises like whispers close at my ear—nothing more."

"You are not at all frightened?"

"I! not a bit of it, sir," and the man's bold look reassured me on one point—viz., that happen what might, he would not desert me.

We were in the hall, the street-door closed, and my attention was now drawn to my dog. He had at first run in eagerly enough, but had sneaked back to the door, and was scratching and whining to get out. After patting him on the head, and encouraging him gently, the dog seemed to reconcile himself to the situation, and followed me and F—— through the house, but keeping close at my heels instead of hurrying inquisitively in advance, which was his usual and normal habit in all strange places. We first visited the subterranean apartments, the kitchen and other offices, and especially the cellars, in which last there were two or three bottles of wine still left in a bin, covered with cobwebs, and evidently, by their appearance, undisturbed for many years. It was clear that the ghosts were not wine-bibers. For the rest we discovered nothing of interest. There was a gloomy little backyard with very high walls. The stones of this yard were very damp; and what with the damp, and what with the dust and smoke-grime on the pavement, our feet left a slight impression where we passed.

And now appeared the first strange phenomenon witnessed by myself in this strange abode. I saw, just before me, the print of a foot suddenly form itself, as it were. I stopped, caught hold of my servant, and pointed to it. In advance of that footprint as suddenly dropped another. We both saw it. I advanced quickly to the place; the footprint kept advancing before me, a small footprint—the foot of a child; the impression was too faint thoroughly to distinguish the shape, but it seemed to us both that it was the print of a naked foot. This phenomenon ceased when we arrived at the opposite wall, nor did it repeat itself on returning. We remounted the stairs, and entered the rooms on the ground floor, a dining-parlor, a small back parlor, and a still smaller third room that had been probably appropriated to a footman—all still as death. We then visited the drawing-rooms, which seemed fresh and new. In the front room I seated myself in an armchair. F—— placed on the table the candlestick with which he had lighted us. I told him to shut the door. As he turned to do so, a chair opposite to me moved from the wall quickly and noiselessly, and dropped itself about a yard from my own chair, immediately fronting it.

"Why, this is better than the turning tables," said I, with a half-laugh; and as I laughed, my dog put back his head and howled.

F——, coming back, had not observed the movement of the chair. He employed himself now in stilling the dog. I continued to gaze on the chair, and fancied I saw on it a pale blue misty outline of a human figure, but an outline so indistinct that I could only distrust my own vision. The dog now was quiet.

"Put back that chair opposite me," said I to F——; "put it back to the wall."

F—— obeyed. "Was that you, sir?" said he, turning abruptly.

"I!—what?"

"Why, something struck me. I felt it sharply on the shoulder—just here."

"No," said I. "But we have jugglers present, and though we may not discover their tricks, we shall catch *them* before they frighten *us.*"

We did not stay long in the drawing-rooms—in fact, they felt so damp and so chilly that I was glad to get to the fire upstairs. We locked the doors of the drawing-rooms—a precaution which, I should observe, we had taken with all the rooms we had searched below. The bedroom my servant had selected for me was the best on the floor—a large one, with two windows fronting the street. The four-posted bed, which took up no inconsiderable space, was opposite to the fire, which burnt clear and bright; a door in the wall to the left, between the bed and the window, communicated with the room which my servant appropriated to himself. This last was a small room with a sofa-bed, and had no communication with the landing-place—no other door but that which conducted to the bedroom I was to occupy. On either side of my fireplace was a cupboard, without locks, flush with the wall and covered with the same dull-brown paper. We examined these cupboards—only hooks to suspend female dresses—nothing else; we sounded the walls—evidently solid—the outer walls of the building. Having finished the survey of these apartments, I warmed myself a few moments, and lighted my cigar, I then, still accompanied by F——, went forth to complete my reconnoiter. In the landing-place there was another door; it was closed firmly. "Sir," said my servant, in surprise, "I unlocked this door with all the others when I first came; it cannot have got locked from the inside, for—"

Before he had finished his sentence, the door, which neither of us then was touching, opened quietly of itself. We looked at each other a single instant. The same thought seized both—some human agency might be detected here. I rushed in first, my servant followed. A small blank dreary room without furniture—few empty boxes and hampers in a corner—a small window—the shutters closed—not even a fireplace—no other door than that by which we had entered—no carpet on the floor, and the floor seemed very old, uneven, worm-eaten, mended here and there, as was shown by the whiter patches on the wood; but no living being, and no visible place in which a living being could have hidden. As we stood gazing round, the door by which we had entered closed as quietly as it had before opened: we were imprisoned.

For the first time I felt a creep of undefinable horror. Not so my servant. "Why, they don't think to trap us, sir; I could break the trumpery door with a kick of my foot."

"Try first if it will open to your hand," said I, shaking off the vague apprehension that had seized me, "while I unclose the shutters and see what is without."

I unbarred the shutters—the window looked on the little backyard I have before described; there was no ledge without—nothing to break the sheer descent of the wall. No man getting out of that window would have found any footing till he had fallen on the stones below.

F——, meanwhile, was vainly attempting to open the door. He now turned round to me and asked my permission to use force. And I should here state, in justice to the servant, that, far from evincing any superstitious terrors, his nerve, composure, and even gaiety amidst circumstances so extraordinary, compelled my admiration, and made me congratulate myself on having secured a companion in every way fitted to the occasion. I willingly gave him the permission he required. But though he was a remarkably strong man, his force was as idle as his milder efforts; the door did not even shake to his stoutest kick. Breathless and panting, he desisted. I then tried the door myself, equally in vain. As I ceased from the effort, again that creep of horror came over me; but this time it was more cold and stubborn. I felt as if some strange and ghastly exhalation were rising up from the chinks of that rugged floor, and filling the atmosphere with a venomous influence hostile to human life. The door now very slowly and quietly opened as of its own accord. We precipitated ourselves into the landing-place. We both saw a large pale light—as large as the human figure but shapeless and unsubstantial—move before us, and ascend the stairs that led from the landing into the attics. I followed the light, and my servant followed me. It entered, to the right of the landing, a small garret, of which the door stood open. I entered in the same instant. The light then collapsed into a small globule, exceeding brilliant and vivid; rested a moment on a bed in the corner, quivered, and vanished.

We approached the bed and examined it—a half-tester, such as is commonly found in attics devoted to servants. On the drawers that stood near it we perceived an old faded silk kerchief, with the needle still left in a rent half repaired. The kerchief was covered with dust; probably it had belonged to the old woman who had last died in that house, and this might have been her sleeping room. I had sufficient curiosity to open the drawers: there were a few odds and ends of female dress, and two letters tied round with a narrow ribbon of faded yellow. I took the liberty to possess myself of the letters. We found nothing else in the room worth noticing—nor did the light reappear; but we distinctly heard, as we turned to go, a pattering footfall on the floor—just before us. We went through the other attics (in all four), the footfall still preceding us. Nothing to be seen—nothing but the footfall heard. I had the letters in my hand: just as I was descending the stairs I distinctly felt my wrist seized, and a faint soft effort made to draw the letters from my clasp. I only held them the more tightly, and the effort ceased.

We regained the bedchamber appropriated to myself, and I then remarked that my dog had not followed us when we had left it. He was thrusting himself close to the fire, and trembling. I was impatient to examine the letters; and while I read them, my servant opened a little box in which he had deposited the weapons I had ordered him to bring; took them out, placed them on a table close at my bed-head, and then occupied himself in soothing the dog, who, however, seemed to heed him very little.

The letters were short—they were dated; the dates exactly thirty-five years ago. They were evidently from a lover to his mistress, or a husband to some young wife. Not only the terms of expression, but a distinct reference to a former voyage, indicated the writer to have been a seafarer. The spelling and handwriting were those of a man imperfectly educated, but still the language itself was forcible. In the expressions of endearment there was a kind of rough wild love; but here and there were dark and unintelligible hints at some secret not of love—some secret that seemed of crime. "We ought to love each other," was one of the sentences I remember, "for how every one else would execrate us if all was known." Again: "Don't let any one be in the same room with you at night—you talk in your sleep." And again: "What's done can't be undone; and I tell you there's nothing against us unless the dead could come to life." Here there was underlined in a better handwriting (a female's), "They do!" At the end of the letter latest in date the same female hand had written these words: "Lost at sea the 4th of June, the same day as————."

I put down the letters, and began to muse over their contents.

Fearing, however, that the train of thought into which I fell might unsteady my nerves, I fully determined to keep my mind in a fit state to cope with whatever of the marvelous the advancing night might bring forth. I roused myself—laid the letters on the table—stirred up the fire, which was still bright and cheering—and opened my volume of Macaulay. I read quickly enough till about half-past eleven. I then threw myself dressed upon the bed, and told my servant he might retire to his own room, but must keep himself awake. I bade him leave open the door between the two rooms. Thus alone, I kept two candles burning on the table by my bed-head. I placed my watch beside the weapons, and calmly resumed my Macaulay. Opposite to me the fire burned clear; and on the hearthrug, seemingly asleep, lay the dog. In about twenty minutes I felt an exceedingly cold air pass by my cheek, like a sudden draught. I fancied the door to my right, communicating with the landing-place, must have got open; but no—it was closed. I then turned my glance to my left, and saw the flame of the candles violently swayed as by a wind. At the same moment the watch beside by revolver softly slid from the table—softly, softly—no visible hand—it was gone. I sprang up, seizing the revolver with the one hand, the dagger with the other: I was not willing that my weapons should share the fate of the watch. Thus armed, I looked round the floor—no sign of the watch. Three slow, loud, distinct knocks were now heard at the bed-head; my servant called out, "Is that you, sir?"

"No; be on your guard."

The dog now roused himself and sat on his haunches, his ears moving quickly backward and forward. He kept his eyes fixed on me with a look so strange that he concentered all my attention on himself. Slowly he rose up, all his hair bristling, and stood perfectly rigid, and with the same wild stare. I had no time, however, to examine the dog. Presently my servant emerged from his room; and if ever I saw horror in the human face, it was then. I should not have recognized him had we met in the street, so altered was every lineament. He passed by me quickly, saying in a whisper that seemed scarcely to come from his lips, "Run—run! It is after me!" He gained the door to the landing, pulled it open, and rushed forth. I followed him into the landing involuntarily, calling him to stop; but, without heeding me, he bounded down the stairs, clinging to the balusters, and taking several steps at a time. I heard, where I stood, the street-door open—heard it again clap to. I was left alone in the haunted house.

It was but for a moment that I remained undecided whether or not to follow my servant; pride and curiosity alike forbade so dastardly a flight. I re-entered my room, closing the door after me, and proceeded cautiously into the interior chamber. I encountered nothing to justify my servant's terror. I again carefully examined the walls, to see if there were any concealed door. I could find no trace of one—not even a seam in the dull-brown paper with which the room was hung. How, then, had the THING, whatever it was, which had so scared him, obtained ingress except through my own chamber?

I returned to my room, shut and locked the door that opened upon the interior one, and stood on the hearth, expectant and prepared. I now perceived that the dog had slunk into an angle of the wall, and was pressing himself close against it, as if literally striving to force his way into it. I approached the animal and spoke to it; the poor brute was evidently beside itself with terror. It showed all its teeth, the slaver dropping from its jaws, and would certainly have bitten me if I had touched it. It did not seem to recognize me. Whoever has seen at the Zoological Gardens a rabbit fascinated by a serpent, cowering in a corner, may form some idea of the anguish which the dog exhibited. Finding all efforts to soothe the animal in vain, and fearing that his bite might be as venomous in that state as in the madness of hydrophobia, I left him alone, placed my weapons on the table beside the fire, seated myself, and recommenced my Macaulay.

Perhaps, in order not to appear seeking credit for a courage, or rather a coolness, which the reader may conceive I exaggerate, I may be pardoned if I pause to indulge in one or two egotistical remarks.

As I hold presence of mind, or what is called courage, to be precisely proportioned to familiarity with the circumstances that lead to it, so I should say that I had been long sufficiently familiar with all experiments that appertain to the Marvelous. I had witnessed many very extraordinary phenomena in various parts of the world—phenomena that would be either totally disbelieved if I stated them, or ascribed to supernatural agencies. Now, my theory is that the Supernatural is the Impossible, and that what is called supernatural is only a something in the laws of nature of which we have been hitherto ignorant. Therefore, if a ghost rise before me, I have not the right to say, "So, then, the supernatural is possible," but rather, "So, then, the apparition of a ghost is, contrary to received opinion, within the laws of nature—*i.e.,* not supernatural."

Now, in all that I had hitherto witnessed, and indeed in all the wonders which the amateurs of mystery in our age record as facts, a material living agency is always required. On the continent you will find still magicians who assert that they can raise spirits. Assume for the moment that they assert truly, still the living material form of the magician is present; and he is the material agency by which, from some constitutional peculiarities, certain strange phenomena are represented to your natural senses.

Accept, again, as truthful, the tales of spirit Manifestation in America— musical or other sounds—writings on paper, produced by no discernible hand—articles of furniture moved without apparent human agency—or the actual sight and touch of hands, to which no bodies seem to belong— still there must be found the MEDIUM or living being, with constitutional peculiarities capable of obtaining these signs. In fine, in all such marvels, supposing even that there is no imposture, there must be a human being like ourselves by whom, or through whom, the effects presented to human beings are produced. It is so with the now familiar phenomena of mesmerism or electro-biology; the mind of the person operated on is affected through a material living agent. Nor, supposing it true that a mesmerized patient can respond to the will or passes of a mesmerizer a hundred miles distant, is the response less occasioned by a material fluid—call it Electric, call it Odic, call it what you will—which has the power of traversing space and passing obstacles, that the material effect is communicated from one to the other. Hence all that I had hitherto witnessed, or expected to witness, in this strange house, I believed to be occasioned through some agency or medium as mortal as myself: and this idea necessarily prevented the awe with which those who regard as supernatural things that are not within the ordinary operations of nature might have been impressed by the adventures of that memorable night.

As, then, it was my conjecture that all that was presented, or would be presented to my senses, must originate in some human being gifted by constitution with the power so to present them, and having some motive so to do, I felt an interest in my theory which, in its way, was rather philosophical than superstitious. And I can sincerely say that I was in as tranquil a temper for observation as any practical experimentalist could be awaiting the effect of some rare, though perhaps perilous, chemical combination. Of course, the more I kept my mind detached from fancy, the more the temper fitted for observation would be obtained; and I therefore riveted eye and thought on the strong daylight sense in the page of my Macaulay.

I now became aware that something interposed between the page and the light—the page was over-shadowed: I looked up, and I saw what I shall find it very difficult, perhaps impossible, to describe.

It was a Darkness shaping itself forth from the air in very undefined outline. I cannot say it was of a human form, and yet it had more resemblance to a human form, or rather shadow, than to anything else. As it stood, wholly apart and distinct from the air and the light around it, its dimensions seemed gigantic, the summit nearly touching the ceiling. When I gazed, a feeling of intense cold seized me. An iceberg before me could not more have chilled me; nor could the cold of an iceberg have been more purely physical. I feel convinced that it was not the cold caused by fear. As I continued to gaze, I thought—but this I cannot say with precision—that I distinguished two eyes looking down on me from the height. One moment I fancied that I distinguished them clearly, the next they seemed gone; but still two rays of a pale-blue light frequently shot through the darkness, as from the height on which I half believed, half doubted, that I had encountered the eyes.

I strove to speak—my voice utterly failed me; I could only think to myself, "Is this fear? it is *not* fear!" I strove to rise—in vain; I felt as if weighed down by an irresistible force. Indeed, my impression was that of an immense and overwhelming power opposed to any volition—that sense of utter inadequacy to cope with a force beyond man's, which one may feel *physically* in a storm at sea, in a conflagration, or when confronting some terrible wild beast, or rather, perhaps, the shark of the ocean. I felt *morally* opposed to my will was another will, as far superior to its strength as storm, fire, and shark are superior in material force to the force of man.

And now, as this impression grew on me—now came, at last, horror—horror to a degree that no words can convey. Still I retained pride, if not courage; and in my own mind I said, "This is horror, but it is not fear; unless I fear I cannot be harmed; my reason rejects this thing, it is an illusion—I do not fear." With a violent effort I succeeded at last in stretching out my hand toward the weapon on the table; as I did so, on the arm and shoulder I received a strange shock, and my arm fell to my side powerless. And now, to add to my horror, the light began slowly to wane from the candles; they were not, as it were, extinguished, but their flame seemed very gradually withdrawn; it was the same with the fire—the light was extracted from the fuel; in a few minutes the room was in utter darkness.

The dread that came over me, to be thus in the dark with that dark Thing, whose power was so intensely felt, brought a reaction of nerve. In fact, terror had reached that climax, that either my senses must have deserted me, or I must have burst through the spell. I did burst through it. I found voice, though the voice was a shriek. I remember that I broke forth with words like these—"I do not fear, my soul does not fear"; and at the same time I found the strength to rise. Still in that profound gloom I rushed to one of the windows—tore aside the curtain—flung open the shutters; my first thought was—LIGHT. And when I saw the moon high, clear, and calm, I felt a joy that almost compensated for the previous terror. There was the moon, there was also the light from the gas-lamps in the deserted slumberous street. I turned to look back into the room; the moon penetrated its shadow very palely and partially—but still there was light. The dark Thing, whatever it might be, was gone—except that I could yet see a dim shadow, which seemed the shadow of that shade, against the opposite wall.

My eye now rested on the table, and from under the table (which was without cloth or cover—an old mahogany round table) there rose a hand, visible as far as the wrist. It was a hand, seemingly, as much of flesh and blood as my own, but the hand of an aged person—lean, wrinkled, small, too—a woman's hand. That hand very softly closed on the two letters that lay on the table: hand and letters both vanished. There then came the same loud measured knocks I heard at the bed-head before this extraordinary drama had commenced.

As those sounds slowly ceased, I felt the whole room vibrate sensibly; and at the far end there rose, as from the floor, sparks or globules like bubbles of light, many-colored—green, yellow, fire-red, azure. Up and down, to and fro, hither, thither, as tiny Will-o'-the-Wisps the sparks moved slow or swift, each at his own caprice. A chair (as in the drawing-room below) was now advanced from the wall without apparent agency, and placed at the opposite side of the table. Suddenly as forth from the chair, there grew a shape—a woman's shape. It was distinct as a shape of life—ghastly as a shape of death. The face was that of youth, with a strange mournful beauty: the throat and shoulders were bare, the rest of the form in a loose robe of cloudy white. It began sleeking its long yellow hair, which fell over its shoulders; its eyes were not turned toward me, but to the door; it seemed listening, watching, waiting. The shadow of the shade in the background grew darker; and again I thought I beheld the eyes gleaming out from the summit of the shadow—eyes fixed upon that shape.

As if from the door, though it did not open, there grew out another shape, equally distinct, equally ghastly—a man's shape—a young man's. It was in the dress of the last century, or rather in a likeness of such dress (for both the male shape and the female, though defined, were evidently unsubstantial, impalpable—simulacra—phantasms); and there was something incongruous, grotesque, yet fearful, in the contrast between the elaborate finery, the courtly precision of that old-fashioned garb, with its ruffles and lace and buckles, and the corpse-like aspect and ghost-like stillness of the flitting wearer. Just as the male shape approached the female, the dark shadow started from the wall, all three for a moment wrapped in darkness. When the pale light returned, the two phantoms were as in the grasp of the shadow that towered between them; and there was a bloodstain on the breast of the female; and the phantom male was leaning on its phantom sword, and blood seemed trickling fast from the ruffles, from the lace; and the darkness of the intermediate Shadow swallowed them up—they were gone. And again the bubbles of light shot, and sailed, and undulated, growing thicker and thicker and more wildly confused in their movements.

The closet door to the right of the fireplace now opened, and from the aperture there came the form of an aged woman. In her hand she held letters—the very letters over which I had seen *the* Hand close; and behind her I heard a footstep. She turned round as if to listen, and then she opened the letters and seemed to read; and over her shoulder I saw a livid face, the face as of a man long drowned—bloated, bleached, seaweed tangled in its dripping hair; and at her feet lay a form as of a corpse, and beside the corpse there cowered a child, a miserable squalid child, with famine in its cheeks and fear in its eyes. And as I looked in the old woman's face, the wrinkles and lines vanished and it became a face of youth—hard-eyed, stony, but still youth; and the Shadow darted forth, and darkened over these phantoms as it had darkened over the last.

Nothing now was left but the Shadow, and on that my eyes were intently fixed, till again eyes grew out of the Shadow—malignant, serpent eyes. And the bubbles of light again rose and fell, and in their disorder, an irregular, turbulent maze, mingled with the wan moonlight. And now from these globules themselves, as from the shell of an egg, monstrous things burst out; the air grew filled with them, larvae so bloodless and so hideous that I can in no way describe them except to remind the reader of the swarming life which the solar microscope brings before his eyes in a drop of water—things transparent, supple, agile, chasing each other, devouring each other—forms like nought ever beheld by the naked eye. As the shapes were without symmetry, so their movements were without order. In their very vagrancies there was no sport; they came round me and round, thicker and faster and swifter, swarming over my head, crawling over my right arm, which was outstretched in involuntary command against all evil beings. Sometimes I felt myself touched, but not by them; invisible hands touched me. Once I felt the clutch as of cold soft fingers at my throat. I was still equally conscious that if I gave way to fear I should be in bodily peril; and I concentrated all my faculties in the single focus of resisting, stubborn will. And I turned my sight from the Shadow— above all, from those strange serpent eyes—eyes that had now become distinctly visible. For there, though in nought else round me, I was aware that there was a WILL, and a will of intense, creative, working evil, which might crush down my own.

The pale atmosphere in the room began now to redden as if in the air of some near conflagration. The larvae grew lurid as things that live in fire. Again the room vibrated; again were heard the three measured knocks; and again all things were swallowed up in the darkness of the dark Shadow, as if out of that darkness all had come, into the darkness all returned.

As the gloom receded, the Shadow was wholly gone. Slowly as it had been withdrawn, the flame grew again into the candles on the table, again into the fuel in the grate. The whole room came once more calmly, healthfully into sight.

The two doors were still closed, the door communicating with the servant's room was still locked. In the corner of the wall into which he had so convulsively niched himself, lay the dog. I called to him—no movement; I approached—the animal was dead; his eyes protruded; his tongue out of his mouth; the froth gathered round his jaws. I took him in my arms; I brought him to the fire. I felt acute grief for the loss of my poor favorite—acute self-reproach; I accused myself of his death; I imagined he had died of fright. But what was my surprise on finding that his neck was actually broken. Had this been done in the dark?—must it not have been by a hand human as mine?—must there not have been a human agency all the while in that room? Good cause to suspect it. I cannot tell. I cannot do more than state the fact fairly; the reader may draw his own inference.

Another surprising circumstance—my watch was restored to the table from which it had been so mysteriously withdrawn; but it had stopped at the very moment it was so withdrawn; nor, despite all the skill of the watchmaker, has it ever gone since—that is, it will go in a strange erratic way for a few hours, and then come to a dead stop—it is worthless.

Nothing more chanced for the rest of the night. Nor, indeed, had I long to wait before the dawn broke. Nor till it was broad daylight did I quit the haunted house. Before I did so, I revisited the little blind room in which my servant and myself had been for a time imprisoned. I had a strong impression—for which I could not account—that from that room had originated the mechanism of the phenomena—if I may use the term— which had been experienced in my chamber. And though I entered it now in the clear day, with the sun peering through the filmy window, I still felt, as I stood on its floor, the creep of the horror which I had first there experienced the night before, and which had been so aggravated by what had passed in my own chamber. I could not indeed bear to stay more than half a minute within those walls. I descended the stairs, and again I heard the footfall before me; and when I opened the street door, I thought I could distinguish a very low laugh. I gained my own home, expecting to find my runaway servant there. But he had not presented himself; nor did I hear more of him for three days, when I received a letter from him, dated from Liverpool to this effect:

"HONORED SIR—I humbly entreat your pardon, though I can scarcely hope that you will think I deserve it, unless—which Heaven forbid—you saw what I did. I feel that it will be years before I can recover myself: and as to being fit for service, it is out of the question. I am therefore going to my brother-in-law at Melbourne. The ship sails tomorrow. Perhaps the long voyage may set me up. I do nothing now but start and tremble, and fancy IT is behind me. I humbly beg you, honored sir, to order my clothes, and whatever wages are due to me, to be sent to my mother's, at Walworth. John knows her address."

The letter ended with additional apologies, somewhat incoherent, and explanatory details as to effects that had been under the writer's charge.

This flight may perhaps warrant a suspicion that the man wished to go to Australia, and had been somehow or other fraudulently mixed up with the events of the night. I say nothing in refutation of that conjecture; rather, I suggest it is as one that would seem to many persons that most probable solution of improbable occurrences. My belief in my own theory remained unshaken. I returned in the evening to the house, to bring away in a hack cab the things I had left there, with my poor dog's body. In this task I was not disturbed, nor did any incident worth note befall me, except that still, on ascending and descending the stairs, I heard the same footfall in advance. On leaving the house, I went to Mr. J——'s. He was at home. I returned him the keys, told him that my curiosity was sufficiently gratified, and was about to relate quickly what had passed, when he stopped me, and said, though with much politeness, that he had no longer any interest in a mystery which none had ever solved.

I determined at least to tell him of the two letters I had read, as well as of the extraordinary manner in which they had disappeared, and I then inquired if he thought they had been addressed to the woman who had died in the house, and if there were anything in her early history which could possibly confirm the dark suspicions to which the letters gave rise. Mr. J—— seemed startled, and, after musing a few moments, answered, "I am but little acquainted with the woman's earlier history, except, as I before told you, that her family were known to mine. But you revive some vague reminiscences to her prejudice. I will make inquiries, and inform you of their result. Still, even if we could admit the popular superstition that a person who had been either the perpetrator or the victim of dark crimes in life could revisit, as a restless spirit, the scene in which those crimes had been commited, I should observe that the house was infested by strange sights and sounds before the old woman died—you smile—what would you say?"

"I would say this, that I am convinced, if we could get to the bottom of these mysteries, we should find a living human agency."

"What! you believe it is all an imposture? for what object?"

"Not an imposture in the ordinary sense of the word. If suddenly I were to sink into a deep sleep, from which you could not awake me, but in that sleep could answer questions with an accuracy which I could not pretend to when awake—tell you what money you had in your pocket—nay, describe your very thoughts—it is not necessarily an imposture, any more than it is necessarily supernatural. I should be, unconsciously to myself, under a mesmeric influence, conveyed to me from a distance by a human being who had acquired power over me by previous *rapport*."

"But if a mesmerizer could so affect another living being, can you suppose that a mesmerizer could also affect inanimate objects: move chairs—open and shut doors?"

"Or impress our senses with the belief in such effects—we never having been *en rapport* with the person acting on us? No. What is commonly called mesmerism could not do this: but there may be a power akin to mesmerism, and superior to it—the power that in the old days was called Magic. That such a power may extend to all inanimate objects of matter I do not say; but if so, it would not be against nature—it would be only a rare power in nature which might be given to constitutions with certain peculiarities, and cultivated by practice to an extraordinary degree. That such a power might extend over the dead—that is, over certain thoughts and memories that the dead may still retain—and compel, not that which ought properly to be called the SOUL, and which is far beyond human reach, but rather a phantom of what has been most earth-stained on earth, to make itself apparent to our senses—is a very ancient though obsolete theory, upon which I will hazard no opinion. But I do not conceive the power would be supernatural. Let me illustrate what I mean from an experiment which Paracelsus describes as not difficult, and which the author of the *Curiosities of Literature* cites as credible: a flower perishes; you burn it. Whatever were the elements of that flower while it lived are gone, dispersed, you know not wither; you can never discover nor recollect them. But you can, by chemistry, out of the burnt dust of that flower, raise a spectrum of the flower, just as it seemed in life. It may be the same with the human being. The soul has as much escaped you as the essence or elements of the flower. Still you may make a spectrum of it.

"And this phantom, though in the popular superstition it is held to be the soul of the departed, must not be confounded with the true soul; it is but eidolon of the dead form. Hence, like the best attested stories of ghosts or spirits, the thing that most strikes us is the absence of what we hold to be soul; that is, of superior emancipated intelligence. These apparitions come for little or no object—they seldom speak when they do come; if they speak, they utter no ideas above those of an ordinary person on earth. American spirit-seers have published volumes of com- munications in prose and verse, which they assert to be given in the names of the most illustrious dead—Shakespeare, Bacon—heaven knows whom. Those communications, taking the best, are certainly not a whit of higher order than would be communications from living persons of fair talent and education; they are wondrously inferior to what Bacon, Shakespeare, and Plato said and wrote when on earth. Nor, what is more noticeable, do they ever contain an idea that was not on the earth before. Wonderful, therefore, as such phenomena may be (granting them to be truthful), I see much that philosophy may question, nothing that it is incumbent on philosophy to deny, viz., nothing supernatural. They are but ideas conveyed somehow or other (we have not yet discovered the means) from one mortal brain to another. Whether, in so doing, tables walk of their own accord, or fiend-like shapes appear in a magic circle, or bodyless hands rise and remove material objects, or a Thing of Darkness, such as presented itself to me, freeze our blood—still am I persuaded that these are but agencies conveyed, as if by electric wires, to my own brain from the brain of another. In some constitutions there is a natural chemistry, and these constitutions may produce chemic wonders—in others a natural fluid, call it electricity, and these may produce electric wonders.

"But the wonders differ from Normal Science in this—they are alike objectless, purposeless, puerile, frivolous. They lead on to no grand results; and therefore the world does not heed, and true sages have not cultivated them. But sure I am, that of all I saw or heard, a man, human as myself, was the remote originator; and was, I believe, unconscious himself as to the exact effects produced, for this reason: no two persons, you say, have ever told you that they experienced exactly the same thing. Well, observe, no two persons ever experience exactly the same dream. If this were an ordinary imposture, the machinery would be arranged for results that would but little vary; if it were a supernatural agency permitted by the Almighty, it would surely be for some definite end. These phenomena belong to neither class; my persuasion is, that they originate in some brain now far distant; and that that brain had no distinct volition in anything that occurred; that what does occur reflects but its devious, motley, ever-shifting, half-formed thoughts; in short, that it has been but the dreams of such a brain put into action and invested with a semi-substance. That this brain is of immense power, that it can set matter into movement, that it is malignant and destructive, I believe; some material force must have killed my dog; the same force might, for aught I know, have sufficed to kill myself, had I been as subjugated by terror as the dog—had my intellect or my spirit given me no countervailing resistance in my will."

"It killed your dog! That is fearful! Indeed it is strange that no animal can be induced to stay in that house; not even a cat. Rats and mice are never found in it."

"The instincts of the brute create influences deadly to their existence. Man's reason has a sense less subtle, because it has a resisting power more supreme. But enough; do you comprehend my theory?"

"Yes, though imperfectly—and I accept any crochet (pardon the word), however odd, rather than embrace at once the notion of ghosts and hobgoblins we imbibed in our nurseries. Still, to my unfortunate house the evil is the same. What on earth can I do with the house?"

"I will tell you what I would do. I am convinced from my own internal feelings that the small unfurnished room at right angles to the door of the bedroom which I occupied, forms a starting point or receptacle for the influences which haunt the house; and I strongly advise you to have the walls opened, the floor removed—nay, the whole room pulled down. I observe that it is detached from the body of the house, built over the small backyard, and could be removed without injury to the rest of the building."

"And you think, if I did that—"

"You would cut off the telegraph wires. Try it. I am so persuaded that I am right, that I will pay half the expense if you will allow me to direct the operations.

"Nay, I am well able to afford the cost; for the rest, allow me to write to you."

About ten days afterward I received a letter from Mr. J——, telling me that he had visited the house since I had seen him; that he had found the two letters I had described replaced in the drawer from which I had taken them; that he had read them with misgivings like my own; that he had instituted a cautious inquiry about the woman to whom I rightly conjectured they had been written. It seemed that thirty-six years ago (a year before the date of the letters) she had married, against the wish of her relations, an American of very suspicious character, in fact, he was generally believed to have been a pirate. She herself was the daughter of very respectable tradespeople, and had served in the capacity of nursery governess before her marriage. She had a brother, a widower, who was considered wealthy, and who had one child of about six years old. A month after the marriage, the body of this brother was found in the Thames, near London Bridge; there seemed some marks of violence about his throat, but they were not deemed sufficient to warrant the inquest in any other verdict than that of "found drowned."

The American and his wife took charge of the little boy, the deceased brother having by his will left his sister the guardian of his only child—and in the event of the child's death, the sister inherited. The child died about six months afterward—it was supposed to have been neglected and ill-treated. The neighbors deposed to have heard it shriek at night. The surgeon who had examined it after death said that it was emaciated as if from want of nourishment, and the body was covered with livid bruises. It seemed that one winter night the child had sought to escape—crept out into the backyard—tried to scale the wall—fallen back exhausted, and been found at morning on the stones in a dying state. But though there was some evidence of cruelty, there was none of murder; and the aunt and her husband had sought to palliate cruelty by alleging the exceeding stubbornness and perversity of the child, who was declared to be half-witted. Be that as it may, at the orphan's death the aunt inherited her brother's fortune. Before the first wedded year was out the American quitted England abruptly, and never returned to it. He obtained a cruising vessel, which was lost in the Atlantic two years afterward. The widow was left in affluence; but reverses of various kinds had befallen her; a bank broke—an investment failed—she went into a small business and became insolvent—then she entered into service, sinking lower and lower, from housekeeper down to maid-of-all work—never long retaining a place, though nothing decided against her character was ever alleged. She was considered sober, honest, and peculiarly quiet in her ways; still nothing prospered with her. And so she had dropped into the workhouse, from which Mr. J—— had taken her, to be placed in charge of the very house which she had rented as mistress in the first year of her wedded life.

Mr. J—— added that he had passed an hour alone in the unfurnished room which I had urged him to destroy, and that his impressions of dread while there were so great, though he had neither heard nor seen anything, that he was eager to have the walls bared and the floor removed as I had suggested. He had engaged persons for the work, and would commence any day I would name.

The day was accordingly fixed. I repaired to the haunted house—he went into the blind dreary room, took up the skirting, and then the floors.

Under the rafters, covered with rubbish, was found a trap-door, quite large enough to admit a man. It was closely nailed, with clamps and rivets of iron. On removing these we descended into a room below, the existence of which had never been suspected. In this room there had been a window and a flue, but they had been bricked over, evidently for many years. By the help of candles we examined this place; it still retained some mouldering furniture—three chairs, an oak settle, a table—all of the fashion of about eighty years ago. There was a chest of drawers against the wall, in which we found, half-rotted away, old-fashioned articles of a man's dress, such as might have been worn eighty or a hundred years ago by a gentleman of some rank—costly steel buckles and buttons, like those yet worn in court-dresses, a handsome court sword—in a waistcoat which had once been rich with gold-lace, but which was now blackened and foul with damp, we found five guineas, a few silver coins, and a ivory ticket, probably for some place of entertainment long since passed away. But our main discovery was in a kind of iron safe fixed to the wall, the lock of which it cost us much trouble to get picked.

In this safe were three shelves, and two small drawers. Ranged on the shelves were several small bottles of crystal, hermetically stopped. They contained colorless volatile essences, of the nature of which I shall only say that they were not poisons—phosphor and ammonia entered into some of them. There were also some very curious glass tubes, and a small pointed rod of iron, with a large lump of rock-crystal, and another of amber— also a lodestone of great power.

In one of the drawers we found a miniature portrait set in gold, and retaining the freshness of its colors most remarkably, considering the length of time it had probably been there. The portrait was that of a man who might be somewhat advanced in middle life, perhaps forty-seven or forty-eight.

It was a remarkable face—a most impressive face. If you could fancy some mighty serpent transformed into a man, perserving in the human lineaments the old serpent type, you would have a better idea of that countenance than long descriptions can convey: the width and flatness of forehead—the tapering elegance of contour disguising the strength of the deadly jaw—the long, large, terrible eyes, glittering and green as the emerald— and withal a certain ruthless calm, as if from the consciousness of an immense power.

Mechanically I turned round the miniature to examine the back of it, and on the back was engraved a pentacle; in the middle of the pentacle a ladder, and the third step of the ladder was formed by the date 1765. Examining still more minutely, I detected a spring; this, on being pressed, opened the back of the miniature as a lid. Withinside the lid were engraved, "Marianna to thee—be faithful in life and in death to———." Here follows a name that I will not mention, but it was not unfamiliar to me. I had heard it spoken of by old men in my childhood as the name borne by a dazzling charlatan who had made a great sensation in London for a year or so, and had fled the country on the charge of a double murder within his own house—that of his mistress and his rival. I said nothing of this to Mr. J——, to whom reluctantly I resigned the miniature.

We had found no difficulty in opening the first drawer within the iron safe; we found great difficulty in opening the second: it was not locked, but it resisted all efforts, till we inserted in the chinks the edge of a chisel. When we had thus drawn it forth we found a very singular apparatus in the nicest order. Upon a small thin book or rather tablet, was placed a saucer of crystal: this saucer was filled with a clear liquid—on that liquid floated a kind of compass, with a needle shifting rapidly round; but instead of the usual points of a compass were seven strange characters, not very unlike those used by astrologers to denote the planets.

A peculiar, but not strong nor displeasing odor came from this drawer, which was lined with a wood that we afterward discovered to be hazel. Whatever the cause of this odor, it produced a material effect on the nerves. We all felt it, even the two workmen who were in the room—a creeping tingling sensation from the tips of the fingers to the roots of the hair. Impatient to examine the tablet, I removed the saucer. As I did so the needle of the compass went round and round with exceeding swiftness, and I felt a shock that ran through my whole frame, so that I dropped the saucer on the floor. The liquid was split—the saucer was broken— the compass rolled to the end of the room—and at that instant the walls shook to and fro, as if a giant had swayed and rocked them.

The two workmen were so frightened that they ran up the ladder by which we had descended from the trap-door; but seeing that nothing more happened, they were easily induced to return.

Meanwhile I had opened the tablet: it was bound in plain red leather, with a silver clasp; it contained but one sheet of thick vellum, and on that sheet were inscribed within a double pentacle, words in old monkish Latin, which are literally to be translated thus: "On all that it can reach within these walls—sentient or inanimate, living or dead—as moves the needle, so work my will! Accursed be the house, and restless be the dwellers therein."

We found no more. Mr. J—— burnt the tablet and its anathema. He razed to the foundations the part of the building containing the secret room with the chamber over it. He had then the courage to inhabit the house himself for a month, and a quieter, better-conditioned house could not be found in all London. Subsequently he let it to advantage, and his tenant has made no complaints.

Afterword

"Exorcism" is from Greek words meaning "to cause to swear an oath."
You swear an oath by affirming something in the name of the gods. This
means that if you tell a lie, the indignant gods, angry at having their names
called upon uselessly or falsely ("in vain," the usual expression is), will
punish you.

When evil spirits have appropriated some person or some place, they
can be driven out, usually, by calling upon the name of God, and therefore
that can be considered an exorcism, too.

Not all exorcisms need make use of spiritual tools only, by the way.
There was a time when, after someone had died in a particular house,
of plague or of some other virulent disease, that house would be subjected
to burning pitch or sulfur in the hope that the spirits that caused the disease
would find the fumes as unpleasant as human beings would and would
leave the house. And if we read "germs" for "spirits," it might work. The
fumes might kill them, although I've often wondered how long it took
before the house became truly habitable after such treatment.

Similarly, exterminators exorcise cockroaches and mice by the use of
poison pellets or poison gas of one sort or another.

Nevertheless the word is used primarily for the spiritual removal of
spiritual dangers and came into particular prominence in recent years with
the motion picture The Exorcist *and its imitations.—I.A.*

Additional Reading

Sir Andrew Caldecott, "A Room in the Rectory," in *Not Exactly Ghosts*
(London: Arnold, 1947).

R. S. Hawker, "The Botathen Ghost," in *The Haunted and the Haunters,*
Ernest Rhys, ed. (London: Daniel O'Connor, 1921).

Richard Matheson, "From Shadowed Places," in *Shock II* (New York:
Dell Books, 1964).

Seabury Quinn, "The Wolf of Saint Bonnot," in *The Phantom-Fighter*
(Sauk City, Wisc.: Mycroft and Moran, 1966).

Isaac Bashevis Singer, "The Dead Fiddler," in *The Collected Stories of*
Isaac Bashevis Singer (New York: Farrar, Strauss, 1982).

10

Hand of Glory

Manly Wade Wellman
The Dead Man's Hand

Now open lock To the Dead Man's knock!
Fly bar and bolt and band!
Nor move nor swerve Joint, muscle or nerve
At the spell of the Dead Man's Hand!
Sleep, all who sleep!— Wake, all who wake!
But be as the Dead for the Dead Man's sake!

—Thomas Ingoldsby, *The Hand of Glory*

The men in front of the store were all laughing in the sunset, but not one of them sounded cheerful.

"Y'hear this, Sam?" someone asked a latecomer. "Stranger askin' the way to Old Monroe's. Must be the one who bought the place."

More laughter, in which the latecomer joined. Berna's father turned grim and dangerous enough to counterbalance all their mockery. He was hard and gaunt in his seersucker suit, with a long nose, a long chin, and a foxtrap mouth between them.

"I know the joke," he said, leaning over his steering wheel. "You think the place is haunted."

"No," cackled a dried little gaffer on an upturned nail-keg. "Haunted ain't the word. Curst, more like it. Me, I ain't got many more nights to live, and I wouldn't spend none of 'em at Old Monroe's."

"I know all about that silly story," announced Berna's father.

"All?" teased someone else. "Silly story?"

"And I'm thankful it's so well believed. That's how I was able to buy the farm so cheap."

"I wonder," mumbled the little old man, "if you bought it from who owns it rightful. 'Fter all, way I heard it, Old Monroe's deal was only for his lifetime—long enough in all conscience." He spat at a crack in the boardwalk. "When it comes to that, whoever bargained for Old Monroe's soul made a fool trade, for Old Monroe's soul was a sure shot anyway to go to—"

"If you're all through laughing," interrupted Berna's father savagely, "maybe someone will remember enough manners to direct us."

"Please, gentlemen," added Berna timidly from beside her father. She was slender where he was gaunt, appealing where he was grim. Her dark wide eyes sought a loiterer, who removed his palmleaf hat.

"If you're set on it," said this one, "you follow the street out, along the pavement. Miss the turn into Hanksville, then go left on a sand road. Watch for a little stone bridge over a run, with a big bunch of willows. Across the run, beyond them willows, is a private road. All grown up, and not even rabbit hunters go there. Well, at the other end is your new house, and I wish you luck." He fiddled with the hat. "You'll need it."

"Thank you kindly," said Berna's father. "My name's Ward Conley. I'll be your neighbor at the Old Monroe farm. And if you think you'll play any ghost jokes around there at night, remember I'm moving in with a shotgun, which I can use tolerably well."

He started the car. Berna heard the men start talking again, not laughing now.

"I didn't think," she ventured as they drove out of the little town in the last red sunglow, "that the story we heard was taken so seriously." She looked at her father. "I didn't even pay attention when the farm broker mentioned it. Tell me all of it."

"Nervous, Berna?" demanded Ward Conley.

"No. Just curious."

"It's the sort of yarn that's pinned on some house in every district where history's old enough, and ghost-believing gawks are plentiful enough. What I heard was that the former owner, the one they called Old Monroe, came here eighty years ago and took a piece of land that seemed worthless. By working and planning he made it pay richly. He never got married, never mixed with his neighbors, never spent much of what he took in, and he lived to be more than a hundred. Knowing so little about him, the corn-crackers hereabouts made up their own story. That Old Monroe made a sort of bargain with—well—"

"With the devil?"

"Maybe. Or anyway some old Indian spirit of evil. They said the bargain included a magic-built house, the richest of crops, and more money than anyone for miles around. Old Monroe got the last named, anyway. When he died, he died raving. Most hermits and misers are crazy. Since then nobody goes near the place. A second cousin up in Richmond inherited, and sold to us for a song."

"A bargain with devils," mused Berna. "It sounds like Hawthorne."

"It sounds like foolishness," snapped Conley. "Any devils come bargaining around, I'm enough of a business man to give them the short end of the deal."

† † †

In a city to the north, big John Thunstone listened earnestly as he leaned across a desk.

"You don't mean to tell me, Mr. Thunstone," said the professor opposite, "that you're really serious about the Shonokin myths?"

"I discount nothing until I know enough to judge," replied Thunstone. "The hint I picked up today is shadowy. And you're the only man who has made an intelligent study of the subject."

"Only the better to finish my American folkways encyclopedia," deprecated the other. "Well the Shonokins are supposed to be a race of magicians that peopled America before the Red Indians migrated from—wherever they migrated from. One or two commentators insist that Shonokin wizardry and enmity is the basis for most of the Indian stories of supernatural evils, everything from the Wendigo to those nasty little tales about singing snakes and the Pukwitchee dwarfs. All mention we get of Shonokins today— and it's mighty slim—we get third or fourth hand. From old Indians to recent ones, through them by way of first settlers to musty students like me. There's an amusing suggestion that Shonokins, or their descendants, actually exist today here and there. Notably in the neighborhood of—"

"I wonder," broke in John Thunstone, rather mannerlessly for him, "if that isn't the neighborhood I'm so curious about."

† † †

In the dusk the Conley car passed the Hanksville turn, gained the sand road and crossed the stone bridge. Beyond the willows showed a dense-grown hedge of thorny trees, with a gap closed by a single hewn timber on forked stakes. The timber bore a signboard, and by the glow of the headlights Berna could read the word "PRIVATE." Conley got out, unshipped the barrier, then returned to drive them along a brush-lined road with ruts full of rank, squelchy grass.

A first journey over a strange trail always seems longer than it is. Berna felt that ages had passed before her father stepped on the brake. "There's our home," he said.

At almost the same moment the moon rose, pale and sheeny as a disk of clean, fresh bone.

The pale light showed them a house, built squarely like old plantation manors, but smaller. It had once been painted gray, and still looked well kept and clean. No windows were broken, the pillars of the porch were still sturdy. Around it clung dark, plump masses of shrubbery and, farther back, tall flourishing trees. A flagged path led up to the broad steps. Berna knew she should be pleased. But she was not.

From the rear seat Conley dug their suitcases and rolls of bedding. Berna rummaged for the hamper that held their supper.

She followed her father up the flagstone way, wondering why the night seemed so cool for this season. Conley set down his burdens, then mounted the porch to try the door.

"Locked," he grumbled. "The broker said there was never a key." He turned and studied a window. "We'll have to break the glass."

"May I help?" inquired a gentle voice, and into view, perhaps from the massed bushes at the porch-side, strolled a man.

He did not stand in the full moonlight, and later Berna would wonder how she knew he was handsome. Slim white-clad elegance, face of a healthy pallor under a wide hat, clear-cut features, deep eyes and brows both heavy and graceful—these impressions she received. Conley came down off the porch.

"I'm Ward Conley, the new owner of this farm," he introduced himself briskly. "This is my daughter, Berna."

The stranger bowed. "I am a Shonokin."

"Glad to know you, Mr. Shannon."

"Shonokin," corrected the man.

"People in town said that nobody dared come here," went on Conley.

"They lied. They usually lie." The man's deep eyes studied Berna, they may have admired. She did not know whether to feel confused or resentful. "Mr. Conley," continued the gentle voice, "you are having difficulty?"

"Yes. The door's jammed or locked."

"Let me help." The graceful figure stepped up on the porch, bending over something. A light glared. He seemed to be holding a little sheaf of home-dipped tapers, such as Berna had seen in very old-fashioned farmhouses. They looked knobby and skimpy, but their light was almost blinding. He held it close to the lock as he stooped. He did not seem to move, but after a moment he turned.

"Now your door is open," he told them. And so it was, swinging gently inward.

"Thanks, Mr. Shonokin," said Conley, more warmly than he had spoken all evening. "Won't you step inside with us?"

"Not now." Bowing again, the man swept his fingertips over the lights he held, snuffing them out. Descending the steps lithely, he walked along the stone flags. At the far end he paused and lifted his hat. Berna saw his hair, long, wavy and black as soot. He was gone.

"Seems like a nice fellow," grunted Conley. "How about some candles of our own, Berna?"

She gave him one from the hamper, and he lighted it and led her inside.

† † †

"I know that it's a considerable journey, and that the evidence is slim," John Thunstone was telephoning at Pennsylvania Station. "But I'll get the full story, on the exact spot. I'm sorry you and Dr. Trowbridge can't come. I'll report when I get back." He listened a moment, then chuckled in his trim mustache. "Haven't I always returned. Now, goodbye, or I'll miss my train."

† † †

Ward Conley lifted his wax candle overhead and grunted approvingly. "I was a little worried, Berna, about buying the place sight unseen, even at a figure that would make the worst land profitable." His eyes gleamed. "But this is worth coming home to, hah?"

The old furniture looked comfortable and in good shape. Berna wondered if the rich carpet in the hall was not valuable. In the room beyond was a table of dark wood, with sturdy chairs around it, and farther on glass-doored closets with china and silver and the white of folded linen. Conley dragged down a hanging lamp.

"Oil in it, and the wick ready trimmed," he announced. With his candle he lighted the lamp and drew it up to the ceiling. "Berna, someone's put this place in apple-pie order for us. Even swept and dusted. Might it have been Mr. Shonokin's family? Neighborly, I call it." His stern face was relaxing. They walked into a kitchen, well appointed but cool. There was firewood in the box. Berna set down her hamper. Then they mounted to the upper floor.

"The beds are made," Conley exulted. "This front room will be yours, Berna. I'll take the next one. Suppose we eat now, and poke around more tomorrow. I want to be up early, out at the barn and in the fields."

Returning to the kitchen, they brought out sandwiches and fruit and a jugful of coffee. "It's getting cold," pronounced Conley, peering into the jug. "Let's fire up the range and heat it."

Berna believed that the coffee was hot enough, but she was glad that her father had made an excuse for a fire. The kitchen was downright shuddery. Even while the kindling blazed up, she got a sweater from her suitcase and put it on. They ate in silence, for Conley disliked conversation while he was at the important business of eating. When Berna had brushed up the crumbs, he yawned.

"Bed now," he decreed, and again took up the candle. Walking through the front room, he drew down the lamp and blew it out. Berna kept close to his heels as they mounted the stairs. The little moving flame that Conley held up made a host of strange and stealthy shadows around them.

Alone in the room assigned her, Berna drew back the bedclothes. They were so chilly within as to seem damp, but she had brought up a blanket roll from the car. She made the bed afresh, and before creeping in she knelt down. Her prayer was the one taught her as a child, while her mother still lived:

> *"Matthew, Mark, Luke and John,*
> *Bless the bed I lie upon.*
> *There are four corners to my bed,*
> *There are four saints around my head—*
> *One to watch and one to pray,*
> *And two to bear my soul away."*

She remembered her flutter of dread at the last two lines. Though serious and thoughtful, Berna was young. She did not want her soul to be borne away yet. And she felt a close silence about her, as of many lurking watchers.

Of a sudden, there popped into her mind a tag of another bedtime prayer, heard in the long ago from a plantation mammy. She repeated that, too:

> *"Keep me from hoodoo and witch,*
> *And lead my path from the poorhouse gate. . . ."*

The tenseness seemed to evaporate around her. Berna got into bed, listened a while to the sighing of a breeze-shaken tree outside her window, and finally slept soundly until her father's fist on the door told her that it was dawn and time to be up.

They had fried eggs and bacon in the kitchen that remained cool despite the fire that had smouldered in the range all night.

Wiping his mouth at the end of the meal, Ward Conley tramped to the back door and tugged at the knob. It refused to budge, though he heaved and puffed.

"I wish that Shonokin man was back here to open this, too," he said at last. "Well, let's use the front door."

Out they went together. The early morning was bright and dry, and Berna saw flowers on the shrubs, blue, red and yellow, that were beyond her knowledge of garden botany. They walked around the side of the house and saw a quiet barnyard, with a great red barn and smaller sheds. Beyond these extended rich-seeming fields.

"Something's been planted there," said Conley, shading his eyes with his hand. "If anybody thinks he can use my fields—well, he'll lose the crop he put in. Berna, go back to the house and make a list of the things we need. I'll drive into town later, either Hanksville or that little superstition-ridden rookery we passed through yesterday."

He strolled off, hands in pockets, toward the land beyond the barnyard. Berna again walked around the house and in through the front door. For the first time she was alone in her new home, and fancied that her footsteps echoed loudly, even on the rug in the hall. Back in the kitchen she washed the dishes—there was a sink, with running water from somewhere or other—then sat at the kitchen table to list needed articles as her father had directed.

There was a slight sound at the door, as if a bird had fluttered against it. Berna glanced up, wide-eyed.

That was all. She sat where she was, pencil in fingers, eyes starting and unwinking. She did not move. There was no feeling of stiffness or confinement or weight. Trying, in the back of her amazed and terrified mind, to diagnose, she decided it was like the familiar grammar-school experiment—you clasp your hands and say "I cannot, I cannot," until you find yourself unable to move your fingers from each other. Berna may have breathed, her heart may have beaten. She could not be sure, then or later.

The door, that had not budged for her father's struggles, was gently swaying open. In stepped Mr. Shonokin, smiling over the glow of his peculiar little sheaf of tapers. He snuffed them, slid the sheaf into his pocket. And Berna could move again.

Only her eyes moved at first, quartering him over. He wore the white suit, beautifully cut, and of a fabric Berna could not identify—if it were fabric and not some sort of skin, delicately thin and soft and perfectly bleached. His hands, which hung gracefully at his side, were long and a little strange; perhaps the ring fingers were unnaturally long, longer than the middle fingers. One of them held his wide hat, and the uncovered locks of dead black hair fell in soft waves over Mr. Shonokin's broad brow. As Berna's eyes came to his, he smiled.

"I've been talking to your father," he said, "and now I want to talk to you."

She got to her feet, grateful for the restored power to do so. "Talk?" she echoed. "Talk of what?"

"This place of yours," he told her, laying his hat on the table. "You see, the title isn't exactly clear."

She shook her head at once. She knew her father better than that.

"It's completely clear, Mr. Shonokin. All in order, back to the original grant from the Indians."

"Ah," said Shonokin, still gently. "But where did the Indians get their title? Where? I'll tell you. From us, the Shonokins."

Berna was still trembling, from that strange moment of tranced inaction. She had been hypnotized, she told herself, like Trilby in the book. It must not happen again. She would face this stranger with resolution and defiance.

"You don't mean to claim," she replied, with an attempt at loftiness, "that your family was in this part of the country before the Indians."

"We were everywhere before the Indians," he assured her, and smiled. His teeth were white, perfect, and ever so slightly pointed, even the front teeth that should be square-edged like chisels.

"Then you're Indian yourself," she suggested, but he shook his head.

"Shonokins are not Indians. They are not—" He paused, as if choosing his words. "We are not like any race you know. We are old, even when we are young. We took this country from creatures too terrible for you to imagine, even though they are dead and leave only their fossil bones. We ruled well, in ways you can't understand." That sounded both sad and superior. "For reasons that you can't understand, either, we were once tired of ruling. That is when we allowed the Indians to come, retaining only limited domains. This is one of them."

"This farm?" prompted Berna. She still held the pencil, so tightly that her fingers were bruising against it.

"This farm," said her visitor. "The Indians never had any right to it. It is ground sacred to the Shonokins, where their wisdom and rule will continue forever. And so any deed dating back to Indians is not lawful. I told your father that, and it's the truth, however stupid and furious he may be."

"Suppose," said Berna, "that you say to my father that you think he's stupid. Tell him to his face. I'd like to see what he does to you then."

"I did tell him," replied the man they knew as Mr. Shonokin. "And he did nothing. He was frozen into silence, as you were just now, when I held up—" His strange-shaped hand moved toward his side pocket, where he had put that strange sheaf of tapers.

"Suppose," went on Berna, "that you get out of this house and off this property."

It was bold, fierce talk for a quiet girl like Berna, but she felt she was managing it splendidly. She took a step toward him. "Yes, right now."

His pointed teeth smiled at her again. He backed smoothly toward the open door and paused on the sill. "You're hasty," he protested gently. "We want only to be fair. You may enjoy this place—enjoy it very much, as Old Monroe did—if you simply and courteously make the same agreement."

"Sell our souls?" Berna snapped, as she had never snapped at anyone before in all her life.

"The Shonokins," he said, "do not recognize the existence of any such thing as a soul."

He was gone, as abruptly as he had gone from the end of the path last night.

Berna sat down, her heart stuttering inside her. After a minute, her father came in. He, too, sat down. Berna wondered if she were as pale as he.

"That—that—that trick-playing, sneering skunk," he panted. "No man can try things like that on Ward Conley." He looked around. "Did he come in here? Is he still here? If he is, I'm going to get the shotgun."

"He's gone," Berna replied. "I made him go. But who is he? Did he tell you that preposterous story?"

As she spoke, she knew she had believed it all, about the Shonokins who had ruled before the Indians, who wanted to rule again, and who claimed this land, on which nobody could live except as their tenant and vassal.

"He put some sort of a trance or spell on me," said Conley, still breathing hard. "If he hadn't been able to do it, I'd have killed him—there's a hayfork out there in the barn. And he wanted me to believe I'd do some hokus-pokus for him, to be allowed to live here on my own land. Berna," said Conley suddenly, "I think he'll be sneaking back here again. And I'm going to be ready for him."

"Let me go to town when you go," she began, but Conley waved the words aside.

"You'll drive in alone and shop for whatever we need. Because I stay right here, waiting for Mr. Smart Aleck Shonokin." Rising, he walked into the front room, where much of the luggage was still stacked. He returned with his shotgun, fitting it together. It was a well-kept repeater. Ponderously he pumped a shell into the chamber.

"We'll see," promised Conley balefully, "how much lead he can carry away with him."

And so Berna drove the car to the village. At the general store in front of which loiterers had mocked the evening before, she bought flour, potatoes, meat, lard, tinned goods. Her father had stipulated nails and a few household tools, and on inspiration Berna bought two heavy new locks. When she returned, Conley approved this last purchase and installed the locks, one at the front door and one at the back.

"The windows can all be latched, too," he reported. "Let him jimmy his way inside now. I'll give a lot to have him try it." When he had finished his work, Conley picked up the shotgun again, cradling it across his knees. "Now we're all ready for a call from Mr. Shonokin."

But he was tense, nervous, jumpy. Berna cut herself peeling vegetables for supper, and dreaded the dropping of the sun toward the western horizon.

† † †

At Hanksville, several townsfolk had ambled out to see the afternoon train arrive. They stared amiably at the one disembarking passenger, a broad giant of a man with a small mustache, who addressed them in a voice that sounded purposeful and authoritative.

"Old Monroe's," they echoed his first question. "Lookee, mister, nobody ever goes there."

"Well, I'm going there at once. A matter of life and death. Will anybody let me rent his automobile?"

Nobody answered that at all.

"How do you get there?" he demanded next, and someone told about the crossing, the sanded road, the stone bridge, the clump of willows, the side trail.

"And how far?"

Ten miles, opined one. A companion thought it might be nearer twelve.

John Thunstone looked up at the sinking sun. "Then I have no time to waste," he said, "for I'll have to walk it."

He strode off through Hanksville. Those who had spoken with him now watched him go. Then they turned to each other, shook their heads, and made clicking sounds with their tongues.

† † †

It was not easy for Conley to explain to Berna all that had passed between him and Shonokin. In the first place, Conley had been both furious and alarmed, and was still so. In the second, there was much he could not understand.

It seemed that the visitor had bobbed up at Conley's elbow, with that talent he had for appearing and disappearing so quickly. He had courteously admired the growing fields of corn and beans, and when Conley had repeated his complaint that someone was making free with the ground, had assured Conley that these things had been planted and were growing for the Conleys alone. He, Shonokin, took credit for the putting in and advancement of what looked like a prize crop.

"And then," Conley told Berna, "he took up the question of payment. I said, of course, that I'd be glad to give him something for his trouble. Whatever was fair, I said. And he out with an idea you'd never believe— not even though I swear to every word he said."

Shonokin wanted the Conleys to live comfortably, pleasantly, even richly. He was willing to give assurance that there would never be anything to limit or endanger their material prosperity. But, here and now, Conley must admit by signed paper his indebtedness and dependency.

"Dependency!" Conley fairly exploded, describing the scene to his daughter. "Dependency—on that young buck I never even saw before last night! I just stood there, wondering which word to say first, and he went on with the idea that he and his bunch—whoever the Shonokins might be—would make themselves responsible for the crops and the profits of this place, deciding what would be raised and see that it succeeded. Then I blew up."

He paused, and his face went a shade whiter. He looked old.

"I told you what came after that. I grabbed for the hayfork. But he held up his hand, that hand he carries that gives off light."

"The little candles?" prompted Berna.

"It's a hand, I tell you, a sort of skinny hand. It has lights on the fingers. I froze like a wooden Indian in front of a cigar store. And he grinned that ugly way he has, and told me that I now had time to think it over quietly; that I'd better be a good tenant, and that he and we could be a wonderful help to each other if we didn't lose any energy by quarreling. I couldn't move until he walked away out of sight."

Conley shuddered. "What," he demanded savagely, "is he driving at? Why does he want to run our affairs?"

That question, reflected Berna to herself, had been asked countless times in the world's history by people who could not understand tyranny. Tyrants alone could understand, for they lived tormented by the urge and appetite and insistence to dominate others.

"He won't come back," she said, trying to be confident and not succeeding.

"Yes, he will," replied Conley balefully, "and I'll be ready for him." He patted the shotgun in his lap. "Is supper about done?"

It was, but they had little appetite. Afterwards Berna washed the dishes. She thought she had never felt such cold water as gushed from the faucet. Conley went into the front room, and when Berna joined him he sat in a solid old rocking chair, still holding the shotgun.

"The furniture's nice," said Berna lamely.

"Reminds me of another thing that skunk said," rejoined Conley. "That his Shonokins had made all the furniture, as well as the house. That it—the furniture—was really theirs and would do what they said. What did he mean?"

Berna did not know, and did not reply.

"Those new locks weren't made by him," Conley went on. "They won't obey him. Let him try to get in."

When Conley repeated himself thus aimlessly, it meant that he was harrassed and daunted. They sat in the gathering gloom, that the hanging lamp could not dispel successfully. Berna wished for a radio. There was one in the car, and this was a night for good programs. But she would not have ventured into the open to meet the entire galaxy of her radio favorites in person. Later on perhaps they'd buy a cabinet radio for this room, she mused; if they lasted out the evening, and the next day and the days and nights to follow, if they could successfully avoid or defeat the slender dark man who menaced them.

Conley had unpacked their few books. One lay on the sideboard near Berna's chair, a huge showy volume of Shakespeare's works that a book agent had sold to Berna's mother years ago. Berna loved Shakespeare no more and no less than most girls of limited education and experience. But she remembered the words of a neighbor, spoken when the book was bought; Shakespeare could be used, like the Bible, for "casting sortes." It was an old-country custom, still followed here and there in rural America. You opened the book at random and hastily clapped your finger on a passage, which answered whatever troubled you. Hadn't the wife of Enoch Arden done something like that, or did she remember her high school English course rightly?

She lifted the volume into her lap. It fell open of itself. Without looking at the fine double-columned type, she put out her forefinger quickly. She had opened to *Macbeth*. At the head of the page was printed: *Act I, Scene 3.* She stooped to read in the lamplight;

> *Were such things here as we do speak about,*
> *Or have we eaten on the insane root,*
> *That takes the reason prisoner?*

That was close enough to what fretted her and her father. Shakespeare, what she knew of him, was full of creepy things about prophecies, witches, phantoms, and such. The "insane root"—what was that? It had a frightening sound to it. Anyway, Shonokin had momentarily imprisoned their minds with his dirty tricks of hypnotism. Again she swore to herself not to be caught another time. She had heard that a strong effort of will could resist such things. She took hold of the book to replace it on the sideboard.

She could not.

As before, her eyes could not blink, her muscles could not stir. She could only watch as, visible through the hallway beyond, the front door slowly moved open and showed the dead pale light that Shonokin could evoke.

He glided in, white-clad, elegantly slender, grinning. He held his light aloft, and Conley had been right. It was shaped like a hand. What had seemed to be a joined bunch of tapers were the five fingers, each sprouting a clear flame. Berna saw how shriveled and shrunken those fingers were, and how bones and tendons showed through the coarse skin of their backs. Shonokin set the thing carefully on a stand by the door to the hallway. It was flat at the wrist end, it stayed upright like the ugliest of little candlesticks.

Shonokin walked closer, gazing in hushed triumph from the paralyzed Conley to the paralyzed Berna.

"Now we can settle everything," he said in his gentle voice, and stuck a terrible little laugh on the end of the words. He paused just in front of Berna's fixed eyes. She could study that white suit now, could see the tiny pore-openings in the strange integument from which it was tailored. His slender hands, too, with their abnormally long ring fingers—they did not have human nails but talons, narrow and curved and trimmed most carefully to cruel points, as if for better rending.

"Mr. Conley is beyond any reasonable discussion," the creature was saying. "He is an aging man, harsh and boastful and narrow from his youth upwards. But Berna—" His eyes slid around to her. Their pupils had a lean perpendicularity, like the pupils of a cat. "Miss Berna is young," he went on. "She is not reckless or greedy or violent. She will listen and obey, even if she does not fully understand, the wise advice of the Shonokins."

He rested his hands, fingers spread, on the heavy table. It seemed to stir at his touch, like a board on ripply water.

"She will obey the better," said their captor, "when she sees how simply we go about removing her father, with his foolish opposition. Conley," and the eyes shifted to the helpless man, "you were so mannerless today as to doubt many of the things I told you. Most of all you seemed to scorn the suggestion that this furniture can move at my bidding. But watch."

The slender hand was barely touching the table-top. Shonokin drew together his spread fingertips, the sharp horny talons scraping softly on the wood. Again the table creaked, quivered, and moved.

Spiritualism, Berna insisted to herself. Mediums did that sort of illusion for customers at paid seances. Men like Dr. Dunninger and John Mulholland wrote articles in the newspapers, explaining the trickery. This Shonokin person must be a professional sleight-of-hand performer. He made as if to lift the hand. The table shifted again, actually rising with the gesture, as if it were of no weight and gummed to his fingers.

"You see that it does obey," the gentle voice pointed out. "It obeys, and now I give you the full measure of proof, Conley. This table is going to kill you."

Shonokin stepped toward Conley's rocking chair, and the table stepped with him.

"It is heavy, Conley, though I make it seem light. Its wood is dark and ancient, and almost as solid and hard as metal. This table can kill you, and nobody can sensibly call the death murder. How could your law convict or punish an insensible piece of furniture, however weighty?"

Again he stepped toward Conley. Again the table kept pace. It was like some squat, obedient farm beast, urged along by its master's touch on its flank.

"You will be crushed, Conley. Berna, do you hear all this? Make careful note of it, and tell it to yourself often; for when things are all over, you will realize that you cannot tell it to others. Nobody will believe the real nature of your father's death. It cannot appear otherwise than a freak accident—a heavy table tipped over upon him, crushing him. What narrow-brained sheriff or town marshal would listen if you told the truth?"

Even if she had been able to speak, Berna could not have denied his logic.

"And after your father is dead, you will be recognized as mistress here. You will have learned to obey my people and me, recognize our leadership and guidance. This farm is both remote and rich. It will form our gathering point for what we wish to do in the world again. But first—"

Once more his hand shifted. The table began slowly to rear its end that was closest to where Conley sat.

It was long and massive, and it creaked ominously, like an ancient drawbridge going up. The thick legs that rose in the air seemed to move, like the forefeet of a rearing, pawing horse. Or was that a flicker of pale light from the candle-hand yonder?

"Nearer," said Shonokin, and the table pranced forward, its upper legs quivering. They would fall in a moment like two pile-drivers. "Nearer. Now—"

Something moved, large and broad but noiseless, in at the front door. An arm darted out, more like a snake than an arm. The candle-hand flew from where it had been placed, struck the floor, and a foot trod on it. All five of its flames went out at once.

Shonokin whirled, his hand leaving the table. It fell over sidewise, with a crash that shook the windows. One second later came a crash still louder.

Conley had risen from his chair, jammed the muzzle of the shotgun against Shonokin's ribs, and touched the trigger. The charge almost blew the slender man in two.

It took all of John Thunstone's straining thews to set the table right again. Then he sat on its edge, speaking to Conley and Berna, who sagged in their chairs too exhausted for anything but gratitude.

"The magic used was very familiar," Thunstone was saying. "The 'hand of glory' is known in Europe and in old Mexico, too." He glanced at the grisly trodden-out thing, still lying on the floor. "You'll find it described in Spence's *Encyclopedia of Occultism,* and a rhymed tale about it in *Ingoldsby Legends.* The hand of a dead murderer—and trust people like the Shonokins to be able to secure that—is treated with saltpeter and oils to make it inflammable. We needn't go into the words that are said over it to give it the power. Lighted by the proper sorcerer, it makes locks open, and all inside the house remain silent as death."

"You were able to move," reminded Conley.

"Because I came in after the hand had laid the spell. I wasn't involved, any more than your visitor himself," and Thunstone glanced at the silent, slender body covered by a blanket on the floor.

"Is the hand of glory also Shonokin magic?" asked Berna. "Did they perhaps learn it first, and teach it to those other peoples?"

"About the Shonokins I know very little more than you yourselves seem to have heard. It seems evident that they do exist, and that they plan to be active in the world, and that they do feel a claim on this land of yours, and so on. But the death of one of them may deter the others."

"How?" asked Conley.

"You and I will bury him, under the flagstones at the far end of your walk. His body will keep other Shonokins from your door. They are a magic-minded lot, and a dangerous one, but they fear very few things more than they fear their own dead."

"What will the law say?" quavered Berna.

"Nothing, if you do not speak, and how can you speak? From outside I heard this one say, very truthfully, that the real story would never be believed, even in this superstitious district. Let it go with what I suggest. Justice has certainly been done. I doubt if you will be bothered by more Shonokins, though they may be heard from elsewhere."

"But what are they?" cried Berna. "What?"

Thunstone shook his great head. "My studies are anything but complete. All I know is that they are an old people and clever, very sure of their superiority, and that the ways they hope to follow are not our ways. Mr. Conley, are you ready?"

Conley departed to fetch spade and pick. Alone with Thunstone and the body under the blanket, Berna spoke:

"I don't know how to say how thankful I am—"

"Then don't try," he smiled. Berna laid her little hand on his huge arm.

"I will pray for you always," she promised.

"Prayers are what I greatly need," replied Thunstone, very thankfully on his own part.

Afterword

But, just as there are world languages spoken by hundreds of millions of people, and small isolated languages spoken only by a few thousand people in some hidden valley, so there are occult practices that are worldwide and others that are regional and local.

Manly Wade Wellman specialized in writing stories about some of the superstitions and mysticisms among the more primitive hill-people of the United States. He even created new legends such as the "Shonokins."

But just as there are small isolated languages spoken only by a few thousand people in some hidden valley, so there are world languages spoken by hundreds of millions of people and occult practices that are regional and worldwide.

A "Glory Hand," as Wellman explains, is fairly widely known. Perhaps it is natural to suppose that "the hand of a dead murderer" has absorbed a spiritual principle of evil and has a life of its own thereafter.—I.A.

Additional Reading

Sir Gilbert Edward Campbell, "The Thief's Taper," in *Wild and Weird Tales of Imagination and Mystery: Russians, English, and Italian* (London: Ward, Lock, 1889).

August Derleth, "Glory Hand," in *Someone in the Dark* (Sauk City, Wisc.: Arkham House, 1941).

R. H. Malden, "The Blank Leaves," in *Nine Ghosts* (London: Arnold, 1943).

Seabury Quinn, "The Hand of Glory," in *The Hellfire Files of Jules de Grandin* (New York: Popular Library, 1976).

Manly Wade Wellman, "Larroes Catch Meddlers," in *Worse Things Waiting* (Chapel Hill, N.C.: Carcosa, 1973).

11

Life Bonds and Tokens

Ray Bradbury
The Scythe

Quite suddenly there was no more road. It ran down the valley like any other road, between slopes of barren, stony ground and live oak trees, and then past a broad field of wheat standing alone in the wilderness. It came up beside the small white house that belonged to the wheat field and then just faded out, as though there was no more use for it.

It didn't matter much, because just there the last of the gas was gone. Drew Erickson braked the ancient car to a stop and sat there, not speaking, staring at his big, rough farmer's hands.

Molly spoke, without moving where she lay in the corner beside him. "We must of took the wrong fork back yonder."

Drew nodded.

Molly's lips were almost as white as her face. Only they were dry, where her skin was damp with sweat. Her voice was flat, with no expression in it.

"Drew," she said. "Drew, what are we a-goin' to do now?"

Drew stared at his hands. A farmer's hands, with the farm blown out from under them by the dry, hungry wind that never got enough good loam to eat.

The kids in the back seat woke up and pried themselves out of the dusty litter of bundles and bedding. They poked their heads over the back of the seat and said:

"What are we stoppin' for, Pa? Are we gonna eat now, Pa? Pa, we're awful hungry. Can we eat now, Pa?"

Drew closed his eyes. He hated the sight of his hands.

Molly's fingers touched his wrist. Very light, very soft. "Drew, maybe in the house there they'd spare us somethin' to eat?"

A white line showed around his mouth. "Beggin'," he said harshly. "Ain't none of us ever begged before. Ain't none of us ever goin' to."

Molly's hand tightened on his wrist. He turned and saw her eyes. He saw the eyes of Susie and little Drew, looking at him. Slowly all the stiffness went out of his neck and his back. His face got loose and blank, shapeless like a thing that has been beaten too hard and too long. He got out of the car and went up the path to the house. He walked uncertainly, like a man who is sick, or nearly blind.

The door of the house was open. Drew knocked three times. There was nothing inside but silence, and a white window curtain moving in the slow, hot air.

He knew it before he went in. He knew there was death in the house. It was that kind of silence.

He went through a small, clean living room and down a little hall. He wasn't thinking anything. He was past thinking. He was going toward the kitchen, unquestioning, like an animal.

Then he looked through an open door and saw the dead man.

He was an old man, lying out on a clean white bed. He hadn't been dead long; not long enough to lose the last quiet look of peace. He must have known he was going to die, because he wore his grave clothes— an old black suit, brushed and neat, and a clean white shirt and a black tie.

A scythe leaned against the wall beside the bed. Between the old man's hands there was a blade of wheat, still fresh. A ripe blade, golden and heavy in the tassel.

Drew went into the bedroom, walking soft. There was a coldness on him. He took off his broken, dusty hat and stood by the bed, looking down.

The paper lay open on the pillow beside the old man's head. It was meant to be read. Maybe a request for burial, or to call a relative. Drew scowled over the words, moving his pale, dry lips.

To him who stands beside me at my death bed: Being of sound mind, and alone in the world as it has been declared, I, John Buhr, do give and bequeath this farm, with all pertaining to it, to the man who is to come. Whatever his name or origin shall be, it will not matter. The farm is his, and the wheat; the scythe, and the task ordained thereto. Let him take them freely, and without question—and remember that I, John Buhr, am only the giver, not the ordainer. To which I set my hand and seal this third day of April, 1938. (Signed) John Buhr. *Kyrie eléison!*

Drew walked back through the house and opened the screen door. He said, "Molly, you come in. Kids, you stay in the car."

Molly came inside. He took her to the bedroom. She looked at the will, the scythe, the wheat field moving in a hot wind outside the window. Her white face tightened up and she bit her lips and held onto him. "It's too good to be true. There must be some trick to it."

Drew said, "Our luck's changin', that's all. We'll have work to do, stuff to eat, somethin' over our heads to keep rain off." He touched the scythe. It gleamed like a halfmoon. Words were scratched on its blade: WHO WIELDS ME—WIELDS THE WORLD! It didn't mean much to him, right at that moment.

"Drew," Molly asked, staring at the old man's clasped hands, "why— why's he holdin' that wheat-stalk so hard in his fingers?"

Just then the heavy silence was broken by the sound of the kids scrambling up the front porch. Molly gasped.

† † †

They lived in the house. They buried the old man on a hill and said some words over him, and came back down and swept the house and unloaded the car and had something to eat, because there was food, lots of it, in the kitchen; and they did nothing for three days but fix the house and look at the land and lie in the good beds, and then look at one another in surprise that all this was happening this way, and their stomachs were full and there was even a cigar for him to smoke in the evenings.

There was a small barn behind the house and in the barn a bull and three cows; and there was a well-house, a spring-house, under some big trees that kept it cool. And inside the well-house were big sides of beef and bacon and pork and mutton, enough to feed a family five times their size for a year, two years, maybe three. There was a churn and a box of cheese there, and big metal cans for the milk.

On the fourth morning Drew Erickson lay in bed looking at the scythe, and he knew it was time for him to work because there was ripe grain in the long field; he had seen it with his eyes, and he did not want to get soft. Three days sitting were enough for any man. He roused himself in the first fresh smell of dawn and took the scythe and held it before him as he walked out into the field. He held it up in his hands and swung it down.

It was a big field of grain. Too big for one man to tend, and yet one man had tended it.

At the end of the first day of work, he walked in with the scythe riding his shoulder quietly, and there was a look on his face of a puzzled man. It was a wheat field the like of which he had never seen. It ripened only in separate clusters, each set off from the others. Wheat shouldn't do that. He didn't tell Molly. Nor did he tell her the other things about the field. About how, for instance, the wheat rotted within a few hours after he cut it down. Wheat shouldn't do that, either. He was not greatly worried. After all, there was food at hand.

The next morning the wheat he had left rotting, cut down, had taken hold and came up again in little green sprouts, with tiny roots, all born again.

Drew Erickson rubbed his chin, wondered what and why and how it acted that way, and what good it would be to him—he couldn't sell it. A couple of times during the day he walked far up in the hills to where the old man's grave was, just to be sure the old man was there, maybe with some notion he might get an idea there about the field. He looked down and saw how much land he owned. The wheat stretched three miles in one direction toward the mountains, and was about two acres wide, patches of it in seedlings, patches of it golden, patches of it fresh cut by his hand. But the old man said nothing concerning this; there were a lot of stones and dirt in his face now. The grave was in the sun and the wind and silence. So Drew Erickson walked back down to use the scythe, curious, enjoying it because it seemed important. He didn't know just why, but it was. Very, very important.

He couldn't just let the wheat stand. There were always new patches of it ripened, and in his figuring out loud to no one in particular he said, "If I cut the wheat for the next ten years, just as it ripens up, I don't think I'll pass the same spot twice. Such a damn big field." He shook his head. "That wheat ripens just *so*. Never too much of it so I can't cut all the ripe stuff each day. That leaves nothin' but green grain. And the next mornin', sure enough, another patch of ripe stuff. . . ."

It was damned foolish to cut the grain when it rotted as quick as it fell. At the end of the week he decided to let it go a few days.

He lay in bed late, just listening to the silence in the house that wasn't anything like death silence, but a silence of things living well and happily.

He got up, dressed, and ate his breakfast slowly. He wasn't going to work. He went out to milk the cows, stood on the porch smoking a cigarette, walked about the backyard a little and then came back in and asked Molly what he had gone out to do.

"Milk the cows," she said.

"Oh, yes," he said, and went out again. He found the cows waiting and full, and milked them and put the milk cans in the spring-house, but thought of other things. The wheat. The scythe.

All through the morning he sat on the back porch rolling cigarettes. He made a toy boat for little Drew and one for Susie, and then he churned some of the milk into butter and drew off the buttermilk, but the sun was in his head, aching. It burned there. He wasn't hungry for lunch. He kept looking at the wheat and the wind bending and tipping and ruffling it. His arms flexed, his fingers, resting on his knees as he sat again on the porch, made a kind of grip in the empty air, itching. The pads of his palms itched and burned. He stood up and wiped his hands on his pants and sat down and tried to roll another cigarette and got mad at the mixings and threw it all away with a muttering. He had a feeling as if a third arm had been cut off of him, or he had lost something of himself. It had to do with his hands and his arms.

He heard the wind whisper in the field.

By one o'clock he was going in and out of the house, getting underfoot, thinking about digging an irrigation ditch, but all the time really thinking about the wheat and how ripe and beautiful it was, aching to be cut.

"Damn it to hell!"

He strode into the bedroom, took the scythe down off its wall-pegs. He stood holding it. He felt cool. His hands stopped itching. His head didn't ache. The third arm was returned to him. He was intact again.

It was instinct. Illogical as lightning striking and not hurting. Each day the grain must be cut. It had to be cut. Why? Well, it just did, that was all. He laughed at the scythe in his big hands. Then, whistling, he took it out to the ripe and waiting field and did the work. He thought himself a little mad. Hell, it was an ordinary-enough wheat field, really, wasn't it? Almost.

†   †   †

The days loped away like gentle horses.

Drew Erickson began to understand his work as a sort of dry ache and hunger and need. Things built in his head.

One noon, Susie and little Drew giggled and played with the scythe while their father lunched in the kitchen. He heard them. He came out and took it away from them. He didn't yell at them. He just looked very concerned and locked the scythe up after that, when it wasn't being used.

He never missed a day, scything.

Up. Down. Up, down, and across. Back and up and down and across. Cutting. Up. Down.

Up.

Think about the old man and the wheat in his hands when he died.

Down.

Think about this dead land, with wheat living on it.

Up.

Think about the crazy patterns of ripe and green wheat, the way it grows!

Down.

Think about . . .

The wheat whirled in a full yellow tide at his ankles. The sky blackened. Drew Erickson dropped the scythe and bent over to hold his stomach, his eyes running blindly. The world reeled.

"I've killed somebody!" he gasped, choking, holding his chest, falling to his knees beside the blade. "I've killed a lot—"

The sky revolved like a blue merry-go-round at the county fair in Kansas. But no music. Only a ringing in his ears.

Molly was sitting at the blue kitchen table peeling potatoes when he blundered into the kitchen, dragging the scythe behind him.

"Molly!"

She swam around in the wet of his eyes.

She sat there, her hands open, waiting for him to finally get it out.

"Get the things packed!" he said, looking at the floor.

"Why?"

"We're leaving," he said, dully.

"We're leaving?" she said.

"That old man. You know what he did here? It's the wheat, Molly, and this scythe. Every time you use the scythe on the wheat a thousand people die. You cut across them and—"

Molly got up and put the knife down and the potatoes to one side and said, understandingly, "We traveled a lot and haven't eaten good until the last month here, and you been workin' every day and you're tired—"

"I hear voices, sad voices, out there. In the wheat," he said. "Tellin' me to stop. Tellin' me not to kill them!"

"Drew!"

He didn't hear her. "The field grows crooked, wild, like a crazy thing. I didn't tell you. But it's wrong."

She stared at him. His eyes were blue glass, nothing else.

"You think I'm crazy," he said, "but wait 'til I tell you. Oh, God, Molly, help me; I just killed my mother!"

"Stop it!" she said firmly.

"I cut down one stalk of wheat and I killed her. I felt her dyin', that's how I found out just now—"

"Drew!" Her voice was like a crack across the face, angry and afraid now. "Shut up!"

He mumbled. "Oh—Molly—"

The scythe dropped from his hands, clamored on the floor. She picked it up with a snap of anger and set it in one corner. "Ten years I been with you," she said. "Sometimes we had nothin' but dust and prayers in our mouths. Now, all this good luck sudden, and you can't bear up under it!"

She brought the Bible from the living room.

She rustled its pages over. They sounded like the wheat rustling in a small, slow wind. "You sit down and listen," she said.

A sound came in from the sunshine. The kids, laughing in the shade of the large live oak beside the house.

She read from the Bible, looking up now and again to see what was happening to Drew's face.

She read from the Bible each day after that. The following Wednesday, a week later, when Drew walked down to the distant town to see if there was any General Delivery mail, there was a letter.

He came home looking two hundred years old.

He held the letter out to Molly and told her what it said in a cold, uneven voice.

"Mother passed away—one o'clock Tuesday afternoon—her heart—"

† † †

All that Drew Erickson had to say was, "Get the kids in the car, load it up with food. We're goin' on to California."

"Drew——" said his wife, holding the letter.

"You know yourself," he said, "this is poor grain land. Yet look how ripe it grows. I ain't told you all the things. It ripens in patches, a little each day. It ain't right. And when I cut it, it rots! And next mornin' it comes up without any help, growin' again! Last Tuesday, a week ago, when I cut the grain it was like rippin' my own flesh. I heard somebody scream. It sounded just like— And now, today, this letter."

She said, "We're stayin' here."

"Molly."

"We're stayin' here, where we're sure of eatin' and sleepin' and livin' decent and livin' long. I'm not starvin' my children down again, ever!"

The sky was blue through the windows. The sun slanted in, touching half of Molly's calm face, shining one eye bright blue. Four or five water drops hung and fell from the kitchen faucet slowly, shining, before Drew sighed. The sigh was husky and resigned and tired. He nodded, looking away. "All right," he said. "We'll stay."

He picked up the scythe weakly. The words on the metal leaped up with a sharp glitter.

WHO WIELDS ME—WIELDS THE WORLD!

"We'll stay. . . ."

† † †

Next morning he walked to the old man's grave. There was a single fresh sprout of wheat growing in the center of it. The same sprout, reborn, that the old man had held in his hands weeks before.

He talked to the old man, getting no answers.

"You worked the field all your life because you *had* to, and one day you came across your own life growin' there. You knew it was yours. You cut it. And you went home, put on your grave clothes, and your heart gave out and you died. That's how it was, wasn't it? And you passed the land on to me, and when I die, I'm supposed to hand it over to someone else."

Drew's voice had awe in it. "How long a time has this been goin' on? With nobody knowin' about this field and its use except the man with the scythe . . . ?"

Quite suddenly he felt very old. The valley seemed ancient, mummified, secretive, dried and bent and powerful. When the Indians danced on the prairie it had been here, this field. The same sky, the same wind, the same wheat. And, before the Indians? Some Cro-Magnon, gnarled and shag-haired, wielding a crude wooden scythe, perhaps, prowling down through the living wheat. . . .

Drew returned to work. Up, down. Up, down. Obsessed with the idea of being the wielder of *the* scythe. He, himself! It burst upon him in a mad, wild surge of strength and horror.

Up! WHO WIELDS ME! Down! WIELDS THE WORLD!

He had to accept the job with some sort of philosophy. It was simply his way of getting food and housing for his family. They deserved eating and living decent, he thought, after all these years.

Up and down. Each grain a life he neatly cut into two pieces. If he planned it carefully—he looked at the wheat—why, he and Molly and the kids could live forever!

Once he found the place where the grain grew that was Molly and Susie and little Drew he would never cut it.

And then, like a signal, it came, quietly.

Right there, before him.

Another sweep of the scythe and he'd cut them away.

Molly, Drew, Susie. It was certain. Trembling, he knelt and looked at the few grains of wheat. They glowed at his touch.

He groaned with relief. What if he had cut them down, never guessing? He blew out his breath and got up and took the scythe and stood back away from the wheat and stood for a long while looking down.

Molly thought it awfully strange when he came home early and kissed her on the cheek, for no reason at all.

† † †

At dinner, Molly said, "You quit early today? Does—does the wheat still spoil when it falls?"

He nodded and took more meat.

She said, "You ought to write to the Agriculture people and have them come look at it."

"No," he said.

"I was just suggestin'," she said.

His eyes dilated. "I got to stay here all my life. Can't nobody mess with that wheat; they wouldn't know where to cut and not to cut. They might cut the wrong parts."

"What wrong parts?"

"Nothin'," he said, chewing slowly. "Nothin' at all."

He slapped his fork down, hard. "Who knows *what* they might want to do! Those government men! They might even—might even want to plow the whole field under!"

Molly nodded. "That's just what it needs," she said. "And start all over again, with new seed."

He didn't finish eating. "I'm not writin' any gover'ment, and I'm not handin' this field over to no stranger to cut, and that's that!" he said, and the screen door banged behind him.

† † †

He detoured around that place where the lives of his children and his wife grew up in the sun, and used his scythe on the far end of the field where he knew he would make no mistakes.

But he no longer liked the work. At the end of an hour he knew he had brought death to three of his old, loved friends in Missouri. He read their names in the cut grain and couldn't go on.

He locked the scythe in the cellar and put the key away. He was done with the reaping, done for good and all.

† † †

He smoked his pipe in the evening, on the front porch, and told the kids stories to hear them laugh. But they didn't laugh much. They seemed withdrawn, tired and funny, like they weren't his children any more.

Molly complained of a headache, dragged around the house a little, went to bed early and fell into a deep sleep. That was funny, too. Molly always stayed up late and was full of vinegar.

The wheat field rippled with moonlight on it, making it into a sea.

It wanted cutting. Certain parts needed cutting *now*. Drew Erickson sat, swallowing quietly, trying not to look at it.

What'd happen to the world if he never went in the field again? What'd happen to people ripe for death, who waited the coming of the scythe?

He'd wait and see.

Molly was breathing softly when he blew out the oil lamp and got to bed. He couldn't sleep. He heard the wind in the wheat, felt the hunger to do the work in his arms and fingers.

In the middle of the night he found himself walking in the field, the scythe in his hands. Walking like a crazy man, walking and afraid, half-awake. He didn't remember unlocking the cellar door, getting the scythe, but here he was in the moonlight, walking in the grain.

Among these grains there were many who were old, weary, wanting so very much to sleep. The long, quiet, moonless sleep.

The scythe held him, grew into his palms, forced him to walk.

Somehow, struggling, he got free of it. He threw it down, ran off into the wheat, where he stopped and went down on his knees.

"I don't want to kill anymore," he said. "If I work with the scythe I'll have to kill Molly and the kids. Don't ask me to do that!"

The stars only sat in the sky, shining.

Behind him, he heard a dull, thumping sound.

Something shot up over the hill into the sky. It was like a living thing, with arms of red color, licking at the stars. Sparks fell into his face. The thick, hot odor of fire came with it.

The house!

Crying out, he got sluggishly, hopelessly, to his feet, looking at the big fire.

The little white house with the live oaks was roaring up in one savage bloom of fire. Heat rolled over the hill and he swam in it and went down in it, stumbling, drowning over his head.

By the time he got down the hill there was not a shingle, bolt or threshold of it that wasn't alive with flame. It made blistering, cracking, fumbling noises.

No one screamed inside. No one ran around or shouted.

He yelled in the yard."Molly! Susie! Drew!"

He got no answer. He ran close in until his eyebrows withered and his skin crawled hot like paper burning, crisping, curling up in tight little curls.

"Molly! Susie!"

The fire settled contentedly down to feed. Drew ran around the house a dozen times, all alone, trying to find a way in. Then he sat where the fire roasted his body and waited until all the walls had sunken down with fluttering crashes, until the last ceilings bent, blanketing the floors with molten plaster and scorched lathing. Until the flames died and smoke coughed up, and the new day came slowly; and there was nothing but embering ashes and an acid smoldering.

Disregarding the heat fanning from the leveled frames, Drew walked into the ruin. It was still too dark to see much. Red light glowed on his sweating throat. He stood like a stranger in a new and different land. Here— the kitchen. Charred tables, chairs, the iron stove, the cupboards. Here— the hall. Here the parlor and then over here was the bedroom where—

Where Molly was still alive.

She slept among fallen timbers and angry-colored pieces of wire spring and metal.

She slept as if nothing had happened. Her small white hands lay at her sides, flaked with sparks. Her calm face slept with a flaming lath across one cheek.

Drew stopped and didn't believe it. In the ruin of her smoking bedroom she lay on a glittering bed of sparks, her skin intact, her breast rising, falling, taking air.

"Molly!"

Alive and sleeping after the fire, after the walls had roared down, after ceilings had collapsed upon her and flame had lived all about her.

His shoes smoked as he pushed through piles of fuming litter. It could have seared his feet off at the ankles, he wouldn't have known.

"Molly . . ."

He bent over her. She didn't move or hear him, and she didn't speak. She wasn't dead. She wasn't alive. She just lay there with the fire surrounding her and not touching her, not harming her in any way. Her cotton nightgown was streaked with ashes, but not burnt. Her brown hair was pillowed on a tumble of red-hot coals.

He touched her cheek, and it was cold, cold in the middle of hell. Tiny breaths trembled her half-smiling lips.

The children were there, too. Behind a veil of smoke he made out two smaller figures huddled in the ashes sleeping.

He carried all three of them out to the edge of the wheat field.

"Molly. Molly, wake up! Kids! Kids, wake up!"

They breathed and didn't move and went on sleeping.

"Kids, wake up! Your mother is—"

Dead? No, not dead. But—

He shook the kids as if they were to blame. They paid no attention; they were busy with their dreams. He put them back down and stood over them, his face cut with lines.

He knew why they'd slept through the fire and continued to sleep now. He knew why Molly just lay there, never wanting to laugh again.

The power of the wheat and the scythe.

Their lives, supposed to end yesterday, May 30th, 1938, had been prolonged simply because he refused to cut the grain. They should have died in the fire. That's the way it was meant to *be*. But since he had not used the scythe, nothing could hurt them. A house had flamed and fallen and still they lived, caught halfway, not dead, not alive. Simply—waiting. And all over the world thousands more just like them, victims of accidents, fires, disease, suicide, waited, slept just like Molly and her children slept. Not able to die, not able to live. All because a man was afraid of harvesting the ripe grain. All because one man thought he could stop working with a scythe and never work with that scythe again.

He looked down upon the children. The job had to be done every day and every day with never stopping but going on, with never a pause, but always the harvesting, forever and forever and forever.

All right, he thought. All right. I'll use the scythe.

He didn't say good-by to his family. He turned with a slow-feeding anger and found the scythe and walked rapidly, then he began to trot, then he ran with long jolting strides into the field, raving, feeling the hunger in his arms, as the wheat whipped and flailed his legs. He pounded through it, shouting. He stopped.

"Molly!" he cried, and raised the blade and swung it down.

"Susie!" he cried. "Drew!" And swung the blade down again.

Somebody screamed. He didn't turn to look at the fire-ruined house.

And then, sobbing wildly, he rose above the grain again and again and hewed to left and right and to left and to right and to left and to right. Over and over and over! Slicing out huge scars in green wheat and ripe wheat, with no selection and no care, cursing, over and over, swearing, laughing, the blade swinging up in the sun and falling in the sun with a singing whistle! Down!

Bombs shattered London, Moscow, Tokyo.

The blade swung insanely.

And the kilns of Belsen and Buchenwald took fire.

The blade sang, crimson wet.

And mushrooms vomited out blind suns at White Sands, Hiroshima, Bikini, and up, through, and in continental Siberian skies.

The grain wept in a green rain, falling.

Korea, Indo-China, Egypt, India trembled; Asia stirred, Africa woke in the night. . . .

And the blade went on rising, crashing, severing, with the fury and the rage of a man who has lost and lost so much that he no longer cares what he does to the world.

Just a few short miles off the main highway, down a rough dirt road that leads to nowhere, just a few short miles from a highway jammed with traffic bound for California.

Once in a while during the long years a jalopy gets off the main highway, pulls up steaming in front of the charred ruin of a little white house at the end of the dirt road, to ask instructions from the farmer they see just beyond, the one who works insanely, wildly, without ever stopping, night and day, in the endless fields of wheat.

But they get no help and no answer. The farmer in the field is too busy, even after all these years; too busy slashing and chopping the green wheat instead of the ripe.

And Drew Erickson moves on with his scythe, with the light of blind suns and a look of white fire in his never-sleeping eyes, on and on and on. . . .

Afterword

Primitive people did not come to the natural conclusion that inanimate events were the product of inanimate forces. In the world around them, things happened because people made them happen. If things happened without human cause, then there must be some unseen superhuman cause.

The sun moved across the sky because it was a fiery chariot driven by a god. The lightning flashed because it was a vast spear thrown by a god. The wind blew because some god was puffing his cheeks.

This made all the more sense because some inanimate events, such as rainstorms and diseases, seemed to come and go arbitrarily, and what could be so whimsical and unpredictable as a human or superhuman agency.

Even death was superhumanized in this fashion. The Greek god of time, Kronos, was pictured with an hourglass and a scythe. The hourglass signified the passing of time, and the scythe signified death, since with time, human beings were inevitably cut down as grain was cut down by a scythe.

The Angel of Death, divorced from time, is a figure in many myth-systems. Thus, when God smote Israel with a plague, he did so by the hand of the Angel of Death. "And when the angel stretched out his hand upon Jerusalem to destroy it, the Lord repented him of the evil, and said to the angel that destroyed the people, It is enough" (2 Sam. 24:16).

Incidentally, an editor can't help having opinions. Of the stories in this book, this by Bradbury is the one I consider the best.—I.A.

Additional Reading

Robert Arthur, "The Crystal Bell," in *Ghosts and More Ghosts* (New York: Random House, 1963).

Oliver La Farge, "Spud and Cochice," in *A Pause in the Desert* (Boston: Houghton Mifflin, 1957).

M. P. Shiel, "Vaila," in *Shapes in the Fire: Being a Mid-Winter-Night's Entertainment in Two Parts and an Interlude* (London: John Lane, 1896).

Manly Wade Wellman, "His Name on a Bullet," in *Worse Things Waiting* (Chapel Hill, N.C.: Carcosa, 1973).

Henry S. Whitehead, "The Tree Man," in *Jumbee and Other Uncanny Tales* (Sauk City, Wisc.: Arkham House, 1944).

12

Personality Transfer

Arthur Conan Doyle
The Great Keinplatz Experiment

Of all the sciences which have puzzled the sons of men, none had such an attraction for the learned Professor von Baumgarten as those which relate to psychology and the ill-defined relations between mind and matter. A celebrated anatomist, a profound chemist, and one of the first physiologists in Europe, it was a relief for him to turn from these subjects and to bring his varied knowledge to bear upon the study of the soul and the mysterious relationship of spirits. At first, when as a young man he began to dip into the secrets of mesmerism, his mind seemed to be wandering in a strange land where all was chaos and darkness, save that here and there some great unexplainable and disconnected fact loomed out in front of him. As the years passed, however, and as the worthy Professor's stock of knowledge increased, for knowledge begets knowledge as money bears interest, much which had seemed strange and unaccountable began to take another shape in his eyes. New trains of reasoning became familiar to him, and he perceived connecting links where all had been incomprehensible and startling. By experiments which extended over twenty years, he obtained a basis of facts upon which it was his ambition to build up a new, exact science which should embrace mesmerism, spiritualism, and all cognate subjects. In this he was much helped by his intimate knowledge of the more intricate parts of animal physiology which treat of nerve currents and the working of the brain; for Alexis von Baumgarten was Regius Professor of Physiology at the University of Keinplatz, and had all the resources of the laboratory to aid him in his profound researches.

Professor von Baumgarten was tall and thin, with a hatchet face and steel-grey eyes, which were singularly bright and penetrating. Much thought had furrowed his forehead and contracted his heavy eyebrows, so that he appeared to wear a perpetual frown, which often misled people as to his character, for though austere he was tender-hearted. He was popular among the students, who would gather round him after his lectures and listen eagerly to his strange theories. Often he would call for volunteers from amongst them in order to conduct some experiment, so that eventually there was hardly a lad in the class who had not, at one time or another, been thrown into a mesmeric trance by his Professor.

Of all these young devotees of science there was none who equalled in enthusiasm Fritz von Hartmann. It had often seemed strange to his fellow-students that wild, reckless Fritz, as dashing a young fellow as ever hailed from the Rhinelands, should devote the time and trouble which he did in reading up abstruse works and in assisting the Professor in his strange experiments. The fact was, however, that Fritz was a knowing and long-headed fellow. Months before he had lost his heart to young Elise, the blue-eyed, yellow-haired daughter of the lecturer. Although he had succeeded in learning from her lips that she was not indifferent to his suit, he had never dared to announce himself to her family as a formal suitor. Hence he would have found it a difficult matter to see his young lady had he not adopted the expedient of making himself useful to the Professor. By this means he frequently was asked to the old man's house, where he willingly submitted to be experimented upon in any way as long as there was a chance of his receiving one bright glance from the eyes of Elise or one touch of her little hand.

Young Fritz von Hartmann was a handsome enough lad. There were broad acres, too, which would descend to him when his father died. To many he would have seemed an eligible suitor; but Madame frowned upon his presence in the house, and lectured the Professor at times on his allowing such a wolf to prowl around their lamb. To tell the truth, Fritz had an evil name in Keinplatz. Never was there a riot or a duel, or any other mischief afoot, but the young Rhinelander figured as a ringleader in it. No one used more free and violent language, no one drank more, no one played cards more habitually, no one was more idle, save in the one solitary subject. No wonder, then, that the good Frau Professorin gathered her Fräulein under her wing, and resented the attentions of such a *mauvais sujet*. As to the worthy lecturer, he was too much engrossed by his strange studies to form an opinion upon the subject one way or the other.

For many years there was one question which had continually obtruded itself upon his thoughts. All his experiments and his theories turned upon a single point. A hundred times a day the Professor asked himself whether it was possible for the human spirit to exist apart from the body for a time and then to return to it once again. When the possibility first suggested itself to him his scientific mind had revolted from it. It clashed too violently with preconceived ideas and the prejudices of his early training. Gradually, however, as he proceeded farther and farther along the pathway of original research, his mind shook off its old fetters and became ready to face any conclusion which could reconcile the facts. There were many things which made him believe that it was possible for mind to exist apart from matter. At last it occurred to him that by a daring and original experiment the question might be definitely decided.

"It is evident," he remarked in his celebrated article upon invisible entities, which appeared in the *Keinplatz wochenliche Medicalschrift* about this time, and which surprised the whole scientific world—"it is evident that under certain conditions the soul or mind does separate itself from the body. In the case of a mesmerised person, the body lies in a cataleptic condition, but the spirit has left it. Perhaps you reply that the soul is there, but in a dormant condition. I answer that this is not so, otherwise how can one account for the condition of clairvoyance, which has fallen into disrepute through the knavery of certain scoundrels, but which can easily be shown to be an undoubted fact. I have been able myself, with a sensitive subject, to obtain an accurate description of what was going on in another room or another house. How can such knowledge be accounted for on any hypothesis save that the soul of the subject has left the body and is wandering through space? For a moment it is recalled by the voice of the operator and says what it has seen, and then wings its way once more through the air. Since the spirit is by its very nature invisible, we cannot see these comings and goings, but we see their effect in the body of the subject, now rigid and inert, now struggling to narrate impressions which could never have come to it by natural means. There is only one way which I can see by which the fact can be demonstrated. Although we in the flesh are unable to see these spirits, yet our own spirits, could we separate them from the body, would be conscious of the presence of others. It is my intention, therefore, shortly to mesmerise one of my pupils. I shall then mesmerise myself in a manner which has become easy to me. After that, if my theory holds good, my spirit will have no difficulty in meeting and communing with the spirit of my pupil, both being separated from the body. I hope to be able to communicate the result of this interesting experiment in an early number of the *Keinplatz wochenliche Medicalschrift.*"

When the good Professor finally fulfilled his promise, and published an account of what occurred, the narrative was so extraordinary that it was received with general incredulity. The tone of some of the papers was so offensive in their comments upon the matter that the angry savant declared that he would never open his mouth again or refer to the subject in any way—a promise which he faithfully kept. This narrative has been compiled, however, from the most authentic sources, and the events cited in it may be relied upon as substantially correct.

It happened, then, that shortly after the time when Professor von Baumgarten conceived the idea of the above-mentioned experiment, he was walking thoughtfully homewards after a long day in the laboratory, when he met a crowd of roistering students who had just streamed out from a beer-house. At the head of them, half-intoxicated and very noisy, was young Fritz von Hartmann. The Professor would have passed them, but his pupil ran across and intercepted him.

"Heh! my worthy master," he said, taking the old man by the sleeve, and leading him down the road with him. "There is something that I have to say to you, and it is easier for me to say it now, when the good beer is humming in my head, than at another time."

"What is it, then, Fritz?" the physiologist asked, looking at him in mild surprise.

"I hear, mein Herr, that you are about to do some wondrous experiment in which you hope to take a man's soul out of his body, and then to put it back again. Is it not so?"

"It is true, Fritz."

"And have you considered, my dear sir, that you may have some difficulty in finding someone on whom to try this? Potztausend! Suppose that the soul went out and would not come back. That would be a bad business. Who is to take the risk?"

"But Fritz," the Professor cried, very much startled by this view of the matter, "I had relied upon your assistance in the attempt. Surely you will not desert me. Consider the honour and glory."

"Consider the fiddlesticks!" the student cried angrily. "Am I to be paid always thus? Did I not stand two hours upon a glass insulator while you poured electricity into my body? Have you not stimulated my phrenic nerves, besides ruining my digestion with a galvanic current round by stomach? Four-and-thirty times you have mesmerised me, and what have I got from all this? Nothing. And now you wish to take my soul out, as you would take the works from a watch. It is more than flesh and blood can stand."

"Dear, dear!" the Professor cried in great distress. "That is very true, Fritz. I never thought of it before. If you can but suggest how I can compensate you, you will find me ready and willing."

"Then listen," said Fritz solemnly. "If you will pledge your word that after this experiment I may have the hand of your daughter, then I am willing to assist you; but if not, I shall have nothing to do with it. These are my only terms."

"And what would my daughter say to this?" the Professor exclaimed, after a pause of astonishment.

"Elise would welcome it," the young man replied. "We have loved each other long."

"Then she shall be yours," the physiologist said with decision, "for you are a good-hearted young man, and one of the best neurotic subjects that I have ever known—that is when you are not under the influence of alcohol. My experiment is to be performed upon the fourth of next month. You will attend at the physiological laboratory at twelve o'clock. It will be a great occasion, Fritz. Von Gruben is coming from Jena, and Hinterstein from Basle. The chief men of science of all South Germany will be there."

"I shall be punctual," the student said briefly; and so the two parted. The Professor plodded homeward, thinking of the great coming event, while the young man staggered along after his noisy companions, with his mind full of the blue-eyed Elise, and of the bargain which he had concluded with her father.

The Professor did not exaggerate when he spoke of the widespread interest excited by his novel psychological experiment. Long before the hour had arrived the room was filled by a galaxy of talent. Besides the celebrities whom he had mentioned, there had come from London the great Professor Lurcher, who had just established his reputation by a remarkable treatise upon cerebral centres. Several great lights of the Spiritualistic body had also come a long distance to be present, as had a Swedenborgian minister, who considered that the proceedings might throw some light upon the doctrines of the Rosy Cross.

There was considerable applause from this eminent assembly upon the appearance of Professor von Baumgarten and his subject upon the platform. The lecturer, in a few well-chosen words, explained what his views were, and how he proposed to test them. "I hold," he said, "that when a person is under the influence of mesmerism, his spirit is for the time released from his body, and I challenge anyone to put forward any other hypothesis which will account for the fact of clairvoyance. I therefore hope that upon mesmerising my young friend here, and then putting myself into a trance, our spirits may be able to commune together, though our bodies lie still and inert. After a time nature will resume her sway, our spirits will return into our respective bodies, and all will be as before. With your kind permission, we shall now proceed to attempt the experiment."

The applause was renewed at this speech, and the audience settled down in expectant silence. With a few rapid passes the Professor mesmerised the young man, who sank back in his chair, pale and rigid. He then took a bright globe of glass from his pocket, and by concentrating his gaze upon it and making a strong mental effort, he succeeded in throwing himself into the same condition. It was a strange and impressive sight to see the old man and the young sitting together in the same cataleptic condition. Whither, then, had their souls fled? That was the question which presented itself to each and every one of the spectators.

Five minutes passed, and then ten, and then fifteen, and then fifteen more, while the Professor and his pupil sat stiff and stark upon the platform. During that time not a sound was heard from the assembled savants, but every eye was bent upon the two pale faces, in search of the first signs of returning consciousness. Nearly an hour had elapsed before the patient watchers were rewarded. A faint flush came back to the cheeks of Professor von Baumgarten. The soul was coming back once more to its earthly tenement. Suddenly he stretched out his long, thin arms, as one awaking from sleep, and rubbing his eyes, stood up from his chair and gazed about him as though he hardly realised where he was. "Tausend Teufel!" he exclaimed, rapping out a tremendous South German oath, to the great astonishment of his audience and to the disgust of the Swedenborgian.

"Where the *Henker* am I then, and what in thunder has occurred? Oh yes, I remember now. One of these nonsensical mesmeric experiments. There is no result this time, for I remember nothing at all since I became unconscious; so you have had all your long journeys for nothing, my learned friends, and a very good joke, too"; at which the Regius Professor of Physiology burst into a roar of laughter and slapped his thigh in a highly indecorous fashion. The audience were so enraged at this unseemly behaviour on the part of their host, that there might have been a considerable disturbance, had it not been for the judicious interference of young Fritz von Hartmann, who had now recovered from his lethargy. Stepping to the front of the platform, the young man apologized for the conduct of his companion.

"I am sorry to say," he said, "that he is a harum-scarum sort of fellow, although he appeared so grave at the commencement of this experiment. He is still suffering from mesmeric reaction, and is hardly accountable for his words. As to the experiment itself, I do not consider it to be a failure. It is very possible that our spirits may have been communing in space during this hour; but, unfortunately, our gross bodily memory is distinct from our spirit, and we cannot recall what has occurred. My energies shall now be devoted to devising some means by which spirits may be able to recollect what occurs to them in their free state, and I trust that when I have worked this out, I may have the pleasure of meeting you all once again in this hall, and demonstrating to you the result." This address, coming from so young a student, caused considerable astonishment among the audience, and some were inclined to be offended, thinking that he assumed rather too much importance. The majority, however, looked upon him as a young man of great promise, and many comparisons were made as they left the hall between his dignified conduct and the levity of his professor, who during the above remarks was laughing heartily in a corner, by no means abashed at the failure of the experiment.

Now although all these learned men were filing out of the lecture-room under the impression that they had seen nothing of note, as a matter fact one of the most wonderful things in the whole history of the world had just occurred before their eyes. Professor von Baumgarten had been so far correct in his theory that both his spirit and that of his pupil had been, for a time, absent from the body. But here a strange and unforeseen complication had occurred. In their return the spirit of Fritz von Hartmann had entered into the body of Alexis von Baumgarten, and that of Alexis von Baumgarten had taken up its abode in the frame of Fritz von Hartmann. Hence the slang and scurrility which issued from the lips of the serious Professor, and hence also the weighty words and grave statements which fell from the careless student. It was an unprecedented event, yet no one knew of it, least of all those whom it concerned.

The body of the Professor, feeling conscious suddenly of a great dryness about the back of the throat, sallied out into the street, still chuckling to himself over the result of the experiment, for the soul of Fritz within was reckless at the thought of the bride whom he had won so easily. His first impulse was to go up to the house and see her, but on second thoughts he came to the conclusion that it would be best to stay away until Madame Baumgarten should be informed by her husband of the agreement which had been made. He therefore made his way down to the Grüner Mann, which was one of the favourite trysting-places of the wilder students, and ran, boisterously waving his cane in the air, into the little parlour, where sat Spiegel and Müller and half a dozen other boon companions.

"Ha, ha! my boys," he shouted. "I knew I should find you here. Drink up, every one of you, and call for what you like, for I'm going to stand treat to-day."

Had the green man who is depicted upon the signpost of that well-known inn suddenly marched into the room and called for a bottle of wine, the students could not have been more amazed than they were by this unexpected entry of their revered professor. They were so astonished that for a minute or two they glared at him in utter bewilderment without being able to make any reply to his hearty invitation.

"Donner and Blitzen!" shouted the Professor angrily. "What the deuce is the matter with you, then? You sit there like a set of stuck pigs staring at me. What is it then?"

"It is the unexpected honour," stammered Spiegel, who was in the chair.

"Honour—rubbish!" said the Professor testily. "Do you think that just because I happen to have been exhibiting mesmerism to a parcel of old fossils, I am therefore too proud to associate with dear old friends like you? Come out of that chair, Spiegel, my boy, for I shall preside now. Beer, or wine, or schnapps, my lads—call for what you like, and put it all down to me."

Never was there such an afternoon in the Grüner Mann. The foaming flagons of lager and the green-necked bottles of Rhenish circulated merrily. By degrees the students lost their shyness in the presence of their Professor. As for him, he shouted, he sang, he roared, he balanced a long tobacco-pipe upon his nose, and offered to run a hundred yards against any member of the company. The Kellner and the barmaid whispered to each other outside the door their astonishment at such proceedings on the part of a Regius Professor of the ancient University of Keinplatz. They had still more to whisper about afterwards, for the learned man cracked the Kellner's crown, and kissed the barmaid behind the kitchen door.

"Gentlemen," said the Professor, standing up, albeit somewhat totteringly, at the end of the table, and balancing his high, old-fashioned wine glass in his bony hand, "I must now explain to you what is the cause of this festivity."

"Hear! hear!" roared the students, hammering their beer glasses against the table; "a speech, a speech!—silence for a speech!"

"The fact is, my friends," said the Professor, beaming through his spectacles, "I hope very soon to be married."

"Married!" cried a student, bolder than the others. "Is Madame dead, then?"

"Madame who?"

"Why, Madame von Baumgarten, of course."

"Ha, ha!" laughed the Professor; "I can see, then, that you know all about my former difficulties. No, she is not dead, but I have reason to believe that she will not oppose my marriage."

"That is very accommodating of her," remarked one of the company.

"In fact," said the Professor, "I hope that she will now be induced to aid me in getting a wife. She and I never took to each other very much; but now I hope all that may be ended, and when I marry she will come and stay with me."

"What a happy family!" exclaimed some wag.

"Yes, indeed; and I hope you will come to my wedding, all of you. I won't mention names, but here is to my little bride!" and the Professor waved his glass in the air.

"Here's to his little bride!" roared the roisterers, with shouts of laughter. "Here's her health. *Sie soll leben—Hoch!*" And so the fun waxed still more fast and furious, while each young fellow followed the Professor's example, and drank a toast to the girl of his heart.

While all this festivity had been going on at the Grüner Mann, a very different scene had been enacted elsewhere. Young Fritz von Hartmann, with a solemn face and a reserved manner, had, after the experiment, consulted and adjusted some mathematical instruments; after which, with a few peremptory words to the janitor, he had walked out into the street and wended his way slowly in the direction of the house of the Professor. As he walked he saw von Althaus, the professor of anatomy, in front of him, and quickening his pace, he overtook him.

"I say, von Althaus," he exclaimed, tapping him on the sleeve, "you were asking me for some information the other day concerning the middle coat of the cerebral arteries. Now I find—"

"Donnerwetter!" shouted von Althaus, who was a peppery old fellow. "What the deuce do you mean by your impertinence! I'll have you up before the Academical Senate for this, sir"; with which threat he turned on his heel and hurried away. Von Hartmann was much surprised at this reception. "It's on account of this failure of my experiment," he said to himself, and continued moodily on his way.

Fresh surprises were in store for him, however. He was hurrying along when he was overtaken by two students. These youths, instead of raising their caps or showing any other sign of respect, gave a wild whoop of delight the instant that they saw him, and rushing at him seized him by each arm and commenced dragging him along with them.

"Gott in Himmel!" roared von Hartmann. "What is the meaning of this unparalleled insult? Where are you taking me?"

"To crack a bottle of wine with us," said the two students. "Come along! That is an invitation which you have never refused."

"I never heard of such insolence in my life!" cried von Hartmann. "Let go my arms! I shall certainly have you rusticated for this. Let me go, I say!" and he kicked furiously at his captors.

"Oh, if you choose to turn ill-tempered, you may go where you like," the students said, releasing him. "We can do very well without you."

"I know you. I'll pay you out," said von Hartmann furiously, and continued in the direction which he imagined to be his own home, much incensed at the two episodes which had occurred to him on the way.

Now, Madame von Baumgarten, who was looking out of the window and wondering why her husband was late for dinner, was considerably astonished to see the young student come stalking down the road. As already remarked, she had a great antipathy to him, and if ever he ventured into the house it was on sufferance, and under the protection of the Professor. Still more astonished was she, therefore, when she beheld him undo the wicket-gate and stride up the garden path with the air of one who is master of the situation. She could hardly believe her eyes, and hastened to the door with all her maternal instincts up in arms. From the upper windows the fair Elise had also observed this daring move upon the part of her lover, and her heart beat quick with mingled pride and consternation.

"Good day, sir," Madame Baumgarten remarked to the intruder, as she stood in gloomy majesty in the open doorway.

"A very fine day indeed, Martha," returned the other. "Now, don't stand there like a statue of Juno, but bustle about and get the dinner ready, for I am well nigh starved."

"Martha! Dinner!" ejaculated the lady, falling back in astonishment.

"Yes, dinner, Martha, dinner!" howled von Hartmann, who was becoming irritable. "Is there anything wonderful in that request when a man has been out all day? I'll wait in the dining-room. Anything will do. *Schinken,* and sausage, and prunes—any little thing that happens to be about. There you are, standing staring again. Woman, will you or will you not stir your legs?"

This last address, delivered with a perfect shriek of rage, had the effect of sending good Madame Baumgarten flying along the passage and through the kitchen, where she locked herself up in the scullery and went into violent hysterics. In the meantime von Hartmann strode into the room and threw himself down upon the sofa in the worst of tempers.

"Elise!" he shouted. "Confound the girl! Elise!"

Thus roughly summoned, the young lady came timidly downstairs and into the presence of her lover. "Dearest!" she cried, throwing her arms round him, "I know this is all done for my sake! It is a *ruse* in order to see me."

Von Hartmann's indignation at this fresh attack upon him was so great that he became speechless for a minute from rage, and could only glare and shake his fists, while he struggled in her embrace. When he at last regained his utterance, he indulged in such a bellow of passion that the young lady dropped back, petrified with fear, into an arm-chair.

"Never have I passed such a day in my life," von Hartmann cried, stamping upon the floor. "My experiment has failed. Von Althaus has insulted me. Two students have dragged me along the public road. My wife nearly faints when I ask her for dinner, and my daughter flies at me and hugs me like a grizzly bear."

"You are ill, dear," the young lady cried. "Your mind is wandering. You have not even kissed me once."

"No, and I don't intend to either," von Hartmann said with decision. "You ought to be ashamed of yourself. Why don't you go and fetch my slippers, and help your mother to dish the dinner?"

"And is it for this," Elise cried, burying her face in her handkerchief— "is it for this that I have loved you passionately for upwards of ten months? Is it for this that I have braved my mother's wrath? Oh, you have broken my heart; I am sure you have!" and she sobbed hysterically.

"I can't stand much more of this," roared von Hartmann furiously. "What the deuce does the girl mean? What did I do ten months ago which inspired you with such a particular affection for me? If you are really so very fond, you would do better to run down and find the *Schinken* and some bread, instead of talking all this nonsense."

"Oh, my darling!" cried the unhappy maiden, throwing herself into the arms of what she imagined to be her lover, "you do but joke in order to frighten your little Elise."

Now it chanced that at the moment of this unexpected embrace von Hartmann was still leaning back against the end of the sofa, which, like much German furniture, was in a somewhat rickety condition. It also chanced that beneath this end of the sofa there stood a tank full of water in which the physiologist was conducting certain experiments upon the ova of fish, and which he kept in his drawing-room in order to ensure an equable temperature. The additional weight of the maiden combined with the impetus with which she hurled herself upon him, caused the precarious piece of furniture to give way, and the body of the unfortunate student was hurled backwards into the tank, in which his head and shoulders were firmly wedged, while his lower extremities flapped helplessly about in the air. This was the last straw. Extricating himself with some difficulty from his unpleasant position, von Hartmann gave an inarticulate yell of fury, and dashing out of the room, in spite of the entreaties of Elise, he seized his hat and rushed off into the town, all dripping and dishevelled, with the intention of seeking in some inn the food and comfort which he could not find at home.

As the spirit of von Baumgarten encased in the body of von Hartmann strode down the winding pathway which led down to the little town, brooding angrily over his many wrongs, he became aware that an elderly man was approaching him who appeared to be in an advanced state of intoxication. Von Hartmann waited by the side of the road and watched this individual, who came stumbling along, reeling from one side of the road to the other, and singing a student song in a very husky and drunken voice. At first his interest was merely excited by the fact of seeing a man of so venerable an appearance in such a disgraceful condition, but as he approached nearer, he became convinced that he knew the other well, though he could not recall when or where he had met him. This impression became so strong with him, that when the stranger came abreast of him he stepped in front of him and took a good look at his features.

"Well, sonny," said the drunken man, surveying von Hartmann and swaying about in front of him, "where the *Henker* have I seen you before? I know you as well as I know myself. Who the deuce are you?"

"I am Professor von Baumgarten," said the student. "May I ask who you are? I am strangely familiar with your features."

"You should never tell lies, young man," said the other. "You're certainly not the Professor, for he is an ugly, snuffy old chap, and you are a big, broad-shouldered young fellow. As to myself, I am Fritz von Hartmann at your service."

"That you certainly are not," exclaimed the body of von Hartmann. "You might very well be his father. But hullo, sir, are you aware that you are wearing my studs and my watch-chain?"

"*Donnerwetter!*" hiccoughed the other. "If those are not the trousers for which my tailor is about to sue me, may I never taste beer again."

Now as von Hartmann, overwhelmed by the many strange things which had occurred to him that day, passed his hand over his forehead and cast his eyes downwards, he chanced to catch the reflection of his own face in a pool which the rain had left upon the road. To his utter astonishment he perceived that his face was that of a youth, that his dress was that of a fashionable young student, and that in every way he was the antithesis of the grave and scholarly figure in which his mind was wont to dwell. In an instant his active brain ran over the series of events which had occurred and sprang to the conclusion. He fairly reeled under the blow.

"Himmel!" he cried, "I see it all. Our souls are in the wrong bodies. I am you and you are I. My theory is proved—but at what an expense! Is the most scholarly mind in Europe to go about with this frivolous exterior? Oh, the labours of a lifetime are ruined!" and he smote his breast in his despair.

"I say," remarked the real von Hartmann from the body of the Professor, "I quite see the force of your remarks, but don't go knocking my body about like that. You received it in excellent condition, but I perceive that you have wet it and bruised it, and spilled snuff over my ruffled shirt-front."

"It matters little," the other said moodily. "Such as we are so must we stay. My theory is triumphantly proved, but the cost is terrible."

"If I thought so," said the spirit of the student, "it would be hard indeed. What could I do with these stiff old limbs, and how could I woo Elise and persuade her that I was not her father? No, thank Heaven, in spite of the beer which has upset me more than ever it could upset my real self, I can see a way out of it."

"How?" gasped the Professor.

"Why, by repeating the experiment. Liberate our souls once more, and the chances are that they will find their way back into their respective bodies."

No drowning man could clutch more eagerly at a straw than did von Baumgarten's spirit at this suggestion. In ferverish haste he dragged his own frame to the side of the road and threw it into a mesmeric trance; he then extracted the crystal ball from the pocket, and managed to bring himself into the same condition.

Some students and peasants who chanced to pass during the next hour were much astonished to see the worthy Professor of Physiology and his favourite student both sitting upon a very muddy bank and both completely insensible. Before the hour was up quite a crowd had assembled, and they were discussing the advisability of sending for an ambulance to convey the pair to hospital, when the learned savant opened his eyes and gazed vacantly around him. For an instant he seemed to forget how he had come there, but next moment he astonished his audience by waving his skinny arms above his head and crying out in a voice of rapture, *"Gott sei gedanket! I am myself again. I feel I am!"* Nor was the amazement lessened when the student, springing to his feet, burst into the same cry, and the two performed a sort of *pas de joie* in the middle of the road.

For some time after that people had some suspicion of the sanity of both the actors in this strange episode. When the Professor published his experiences in the *Medicalshrift* as he had promised, he was met by an intimation, even from his colleagues, that he would do well to have his mind cared for, and that another such publication would certainly consign him to a madhouse. The student also found by experience that it was wisest to be silent about the matter.

When the worthy lecturer returned home that night he did not receive the cordial welcome which he might have looked for after his strange adventures. On the contrary, he was roundly upbraided by both his female relatives for smelling of drink and tobacco, and also for being absent while a young scapegrace invaded the house and insulted its occupants. It was long before the domestic atmosphere of the lecturer's house resumed its normal quiet, and longer still before the genial face of von Hartmann was seen beneath its roof. Perseverance, however, conquers every obstacle, and the student eventually succeeded in pacifying the enraged ladies and in establishing himself upon the old footing. He has now no longer any cause to fear the enmity of Madame, for he is Hauptmann von Hartmann of the Emperor's own Uhlans, and his loving wife Elise had already presented him with two little Uhlans as visible sign and token of her affection.

Afterword

There is a great temptation to distinguish between one's body and one's self. After all, you can lose parts of your body—your teeth, your eyes, your limbs—and still live and be you.

The body, it might seem, is only a form of clothing, a living house, and somewhere inside that clothing, that house, is the something or other that represents the "I." (When I was young, I used to concentrate deeply and try to penetrate to the "I" that lived inside my body, or even perhaps inside my brain, and once, for an exciting moment, I thought I had it—but I didn't.)

This "I," the real individual within the body, can be called an "ego," if you feel like Latin, or the "mind," if you're psychological, or the "soul," if you're in a theological mood; but whatever you call it, it can easily seem to people to be more real than the body.

(To me it seems likely that what makes up the "I" is the complex organization of the fifty trillion cells of the body and of the trillions of molecules within the cells; that death is the disruption of that organization; and that the "I" dies as irrevocably as the body. In fact, the "I" may die when the body is, in almost all its essentials, apparently still intact.)

Nevertheless, to those who find the "I" something immaterial that exists apart from the body, it would seem natural that there might be some way in which the "I"s of two different bodies can be interchanged with, in the case of Doyle's tale, comic results.

"Keinplatz," by the way, is German for "no place."—I.A.

Additional Reading

Isak Dinesen, "The Monkey," in *Seven Gothic Tales* (London: Putnam, 1934).

Jerome K. Jerome, "The Soul of Nicholas Snyders," in *The Passing of the Third Floor Back* (New York: Dodd, Mead, 1908).

Gerald Kersh, "Fantasy of a Hunted Man," in *On an Odd Note* (New York: Ballantine Books, 1958).

H. P. Lovecraft, "The Thing on the Doorstep," in *Best Supernatural Stories of H. P. Lovecraft* (Cleveland, Ohio and New York: World Publishing Co., 1945).

Mary Shelley, "The Transformation," in *Collected Tales and Stories,* Charles E. Robinson, ed. (Baltimore and London: Johns Hopkins University Press, 1976).

13

Possession

Fritz Leiber
Do You Know Dave Wenzel?

When Don Senior said, "There's the bell," and pushed back his chair, Wendy had just upset her bowl, John's hand was creeping across the edge of his plate to join forces with his spoon, and Don Junior had begun to kick the table leg as he gazed into space at an invisible adventure comic.

Katherine spared Don Senior a glance from the exacting task of getting the top layer of mashed carrots back into the bowl while holding off Wendy's jumpy little paws. "I didn't even hear it," she said.

"I'll answer it," Don Senior told her.

Three minutes later Wendy's trancelike spoon-to-mouth routine was operating satisfactorily, John's hand had made a strategic withdrawal, and the rest of the carrots had been wiped up. Don Junior had quietly gone to the window and was standing with his head poked between the heavy rose drapes looking out across the dark lawn—perhaps at more of the invisible adventure, Katherine thought. She watched him fondly. *Little boys are so at the mercy of their dreams. When the "call" comes, they have to answer it. Girls are different.*

Don seemed rather thoughtful when he came back to the table. Suddenly like Don Junior, it occurred to Katherine.

"Who was it, dear?"

He looked at her for a moment, oddly, before replying.

"An old college friend."

"Didn't you invite him in?"

He shook his head, glancing at the children. "He's gone down in the world a long way," he said softly. "Really pretty disreputable."

Katherine leaned forward on her elbows. "Still, if he was once a friend—"

"I'm afraid you wouldn't like him," he said decisively, yet it seemed to Katherine with a shade of wistfulness.

"Did I ever meet him?" she asked.

"No. His name's Dave Wenzel."

"Did he want to borrow money?"

Don seemed not to hear that question. Then, "Money? Oh no!"

"But what did he want to see you about?"

Don didn't answer. He sat frowning.

The children had stopped eating. Don Junior turned from the window. The drapes dropped together behind him.

"Did he go away, Dad?" Don Junior asked.

"Of course."

"But I didn't see him go."

It was quiet for several moments. Then Don Senior said, "He must have cut around the other side of the house."

"How strange," Katherine said. Then, smiling quickly at the children, she asked, "Have you ever seen him since college, Don?"

"Not since the day I graduated."

"Let's see, how long is that?" She made a face of dismay, mockingly. "Oh Lord, it's getting to be a long time. Fourteen, fifteen years. And this is the same month."

Again her husband looked at her intently. "As it happens," he said, "it's exactly the same day."

† † †

When Katherine dropped in at her husband's office the next morning, she was thinking about the mysterious Mr. Wenzel. Not because the incident had stuck in her mind particularly, but because it had been recalled by a chance meeting on the train coming up to town, with another college friend of her husband.

Katherine felt good. It is pleasant to meet an old beau and find that you still attract him and yet have the reassuring knowledge that all the painful and exciting uncertainties of youth are done with.

How lucky I am to have Don, she thought. *Other wives have to worry about women (I wonder how Carleton Hare's wife makes out?) and failure (Is Mr. Wenzel married?) and moods and restlessness and a kind of little-boy rebelliousness against the business of living. But Don is different. So handsome, yet so true. So romantic, yet so regular. He has a quiet heart.*

She greeted the secretary. "Is Mr. McKenzie busy?"

"He has someone with him now. A Mr. Wenzel, I think."

Katherine did not try to conceal her curiosity. "Oh, tell me about him, would you? What does he look like?"

"I really don't know," Miss Korshak said, smiling. "Mr. McKenzie told me there would be a Mr. Wenzel to see him, and I think he came in a few minutes ago, while I was away from the desk. I know Mr. McKenzie has a visitor now, because I heard him talking to someone. Shall I ring your husband, Mrs. McKenzie?"

"No, I'll wait a while." Katherine sat down and pulled off her gloves.

A few minutes later Miss Korshak picked up some papers and went off. Katherine wandered to the door of her husband's office. She could hear his voice every now and then, but she couldn't make out what he was saying. The panel of frosted glass showed only vague masses of light and shadow. She felt a sudden touch of uneasiness. She lifted her hand, which was dusted with freckles almost the same shade as her hair, and knocked.

All sound from beyond the door ceased. Then there were footsteps and the door opened.

Don looked at her blankly for a moment. Then he kissed her.

She went ahead of him into the gray-carpeted office.

"But where is Mr. Wenzel?" she asked, turning to him with a gesture of half-playful amazement.

"He just happened to be finished," Don said lightly, "so he left by the hall door."

"He must be an unusually shy person—and very quiet," Katherine said. "Don, did you arrange with him last night to come and see you here?"

"In a way."

"What is he after, Don?"

Her husband hesitated. "I suppose you could describe him as a kind of crank."

"Does he want to publish some impossible article in your magazine?"

"No, not exactly." Don grimaced and waved a hand as if in mild exasperation. "Oh, you know the type, dear. The old college friend who's a failure and who wants to talk over old times. The sort of chap who gets a morbid pleasure out of dwelling on old ideas and reviving old feelings. Just a born botherer." And he quickly went on to ask her about her shopping, and she mentioned running into Carleton Hare, and there was no more talk of Dave Wenzel.

But when Katherine got home later that afternoon after picking up the children at Aunt Martha's, she found that Don had called to say not to wait dinner. When he finally did get in he looked worried. As soon as the children were asleep, Don and Katherine settled themselves in the living room in front of the fireplace. Don made a fire, and the sharp odor of burning hardwood mingled with the scent of freesias set in a dull blue bowl on the mantlepiece under the Monet.

As soon as the flames were leaping, Katherine asked seriously, "Don, what is this thing about Dave Wenzel?"

He started to make light of the question, but she interrupted, "No, really, Don. Ever since you came back from the door last night, you've had something on your mind. And it isn't at all like you to turn away old friends or shoo them out of your office, even if they have become a bit seedy. What is it, Don?"

"It's nothing to worry about, really."

"I'm not worried, Don. I'm just curious." She hesitated. "And maybe a bit shuddery."

"Shuddery?"

"I have an eerie feeling about Wenzel, perhaps because of the way he disappeared so quietly both times, and then—oh, I don't know, but I do want to know about him, Don."

He looked at the fire for a while and its flames brought orange tints to his skin. Then he turned to her with a shame-faced smile and said, "Oh, I don't mind telling you about it. Only it's pretty silly. And it makes me look silly, too."

"Good," she said with a laugh, turning toward him on the couch and drawing her feet under her. "I've always wanted to hear something silly about you, Don."

"I don't know," he said. "You might even find it a little disgusting. And very small-boy. You know, swearing oaths and all that."

She had a flash of inspiration. "You mean the business of it being fifteen years, to the exact day?"

He nodded. "Yes, that was part of it. There was some sort of agreement between us. A compact."

"Oh good, a mystery," she said with lightly mocked childishness, not feeling as secure as she pretended.

He paused. He reached along the couch and took her hand. "You must remember," he said, squeezing it, "that the Don McKenzie I'm going to tell you about is not the Don McKenzie you know now, not even the one you married. He's a different Don, younger, much less experienced, rather shy and gauche, lonely, a great dreamer, with a lot of mistaken ideas about life and a lot of crazy notions . . . of all sorts."

"I'll remember," she said, returning the pressure of his fingers. "And Dave Wenzel, how am I to picture him?"

"About my age, of course. But with a thinner face and deep-sunk eyes. He was my special friend." He frowned. "You know, you have your ordinary friends in college, the ones you room with, play tennis, go on dates. They're generally solid and reliable, your kind. But then there's a special friend, and oddly enough he's not so apt to be solid and reliable."

Again he frowned. "I don't know why, but he's apt to be a rather disreputable character, someone you're a bit ashamed of and wouldn't want your parents to meet.

"But he's more important to you than anyone, because he shares your crazier dreams and impulses. In fact, you're probably attracted to him in the first place because you feel he possesses those dreams and impulses even more strongly than you do."

"I think I understand," Katherine said wisely, not altogether certain that she did. She heard Don Junior call in his sleep and she listened a moment and looked attentively at her husband. *How extraordinarily bright his eyes are,* she thought.

"Dave and I would have long bull sessions in my room and we'd go for long walks at night, all over the campus, down by the lake front, and through the slum districts. And always the idea between us was to keep alive a wonderful, glamorous dream. Sometimes we'd talk about the books we liked and the weirder things we'd seen. Sometimes we'd make up crazy experiences and tell them to each other as if they were true. But mostly we'd talk about our ambitions, the amazing, outrageous things we were going to do someday."

"And they were—?"

He got up and began to pace restlessly. "That's where it begins to get so silly," he said. "We were going to be great scholars and at the same time we were going to tramp all over the world and have all sorts of adventures."

How like Don Junior, she thought. *But Don Junior's so much younger. When he goes to college, will he still . . . ?*

"We were going to experience danger and excitement in every form. I guess we were going to be a couple of Casanovas, too."

Her humorous "Hmf!" was lost as he hurried on, and despite herself, his words began to stir her imagination. "We were going to do miraculous things with our minds, like a mystic does. Telepathy. Clairvoyance. We were going to take drugs. We were going to find out some great secret that's been hidden ever since the world began. I think if Dave said, 'We'll go to the moon, Don,' I'd have believed him."

He came to a stop in front of the fire. Slitting his eyes, he said slowly, as if summing up, "We were like knights preparing to search for some modern, unknown, and rather dubious grail. And someday in the course of our adventuring we were going to come face to face with the reality behind life and death and time and all those other big ideas."

For a moment, for just a moment, Katherine seemed to feel the spinning world under her and, as if the walls and ceiling had faded, to see her husband's big-shouldered body jutting up against a background of black space and stars.

She thought, *Never before has he seemed so wonderful. And never so frightening.*

He shook his finger at her, almost angrily, she felt. "And then one night, one terrible night before I graduated, we suddenly saw just how miserably weak we were, how utterly impossible of realizing the tiniest of our ambitions. There we were, quite floored by all the minor problems of money and jobs and independence and sex, and dreaming of the sky! We realized that we'd have to establish ourselves in the world, learn how to deal with people, become seasoned men of action, solve all the minor problems, before we could ever tackle the big quest. We gave ourselves fifteen years to bring all those small things under control. Then we were to meet and get going."

Katherine didn't know it was going to happen, but she suddenly started to laugh, almost hysterically. "Excuse me, dear," she mangaged to say after a moment, noting Don's puzzled expression, "but you and your friend did so get the cart before the horse! Back then you had a chance for some adventure, at least you were free. But you had to go and pick on the time when you'd be most tied down." And she started to laugh again.

For an instant Don looked hurt, then he began to laugh with her. "Of course, dear, I understand all that now, and it seems the most ridiculous thing in the world to me. When I opened the door last night and saw Dave standing there expectantly in a sleazy coat, with a lot less hair than I remembered, I was completely dumbfounded. Of course I'd forgotten about our compact years ago, long before you and I were married."

She started to laugh again. "And so I was one of your minor problems, Don?" she asked teasingly.

"Of course not, dear!" He pulled her up from the couch and hugged her boisterously. Katherine quickly closed her mind to the thought *He's changed since I laughed—he's shut something up inside him,* and welcomed the sense of security that flooded back into her at his embrace.

When they were settled again, she said, "Your friend must have been joking when he came around last night. There are people who will wait years for a laugh."

"No, he was actually quite serious."

"I can't believe it. Incidentally, just how well has he done at fulfilling his end of the bargain—I mean, establishing himself in the world?"

"Not well at all. In fact, so badly that, as I say, I didn't want him in the house last night."

"Then I'll bet it's the financial backing for this quest that he's thinking about."

"No, I honestly don't think he's looking for money."

Katherine leaned toward him. She was suddenly moved by the old impulse to measure every danger, however slight. "Tell you what, Don. You get your friend to spruce up a bit and we'll invite him to dinner. Maybe arrange a couple of parties. I'll bet that if he met some women it would make all the difference."

"Oh no, that's out of the question," Don said sharply. "He isn't that sort of person at all. It wouldn't work."

"Very well," Katherine said, shrugging. "But in that case how are you going to get rid of him?"

"Oh, that'll be easy," Don said.

"How did he take it when you refused?"

"Rather hard," Don admitted.

"I still can't believe he was serious."

Don shook his head. "You don't know Dave."

Katherine caught hold of his hand. "Tell me one thing," she said. "How seriously, how really seriously, did you take this . . . compact, when you made it?"

He looked at the fire before he said, "I told you I was a different Don McKenzie then."

"Don," she said, and her voice dropped a little, "is there anything dangerous about this? Is Dave altogether honorable—or sane? Are you going to have any trouble getting rid of him?"

"Of course not, dear! I tell you it's all done with." He caught her in his arms. But for a moment Katherine felt that his voice, though hearty, lacked the note of complete certainty.

† † †

And during the next few days she had reason to think that her momentary feeling had been right. Don stayed late at the office a little more often than usual, and twice when she called him during the day, he was out and Miss Korshak didn't know where to locate him. His explanations, given casually, were always very convincing, but he didn't look well and he'd acquired a nervous manner. At home he began to answer the phone ahead of her, and one or two of the conversations he held over it were cryptic.

Even the children, Katherine felt, had caught something of the uneasiness.

She found herself studying Don Junior rather closely, looking for traits that might increase her understanding of his father. She went over in her mind what she knew of Don Senior's childhood and was bothered at how little there was. (*But isn't that true of many city childhoods?* she asked herself.) Just a good, conscientious boy, brought up mostly by two rather stuffy yet emotional aunts. The only escapade she remembered hearing about was once when he'd stayed at a movie all afternoon and half the night.

She was up against the realization that a whole section of her husband's thoughts were locked off from her. And since this had never happened before she was frightened. Don loved her as much as ever, she was sure of that. But something was eating at him.

Weren't success and a loving wife and children, she wondered, enough for a man? Enough in a serious way, that is, for anyone might have his frivolities, his trivial weaknesses (though actually Don had neither). Or was there something more, something beyond that? Not religion, not power, not fame, but . . .

† † †

She badly needed more people around, so when Carleton Hare called up she impulsively invited him to dinner. His wife, Carleton said, was out of town.

It was one of those evenings when Don called up at the last minute to say he wouldn't be able to get home for dinner. (No, he couldn't make it even for Carleton—something had come up at the printer's. Awfully glad Carleton had come, though. Hoped very much to see him later in the evening, but might be very late—don't wait up.)

After the children were shepherded off and Katherine and Carleton had paraded rather formally into the living room, she asked, "Did you know a college friend of Don's named Dave Wenzel?"

Katherine got the impression that her question had thrown Carleton off some very different line of conversation he had been plotting in his mind. "No, I didn't," he said a little huffily. "Name's a bit familiar, but I don't think I ever met the man."

But then he seemed to reconsider. He turned toward Katherine, so that the knees of his knife-creased gray trousers were a few inches closer to hers along the couch.

"Wait a minute," he said, "Don did have an odd friend of some sort. I think his name may have been Wenzel. Don sometimes bragged about him—how brilliant this man was, what wild exciting experiences he'd had. But somehow, none of us fellows ever met him.

"I hope you won't mind my saying this," he continued with a boyish chuckle that startled Katherine a bit, it was so perfect. "But Don was rather shy and moody at college, not very successful socially and inclined to be put out about it. Some of us even thought this friend of his—yes, I'm sure the name was Wenzel—was just an imaginary person he'd cooked up in his mind to impress us with."

"You did?" Katherine asked.

"Oh yes. Once we insisted on his bringing this Wenzel around to a party. He agreed, but then it turned out that Wenzel had left town on some mysterious and important jaunt."

"Mightn't it have been that he was ashamed of Wenzel for some reason?" Katherine asked.

"Yes, I suppose it might," Carleton agreed doubtfully. "Tell me, Kat," he went on, "how do you get along with a moody, introspective person like Don?"

"Very well."

"Are you happy?" Carleton asked, his voice a little deeper.

Katherine smiled. "I think so."

Carleton's hand, moving along the couch, covered hers. "Of course you are," he said. "An intelligent, well-balanced person like yourself wouldn't be anything else but happy. But how vivid is that happiness? How often, for instance, do you realize what a completely charming woman you are? Aren't there times—not all the time, of course—when, with a simpler, more vital sort of person, you could. . . ."

She shook her head, looking into his eyes with a childlike solemnity. "No, Carleton, there aren't," she said, gently withdrawing her hand from under his.

Carleton blinked, and his head, which had been moving imperceptibly toward hers, stopped with a jerk. Katherine's lips twitched and she started to talk about the children.

During the rest of the evening Carleton didn't by any means give up the attack. But he carried it on in an uninspired fashion, as if merely to comply with the tenets of male behavior. Katherine wanted to burst out laughing, he was so solemn and dogged about it, and once he caught her smiling at him rather hysterically, and he put on an injured look. She tried to pump him, rather cruelly, she felt, about Dave Wenzel and Don, but he apparently knew nothing beyond what he had told her. He left rather early. Katherine couldn't help suspecting that he was relieved to go.

She went to bed. Her somewhat sorry amusement at Carleton Hare faded. The minutes dragged on, as she waited for Don.

A voice woke her. A mumbling distant voice. She was hot with sleep and the dark walls of the bedroom pulsated painfully, as if they were inside her eyes.

At first she thought it was Don Junior. She felt her way into the hall. Then she realized that the voice was coming from downstairs. It would go on for a while, rising a bit, then it would break off several seconds before starting again. It seemed to pulsate with the darkness.

She crept downstairs barefooted. The house was dark. Dimly she could see the white rectangle of the door to Don's study. It was closed and no light showed through the cracks. Yet it was from there that the voice seemed to be coming.

"For the last time I tell you, Dave, I won't. Yes, I've gone back on my word, but I don't care. The whole thing is off."

Katherine's hand trembled on the smooth round of the stair post. It was Don's voice, but tortured, frantic, and yet terribly controlled, like she had never heard it before.

"What's a promise made by a child? Besides, the whole thing's ridiculous, impossible."

She tiptoed toward the door, step by step.

"All right then, Dave, I believe you. We could do everything you say. But I don't want to. I'm going to hold fast to my own."

Now she was crouching by the door and she still couldn't hear the answering voice in the silences. But her imagination supplied it: a whisper that had strength in it, and richness, and mockery, and a certain oily persuasiveness.

"What do I care if my life is drab and monotonous?" Her husband's voice was growing louder. "I tell you I don't want the far cities, and dark streets shimmering with danger. I don't want the gleaming nights and the burning days. I don't want space. I don't want the stars!"

Again silence, and again that suggestion of a resonant whisper, adrip with beauty and evil.

Then, "All right, so the people I know are miserable little worms, men of cardboard and dusty, dry-mouthed puppets. I don't mind. Do you understand, I don't mind! I don't want to meet the people whose emotions are jewels, whose actions are sculptured art. I don't want to know the men like gods. I don't want my mind to meet their minds with a crash like music or the sea."

Katherine was trembling again. Her hand went up and down the door like a moth, hovering, not quite touching it.

"So my mind's small, is it? Well, let it be. Let someone else's consciousness swell and send out tentacles. I don't want the opium dreams. I don't want the more-than-opium dream. I don't care if I never glimpse the great secrets of far shores. I don't care if I die with blinders over my eyes. I don't care, do you hear, I don't care!"

Katherine swayed, as if a great wind were blowing through the door. She writhed as if each word scalded her.

"But I tell you I don't want any woman but Kat!" Her husband's voice was filled with agony. "I don't care how young and beautiful they are. I don't care if they're only twenty. Kat's enough for me. Do you hear that, Dave? Kat's enough. Dave! Stop it, Dave! Stop it!"

There was pounding. Katherine realized she had thrown herself against the door and was beating on it. She grabbed the knob, snatched it open, and darted inside.

There was a whirling of shadows, a gasping exclamation, three pounding footsteps, a great crash of glass, a whish of leaves. Something struck her shoulder and she staggered sideways, found the wall, groped along it, pushed the light switch.

The light hurt. In it, Don's face looked peeled. He was turning back from the big picture window, now a jagged hole of darkness through which the cool night was pouring and a green twig intruded. In it, only a few daggers and corners of glass remained. A chair lay on the floor, overturned. Don stared at her as if she were a stranger.

"Did he . . . jump out?" she asked shakily, wetting her lips.

Don nodded blindly. Then a look of rage grew on his face. He started toward her, taking deliberate steps, swaying a little.

"Don!"

He stopped. Slowly recognition replaced rage. Then he suddenly grimaced with what might have been shame or agony, or both, and turned away.

She moved to him quickly, putting her arms around him. "Oh, what is it, Don?" she said. "Please, Don, let me help you."

He shrank away from her.

"Don," she said hollowly after a moment, forcing the words, "if you really want to go off with this man. . . ."

His back, turned to her, writhed. "No! No!"

"But then what is it, Don? How can he make you act this way? What sort of hold does he have on you?"

He shook his head hopelessly.

"Tell me, Don, please, how can he torment you so? Oh please, Don!"

Silence.

"But what are we going to do, Don? He . . . oh he must be insane," she said, looking uneasily at the window, "to do a thing like that. Will he come back? Will he lurk around? Will he . . . oh, don't you see, Don, we can't have it like that. There are the children. Don, I think we should call the police."

He looked around quickly, his face quite calm. "Oh no, we can't do that," he said quietly. "Under no circumstances."

"But if he keeps on. . . ."

"No," Don said, looking at her intently. "I'll settle the whole matter, myself, Kat. I don't want to talk about it now, but I promise you that it will be settled. And there will be no more incidents like tonight. You have my word on it." He paused. "Well, Kat?"

For a moment she met his eyes. Then, unwillingly—she had the queer feeling that it was the pressure of his stare that made her do it—she dipped her head.

† † †

During the next two weeks there were many times when she desperately wished she had insisted on bringing things to a head that night, for it marked the beginning of a reign of terror that was all the more unnerving because it could not be laid to any very definite incidents. Shadows on the lawn, small noises at the windows, the suggestion of a lurking figure, doors open that should be closed—there is nothing conclusive about such things. But they nibble at courage.

The children felt it, of that Katherine was sure. Don Junior started asking questions about witches and horrors, and he wasn't quite so brave about going upstairs at night. Sometimes she caught him looking at her or at his father in a way that made her wish she didn't have to be so untroubled and cheerful in his presence and could talk to him more freely.

John came to share their bed more often in the middle of the night, and Wendy would wake whimpering.

Don's behavior was very reassuring for the first few days. He was brisk and businesslike, not moody at all, and had an unusually large supply of jokes for the children and of complimentary remarks for her—though Katherine couldn't shake the feeling that these were all carefully prepared and cost him considerable effort. But she couldn't get near him. He showed an artfulness quite unlike his ordinary self at avoiding serious discussions. The two or three times she finally blurted out some question about Dave Wenzel or his feelings, he would only frown and say quickly, "Please don't let's talk about it now. It only makes it harder for me."

She tried to think herself close to him, but when a contact between you and the man you love is broken, thoughts aren't much help. And when you feel that the love is still there, that only makes it the more baffling, for it leaves you nothing to bite against. Don was slipping away from her. He was growing dim. And there was nothing she could do to stop it.

And always the long brittle train of her thoughts would be snapped by some small but ominous incident that set her nerves quivering.

Then the reassuring aspects of Don's behavior began to fade. He became silent and preoccupied, both with her and with the children. His emotions began to show in his face—gloomy, despairing ones, they seemed. The children noticed that, too. At dinner Katherine's heart would sink when she saw Don Junior's glance lift surreptitiously from his plate to his father. And Don didn't look at all well, either. He got thinner and there were dark circles under his eyes, and his movements became fretful and nervous.

He had a habit, too, of staying near the hall when he was at home, so that it was always he who answered the door as well as the telephone.

Sometimes he'd go out late at night, saying he was restless and needed a walk. He might be home in fifteen minutes—or four hours.

Still Katherine made efforts to get through to him. But he seemed to sense what she was going to say, and the look of pain and misery on his face would choke off her question.

Finally she could stand her fear and uncertainty no longer. It was something Don Junior told her that gave her courage to act. He came home from school with a story of a man who had been standing outside the playground at recess and who had walked behind him on the way home.

That evening before dinner, she went to Don and said simply, "I am going to call the police."

He looked at her closely for several seconds and then replied in as calm a voice as hers, "Very well; I only ask you to wait until tomorrow morning."

"It's no use, Don," she said. "I've got to do it. Since you won't tell me what this cloud is that's hanging over you, I must take my own precautions. I don't know what you'll tell the police when they talk to you, but. . . ."

"I'll tell them everything," he said, "tomorrow morning."

"Oh, Don," she said, stiffening her face to hold back emotion. "I don't want to hurt you, but you leave me nothing else to do. I gave in to you before; I gave you time to settle the matter in your own way. I was willing to let whatever it is be a closed door, so long as it was closed, but things have only got worse. If I give in to you now, you'll ask me to give in to you again tomorrow morning. And I can't stand any more of it."

"That's not fair," he said judiciously. "I never set a date before. I am setting one now. It's a very small thing I'm asking of you, Kat. Just a few more hours in which to"—suddenly his face grew very hard—"settle this matter for once and all. Please give me those hours, Kat."

After a moment she sighed and her shoulders slumped. "Very well," she said. "Except I won't have the children in the house tonight. I'll take them to Aunt Martha's."

"That's quite all right," he said. He bowed his head to her and walked up the stairs.

†   †   †

Calling Aunt Martha, spinning an explanation for her, convincing the children that this was the jolliest of impromptu expeditions—these were tasks that Katherine welcomed for the momentary relief they gave. And there were a couple of moments, driving over to Martha's with the children all piled in the front seat beside her, when she felt almost carefree.

She drove home immediately, after repeating to Aunt Martha her story of a sudden invitation she and Don had gotten to a city party given by a publisher whose favor Don particularly courted. When she arrived, Don was gone.

The house had never seemed so empty, so like a trap. But as she crossed the threshold, she gave over the control of herself to that same cold willpower she had depended on earlier that evening in talking to Don. She didn't wander through the house; she didn't let herself stand aimlessly for a moment. She picked up a book and sat down with it in the living room, reading the meaningless words carefully. She did not let her gaze stray occasionally toward the dark windows and doorways, though she knew that would have been normal. That was all.

At ten-thirty she put down her book, went upstairs, bathed, went down to the kitchen, heated some milk, drank it, and went up to bed.

She lay on her back, wide-eyed, motionless, almost without thoughts. Occasionally the lights of a car would sweep across the ceiling. Very rarely, for it was a still night, the leaves outside the window would whisper. She felt that for the rest of her life this sort of trance would substitute for sleep.

It must have been at least three when she heard the key grate in the lock of the front door. She did not move. She heard the door open and close, then cautious steps coming up the stairs and along the hall. A dark shape paused outside the half-open bedroom door, then went on. There was the snick of a light switch and the hall glowed dimly. A little later came the sound of running water.

Katherine got up quietly and looked into the hall. The bathroom door was open and the light was on. Don was standing in front of the wash basin, holding something wrapped in newspapers. She watched him unwrap something that flashed—a long hunting knife.

He inspected it minutely, then laid it down on the newspapers.

He took off his coat and looked it all over, particularly the sleeves. He frowned, soaped a washrag, and rubbed one of the cuffs. Likewise he inspected his trousers and shirt.

He took off his shoes and carefully rubbed them all over, including the soles, with the washrag.

He looked over his hands and bare arms inch by inch. Then he critically studied his face in the mirror, twisting it this way and that.

Katherine swayed. Her wrist knocked the wall. He jerked around, tense, on guard. She went toward him, taking short unsteady steps. "Don," she gasped out, "what have you done?"

There came over his face a look of utter tiredness and apathy. He blinked his eyes flickeringly.

"I did what you wanted me to," he said dully, not looking at her. "I got rid of Wenzel. He'll never trouble you again."

Her gasps formed the words. "No. No."

He lifted his hand toward her. "Dave Wenzel is dead, Katherine," he said very distinctly. "I have finished off Dave Wenzel forever. Do you understand me, Katherine?"

As he spoke the words, the wild tiredness seemed to drain from his eyes, to be replaced (as if he had spoken words of exorcism) by a clear steadiness that she hadn't seen in them for weeks.

But Katherine was no longer just looking into his eyes. The clarity between them had seeped into her mind and she was thinking, *Who was Dave Wenzel? I never heard the doorbell the first time. It never rang. Don Junior didn't see him go, Miss Korshak didn't see him come, Carleton Hare never saw him. I never saw his shadow, I never heard his voice. Don broke the window with the chair, and—the knife is unstained.*

There never was a Dave Wenzel. My husband was hounded by an imaginary man—and now he had exorcised him by an imaginary murder.

"Dave Wenzel is dead," Don repeated. "He had to die—there was no other way. Do you want to call the police?"

She slowly shook her head.

"Good," he said. "That leaves just one more thing, Katherine. You must never ask me about him: who he was or how he died. We must never talk about him again."

Again she slowly nodded.

"And now," he said, "I'd like to go to bed. I'm really quite tired." He started toward the bedroom.

"Wait, Don," she said uncertainly. "The children—"

He turned in the bedroom door. "—are at Aunt Martha's," he finished for her, smiling sleepily. "Did you think I'd forgotten that, Kat?"

She shook her head and came toward him smiling, glad in the present, choking down the first of the thousand questions she would never be able to ask him.

/

Afterword

Suppose we consider the body/personality dichotomy again—this feeling that there is an essential "I" that dwells inside the body.

If that is so, can a strange "I" take over the body and live within it alongside the native "I"? If so, can the strange "I" force the life of the native "I" into other channels? In occult terms, this is called "possession."

There has never been any evidence in favor of the possibility of possession in the occult sense, but there is an eerie resemblance to possession in something that does exist in the real world.

A virus is a small scrap of living matter that resembles both in size and in chemical makeup the chromosome of a cell. It is, very likely, a free-living chromosome.

A virus can invade a cell, and the invading chromosome can bend the cell machinery to its purpose, forcing the cell to manufacture additional units of virus instead of the nucleic acids and proteins it was originally designed to manufacture. In the end, the cell bursts, and in its place are several hundred virus particles, each of which can invade another cell. The cells have been possessed.

Also, physical disturbances such as viruses, injuries, and tumors, and psychological personality disorders such as fugue states and multiple personalities may induce behavioral alterations which outsiders could misdiagnose as possession.—I.A.

Additional Reading

Philip Jose Farmer, "Father's in the Basement," in *The Book of Philip Jose Farmer* (New York: Donald A. Wollheim Books, 1973).

Talmage Powell, "A Hunger in the Blood," in *Curses!,* Isaac Asimov, Charles

G. Waugh, and Martin H. Greenberg, eds. (New York: New American Library, 1989).

Charles Schafhauser, "I'm Yours," in *The Playboy Book of Horror and the Supernatural,* Anonymous, ed. (Chicago: Playboy Press, 1967).

Robert Silverberg, "Passengers," in *The Best of Robert Silverberg* (New York: Pocket Books, 1976).

William W. Stuart, "Inside John Barth," in *The Fifth Galaxy Reader,* H. L. Gold, ed. (Garden City, N.Y.: Doubleday, 1961).

14

Precognition

W. F. Harvey
August Heat

PHENISTONE ROAD, CLAPHAM,

August 20th, 190—. I had what I believe to be the most remarkable day in my life, and while the events are still fresh in my mind, I wish to put them down on paper as clearly as possible.

Let me say at the outset that my name is James Clarence Withencroft.

I am forty years old, in perfect health, never having known a day's illness.

By profession I am an artist, not a very successful one, but I earn enough money by my black-and-white work to satisfy my necessary wants.

My only near relative, a sister, died five years ago, so that I am independent.

I breakfasted this morning at nine, and after glancing through the morning paper I lighted my pipe and proceeded to let my mind wander in the hope that I might chance upon some subject for my pencil.

The room, though door and windows were open, was oppressively hot, and I had just made up my mind that the coolest and most comfortable place in the neighborhood would be the deep end of the public swimming bath, when the idea came.

I began to draw. So intent was I on my work that I left my lunch untouched, only stopping work when the clock of St. Jude's struck four.

The final result, for a hurried sketch, was, I felt sure, the best thing I had done.

It showed a criminal in the dock immediately after the judge had pronounced sentence. The man was fat—enormously fat. The flesh hung in rolls about his chin; it creased his huge, stumpy neck. He was clean shaven (perhaps I should say a few days before he must have been clean shaven) and almost bald. He stood in the dock, his short, stumpy fingers clasping the rail, looking straight in front of him. The feeling that his expression conveyed was not so much one of horror as of utter, absolute collapse.

There seemed nothing in the man strong enough to sustain that mountain of flesh.

I rolled up the sketch, and without quite knowing why, placed it in my pocket. Then with the rare sense of happiness which the knowledge of a good thing well done gives, I left the house.

I believe that I set out with the idea of calling upon Trenton, for I remember walking along Lytton Street and turning to the right along Gilchrist Road at the bottom of the hill where the men were at work on the new tram lines.

From there onward I have only the vaguest recollections of where I went. The one thing of which I was fully conscious was the awful heat, that came up from the dusty asphalt pavement as an almost palpable wave. I longed for the thunder promised by the great banks of copper-colored cloud that hung low over the western sky.

I must have walked five or six miles, when a small boy roused me from my reverie by asking the time.

It was twenty minutes to seven.

When he left me I began to take stock of my bearings. I found myself standing before a gate that led into a yard bordered by a strip of thirsty earth, where there were flowers, purple stock and scarlet geranium. Above the entrance was a board with the inscription—

CHAS. ATKINSON
MONUMENTAL MASON
WORKER IN ENGLISH AND ITALIAN MARBLES

From the yard itself came a cheery whistle, the noise of hammer blows, and the cold sound of steel meeting stone.

A sudden impulse made me enter.

A man was sitting with his back toward me, busy at work on a slab of curiously veined marble. He turned round as he heard tiny steps and stopped short.

It was the man I had been drawing, whose portrait lay in my pocket.

He sat there, huge and elephantine, the sweat pouring from his scalp, which he wiped with a red silk handkerchief. But though the face was the same, the expression was absolutely different.

He greeted me smiling, as if we were old friends, and shook my hand.

I apologized for my intrusion.

"Everything is hot and glary outside," I said. "This seems an oasis in the wilderness."

"I don't know about the oasis," he replied, "but it certainly is hot, as hot as hell. Take a seat, sir!"

He pointed to the end of the gravestone on which he was at work, and I sat down.

"That's a beautiful piece of stone you've got hold of," I said.

He shook his head. "In a way it is," he answered; "the surface here is as fine as anything you could wish, but there's a big flaw at the back, though I don't expect you'd ever notice it. I could never make really a good job of a bit of marble like that. It would be all right in the summer like this; it wouldn't mind the blasted heat. But wait till the winter comes. There's nothing like frost to find out the weak points in stone."

"Then what's it for?" I asked.

The man burst out laughing.

"You'd hardly believe me if I was to tell you it's for an exhibition, but it's the truth. Artists have exhibitions; so do grocers and butchers; we have them too. All the latest little things in headstones, you know."

He went on to talk of marbles, which sort best withstood wind and rain, and which were easiest to work; then of his garden and a new sort of carnation he had bought. At the end of every other minute he would drop his tools, wipe his shining head, and curse the heat.

I said little, for I felt uneasy. There was something unnatural, uncanny, in meeting this man.

I tried at first to persuade myself that I had seen him before, that his face, unknown to me, had found a place in some out-of-the-way corner of my memory, but I knew that I was practicing little more than a plausible piece of self-deception.

Mr. Atkinson finished his work, spat on the ground, and got up with a sigh of relief.

"There! what do you think of that?" he said, with an air of evident pride.

The inscription which I read for the first time was this—

SACRED TO THE MEMORY
OF
JAMES CLARENCE WITHENCROFT.
BORN JAN. 18TH, 1860.
HE PASSED AWAY VERY SUDDENLY
ON AUGUST 20TH, 190—

"In the midst of life we are in death."

For some time I sat in silence. Then a cold shudder ran down my spine. I asked him where he had seen the name.

"Oh, I didn't see it anywhere," replied Mr. Atkinson. "I wanted some name, and I put down the first that came into my head. Why do you want to know?"

"It's a strange coincidence, but it happens to be mine."

He gave a long, low whistle.

"And the dates?"

"I can only answer for one of them, and that's correct."

"It's a rum go!" he said.

But he knew less than I did. I told him of my morning's work. I took the sketch from my pocket and showed it to him. As he looked, the expression of his face altered until it became more and more like that of the man I had drawn.

"And it was only the day before yesterday," he said, "that I told Maria there were no such things as ghosts!"

Neither of us had seen a ghost, but I knew what he meant.

"You probably heard my name," I said.

"And you must have seen me somewhere and have forgotten it! Were you at Clacton-on-Sea last July?"

I had never been to Clacton in my life. We were silent for some time. We were both looking at the same thing, the two dates on the gravestone, and one was right.

"Come inside and have some supper," said Mr. Atkinson.

His wife is a cheerful little woman, with the flaky red cheeks of the country-bred. Her husband introduced me as a friend of his who was an artist. The result was unfortunate, for after the sardines and watercress had been removed, she brought me out a Doré Bible, and I had to sit and express my admiration for nearly half an hour.

I went outside, and found Atkinson sitting on the gravestone smoking.

We resumed the conversation at the point we had left off.

"You must excuse my asking," I said, "but do you know of anything you've done for which you could be put on trial?"

He shook his head.

"I'm not a bankrupt, the business is prosperous enough. Three years ago I gave turkeys to some of the guardians at Christmas, but that's all I can think of. And they were small ones, too," he added as an afterthought.

He got up, fetched a can from the porch, and began to water the flowers. "Twice a day regular in the hot weather," he said, "and then the heat sometimes gets the better of the delicate ones. And ferns, good Lord! they could never stand it. Where do you live?"

I told him my address. It would take an hour's quick walk to get back home.

"It's like this," he said. "We'll look at the matter straight. If you go back home to-night, you take your chance of accidents. A cart may run over you, and there's always banana skins and orange peel, to say nothing of fallen ladders."

He spoke of the improbable with an intense seriousness that would have been laughable six hours before. But I did not laugh.

"The best thing we can do," he continued, "is for you to stay here till twelve o'clock. We'll go upstairs and smoke; it may be cooler inside."

To my surprise I agreed.

† † †

We were sitting in a long, low room beneath the eaves. Atkinson has sent his wife to bed. He himself is busy sharpening some tools at a little oilstone, smoking one of my cigars the while.

The air seems charged with thunder. I am writing this at a shaky table before the open window. The leg is cracked, and Atkinson, who seems a handy man with his tools, is going to mend it as soon as he had finished putting an edge on his chisel.

It is after eleven now. I shall be gone in less than an hour.

But the heat is stifling.

It is enough to send a man mad.

Afterword

It is common to think of the future as something that is as fixed and inevitable as the past. The only difference is that you remember the past or read about it in various chronicles and histories, but don't know what the future will be.

Part of the feeling that the future is fixed and inevitable arises out of the common assumption that God is omniscient and knows everything. This means he must know the future, too, and in fact has designed all of history, from beginning to end, in minute detail, for purposes he alone can understand.

Consequently, there is all this talk about "Fate," and "Kismet," and "If your number is up, you've got to go."

(In actual fact, it is almost certain that the future is what mathematicians now call "chaotic"; that it can't be predicted unless the present is known in the minutest detail. Since the present cannot be known in the minutest detail—not even in theory—the future cannot be predicted.)

The notion of an inevitable future lends itself, however, to interesting stories. Probably a large number of stories have been written concerning the attempt of a person to evade what seems to have been revealed as a very undesirable future—and lo, the very attempt brings about that future. "August Heat" is one of the best of them.—I.A.

Additional Reading

Dana Burnett, "Fog," in *Haunting New England,* Charles G. Waugh, Martin H. Greenberg, and Frank D. McSherry, Jr., eds. (Dublin, N.H.: Yankee Books, 1988).

D. H. Lawrence, "The Rocking-Horse Winner," in *The Ghost Book,* Cynthia Asquith, ed. (London: Hutchinson, 1926).

Ann Mackenzie, "I Can't Help Saying Goodbye," in *Young Mutants,* Isaac Asimov, Martin H. Greenberg, and Charles G. Waugh, eds. (New York: Harper & Row, 1984).

George H. Smith, "The Great Secret," in *Science Fiction A to Z,* Isaac Asimov, Martin H. Greenberg, and Charles G. Waugh, eds. (Boston: Houghton Mifflin Company, 1982).

Jesse Stuart, "Fast-Train Ike," in *Nightmares in Dixie,* Frank D. McSherry, Jr., Charles G. Waugh, and Martin H. Greenberg, eds. (Little Rock, Ark.: Augusta House, 1987).

15

Prophecies Fulfilled

Cornell Woolrich
Speak to Me of Death

Aslick-looking roadster stopped in front of Headquarters at about nine
that night, and its lone occupant sat there in it for a moment before
cutting the ignition, as if trying to make up her mind what to do.

The car had money written all over it, money without flash. The number
was so low it was almost zero. The girl in it took a cigarette out of the
box fitted to the door, pulled a patented lighter out of the dash, inhaled
deeply as if to brace herself. Then she got out and went up the steps between
the two dark-green lights.

She was tall and slim and young. She wore a little leopard-skin jacket
that didn't come below her elbows. The price of it probably ran into three
figures. Her face was pale, paler than powder could have made it. At the
top of the steps she took a second and final drag. Then she dropped the
cigarette, stepped on it, and went in. She asked to see the lieutenant in
charge.

His name was McManus and he brought a chair forward with his
own hands for her in the back room. She was that kind of a girl.

She said, "My name is Ann Bridges." Then she looked down at the
floor. You could see her wrists were trembling, where she held them folded
over one knee. Diamond-splinters flashed around her wristwatch from the
slight vibration.

"Any relative of John T. Bridges?" McManus said.

Ann Bridges looked up again. "I'm his niece," she said. "In fact his
only relative." She took it in her stride, said it almost off-handedly. To

McManus it was a stunning piece of information; it was like finding yourself in the same room with the heir-apparent to a throne. He never thought of doubting her. There was something 14-karat about her that couldn't have been faked.

She said, "It isn't the pleasantest thing in the world to come to the police like this—" she broke off abruptly. Then she went ahead: "I don't even know what there is you people can do about it. But something's got to be done—"

McManus' voice was kind. "You tell me what it is."

"That's the worst part of it. It doesn't sound like anything when you tell it. Anything at all. But it is something!" Her voice rose almost to the point of hysteria. "I can't just stand by and watch him—sink into the grave before my eyes! I *had* to tell somebody—*had* to get it off my chest! I've waited too long as it is!" Her eyes misted. "I've driven down here four nights in a row—and the first three times I lost my nerve, drove on around the block without stopping. I said to myself, 'Ann, they'll think you're crazy, Ann, they'll laugh at you—' "

McManus went over to her and rested a fatherly hand on her shoulder. "We don't laugh at people," he said gently. "We run across anything and everything, in our line—but we don't laugh at people who are in trouble." It wasn't because she was Ann Bridges; it was because she was so young and lovely and there was such distress written on her face.

"Something has hold of us," she said. "Something that started in by being nothing at all, by being just a joke over the luncheon table; something that's grown and grown, until now it's like an octopus throttling us. I can't name it to you, because I don't know what to call it, don't know what it is. It threatens him, not me, but you see I love him, and so the threat is to the two of us."

She gave a little sob deep in her throat.

"Call it a prophecy, call it a prediction, call it fate—call it what you will. I fought against it hard enough, God knows. But the evidence of my own eyes, my own ears, my own senses, is too much for me. And the time's too short now. I'm afraid to take a chance. I haven't got the nerve to bluff it out, to sit pat. You don't gamble with a human life. Today's the 13th, isn't it? It's too close to the 14th; there isn't time-margin enough left now to be skeptical, to keep it to myself any longer. Day by day I've watched him cross off the date on his desk-calendar, drawing nearer to death. There are only two leaves left now, and I want help! Because on the 14th—at the exact stroke of midnight, as the 15th is beginning—"

She covered her face with both arms and shook silently.

"Yes?" urged McManus. "Yes?"

"He's become convinced—oh, and almost I have too—that at exactly midnight on the 14th he's to die. Not just die but meet his death in full vigor and health, a death rushing down to him from the stars he was born under—rushing down even before he existed at all. A death inexorable, inescapable. A death horrid and violent, inconceivable here in this part of the world where we live."

She took a deep, shuddering breath, and whispered the rest of it. *"Death at the jaws of a lion."*

McManus didn't answer for an awfully long time. When he spoke, it wasn't to her at all. He opened the door, called to someone, said, "I'm not to be disturbed—until further orders, hear?"

When he came back to her she said limply, "Thanks—for not laughing, for not smelling my breath, for not hinting that I should see a doctor. Oh, thanks, anyway!"

He took a package of cigarettes out of the desk-drawer, passed them to her. "I know you modern kids," he said paternally. "Smoke up. Pull yourself together. Tell it in your own way. Begin at the beginning—and tell it right straight through—"

† † †

It all started (Ann Bridges said) about an airplane ride. My Uncle John was going to 'Frisco on business, and he'd bought his ticket. He showed it to me at lunch, and I saw that the take-off was dated Friday the 13th. Half-kiddingly I suggested he put off leaving until the day after. There'd been a bad crack-up a week before, but lord! we were joking, not serious about it.

My maid must have overheard us. She came to me later and said, "Beg your pardon, miss, but if that were I, I'd never let him do a thing like that."

I said, "Be your age."

She said, "I know of someone who could warn you, if there is to be any trouble. A man who's gifted with second sight. Why don't you let me take you to him?"

I gave her a cold look and I said, "Just what do I look like to you? Are you seriously suggesting that I go to some flea-bitten fortune-teller with a dirty cloth wrapped around his head and—"

"He's not a fortune-teller," she defended. "He'd resent being called that. He doesn't make a profession of it, and he doesn't take money for it."

"I bet he doesn't refuse it, either," I said cynically.

"He's a good man," she said stoutly, "not a sharper of any kind. He happens to be born with this gift, he can't help that. He doesn't trade on it in any way, in fact he doesn't like to use it. My family and I have known him for years—"

I smiled to myself, as anyone would have. "He's certainly sold himself to you, Elaine," I remarked.

"We won't talk any more about it, miss," she said stiffly. "Only, you remember that time I was in trouble—" She'd got mixed up with some man, and I'd straightened it out for her; it wouldn't be fair for me to give you the details. "You were the only one knew about that, Miss Bridges. I didn't say a word at home, I didn't dare. He took me aside one night and told me the whole thing. He told me how it was going to end up, too. He said the man was going to meet death, and I'd be rid of him once and for all. I fainted dead away on the floor. You remember how we heard two months later he'd been run over on the street?"

I did, but my skepticism wouldn't dent much. "You didn't say a word to me at the time, how was that?"

"He made me promise not to. I've broken my word to him today. He doesn't want it to become known. He hates his gift himself, says it causes him nothing but misery—"

All of which sounded reasonable enough, but I was definitely not impressed. I've had very good common sense all my life, and you have to watch your step—when you own twenty millions.

My uncle took off from Newark early the next morning, and when I got back to the house the maid blurted out: "There's nothing to worry about, Miss Bridges. I—I asked him about this trip, and he said it was safe to make it."

"Oh, you did, did you?" I said severely. "And who told you to?"

"I didn't tell him who it was or anything about it. Just asked him about this morning's plane," she defended. "But Mr. Bridges needn't have gone at all, could have saved himself the trouble. He told me that whoever this party is that's going out there, he or she is doomed to disappointment; nothing will come of it, he'll just have wasted his time."

My uncle's in the import and export business; he'd gone to see about an important consignment of silk from Japan, but the maid couldn't have known that, much less this seer of hers. I'm afraid I snickered rudely right in her face.

Nothing daunted, she rushed on: "But don't let Mr. John come back by air, Miss Bridges, whatever you do! Wire him to take the train instead. The eastbound plane *is* going to run into trouble—he saw it clearly. Not a crack-up, but it's going to be grounded somewhere in the Rockies and half of them are going to die of exposure in the Rockies before they're located. He saw snow piled all around it and people with frozen hands and feet having to have them amputated later—"

I blew up. I said, "One more word out of you, and I'll give you your week's notice!"

She didn't open her mouth from then on, just went around looking sorry for me.

Uncle John had told me he was starting back the following Saturday. Take-off was at seven Pacific Coast Time, ten back here. I'll admit I got a little worried Friday night, wondered whether or not I oughtn't to send that wire after all. I was afraid he'd laugh at me. More than that even,

I hated to give in to her after the way I'd talked. I went to bed without sending the wire. It was too late when I woke up in the morning, he would have started already.

He should have got in about noon Sunday. I drove to the airport to meet him, and he wasn't on the plane. That gave me a nasty turn. I asked at the airport-office, and they told me he'd booked a seat from Chicago east, along with several other people, on this one, and none of them had shown up to make the connection; the 'Frisco plane had been overdue when they left Chicago.

I went home plenty worried. It was in the papers and on the radio already, reported missing somewhere over the Rockies with fourteen people in it!

The maid saw how I was taking it, so finally she came out with: "I suppose I'm discharged, but I knew better than you—I took the liberty of sending Mr. John a wire over your name last night, begging him to come by train instead—"

Discharged? I could have kissed her! But then anxiety raised its head again. "He's stubborn, he'd never listen to a message like that—"

"I—I told him that one of his associates wanted to consult him about a very important matter, and mentioned a place where the planes don't stop, so he'd have to take a train. *He* says," she went on, "that it won't be found for three days, the plane. It wouldn't have meant death, it isn't Mr. John's time yet, but he would have lost both feet and been a helpless cripple for the rest of his—"

All of which evoked a pretty creepy feeling in me. It wasn't helped any when my uncle got off the train three days later, safe and sound. The first words out of his mouth were that he'd made the trip for nothing: a maritime strike had broken out on the Coast and his silk-shipment was tied up indefinitely at Honolulu; he hadn't been able to accomplish a thing.

The snow-bound plane was sighted from the air later that same day, and when the rescue-parties got to it, seven of the fourteen were dead from exposure, and several of the survivors had to have their hands or feet amputated as soon as they got them to a hospital. Just as *he'd* foretold— rescue-date, circumstances, number of casualties, and all! It was uncanny. I didn't want to believe. I fought like anything against believing—and yet there it was.

I told my uncle the whole story of course—who wouldn't have?— and he was as impressed as I was. What we did next was what anyone else would have done after what had happened. We asked the maid to take the two of us to this man, we wanted to see him for ourselves. She wasn't to tell him who we were, just two friends of hers. I even put on an old coat and hat of hers, to look properly working-class, and we left the car home, went there on foot.

It was a big let-down, at first. This fortune-teller was merely a middle-aged man sitting in a furnished room with his suspenders hanging down! His name was Jeremiah Tompkins, about as unimpressive a name as they come. And worst of all, he was just a bookkeeper. Had been, rather, for he wasn't working just then. If I remember correctly, he was reading the want ads in a newspaper when we came in.

I could see my uncle was more disappointed; he was almost resentful. After all, Uncle John is a levelheaded, intelligent businessman. That a figure like this should be able to spout prophecies, should know more than he did himself about what was going to happen to him, was too much for him to swallow.

"Watch," he said to me out of the corner of his mouth, "I'll show you. I'll show you he's just a phony, that all this was just a coincidence. I've got something here that's the best little miracle-eraser in the world!"

And he took out five hundred dollars in cold cash and pressed it into Tompkins' hand. Tompkins had been reading the want ads, remember, and Elaine told me later her people were having him in for meals with them out of sheer pity.

"You've done something for me I can never repay you for," my uncle said as a come-on. "This is just a token of my gratitude. Call on me at any time and I'll be more than glad to—"

Tompkins didn't let him finish. He threw the money down at my uncle's feet. "I don't like being insulted," he said quietly. There was a sort of dignity about the way he said it, at that. "It's like being paid for—for showing a gruesome scar or some deformity. I don't do that for money, and I won't take money for it. This girl here—" he pointed at Elaine— "is a friend of mine. She asked me some questions about a plane and I answered them for her, that's all. Please go. I don't like being made a holy show of."

"But you don't know who I am," my uncle began protestingly.

Tompkins gave a bleak smile and put his hand up to his head, as though he had a headache. Not in that theatrical way clairvoyants do when they're about to "go into their trance," but as though something were hurting him, wouldn't let him alone.

He answered as though he were speaking against his will. "You're John Bridges," he said. "Your mother died when you were fourteen years old, and it was the sight of the beautiful silk kimonos and wrappers she wore that really made you go into the export and import business later on. . . ."

Elaine could have told him all that, was the unspoken thought in my mind.

He turned to me and answered it as though it had been said aloud. I went white and nearly fell through the floor! "But here's something she couldn't have," he said. "About you. You took off your dance-slippers under a restaurant table one night last week and a waiter accidentally kicked one halfway across the room. Rather than admit it was yours, you left in your stocking-feet. And you've got a diamond and ruby necklace with twenty stones in it in a Safety Box No. 1805 at the National Security Bank. Also a bundle of letters you bought back from a gigolo in Paris for fifty thousand francs."

My own uncle didn't know about that!

"I don't ask you to believe in me. I don't care whether you do or not," this Tompkins went on somberly. "I didn't ask you to come here in the first place. You're going to the police about me some day, anyway, and get me in a lot of trouble."

My hands strayed up and down the blank wall trying to find the door where there wasn't any door. My eyes were blurred. I moaned, "Get me out of here!" The whole world was turning upside-down on its axis. I felt like a fly walking on the ceiling.

My uncle took me home. The five hundred stayed there on Tompkins' floor. Elaine brought it back with her when she returned, after we did.

"Wouldn't touch it," she murmured. "What do you think he did, though? Borrowed five dollars from me, to tide himself over."

That business of the $500 sold the fortune-teller to my uncle more than any number of bull's-eye predictions could have. He was convinced now that Jeremiah Tompkins wasn't a phony, a fake, a schemer of any kind. That he was a phenomenon: an ordinary, in fact sub-ordinary, human being with this frightful gift—or blight—of prognostication. In other words, the groundwork of credulity had been laid. The rest followed in due course.

To begin with, Uncle John tried to make the man a gift of money again—no longer to show him up, but in all sincerity and respect now. He mailed him his personal check, for $1000 this time. It came back inside a readdressed envelope, almost by return mail, torn into eight neat pieces. That failing, my uncle got Tompkins a job—and made sure he'd accept it by keeping his own name out of it. He had a friend advertise for a bookkeeper. The friend, without knowing the details, agreed to bar all except one of the applicants who might answer it—Jeremiah Tompkins. In other words, it was a one-man ad. Elaine was posted to call the man's attention to it in the paper, in case it should escape his eye. It all worked out according to plan; he took the job.

"But," I insisted stubbornly to the two of them, "if he's the actual mindreader he seemed to be, how is it he didn't know at once who was in back of this paid ad you showed him? Why couldn't he see that the job came through Uncle John?"

"He doesn't go around all day, reading what's in people's minds— he'd kill himself doing that," Elaine protested, as though I had disparaged the man. "It seems to come to him in flashes, only when he'll let it— and he doesn't like to. It's there in his unconscious self the whole time." She meant subconscious. "And he lets it flicker out once in awhile, or else it gets out in spite of him—I don't know."

Anyway, Tompkins took the job, and if he was a first-class mystic, he wasn't any great shakes as a bookkeeper. My uncle's friend had to let him go in about six weeks. The friend didn't, of course, know the inside story; he claimed the man was too moony and moody—in plain English, shiftless.

Meanwhile Tompkins kept getting under my uncle's skin deeper and deeper. The strike on the Pacific Coast gave signs of going on all the rest of the summer. The silk shipment, which was worth thousands, was stuck there in Honolulu, rotting away. My uncle got an offer from a Japanese dealer in the islands, considerably below its intrinsic value, let alone any profit. It looked like a case of take what he could get or lose the whole thing. It wasn't a question of the money so much, with him, but he hated to come out second best in any transaction, hated to admit himself licked.

He'd already drafted the cable accepting the Jap offer, then at the last minute held it without filing. He went and looked up Tompkins by himself, without confiding in anyone.

I don't know what passed between them. All I know is that Uncle John came home that night and told me he'd cabled the Japs to go to hell; the shipping strike was going to be over in forty-eight hours, right when the deadlock seemed at its worst.

I don't have to remind you what happened. You've read how the Chief Executive himself intervened unexpectedly two days later and the strike was arbitrated and called off between sun-up and sundown. The President's own advisers hadn't known he was going to do it, so it was said. My uncle's consignment beat every other cargo into 'Frisco; and by getting into port first—well, it was quite a windfall. Uncle John got exactly double the usual price for the shipment.

A man in a shabby furnished room, without a job of his own, had saved his firm exactly $200,000 all told!

I kept out of it from then on. I wanted to hang onto my peace of mind; more than that even, my sanity. I didn't want to turn into a neurotic ghost-ridden candidate for a mental clinic. I wouldn't even discuss Tompkins with Uncle John, or let him mention the man to me. So I can't give you the intermediate steps.

But then the thing finally clamped down on my uncle, as anyone might have known it would eventually. Three months ago, I saw the change come over him and asked him what it was. He suddenly retired from business, sold out—or rather gave away his interest for next to nothing. He lost concern in everything and anything. He got haggard. I could see the mortal terror standing out in his eyes, day by day.

He'd gone to Tompkins again about some enormous venture he was contemplating. He was gambling more and more on these "inside tips," growing more reckless all the time. But this time there was a different answer, a catastrophic answer.

The thing under discussion was a long-term transaction, that would have taken about six months to pay off. "It doesn't matter one way or the other," Tompkins told him indifferently, "unless of course it's the firm itself you're thinking about, and not yourself personally." And then very indifferently, as though he'd known it all along: "Because you'll be dead by that time. Your life's coming to an end at midnight on the 14th-to-15th of next March."

I don't know whether Tompkins told it to him all at once, or doled it out piece-meal. I don't know how many times my uncle had to seek him out—plead with him maybe, or grovel on bended knees. I don't know anything at all. Uncle John wouldn't have been human if he hadn't asked the man how he would die, in what manner, and what could be done to prevent it.

"Nothing," was the merciless answer. "You can't stop it from happening, can't evade it. Though you fly to the far ends of the world, though you hide yourself in the depths of the earth, though you gather a thousand men about you to shield you, it will still find you out. It's there—written down for you—*Death by the jaws of a lion.*"

And then Uncle John started going slowly to pieces. Oh, it's not the money, Lieutenant McManus! It's not that he's endowed Tompkins with hundreds of thousands of dollars at a time, that he's dissipating our fortune, my inheritance, trying to buy minutes and *seconds* of life back from a man who admits, himself, that he has no control over it, can do nothing about it. I don't mind that.

It's that he's dying by inches, before my very eyes, day by day. It's that the Spanish Inquisition, the Chinese, the Iroquois, never devised tortures to compare to what he's going through now. It's that it's become communicated to me; I'm terrified, and sick with horror, and beating my hands together in the dark. It's that the sun has gone out and we're two people trapped in a black pit. It's that there's only tomorrow left now. I want help! *I want help!*

† † †

She was so overwrought that she fell forward across his desk, burying her face against it, pounding it helplessly with her little clenched fist, again and again. McManus had to send out for a sedative. When she had drunk the spirits of ammonia, she lay down on a cot in another room and rested, dozed off for a while. McManus covered her up to the chin with his own overcoat, with his own hands.

When he went back again alone to his office, he spat out: "Gad, what things you run into!" Twenty million dollars, eighteen years old, and her very soul taken from her. On the borderline of gibbering idiocy, almost. As for the uncle, McManus could imagine the shape *he* was in.

He sat down at his desk, stayed there staring blankly before him as though he'd forgotten the whole incident.

After about five minutes, he picked up the phone very slowly, and he said even more slowly: "Send Tom Shane in here to me. And Schafer. And Sokolsky. And Dominguez. Send out a short-wave if you have to, I want 'em here right away. Tell 'em to drop whatever they're on, no matter what it is. . . ."

Tom Shane was just a pleasant-looking fellow in a thirty-dollar herring-bone suit. He didn't look dumb and he didn't look bright either. Just a guy you wouldn't mind having a glass of beer with. He lined himself up to the left of the other three.

"Shane," said McManus, "are you afraid of lions?"

"I wouldn't go to bed with one," admitted Shane frankly.

"Shane," said McManus, "do you think you can keep a millionaire from being mangled by a lion at exactly twelve o'clock tomorrow midnight?"

It wasn't really a question. McManus seemed to be talking absent-mindedly while he did a lot of thinking behind the smoke-screen of words. "I may as well tell you now that the 'lion' might take almost any kind of a shape. It might be a bullet. It might be a poisoned cup of coffee. Then again it just might be an honest-to-goodness lion. I could fill that house with fellows like you, have 'em hanging from the chandeliers like mistletoe, but I don't want to do that. Then the 'lion' would only defer its visit, come around some other time, maybe six months from now, when it was least expected. I don't want that to happen; I want it to come when it's due to come, so I can make sure it'll never come again. So there's only one man going up there to that house with those two people, and I don't want him to fall down on the job. It's a double-header too. If this is what I think it is, that girl's as doomed as her uncle. That would mop up the twenty millions nicely, otherwise she could always bring suit to recover what's already been given away of it.

"So, Tom Shane, you go in there in the next room and sit by Ann Bridges, and go home with her when she's feeling fit enough. You're not a detective—you're her boy-friend on a week-end visit as her house-guest, or her new butler, or a traveling-salesman trying to sell her vacuum cleaners, I don't care. But keep those two people alive. Midnight tomorrow's the deadline."

Tom Shane wheeled around and went out without a word. He still didn't look bright, but he didn't look dumb either. Just a well-built guy in a herringbone suit.

McManus said, "Schafer, you're on a girl named Elaine O'Brien— and all her family too. I want to know more about 'em than they know about themselves. And be ready to pinch.

"Sokolsky, you're on a guy named Jeremiah Tompkins. And don't kid yourself by the way he looks that he's no great shakes of a guy. He's the kingpin in this, whatever it is. Don't let him out of your sight. Dictaphones and every trick of the trade. And try not to think while you're at it; the guy's supposed to be a mind-reader. Take somebody else on it with you, it's not going to be any pushover. And be even readier to pinch than Schafer. Tompkins has got to be in custody long before midnight—whether you get anything on him or not."

There was just a guy left that looked a little like Valentino, only better-looking.

"Dominguez," McManus said, "I've gotta lotta little odd-jobs for you. But they're just as important as the other guys' assignments, don't bluff yourself they're not. Find out what zoos there are within a 500-mile radius of here. Check with every one of them and find out if they keep lions. Find out if any have escaped or been swiped."

"Swipe a lion?" breathed the detective.

"Warn the keepers of all of 'em to keep extra watch over their lion cages tonight and all day tomorrow. Report to me. Got that? *Then,* find out at what nightclub Miss Ann Bridges had a slipper kicked across the dance floor two years ago. And what became of it. Also, the mate to it. Use your Latin looks, apply for a job there or something. Find out what waiter picked 'em up after she'd gone, and what he did with them. If you can get hold of him, bring him in. Report to me. *Then,* buttonhole one of the big-shots at the National Security Bank, ask his cooperation, see if you can trace the leak by which the number of Miss Bridges' safe deposit box—1805—and what it had in it, came into the possession of a third party. There's nothing criminal in that, in itself, but it would give us a swell lead.

"Y'got less than twenty-four hours to do all this in! Y'ain't eating and y'ain't sleeping and y'ain't even taking time off to talk from now on! Get going!"

And when he was all by himself once more, McManus picked up the phone and asked for long distance. "Gimme Paris, France," he said matter-of-factly, "the Chief of the *Sûreté.*"

Many blackmailing gigolos have had telephone love-calls, but few have ever been the cause of a transatlantic long-distance phone call from police official to police official!

†   †   †

The University Club Building has two entrances, one on the side street, the other on the avenue. An L-shaped lobby connects them. It's just for men, of course—college men—and women aren't allowed above the mezzanine floor, but the lobby's usually full of them, calling for pinch-hitters to fill in at dances, theatre-parties, house-parties, etc.

Ann Bridges and Tom Shane arrived there simultaneously, she in her car at the main entrance, he in a taxi at the side entrance. He had a cowhide overnight-bag with him, and had changed in the cab itself. He had Princeton written all over him and—no offense—was now veering dangerously toward the dumb side of the not-dumb, not-bright equation. He had a polo coat hanging down his back below the elbows, orange-and-black tie (very narrow diagonals, not loud), the usual thick brogues. If you'd have unbuttoned his jacket, you'd have seen a fraternity pin on the lower tab of his vest. He looked about twenty-three. He jelled perfectly.

The girl was just coming in one side of the lobby as Shane showed up from the other, bag in hand. They were collegiately informal—and loud. He didn't raise his hat; she punched him on the shoulder. "Hi, toots." " 'Lo ducky!" He grabbed her arm and they went sailing outside to her car, two young things without a care in the world.

Heads turned after them. Somebody mentioned her name. Everybody wondered who he was. All this to baffle watchful eyes that otherwise might have seen her drive away from Headquarters with Shane and would have known him to be a detective. A ticket for a traffic violation she had actually received two days previously was screen enough for her visit there tonight. McManus had had the desk sergeant enter a dummy complaint against her in his records, and a Headquarters reporter had fallen for it, phoned a couple of lines about it to his paper.

In the car she took the wheel. Shane pitched his bag into the back seat, lay back on the base of his skull. But as they shot off, he suddenly drew up again.

"Feel well enough to drive?" he asked.

"It'll keep my mind busy till we get there. College men usually let the other fellow do their driving for them anyway. If you're not one to the life—! How did you do it so quickly?"

"Borrowed the outfit from a friend who really went to one—changed in the cab. . . . Who's out there with him?" he asked abruptly.

"We have a cook, and a door-opener; then there's Elaine, and Uncle John's secretary. My uncle will be all right—I know what you're thinking—but he'll be all right until tomorrow night. He wants to live too badly to—to do anything to himself ahead of time. It's tomorrow night we've got to worry about." She drew in her breath fearfully and repeated it a second time: "Tomorrow night."

"Step it up a little," Shane said quietly. "Ninety won't hurt it any." The clock on the dashboard said midnight. The midnight before *the* midnight.

It was a palatial place, lost in the midst of its own grounds. Couldn't see it from the main road, it was so far back, but a private driveway led to it. Lighted by their own private road-lights.

Two granite lions *couchant,* like a sort of omen, were the first things met Shane's eye as he got out in front of the entrance. A little like the lions in front of the Public Library in New York, but smaller. They went up the steps between them.

"I bet it hasn't helped any to have those things staring him in the face every time he went in or out the last few weeks," Shane muttered grimly.

"He's spoken several times of having them removed and replaced by something else," the girl said, "but this terrible lethargy, this fatalism, that's come over him, has prevented his doing even that."

The butler let them in. Shane, taking a snapshot of the man through his mask of collegiate vacuity, decided this wasn't one of those crime-story butlers who are to be suspected at sight. He was an old man—sixty or more—had loyalty written all over him, and looked plenty worried in the bargain.

"How is he, Weeks?" the girl asked in a whisper.

The butler shook his head. "I can't stand much more of it myself, Miss Ann. Just watching him. He's sat in one place ever since you left, staring at a clock on the wall." The old man looked sort of hopefully toward Shane; then, noting the get-up, his hopes seemed to fade a little.

"Yes, he knows about it, Weeks," the girl said; "that's why he's here. Take his bag up—put him in the room next to my uncle."

On each side of the long entrance hall a ceiling-high stained-glass panel was set into the blank wall, with electric lights hidden behind them to throw them into relief. They gleamed out in beautiful medieval tones of ruby, emerald, sapphire and mauve. Each leaded sub-division bore the head of some mythological or heraldic animal—a unicorn, a wild boar, a lion rampant, a phoenix. . . .

She saw Shane looking at the windows as they went by. "They came from England," she said dully. "Some royal abbey or other. Time of the Plantagenets."

Shane didn't know who the Plantagenets were. He wasn't supposed to, anyway. "Pretty old, I guess, eh?" he hazarded. It occurred to him that, judging by the number of decorative animals around, the prophecy might very well have originated right here in the house, in someone's evil, fertile mind.

"*He* ever been here, to your knowledge?" he asked.

"Who, Tompkins? Never."

She took the detective in to see the doomed John Bridges.

Bridges sat in the middle of a big room, and he had gathered three time-pieces around him. A big clock on the wall, a medium-sized one on the table before him, an expensive white-gold watch on his wrist. All three were ticking remorselessly away in the silence, like the mechanism of a time-bomb. There was a minute's difference, Shane noted, between the wall and table clocks. Bridges turned two feverish, burning eyes in hollow sockets toward his niece as she came in.

"Which is right?" he pleaded. "What does yours say?"

"It's twenty-nine past twelve, not half-past," the girl said.

His face lit up joyously. "Oh, Ann!" he cried. "Oh, Ann! that gives me a minute more! Just think, a minute more!"

Tom Shane thought, "For what he's done to this guy already, Tompkins deserves the chair, whether he intends doing anything more or not."

Aloud he said, cheerfully, "You and I, oldtimer, are going to have a good stiff highball together—then we're going up to bed!"

"Yes, yes," Bridges agreed pathetically. "My next-to-the-last night on earth! I must celebrate, I must—" His voice broke dismally. "Oh, help me to forget, fellow, for just five minutes! Just five minutes, that's all I ask!" He opened a drawer, pulled out a checkbook, scribbled hastily in it. "If you can take my mind off it for just five minutes, write your own figure in here over my name! Five thousand, ten thousand, I don't care!"

Shane thought: "I wonder how many times friend Tompkins has cashed in like this?" He went out to mix the highballs himself, and gave Bridges a shot of Scotch that would have lifted a horse off its shoes. McManus' words came back to him: "It may be a poisoned cup of coffee." He sampled the drink himself first, rinsing his mouth with it carefully. The taste was so good he hated to waste it, so he swallowed it.

"Pleasant way of dying, anyway," he consoled himself.

He took the drinks inside. "You go to bed, kid," he told the girl. "Lock your door. It's my job from now on."

She said, "You're swell. Keep us alive," with a funny little catch in her voice as she sidled by him and went up the stairs.

The wall-clock chimed one, with a horrid, shuddery, brazen sound. "Twenty-three hours to go," John Bridges said.

Shane clicked their glasses together with almost enough force to shatter them. "Here's to crime!" he said huskily. He winked one eye deliberately at the doomed man.

†   †   †

3 A.M.—Schafer, lieutenant. Sorry to wake you up, but I've lost this Elaine O'Brien twist, Miss Bridges' maid—

You've lost her? Well, find her again! Whaddye mean by—

It ain't that. I know where she is, but she's no good to us any more. She's dead.

Dead? What happened to her?

She did the Dutch. Took a run to the bathroom just before I closed in on her, and swallowed something. I called an ambulance right away, but it was too late.

So then she *was* implicated! She knew something and was afraid we'd get it out of her!

She didn't know I was on her tail. I had just about located her house, when I heard the screaming start up inside. Time I busted in, it was all over. I'm holding the rest of them. They claim it was the prophecy preying on her mind. She came home tonight and told them she couldn't stand the gaff, waiting around out there for it to happen. I checked on the drugstore where she got the stuff, and she bought it a full three days ago, long before

Miss Bridges came to us. What'll I do with the rest of 'em?

Bring 'em in Schafer—and keep 'em from swallowing things.

† † †

10 A.M.—Dominguez, lieutenant. I took a dishwashing job at the Club Cuckoo, where Miss Bridges lost her shoes. My hands are red as lobsters!

Never mind your hands, I'm no palm-reader. What'd you get?

They knew who she was, so they knew whose shoes they were. First the manager was going to send 'em out to her house next day—after all, they cost about fifty bucks a pair—but a Frenchman fella who was sitting there at one of the tables buttonholes him. This gee gives the manger a lotta malarkey about how he's an old friend of Miss Bridges, knew her in Paris, and he'll see she gets 'em back. I got all this from a waiter, who I gave a tip on the horses to while I was massaging the crockery—

Well, you got something, Don. I was just asking about that very guy at the rate of twenty bucks a syllable. The shakedown racket made Paris too hot for him, so he came over here about two years ago. You gotta description, I suppose?

Yeah. Misplaced eyebrow on his lip. When he's doing the hot spots he wears one eyeglass in his right lamp. Very good-looking. A short little devil, about five—

That's enough. One of his names is Raoul Berger, but he's got twenty others. So he got the shoes?

No. The pay-off is the manager wanted all the credit for himself and hung onto them. But this Frog didn't seem to mind—

Sure he didn't. All he cared about was knowing what had taken place, so he could tip off Tompkins and get under her skin. I'm sending out a general alarm for Berger right away. They're probably working hand-in-glove together, and intend splitting the Bridges millions between 'em at the windup. Probably the idea was originally Berger's, since he'd already shaken her down once in Europe.

Now, about the safe deposit box, chief. I been conferring with Cullinan— he's the manager of that branch of the National Security—and we questioned the vault-keeper. I think I've cleared up pretty definitely about how the number of Miss B's box, 1805, was known—but not its contents. The vault custodian seems straight enough; he's been with them for years. He recalls definitely that one day about a year and a half ago, Miss B took her box into one of the little private cubbyholes that are provided for that purpose down in the vault room. The custodian recalls it, because she came out and absent-mindedly left her key behind her in there. . . . Now, two of these keys are used at a time, see. The custodian has one, and the owner of the box has the other. The number of the box it opens is engraved on the shaft of each key. Well, Miss B stepped right back inside, that day she mislaid her key, and the custodian went with her to help her to look. The key wasn't in there. They came out again—she went through her purse and everything—no sign of it. He stepped in again a second time, and there it was, right on the slab! . . . The custodian's pretty certain that the adjoining booth was occupied at the time, but is hazy about just who was in there. That doesn't matter. The partitions don't run all the way up to the ceiling. Obviously it was our friend Berger, and obviously he'd been in there every time she was, waiting for just such a thing to happen. And when it did, he probably used a fish-hook or a magnet on the end of a string to draw the key up, memorize its number, then replace it again. All to add to Tompkin's buildup with her as a wizard. But about what the contents of the box were, I don't know, unless he used some kind of mirror as a periscope—

More likely she bought that necklace in Paris. Berger'd seen it on her over there, and he figured it would be in the box. Also the letters she'd written to him. Took a guess at it and scored a bull's-eye. To get into the vaults all he'd have to do was rent a box under a phony name for five, six bucks, stuff it with old newspapers, and keep showing up each time she did. Still, it isn't as easy as it sounds. Berger had to stay out of sight—she knew what he looked like—and he had to get in right next door to her each time, not further down the line.

For twenty million bucks I'd go to that much trouble myself.

Get busy on them zoos, or you won't even be earning forty-eight-hundred.

Zoos! That's gratitude for ya!

† † †

5 P.M.—Sokolsky, lieutenant—

It's about time I was hearing from you! Where've you been all this time? What've you got?

A pretty bad case of the jitters, for one thing. And Dobbs—I took him on this detail with me—is about ready to crack wide open. I don't think he'll be any good for the rest of this case.

I ain't asking for a health report, I wanna know—

It's uncanny about that guy—Tompkins, I mean. He—he can see through walls and things—

Less words and more facts!

Yes, sir. We took a room in the same house he lives in. We got a lucky break and got the one right over his. Tompkins was out at the time, so we fixed up a dictaphone and led it up through the ceiling behind the steampipe. The landlady don't like him, on accounta he read what was in her mind when she insured her third husband so heavily, after losing two in a year, and also 'cause he's hep that the color of the hair she goes around wearing ain't her own. She didn't tell me this; I put two and two together from the remarks she let drop. Anyway, I got around her and found out some French cake-eater's been calling on Tompkins off and on for the past year or so.

Your voice makes sweet music! We're getting places fast, now!

The landlady thinks this Frenchy is the nuts, but that's neither here nor there. The point is, he's the only person at all—outside of the O'Brien girl and the old man Bridges himself—who has been near Tompkins since he's living in the house. . . .

Well, the O'Brien girl's out of it now. I don't think she was in on it, anyway. Just a stooge they used to pump facts out of about the Bridges family. I think maybe she found out there was something phony up, after it was too late, and realizing what she'd done to her benefactors, committed the old harry. Go ahead, Sock, what else?

I gave Tompkins' room a good going-over while I was in there, and came across any number of checks made out by Bridges. Way up in the high brackets too, telephone numbers! The only thing that don't jell right, was some of 'em were dated six months or more back. He hauls 'em in all right, but don't seem to bother cashing 'em! Maybe he's just cagey, afraid to go too heavy yet while Bridges is still alive. Maybe he's saving them all up until B and the girl have been done away with!

Will those checks build us a case against him and his French shill! What'd you do with them?

I was afraid he'd miss them if I impounded them this soon. Dobbs and I rushed a few of the biggest ones out, had 'em photostated, and then replaced 'em again.

Good work!

Tompkins came in about midnight, just as we were getting through, so we beat it upstairs to listen in. About two in the morning this French pal of his pays him a visit. Dobbs took down everything in shorthand, until he went haywire, and I'll read it to you.

Tompkins says, "You again? What do you want now?"

"Endorse me another one of them checks—I'm running short."

T refuses at first, says he don't want Bridges' money, and Frenchy has no right to it either. Frenchy pulls a gun on him or something, and makes him do it. Then Frenchy says, "Now you get hold of Bridges tomorrow and have him change his will, while there's still time. I'll supply the lawyer, a friend of mine. He's to turn over everything to you, see? Kid him that you'll call off the prophecy if he does it."

Tompkins says, "But I can't. It's not in my power. It's there. It's going to happen."

The French guy does a slow burn. "You think I believe that stuff? Save that for him! You do what I tell you, or—"

Tompkins answers quietly, "You're not going to get hold of his money, Berger. You're not going to live long enough to. Why, you're going to die even sooner than he is! His time is tomorrow night, but yours is right tonight! You're never even going to get out of this house alive. There are two dicks in the room over us right now, listening to every word we say— their names are Sokolsky and Dobbs—"

The notes break off there, because Dobbs keeled over right at the mike and pulled a dead faint on the floor. Yeah, honest! It gave me a pretty stiff jolt myself. Just seeing the leadwire of the dictaphone, which I'm sure he didn't, wouldn't have given this Tompkins our names—nor how many of us there were.

I'll have to quote the rest from memory: "Death," says Tompkins, "is rushing at you right now, I hear the beat of his swift wings. I feel it, I see it, it's on its way. You have only minutes left. And for me there is imprisonment waiting, and lingering death in a little stone room—"

I heard the Frenchman yell out, "So you framed me, you dirty double-crossing lug! Well, see if you saw this in your crystal ball!"

And with that the gun goes off, and nearly busts my eardrum. The Frenchman has shot him.

I didn't wait to hear any more. I unlimbered my own gun and lit out and down the stairs hell-bent for leather. Berger had beaten me out to the stairs; he was already a flight below me.

I yelled, "Hold it! Stay where you are!" Instead he turned and fired at me, and I fired at the same time he did. He fell all the rest of the way down to the ground floor, and when I got to him he was dead.

Tompkins came out of his room unhurt, but with a powder burn across his forehead. Berger must have fired at point-blank range, and still didn't hit him! He started coming down slowly to where I was, with nothing in his hands. Dobbs had come to, and came down behind him, looking like he'd seen a ghost.

Well, this is the hardest part to believe; look, you can suspend me if you want to, but it's the God's honest truth. This man Tompkins came all the way down to where I was bending over the body at the foot of the stairs. I straightened up and covered him with my gun. It didn't faze him in the least, he kept moving right on past me toward the street-door. Not quickly, either; as slowly as if he was just going out for a walk. He said, "It isn't my time yet. You can't do anything to me with that."

I said, "I can't, eh? You take one step away from me, and it'll not only be your time, but you'll be a minute late!"

Dobbs was practically useless; he almost seemed to be afraid of the guy.

Tompkins turned his back on me and took that one step more. I fired a warning shot over his head. He put his hand on the doorknob. So I lowered the gun and fired at the back of his knee, to bring him down. The bullet must have gone right through between his legs. I heard it hit wood along the door-frame. Tompkins opened the door and stepped into the opening, and I got mad. I reared after him and fired point-blank at the back of head. He wasn't five yards away from me. It was brutal—

would have been murder and I'm willing to admit it myself, even though technically he was resisting arrest! I'm telling you he didn't even stagger; it never even got him. He went on through and the darkness swallowed him up.

I leaned there against that door for a minute seeing ghosts, then I ran out after him. He was clean gone, not a sign of him up or down the block.

I'm in a frame of mind where I don't care what you do to me. My job is to get flesh-and-blood guys that know a bullet when they feel one, not protoplasms that don't even know enough to lie down when they're hit. . . .

Awright, Sokolsky, pull yourself together. Bring in the stiff and rinse yourself out with a jolt of rye; maybe it'll help you carry out instructions better next time! All I know is you let Tompkins slip right through your fingers, and we're right back where we were. We got to start all over again. We've stopped the crook, but the maniac or screwball or whatever you want to call him, the more dangerous of the two, is at large. And every minute he stays that way, Bridges and his niece are in danger of their lives! Tompkins wasn't bluffing when he walked out that door. He believes in that hooey himself; and if the prophecy don't work, he'll help it work! We've got seven hours to pick him up again, out of seven million people!

†   †   †

"Don't!" Shane yelled at the man roughly. "Take your eyes off that clock! You're starting to get me myself, doing that! I'm only human!" He took a quick step over to the table and turned the instrument face down.

John Bridges gave a skull-like grin, all teeth and no mirth. "You're only human—that's right. That's the truest thing ever said, son. You're a detective too, aren't you, son? That's why you've been hanging around here all day. Don't try to tell me, I know. This poor child here thinks you can save me. *You* think you can save me, too. You poor fools! Nothing can—nothing! *He* said I'm to die, and I've got to die."

"He's lying through his teeth!" Shane yelled hotly. "That Tompkins is a faker and a crook and a skunk. He'll fry in hell, before anything gets near you. I'll live to see it, and so will she—and so will you!"

Bridges' head fell forward, over his lap. "Will it hurt much?" he whined. "I guess it must. Those terrible fangs in their mouths! Those sharp, cruel claws, tearing your skin to ribbons! But it won't be the claws—it's the jaws that will mangle me, worry me like a cat worries a mouse! By the *jaws* of a lion, he said—by the *jaws* of a lion!"

Ann Bridges put her hands over her ears. "Don't," she murmured quietly. She gave Shane a look. "I'm trying so hard to—to stay all in one piece."

Shane poured a dynamic drink, all Scotch with just a needle of seltzer. He handed it to Bridges with a stony face. "Give yourself a little bravemaker," he suggested in an undertone.

The millionaire deliberately thrust the glass away from him. Liquor spilled all over the carpet; the glass bounced and rocked on its side without breaking. "Alcohol! Trying to ward off death with bottled slops!"

Shane took out his gun, pointed it butt-first at the old millionaire. "Don't this mean anything to you? Don't it mean anything to you that every window and door of this house is locked fast, that there's an electric alarm on them? That there's dozens of armed men within call hidden all around this estate, ready to jump in and grab anyone or anything the minute it shows? That we're sealed up tight, just the five of us?"

The secretary had lit out in panic sometime during the previous night. Just as Elaine O'Brien had fled. Shane had found a note from him that morning, saying he couldn't stand it, resigning the job.

Bridges cackled horribly, like a chicken about to have its neck wrung. "Five against Fate. Five against the stars. And what a five! A fat Finnish cook, an old-man butler, a slip of a girl, a loud-mouthed boy with a gun, and I—!"

"Fate, hell! Stars, hell!" Shane smashed the butt of his gun fiercely at the face of the clock on the wall. Thick glass dribbled off it. "That for Fate, and that for the stars!"

Something happened to the clock. The damaged mechanism started whirring violently, the hands began to fluctuate—the hour-hand slowly, the minute-hand more rapidly. They telescoped, jammed together in a straight line pointing at the top of the dial, stayed that way. The whirring sound stopped, the apparatus went dead.

Bridges pointed a bloodless finger at the omen; he didn't have to say anything.

In the silence the old butler came to the door, stood looking in at them a minute. "Dinner is served," he said hollowly.

"The Last Supper," Bridges shuddered. He got up, swayed, tottered toward the dining room. "Eat, drink, let us be merry, for—tonight we die!"

Ann Bridges ran to the detective, clung to him. What difference did it make, at a time like this, that Shane was still a stranger to her, that she hadn't even known him twenty-four hours before?

"And I still say it was just a coincidence," he muttered pugnaciously. "You say it too! Look at me and say it! It was just a coincidence. That happened to be the nearest place on the dial where they both met exactly, those two hands. My blows dented them. They got stuck there just as the works died, that was all. Stay sane whatever you do. Say it over and over. It was just a coincidence!"

Outside the tall French windows, in the velvety night-sky, the stars in all their glory twinkled derisively in at them.

† † †

10:45 P.M.—Dominguez, Mac. I've been trying to get through to you for fifteen minutes. Must be some trouble along the line somewhere. I'm way the hell out at a little crossroads called Sterling Junction—yeah, it's only about ten miles from the Bridges' place, in the other direction. Very bad grief. Checking the zoos like you told me, I dig up a traveling road-show— a carnival or whatever you want to call it—making a one-night-stand here.

Now they had two lions—yes, I said *had,* that's the grief. Two monsters, a male and a female, both in one cage. My check-up was a postmortem. They'd both busted out not twenty minutes before—don't know if the cage was left open through the keeper's carelessness, or deliberately tampered with. I beat it right up here to find out what I could. The female was shot dead just outside the carnival-grounds but the male got away clean. A posse is out after it with everything from shotguns to fire-extinguishers, hoping to rub it out before it gets anyone. They think it's heading toward the Bridges' estate. Someone in a Ford reported sighting what he mistook to be an enormous tawny dog with iridescent green eyes in the underbrush as he went by.

Earlier in the evening, the keeper tells me, there was a peculiar-looking duck mooning around the lion cage. Kept staring at them like he was trying to hypnotize the two brutes. The keeper caught this guy teasing them with a bit of goods torn from a woman's dress, flitting it at them through the bars. He sent him about his business, without having sense enough to try and find out what the idea was. It may have been our friend Tompkins, then again it may not. Plenty of village half-wits can't resist riling caged animals like that.

D'you suppose brutes like that can be mesmerized or hypnotized in some way? D'you suppose they can be given the scent of one particular person, through a bit of clothing, like bloodhounds? Yeah, I know, but then this whole affair is so screwy from first to last, nothing would surprise me any more. You better contact Shane right away and let him know he's up against the real thing, not a metaphor any more. There's a lot of difference between a man-eater like that and a little runt like Tompkins, when it comes to a showdown!

† † †

John Bridges was slumped in a big overstuffed chair by now, staring wild-eyed at nothing. Shane was perched on the chair arm, his gun resting on his thigh, finger around the trigger, safety off. Ann Bridges was standing behind the chair, leaning over it, pressing soothing hands to her uncle's forehead.

The portières were drawn across the French windows now, veiling the stars outside—they were there nevertheless. In addition, a ponderous book-case blocked one window, a massive desk the other. The double-doors were locked on the inside, and the key to them was in Shane's vest pocket.

The butler and the Finnish cook were, at their own request, locked in the scullery. If death must come to the head of the house, perhaps it would pass them by. They were not marked for it.

It was the awful silence that was so hard to bear. They couldn't get the old millionaire to say anything any more. Their own voices—Shane's and Ann's—were a mockery in their ears, so they quit trying to talk after a while. Bridges wouldn't drink either, and even if he had, he was past receptivity by now; it wouldn't have affected him.

The girl's face was the color of talcum. Her uncle's was a death mask, a bone structure overlaid by parchment. Shane's was granite, with a glistening line of sweat just below his hair line. He'd never forget this night, the detective knew, no matter what else happened for the rest of his life. They were all getting scars on their souls, the sort of scars people got in the Dark Ages, when they believed in devils and black magic.

The travesty of food and drink that Shane had swallowed at that shadowy supper-table a while before was sticking in his craw. How can wine warm you when the toast is death at midnight? He'd tried to urge the girl to leave while there was time, to get out and let the two of them face it alone. He hadn't been surprised at her staunch refusal; he admired her all the more for it. He would nevertheless have overridden her by physical force if necessary—the atmosphere had grown so macabre, so deadly— but for one fact, one all-important fact that he hadn't mentioned.

When he'd tried to contact McManus, to have a special bodyguard sent out to take Ann away, he found out that the phone was dead. They were cut off here. She couldn't go alone, of course; that would have been worse than staying.

They had a clock with them in the room again. Bridges begged and pleaded so hard for one, that Shane had reversed his edict. The mental agony of Bridges, and the strain on Ann and himself, he noticed, were much worse without a clock than with one. It was far better to know just how much time there was left. Shane had brought in a large one with a pendulum, from the entrance hall. It was fourteen minutes to twelve, now.

Tick, tick, tick, tick, tick—and it was thirteen minutes to twelve. The pendulum, like a harried gold planet, kept flashing back and forth behind the glass pane that cased it. Ann kept manipulating her two solacing hands over the doomed man's temples, stroking gently,

"It goes so fast, so fast," John Bridges groaned, eyes on the clock. The minute-hand, shaped like a gold spearhead, had just notched forward again—twelve to twelve.

"Damn!" Shane said with a throaty growl, "Damn!" He began to switch the muzzle of his gun restlessly up and down on his thigh. Something to shoot at, he thought; gimme something to shoot at! A drop of sweat ran vertically down his forehead as far as the bridge of his nose, then off into one of the tear-ducts beside it.

Tick, tick, tick—whish, whish, whish—eleven to twelve.

Bridges said suddenly, without taking his eyes off the clock: "Son—Shane, or whatever your name is—call Warren 2424 in the city for me. Ask *him* once more—oh, I've asked him so many times, so many thousand times already—but ask him once more, for the last time, if there isn't any hope for me? Ask him if I've got to go, if he still sees it?"

Shane said, "Who?" But he knew who. Bridges wasn't aware yet that Tompkins was no doubt in custody long ago, that McManus had probably seen to that item right after Ann's visit, first thing.

"Tompkins," the dead man in the chair answered. "I haven't—haven't heard from him in two days now. And if—if there isn't any hope, then say goodby for me."

Shane said curiously, sparring for time because he knew the phone was dead, "You want me to unlock those doors, go out there into the other room where the phone is?"

"Yes, yes," Bridges said. "It's still safe, we have—yes, there's ten minutes yet. You can be back in here inside of a minute. His landlady will answer. Tell her hurry and bring him down to the phone—"

Shane snapped his fingers mentally, got off the arm of the chair. "Maybe I can bring this baby back to life," he thought. "Why didn't I think of this before?" He gave the girl a look. "Stay right by him, where you are, Miss Ann. I'll just be outside the door."

He took the door key out, opened the two tall halves, stepped quickly to the phone in the room beyond. The lights were on all over the house, everything was still.

The phone was still dead, of course. One of the lines must be down somewhere. He said loudly into the silent mouthpiece, "Give me Warren 2424, hurry it up!" He feigned a pause, then he said: "Bring Jeremiah Tompkins to the phone, quickly! This call is from John Bridges."

He faked another wait, slightly longer this time. He could hear the clock ticking remorselessly away in there where Ann Bridges and her uncle were, everything was so quiet. He kept his gun out in his right hand; the phone was a hand-set. A gust of wind or something scuffed and snuffed at one of the French windows over on the other side of the house; instantly his gun was pointing in that direction, like the magnetic needle of a compass. There was something almost animal-like about the sound—*Phoof!* like that. A snuffle.

It wasn't repeated, and the fact that he was staging an act out here, a lifesaving act, took Shane's mind off the interruption. He said aloud, into empty space: "Tompkins? I'm talking on behalf of Mr. Bridges. Does that still hold good, for tonight at twelve? It's nearly that now, you know."

There was a long mirror-panel in the wall over him. In it he could see the room he had left, see the two of them in there, the girl and her uncle, tense, bending forward, drinking in every word he uttered.

"Fight fire with fire," he thought. "I don't know why McManus didn't sweat Tompkins down to the bone, then make him eat this prophecy to Bridges' face. That would have undone the damage quicker than anything else!"

He raised his voice. "That's more like it!" he said. "When did you find this out? Re-checked, eh? You should have let him know first thing— he's been worried sick! I'll tell him right away!" He hung up, wondering just how good an actor he was going to be.

He went briskly in again, gave them the bridgework. He could tell by the girl's face that, woman-like, she saw through the bluff; maybe she had found out already that the phone was n.g. But if he could only sell the death-candidate himself—

"It's all off!" he announced cheerfully. "Tompkins just told me so himself. There's been a change in—in, uh, the stars. He's not getting the death-vibrations any more. Can't possibly be midnight tonight. He'll tell you all about it himself when he—" Something in the old man's face stopped him. "What's the matter, what're you looking at me like that for? Didn't you hear what I just said?"

John Bridges' head was thrown wearily back, mouth open. He began to roll it slowly from side to side in negation. "Don't mock me," he said. "Death's too serious to be mocked like that. I just remembered—after I sent you out there—his landlady had that phone taken out a month ago. Too much trouble calling roomers to it all the time, she said. There is no phone at all now in the house where Tompkins lives."

Shane took it like a man. He turned away without a word, closed the doors again behind him, leaned his back against them. Tossing the key up and down in the hollow of his hand, he smiled mirthlessly out of the corner of his mouth.

The figure in the chair was holding out a hand toward him, a trembling hand. "It's five-to," he quavered. "I'm going to say goodby now. Thank you for sticking by me anyway, son. Ann, my dear, come around in front of me. Kiss me goodby."

Shane said in a hoarse, offensive voice: "What'll you have for breakfast?" He ignored the outstretched hand.

Bridges didn't answer. The girl crouched down before him and he kissed her on the forehead. "Goodby, dear. Try to be happy. Try to forget— whatever horror you're about to witness in the next few minutes."

Shane said belligerently, trying to rally him: "Not to want to die is one thing. Not to lift a finger to keep from dying is another! Were you always like this, all your life?"

The doomed man said, "It's easy to be brave with forty years ahead of you. Not so easy with only four minutes—"

The tick of the clock, the hiss of its pendulum, seemed louder than all their voices. Three minutes to twelve . . . two minutes. John Bridges' eyes were like billiard balls in his head, so rounded, so hard, so white, straining toward those two hands closing in on one another. Shane's trigger-finger kept twitching nervously, aching to pull, to let go—but in which direction he didn't know, couldn't tell.

That was the worst part of it, there wasn't anything to shoot at!

One minute to go. The space between the two hands was a sliver of white, a paring, a thread. Three pairs of eyes were on it. Dying calf-eyes; frightened woman's eyes; hard, skeptical policeman's eyes that refused to believe.

Then suddenly the space was gone. The two hands had blended into one.

A bell, a pair of them, rang out jarringly. The phone that Shane had thought dead, that *had* been dead until now, was pealing on the other side of the door. The shock lifted him off his heels. The girl jolted too. Bridges alone gave no sign, seemed already half into the other world.

Bong! the clock went mellowly, majestically.

Before the vibration had died away Shane was already outside at the signaling instrument, gun-hand watchfully fanning the empty air around him. A trick? A trap to draw him away? He'd thought of that. But Bridges and the girl were in full sight of him; to get to them anything would have to pass him first. And he had to find out what this call was.

It must be vital, coming at just this precise—

It was vital. *Bong!* went the clock a second time, over McManus' distant voice in his ears: "Hello! Shane—Shane? Line was down, couldn't get through to you till now. Been trying for an hour. . . . Everything's under control, Shane. We've beaten the rap, the guy's saved! No time to tell you now. I'll be out there the quickest I can—"

Bong! cut across the voice, third stroke of the hour.

"Hurry, chief," said Shane. "The poor guy is sweating his very life away with terror. I want to tell him it's all O.K."

"General alarm was out for Tompkins. At half-past ten tonight he walks in here of his own accord, gives himself up! Yeah, Headquarters! Said he knew he'd be arrested anyway. Was he! He's still spouting Bridges has to die. Also that he's going to conk out himself, in jail waiting for his trial to come up. The latter he has my best wishes on. Here's something for you, kid, after what you must have gone through out there tonight—according to Tompkins, you're marrying twenty-million bucks inside a year. Ann Bridges, before the year is out!"

Bong!

"Oh, one other thing. I just got word they shot a lion that was heading your way, cornered it on the outskirts of the estate. A real one that broke out of its cage earlier tonight. We thought at first Tompkins had something to do with it, but he's been able to prove he wasn't anywhere near there when it happened. Just one of those spooky coincidences—"

The girl's frenzied scream seared through Shane like cauterization. He dropped the phone like a bar of red-hot iron, whirled. Bridges flashed by before he could stop him. The old man whisked out the other door, and turned down the entrance-hall like something bereft of its senses.

"Hold him! He's gone out of his mind!" Ann Bridges screamed.

Bong! sounded dismally.

Shane raced after him. Glass crashed far down the lighted hall. Bridges was standing there, stock still, when Shane turned into the hallway. The millionaire seemed to be leaning over against the wall, up where those two stained-glass panels were.

The detective didn't see what had happened until he got there. Then he stood frozen, unable to breathe. For John Bridges was headless, or seemed to be; he ended at the neck. . . . Then Shane saw that was because he'd thrust his head through one of those leaded panes, clear to the other side.

Jagged teeth of thick, splintered glass held his neck in a vise, had pierced his jugular. You could see the dark shadow running down the inside of the lighted pane that was the millionaire's life-blood.

He was gone, gone. . . . And the square of glass he'd chosen, in his blind, headlong flight, out of all the squares, was that one of the lion rampant!

Bong!

The mane and rabid eyes and flat, feline nostrils of the beast still showed undestroyed above John Bridges' gashed neck, as though the painted image were swallowing the man bodily. And for fangs now, instead of painted ones there were jagged spears of glass, thrusting into Bridges' flesh from all sides of the orifice he himself had created.

Shane felt the cold horror which washed his spine and turned his blood into ice water.

Death by the jaws of a lion!

Bong! the clock went for the twelfth time, and then all was silence.

† † †

McManus raised worried eyes above the report he was making out. "What'll I put in here? Would you call it murder by mental suggestion?"

"I'm not so sure," Shane answered low.

"Are you starting to go superstitious on me too?" the lieutenant snapped. But his eyes went uneasily toward the window, beyond which the stars were paling into dawn.

They both kept looking troubledly out and up, at those distant inscrutable pin-points of brilliance, that no man can defy or alter.

Afterword

We are back to the subject of the future. Another form of extrasensory perception is the ability to be aware of something that has not yet taken place—to see the future, in other words. This is called "precognition," from Latin words meaning "to know before."

This is a very desirable ability, it would seem, for one of the great insecurities under which human beings live is uncertainty concerning the future. We don't know what lies in wait for us, what threatens us, what is on the point of snatching away something we hold dear. If we only knew what it might be, we might work out a method for avoiding or subverting it.

But sometimes precognition is not clear. It views things through a translucent medium, not a transparent one, and the prediction of the future is therefore stated in elliptical terms. Sometimes, in fact, the prediction is by a malevolent agency that tells the truth in such a way that it deliberately deceives.

Thus the witches tell Macbeth that "none of woman born" shall harm him. That's true, but MacDuff was not born of woman in the usual fashion but was delivered by Caesarean section. When Macbeth learns this he complains that the witches "palter with us in a double sense."

Sometimes, of course, the seer means well, but his uncertain vision deludes and misleads just the same. Combine this with the inevitability of the future, and the attempt to avoid a danger interpreted literally may lead to falling into the same danger interpreted symbolically.—I.A.

Additional Reading

Algernon Blackwood, "By Water," in *Day and Night Stories* (London: Cassell, 1917).

Wilkie Collins, "Mad Monckton," in *Curses!* Isaac Asimov, Charles G. Waugh, and Martin H. Greenberg, eds. (New York: New American Library, 1989).

Mrs. Gaskell, "The Doom of the Griffiths," in *Isaac Asimov Presents the Best Horror and Supernatural Stories of the 19th Century,* Isaac Asimov, Charles G. Waugh, and Martin H. Greenberg, eds. (New York: Beaufort Books, Inc., 1983).

Sir H. Rider Haggard, "Black Heart and White Heart," in *Witches,* Isaac Asimov, Martin H. Greenberg, and Charles C. Waugh, eds. (New York: New American Library, 1984).

"Oliver," "The Red Pipe," in *Catholic World* 99, July & Aug. 1914.

16

Reading the Future

Avram Davidson
The Woman Who Thought She Could Read

About a hundred years ago a man named Vanderhorn built the little
house. He built it one and half stories high, with attached and detached
sheds snuggling around it as usual; and he covered it with clapboards cut
at his own mill—he had a small sawmill down at the creek, Mr. Vanderhorn
did. After that he lived in the little house with his daughter and her husband
(being a widower man) and one day he died there. So the daughter and
son-in-law, a Mr. Hooten or Wooten or whatever it was, they came into
his money which he made out of musket stocks for the Civil War, and
they built a big new house next to the old one, only further back from
the street. This Mr. Wooten or Hooten or something like that, *he* didn't
have any sons, either; and *his* son-in-law turned the sawmill into a buggy
factory. Well, you know what happened to *that* business! Finally, a man
named Carmichael, who made milk wagons and baggage carts and pie-
wagons, he bought the whole Vanderhorn estate. He fixed up the big house
and put in apartments, and finally he sold it to my father and went out
of business. Moved away somewhere.

I was just a little boy when we moved in. My sister was a lot older.
The *old* Vanderhorn house wasn't part of the property any more. A lady
named Mrs. Grummick was living there and Mr. Carmichael had sold
her all the property the width of her house from the street on back to
the next lot which faced the street behind ours. I heard my father say
it was one of the narrowest lots in the city, and it was separated from
ours by a picket fence. In the front of the old house was an old weeping

willow tree and a big lilac bush like a small tree. In back were a truck garden and a few flowerbeds. Mrs. Grummick's house was so near to our property that I could look right into her window, and one day I did, and she was sorting beans.

Mrs. Grummick looked out and smiled at me. She had one of those broad faces with high cheekbones, and when she smiled her little bright black eyes almost disappeared.

"Little boy, hello!" she said. I said Hello and went right on staring, and she went right on sorting her beans. On her head was a kerchief (you have to remember that this was before they became fashionable) and there was a tiny gold earring in each plump earlobe. The beans were in two crocks on the table and in a pile in front of her. She was moving them around and sorting them into little groups. There were more crocks on the shelves, and glass jars, and bundles of herbs and strings of onions and peppers and bunches of garlic all hanging around the room. I looked through the room and out the window facing the street and there was a sign in front of the little house, hanging on a sort of one-armed gallows. *Anastasia Grummick, Midwife,* it said.

"What's a midwife?" I asked her.

"Me," she said. And she went on pushing the beans around, lining them up in rows, taking some from one place and putting them in another.

"Have you got any children, Mrs. Grummick?"

"One. I god one boy. *Big* boy." She laughed.

"Where is he?"

"I think he come home today. I *know* he come home today." Her head bobbed.

"How do you know?"

"I know because I know. He come home and I make a bean soup for him. You want go errand for me?"

"All right." She stood up and pulled a little change purse out of her apron pocket, and counted out some money and handed it to me out of the window.

"Tell butcher Mrs. Grummick want him to cut some meat for a bean soup. He knows. Mr. Schloutz. And you ged iche-cream comb with nickel, for you."

I started to go, but she gave me another nickel. "Ged *two* iche-cream combs. I ead one, too." She laughed. "One, too. One, two, three—Oh, Englisht languish!" Then she went back to the table, put part of the beans back in the crocks, and swept the rest of them into her apron. I got the meat for her and ate my French vanilla and then went off to play.

A few hours later a taxicab stopped in front of the little gray house and a man got out of it. A big fellow. Of course, to a kid, all grown-ups are real big, but he was *very* big—tremendous, he was, across, but not so tall. Mrs. Grummick came to the door.

"Eddie!" she said. And they hugged and kissed, so I decided this was her son, even before he called her "Mom."

"Mom," he said, "do I smell bean soup?"

"Just for you I make it," she said.

He laughed. "You knew I was coming, huh? You been reading them old beans again, Mom?" And they went into the house together.

I went home, thinking. My mother was doing something over the washtub with a ball of bluing. "Mama," I said "can a person read beans?"

"Did you take your milk of magnesia?" my mother asked. Just as if I hadn't spoken. "Did you?"

I decided to bluff it out. "Uh-huh," I said.

"Oh *no* you didn't. Get me a spoon."

"Well, why do you ask if you ain't going to believe me?"

"Open up," she ordered. "More. Swallow it. Take the rest. All of it. If you could see your face! Suppose it froze and stayed like that? Go and wash the spoon off."

†   †   †

Next morning Eddie was down in the far end of the garden with a hoe. He had his shirt off. Talk about shoulders! Talk about arms! Talk about a chest! My mother was out in front of our house, which made her near Eddie's mother out in back of hers. Of course my mother had to know everybody's business.

"That your son, Mrs. Grummick?"

"My son, yes."

"What does he do for a living?"

"Rachel."

"No, I mean your *son* . . . what does he do. . . ."

"He rachel. All over country. I show you."

She showed us a picture of a man in trunks with a hood over his head. "The Masked Marvel! Wrestling's Greatest Mystery!" The shoulders, arms, and chest—they could only have been Eddie's. There were other pictures of him in bulging poses, with names like, oh, The Slav Slayer, Chief Thunderwing, Young Kehoe, and so on. Every month Eddie Grummick sent his mother another photograph. It was the only kind of letter he sent because she didn't know how to read English. Or any other language, for that matter.

Back in the vegetable patch Eddie started singing a very popular song at that time, called "I Faw Down And Go *Boom!*"

†   †   †

It was a hot summer that year, a long hot summer, and September was just as hot as July. One shimmering, blazing day Mrs. Grummick called my father over. He had his shirt off and was sitting under our tree in his BVD top. We were drinking lemonade.

"When I was a kid," he said, "we used to make lemonade with brown sugar and sell it in the streets. We used to call out

> Brown lemonade
> Mixed in the shade
> Stirred by an old maid.

People used to think that was pretty funny."

Mrs. Grummick called out: "Hoo-hoo! Mister! Hoo-hoo!"

"Guess she wants *me,*" my father said. He went across the lawn. "Yes ma'am. . . ." he was saying. "Yes ma'am."

She asked, "You buy coal yed, mister?"

"*Coal?* Why, no-o-o . . . not *yet.* Looks like a pretty mild winter ahead, wouldn't you say?"

She pressed her lips together, closed her eyes and shook her head. "No! Bedder you buy soon coal. Lots coal. Comes very soon bad wedder. Bad!"

My father scratched his head. "Why, you sound pretty certain, Mrs. Grummick, but—uh—"

"I *know,* mister. If I say id, if I tell you, I *know.*"

Then I piped up and asked, "Did you read it in the beans, Mrs. Grummick?"

"Hey!" She looked at me, surprised. "How you know, liddle boy?"

My father said, "You mean you can tell a bad winter is coming from the *beans?*"

"Iss true. I know. I read id."

"*Well,* now, that's very interesting. Where I come from, used to be a man—a weather prophet, they called him—*he* used to predict the weather by studying skunk stripes. Said his grandfather'd learned it from the Indians. How wide this year, how wide last year. Never failed. So you use beans?"

So I pushed my oar in and I said, "I guess you don't have the kind of beans that the man gave Jack for the cow and he planted them and they were all different colors. Well, a beanstalk grew way way up and he climbed—"

Father said, "Now don't bother Mrs. Grummick, sonny," but she leaned over the fence and picked me up and set me down on her side of it.

"You, liddle boy, come in house and tell me. You, mister: buy coal."

Mrs. Grummick gave me a glass of milk from the nanny goat who lived in one of the sheds, and a piece of gingerbread, and I told her the story of Jack and the beanstalk. Here's a funny thing—she believed it. I'm sure she did. It wasn't even what the kids call Making Believe, it was just a pure and simple belief. Then she told *me* a story. This happened on the other side, in some backwoods section of Europe where she came from. In this place they used to teach the boys to read, but not the girls. They figured, what did they need it for? So one day there was this little girl, her brothers were all off in school and she was left at home sorting beans. She was suppossed to pick out all the bad beans and the worms, and when she thought about it and about everything, she began to cry.

Suddenly the little girl looked up and there was this old woman. She asked the kid how come she was crying. Because all the boys can learn to read, but not me. Is *that* all? the old lady asked.

Don't cry, she said. *I'll* teach you how to read, only not in books, the old lady said. Let the *men* read books, books are new things, people could read before there were books. Books tell you what *was,* but you'll be able to tell what's *going* to be. And this old lady taught the little girl how to read the beans instead of the books. And I kind of have a notion that Mrs. Grummick said something about how they once used to read *bones,* but maybe it was just her accent and she meant beans. . . .

And you know, it's a funny thing, but, now, if you look at dried beans, you'll notice how each one is maybe a little different shape or maybe the wrinkles are a little different. But I was thinking that, after all, an "A" is an "A" even if it's big or small or twisted or. . . .

But that was the story Mrs. Grummick told me. So it isn't remarkable, if she could believe *that* story, she could easily believe the Jack and the beanstalk one. But the funny thing was, all that hot weather just vanished one day suddenly, and from October until almost April we had what you might call an ironbound winter. Terrible blizzards one right after another. The rivers wre frozen and the canals were frozen and even the railroads weren't running and the roads were blocked more than they were open. And coal? Why, you just couldn't *get* coal. People were freezing to death right and left. But Mrs. Grummick's little house was always warm and it smelled real nice with all those herbs and dried flowers and stuff hanging around in it.

† † †

A few years later my sister got married. And after then, in the summertime, she and her husband Jim used to come back and visit with us. Jim and I used to play ball and we had a fine time—they didn't have any children, so they made much of me. I'll always remember those happy summers.

Well, you know, each summer, a few of the churches used to get together and charter a boat and run an excursion. All the young couples used to go, but my sister always made some excuse. See, she was always afraid of the water. This particular summer the same thing happened, but her friends urged her to come. My brother-in-law, he didn't care one way or the other. And then, with all the joking, someone said, Let's ask Mrs. Grummick to read it in the beans for us. It had gotten known, you see. Everybody laughed, and more for the fun of it than anything else, I suppose, they went over and spoke to her. She said that Sister and Jim could come inside, but there wasn't room for anybody else. So we watched through the window.

Mrs. Grummick spread her beans on the table and began to shove them around here and there with her fingers. Some she put to one side and the rest she little by little lined up in rows. Then she took from one row and added to another row and changed some around from one spot to another. And meanwhile, mind you, she was muttering to herself, for all the world like one of these old people who reads by putting his finger on each word and mumbling it. And what was the answer?

"Don't go by the water."

And that was all. Well, like I say, my sister was just looking for any excuse at all, and Jim didn't care. So the day of the excursion they went off on a picnic by car. I'd like to have gone, but I guess they sort of wanted to be by themselves a bit and Jim gave me a quarter and I went to the movies and bought ice-cream and soda.

I came out and the first thing I saw was a boy my own age, by the name of Bill Baumgardner, running down the street crying. His shirt was out and his nose was running and he kept up an awful grinding kind of howl. I called to him but he paid no attention. I still don't know where he was running from or where to and I guess maybe he didn't know either. Because he'd been told, by some old fool who should've known better, that the excursion boat had caught on fire, with his parents on it. The news swept through town and almost everybody with folks on the boat was soon in as bad a state as poor Billy.

First they said everybody was burned or drowned or trampled. Later on it turned out to be not that bad—but it was bad enough.

Oh, my folks were shook up, sure enough, but it's easier to be calm when you know it's not your own flesh and blood. I recall hearing the church clock striking six and my mother saying, "I'll never laugh at Mrs. Grummick again as long as I live." Well, she never did.

Almost everyone who had people on the boat went up the river to where it had finally been run ashore, or else they waited by the police station for news. There was a deaf lady on our street. I guess her daughter got tired of its being so dull at home and she'd lied to her mother, told her she was going riding in the country with a friend. So when the policeman came and told her—shouted at her they'd pulled out the girl's body, she didn't know what he was talking about. And when she finally understood she began to scream and scream and scream.

The policeman came over toward us and my mother said, "I'd better get over there," and she started out. He was just a young policeman and his face was pale. He held up his hand and shook his head. Mother stopped and he came over. I could hear how hard he was breathing. Then he mentioned Jim's name.

"Oh, no," my mother said, very quickly. "They didn't *go* on the boat." He started to say something and she interrupted him and said, "But I tell you, they didn't *go*—" and she looked around, kind of frantically, as if wishing someone would come and send the policeman away.

But no one did. We had to hear him out. It was Sister and Jim, all right. A big truck had gotten out of control ("—but they didn't go on the boat," my mother kept repeating, kind of stupidly. "They had this warning and so—") and smashed into their car. It fell off the road into the canal. The police were called right away and they came and pulled it out ("Oh, *oh!* Then they're all *right!*" my mother cried. *Then* she was willing to understand.) But they weren't all right. They'd been drowned.

So we forgot about the deaf neighbor lady because my mother, poor thing, *she* got hysterical. My father and the policeman helped her inside and after a while she just lay there on the couch, kind of moaning. The door opened and in tiptoed Mrs. Grummick. She had her lower lip tucked in under her teeth and her eyes were wide and she was kind of rocking her head from side to side. In each hand she held a little bottle—smelling salts, maybe, and some kind of cordial. I was glad to see her and I think my father was. I *know* the policeman was, because he blew out his cheeks, nodded very quickly to my father, and went away.

Mother said, in a weak, thin voice: "They didn't go on the boat. They didn't go because they had a warning. That's why—" Then she saw Mrs. Grummick. The color came back to her face and she just leaped off the couch and tried to hit Mrs. Grummick, and she yelled at her in a hoarse voice I'd never heard and called her names—the kind of names I was just beginning to find out what they meant. I was, I think, more shocked and stunned to hear my mother use them than I was at the news that Sister and Jim were dead.

Well, my father threw his arms around her and kept her from reaching Mrs. Grummick and I remember I grabbed hold of one hand and how it tried to get away from me.

"You *knew!*" my mother shouted, struggling, her hair coming loose. "*You* knew! You read it there, you witch! And you didn't tell! You didn't tell! She'd be alive now if she'd gone on the boat. They weren't all killed, on the boat—But you didn't say a *word!*"

Mrs. Grummick's mouth opened and she started to speak. She was so mixed up, I guess, that she spoke in her own language, and my mother screamed at her.

My father turned his head around and said, "You'd better get out."

Mrs. Grummick made a funny kind of noise in her throat. Then she said, "But, Lady—mister—no I tell you only what I see—I read there, *'Don't go by the water.'* I only can say what I see in front of me, only what I read. Nothing else. Maybe it mean one thing or maybe another. I only can read it. Please, lady—"

But we knew we'd lost them, and it was because of her.

"They ask *me,*" Mrs. Grummick said. "They *ask* me to read."

My mother kind of collapsed, sobbing. Father said, "Just get out of here. Just turn around and get out."

I heard a kid's voice saying, high, and kind of trembling, "We don't want your here, you old witch! *We hate you!*"

Well, it was *my* voice. And then her shoulders sagged and she looked for the first time like a real old woman. She turned around and shuffled away. At the door she stopped and half faced us. "I read no more," she said. "I never read more. Better not to know at all." And she went out.

Not long after the funeral we woke up one morning and the little house was empty. We never heard where the Grummicks went and it's only now that I begin to wonder about it and to think of it once again.

Afterword

We are still concerned with predicting the future. However, in "reading the future," seers do not depend on precognitive abilities, but rather use some sort of agent such as beans, tea leaves, palms, or cards to help them interpret what is to come.

Such predictions are consistently found no better than chance. In addition, as this story illustrates, it is possible for the seer to be totally benevolent and to be the victim of her own imperfect or incomplete vision, if not through direct harm, then through the infliction of unbearable guilt.—I.A.

Additional Reading

Josephine Daskam Bacon, "Oracles," in *Woman's Home Companion* 38, Nov. 11, 1911.

Nathaniel Hawthorne, "The Prophetic Pictures," in *Twice-Told Tales* (Boston: American Stationers Co., 1837).

O. Henry, "Tobin's Palm," in *Complete Works of O. Henry* (Garden City, N.Y.: Doubleday and Company, Inc., 1953).

Karel Kapek, "The Fortune Teller," in *Tales of the Occult,* Jack C. and Barbara H. Wolf, eds. (New York: Fawcett, 1975).

Oscar Wilde, "Lord Arthur Savile's Crime," in *Lord Arthur Savile's Crime and Other Stories* (London: James R. Osgood, McIlvaine, 1891).

17

Reincarnation

C. L. Moore
Tryst in Time

Eric Rosner at twenty had worked his way round the world on cattle
boats, killed his first man in a street brawl in Shanghai, escaped a
firing squad by a hairbreadth, stowed away on a pole-bound exploring
ship.

At twenty-five he had lost himself in Siberian wilderness, led a troup
of Tatar bandits, commanded a Chinese regiment, fought in a hundred
battles, impartially on either side.

At thirty there was not a continent nor a capital that had not known
him, not a jungle nor a desert nor a mountain range that had not left
scars upon his great Viking body. Tiger claws and the Russian knout, Chinese
bullets and the knives of savage black warriors in African forests had written
their tales of a full and perilous life upon him. At thirty he looked backward
upon such a gorgeous, brawling, color-splashed career as few men of sixty
can boast. But at thirty he was not content.

Life had been full for him, and yet as the years passed he was becoming
increasingly aware of a need for something which those years were empty
of. What it was he did not know. He was not even consciously aware
of missing anything, but as time went on he turned more and more to
a search for something new—anything new. Perhaps it was his subconscious
hunting blindly for what life had lacked.

There was so very little that Eric Rosen had not done in his thirty
riotous years that the search for newness rapidly became almost feverish,
and almost in vain. Riches he had known, and poverty, much pleasure

and much pain, and the extremes of human experience were old tales to him. Ennui replaced the zest for living that had sent him so gayly through the exultant years of his youth. And for a man like Eric Rosner ennui was like a little death.

Perhaps, in part, all this was because he had missed love. No girl of all the girls that had kissed him and adored him and wept when he left them had mattered a snap of the fingers to Eric Rosner. He searched on restlessly.

In this mood of feverish hunting for new things, he met the scientist, Walter Dow. It happened casually, and they might never have met a second time had not Eric said something offhand about the lack of adventure which life had to offer a man. And Dow laughed.

"What do you know about adventure?" he demanded. He was a little man with a shock of prematurely white hair and a face that crinkled into lines of derision as he laughed. "You've spent your life among dangers and gunfire—sure! But that's not real adventure. Science is the only field where true adventure exists. I mean it! The things that are waiting to be discovered offer fields of excitement like nothing you ever heard of. One man in a lifetime couldn't begin to touch the edges of what there is to know. I tell you I—"

"Oh, sure," interrupted Eric lazily. "I see what you mean. But all that's not for me. I'm a man of action; I haven't any brains. Hunching over a microscope isn't my idea of fun."

†   †   †

The argument that began then developed into a queer sort of antagonistic friendship which brought the two men together very often in the weeks that passed. But they were to know one another much more intimately than that before the true urgency of what lay in the minds of each became clear to the other.

Walter Dow had spent a lifetime in the worship of one god—inertia. "There is a bedrock," he used to say reverently, "over which the tides of time ebb and flow, over which all things material and immaterial, as the layman sees them, change and fade and form again. But the bedrock remains. Complete inertia! What couldn't we do if we attained it!"

"And what," asked Eric, "is inertia?"

Dow shot him a despairing glance.

"Everybody knows what inertia is. Newton's first law of motion is the law of inertia, stating that every body remains in a state of rest or of uniform motion in a straight line unless impressed forces change it. That's what makes people in a moving car swerve to one side when the car goes round a bend. It's what makes it so difficult for a horse to start a heavy load moving, though once it's in motion the strain eases. There's nothing that doesn't obey the law—nothing!

"But Newton didn't dream what measureless abysses of force lay behind his simple statement. Or what an understatement it was. Describing inertia by stating Newton's law is like describing the sea by saying there's foam on the waves. The inertia force is inherent in everything, just as there's moisture in everything. But behind that inertia, manifest so obscurely in matter, is a vastness of power much greater comparatively than the vastnesses of the seas which are the storehouses for the relatively tiny amounts of moisture in everything you see.

"I can't make you understand; you don't speak the language. And I sometimes wonder if I could explain even to another physicist all that I've discovered in the past ten years. But I do very firmly believe that it would be possible to anchor to that bedrock of essential, underlying inertia which is the base upon which matter builds and—and allow time itself to whirl by!"

"Yeah, and find yourself floating in space when you let go." Eric grinned. "Even I've heard that the universe is in motion through space. I don't know about time, but I'm pretty sure space would block your little scheme."

"I didn't mean you'd have to—to dig your anchor right into the rock," explained Dow with dignity. "It'd be a sort of a drag to slow you down, not a jerk that would snatch you right off the Earth. And it'd involve—immensities—even then. But it could be done. It will be done. By Heaven, I'll do it!"

Eric's sunburned face sobered.

"You're not kidding?" he asked. "A man could—could drag his anchor and let time go by, and 'up-anchor' in another age? Say! Make me an anchor, and I'll be your guinea pig!"

Dow did not smile.

"That's the worst of it," he said. "All this is pure theory and will have to remain that, in spite of all I've bragged. It would be absolutely blind experimenting, and the very nature of the element I'm experimenting with precludes any proof of success or failure. I could—to be frank with you I *have*—sent objects out through time—"

"You have!" Eric leaned forward with a jerk and laid an urgent hand on Dow's arm. "You really have?"

"Well, I've made them vanish. I think it proves I've succeeded, but I have no way of knowing. The chances are countless millions to one against my landing an experiment in my own immediate future, with all the measureless vastness of time lying open. And, of course, I can't guide it."

"Suppose you landed in your own past?" queried Eric.

Dow smiled.

"The eternal question," he said. "The inevitable objection to the very idea of time travel. Well, you never did, did you? You know it never happened! I think there must be some inflexible law which forbids the same arrangement of matter, the pattern which is one's self, from occupying the same space-time more than once. As if any given section of space-time were a design in which any arrangement of atoms is possible, except that no pattern may appear exactly twice.

"You see, we know of time only enough to be sure that it's far beyond any human understanding. Though I think the past and the future may be visited, which on the face of it seems to predicate an absolutely preordained future, a fixed and unchangeable past—yet I do not believe that time is arbitrary. There must be many possible futures. The one we enter upon is not the only way. Have you ever heard that theory explained? It's not a new one—the idea that at every point of our progress we confront crossroads, with a free choice as to which we take. And a different future lies down each.

"I can transport you into the past, and you can create events there which never took place in the past we know—but the events are not new. They were ordained from the beginning, *if* you took that particular path. You are simply embarking upon a different path into a different future, a fixed and preordained future, yet one which will be strange to you because it lies outside your own layer of experience. So you have infinite freedom in all your actions, yet everything you can possibly do is already fixed in time."

"Why, then—then there's no limit to the excitement a man could find in navigating time," said Eric almost reverently. And then in sudden urgency, "Dow, you've got to fix it up for me! This is what I've been hunting!"

"Are you crazy, boy? This is nothing that can ever be proved safe except by the actual experiment, and the experiment could never return. You know that, don't you? From what blind groping I've done, it seems to me that time is not a constant flow, but an ebb and flux that can't be measured. It would be hard to explain to you. But you couldn't return—couldn't guide yourself. You wouldn't dare try it!"

"I'm fed up with certainty and safety! And as for returning, what have I here to return to? No, you can't scare me. I've got to try it!"

"Absolutely no," said Dow firmly.

† † †

But three months later he was standing under the great skylight of his laboratory, watching Eric buckle a flat metal pack on his heavy young shoulders. Though reluctance still lined the scientist's face, under its shock of white hair he was alight almost as hotly as the younger man, with the tremendous adventure of what was about to happen. It had taken weeks of persuasion and argument, and he was not wholly at ease even yet about the experiment, but the fever that burned in Eric Rosner was not to be denied.

Now that the way was open, it seemed to Eric that all his life he had lived toward this moment in the laboratory. The need for this launching upon time's broad river was what had driven him restless and feverish through the petty adventures which life had shown him. Peace was upon him now for the first time in months. There was something rather awe-inspiring about it.

"Look here," broke in Walter Dow upon the raptness of his mood, "Are you sure you understand?"

"I don't understand anything about the works, and I don't much care," said Eric. "All I know is I'm to snap these switches here"—he laid big sunburned hands on the two rods at his belt—"when I want to move along. That will throw out the anchor. Right?"

"As far as it goes, yes. That will increase your inertia sufficiently to make you immune to time and space and matter. You will be inert mentally and physically. You'll sink down, so to speak, to the bedrock, while time flows past you. I have in this pack on your back, connecting with the switches in the belt, the means to increase your inertia until no outside force can interrupt it. And a mechanism there will permit the switches to remain thrown until one small part, insulated from the inertia in a tiny time space of its own, trips the switches again and up-anchors. And if my calculations are correct—and I *think* they are—there you'll be in some other age than ours. You can escape from it by throwing the switches again and returning to inertia, to be released after an interval by the automatic insulated mechanism in your pack. Got it?"

"Got it!" Eric grinned all over his good-looking, sunburned face. "Everything ready now?"

"Yes—yes, except that—are you sure you want to risk it? This may be plain murder, boy! I don't know what will happen!"

"That's the beauty of it—not knowing. Don't worry, Walter. Call it suicide, not murder, if that helps you any. I'm going now. Good-by."

Dow choked a little as he gripped the younger man's hand hard, but Eric's face was shining with the fever to be gone, and at the last the scientist was almost reconciled by the sight of that rapt face. Almost he saw in the last instant before the the switches closed a purpose vaster than his own, sweeping the work of his hands and the exultant young man before him into a whole that fulfilled some greater need than he could guess.

Then Eric's hands dropped to his belt. One last instant he stood there, tall under the clear radiance of the skylight, blond and sunburned, the tale of his riotous, brawling life clear upon his scarred, young face, but upon it, too, a raptness and an eagerness that sent a quick stab of unreasoning hope through the scientist's mind. Surely success would crown this experiment. Surely all the vital, throbbing aliveness, the strength and seasoned toughness of this brawny young man before him could not snuff into nothing as the switches closed. Danger awaited him—yes, danger against which the gun at his belt might not avail at all. But splendor, too. Splendor—envy clouded Dow's eyes for a moment, as the switches closed.

†   †   †

Past Eric's eyes eternity ebbed blindingly. Rushing blankness closed over him, but he was conscious of infinite motion, infinite change passing over him, by him, through him, as events beyond imagination streamed past that anchorage in inertia's eternal bedrock. For a timeless eternity it lasted. And then—and then—

A confusion of noises from very far away began to sound in his ears. That rushing blurriness abated and slowed and by degrees took on a nebulous shape. He was looking down from a height of about thirty feet upon a street scene which he identified roughly as Elizabethan by the costumes of those who moved through the crowd below him.

Something was wrong. The machine could not have worked perfectly somehow, for he did not feel that he was actually present. The scene was uncertain and wavery, like a faulty film reflecting upon an uneven screen. There must have been an obstruction somewhere in that particular time section, though what it was he never knew.

He leaned forward for a few minutes, looking down eagerly through the hazy uncertainty that shrouded the place. He did not seem to himself to be resting on anything; yet he was conscious of that forward bending as he looked down. It was inexplicable.

The noises rose up to him now loudly, now softly, from the shifting, pushing throng. Shopkeepers bawled their wares from both sides of the street. Apprentice boys darted to and fro through the crowd, waylaying passers-by.

A girl in a scarlet cloak flung open a window and leaned out to wave a message to someone below, her bright hair falling about her face. In the room behind her, dimly seen, another girl moved forward and flung both arms about her waist, laughing, dragging her back. Their merriment rose clearly to Eric's ears.

But all this was not real. That cloudiness hazed it over time and again, until his eyes ached from trying to follow what was happening. Regretfully, he reached for the switch at his belt, and in a breath the whole place shimmered and vanished. Oblivion in a torrent poured over him as the centuries plunged by over the bedrock inertia to which he was anchored.

The automatic workings of the time machine on his shoulders clicked on. Then the switches threw themselves and the blankness cleared from Eric's mind again. He found himself staring through a screen of leaves upon a grassy meadow through which trickled a small brook. He was tangibly, actually here this time, standing on soft turf and feeling the stir of a breeze through the leaves.

Over the slope of the meadow before him dingy white sheep moved slowly. A little curly-haired boy in a brief leather garment leaned on the grass drowsily, watching them. Sun lay yellow over the whole scene. It was peaceful and dreamy as an idyl, but for some obscure reason Eric's hands moved to his belt almost of their own accord, a feeling of disappointment stirring vaguely in his mind. This was not what he sought. Sought? Was he seeking? Almost one might think so, he told himself.

The thought troubled him as he clicked the switches at his belt. What was it that by its absence here made him dismiss the idyllic scene with a glance? He was hunting something, restlessly searching through the ages for—something. Then the tidal rush of the centuries over his anchorage blotted out wonder and all else in its oblivion.

† † †

Sunlight like a physical blow crashed down about him—blazing hot sun that beat violently upon marble pavement and struck blindingly up again into his eyes. For a few seconds he was aware of nothing more than this intolerable glare. Gradually out of the blazing heat the lines of marble walls became clear about him. He stood upon the floor of a dazzling white marble pit about twenty feet square. Against the opposite wall lay a man whose naked, blood-spattered body was so still under the down-blazing heat that Eric could not be sure that he was alive.

He had seen this much before the rising babble of excited voices above him mounted loud enough to pierce his dazed surprise. He looked up. Leaning over the pit's rim were faces—faces and arms and here and there a trail of velvet robe, a bright scarf's fringe. They were the faces of aristocrats, fine and dissipated and cruel. But all expression was wiped from every one now.

In that first glance he had of them he thought they must be Romans. He had little to judge by save their hair dressing, and only a momentary glimpse of that; for, as he raised his head, his eyes met the strange, smoke-blue eyes of a woman who leaned upon the marble rim just in front of him, and above. A little space separated her from those on each side. He had the swift impression that she was of higher rank than the rest—some fleeting touch of arrogance and pride in the face looking down on him. And it was a familiar face. Why he could not guess, but in that glimpse of her he was sure that he had seen those features somewhere before, and recently.

Then she lifted one bare arm upon whose whiteness the sun struck dazzlingly, and pointed downward. From behind her came the sound of metal upon stone, and in the blinding light he saw a man's arm move swiftly. The sun struck upon a long shaft of steel. The spear was hurtling straight for his breast as his hands flew to his belt. The switches clicked, and in one great sweeping blur the whole scene vanished.

After that came a blurry interval of unthinkable inertness. The centuries poured past. Then reality burst upon him again as the switches clicked off. He choked suddenly and gasped as air thicker and moister than the air of a tropical swamp smothered his lungs. He stood there for a moment struggling with it, forcing himself to evener breathing, as his bewildered gaze swept the scene before him.

He stood in a square of ruined walls that must once have been a small building, though roof and sides had vanished now and little was left but a crumbling square outlining the long-fallen house. To one side a higher heap of stone, which was all that was left of the western wall, obstructed his view of what lay beyond. Over the fallen blocks before him he could see a vast paved square dotted with other buildings fallen into ruin. And beyond these, under a heavily clouded sky through which the obscured sun poured in a queer, grayly radiant light, buildings of barbaric colors and utterly alien architecture lifted their Cyclopean heights, massive as the walls of Karnak, but too strangely constructed to awake any memories.

Even at this distance he recognized those darker blotches upon the tremendous walls as the sign of a coming dissolution. It was a city more awfully impressive than any he had ever dreamed of, standing gigantic under the low, gray sky of this swamplike world—but its glory was past. Here and there gaps in the colossal walls spoke of fallen blocks and ruined buildings. By the thick, primordial air and the small swamp and the unrecognizable architecture he knew that he gazed upon a scene of immortal antiquity, and his breath came quicker as he stared, wondering where the people were whose Cyclopean city this was, what name they bore and if history had ever recorded it.

†   †   †

A medley of curious sounds coming nearer awoke him from the awed trance into which he had sunk. Feet shuffling over pavement, the clang of metal shivering against metal, hoarse breathing, and a strange, intermittent hissing he could not account for. It came from that part of the great square which the crumbling wall beside him hid.

That queer hissing sounded loud. Someone yelled in a growling guttural, and he heard the beat of running feet, staggering and uncertain, coming nearer. Then a figure that was a dazzle of white and scarlet flashed through the aperture in the crumbling wall where a door must once have been. It was a girl. Her choked breath beat loud in the narrow place, and the scarlet that stained and streaked her was bright blood that gushed in ominous spurts from a deep gash in her side. She was incredibly white in the sunless day of this primordial city. Afterward he could never remember much more than that—her dazzling whiteness and the blood pumping in measured spurts from severed arteries—and the smoke blueness of her eyes.

He did not know what she had worn, or anything else about her, for his eyes met the smoky darkness of hers, and for a timeless moment they stared at one another, neither moving. He knew her. She was that royal Roman who had condemned him to death in the sun-hot pit; she was the laughing, red-cloaked girl who had leaned from the Elizabethan window. Incredibly, unquestionably, they three were the same blue-eyed girl.

A yell and a scrambling sound outside roused her from her tranced stare. He wondered wildly if he had not seen puzzled recognition in her filming eyes in that one long instant before she swung staggering toward the door. He knew she was dying as she turned, but some inner compulsion held him back, so that he did not offer to support her, only stood watching. After all, there was no help for her now. The smoke-blue eyes were glazing and life gushed scarlet out of her riven side.

He saw her reel back against the broken wall, and again he heard that strange hissing as her right hand rose and from a shining cylinder grasped in it a long stream of blue heat flared. There was a yell from outside. A throbbing silence broken only by the spatter of the girl's blood on the pavement. And then something very strange happened.

She turned and glanced over her shoulder and her eyes met his. Something choked in his throat. He was very near understanding a great many things in that instant while her filming blue gaze held his—why he had felt so urgently all his life long the need of something he had never neared, until now—words rushed to his lips, but he never spoke them. The instant passed in a flash.

The girl in that illuminating moment must have realized something yet hidden from him, for her lips trembled and an infinite tenderness softened her glazing eyes. And at the same instant her hand rose again, and for the last time he heard that searing hiss. She had turned her nameless weapon upon herself.

In a flare of blue brilliance he saw her literally melt before his eyes. The stones glowed hot, and the smell of burned flesh filled the inclosure. And Eric went sick with a sensation of devastating loss. She was dead— gone—out of all reach now, and the universe was so empty that—he had no time to waste on his own emotion, for through the broken wall was pouring a mob of shambling things that were not yet men.

Big, hairy, apish brutes brandishing clubs and heavy stones, they surged in a disordered mob through the ruined stones. One or two of them carried curiously shaped rusty swords of no recognizable pattern. And Eric understood.

Dying, the girl would not leave even her untenanted body to their defilement. Pride had turned her hand to lay the consuming beam upon herself—an inbred pride that could have come only from generations of proud ancestry. It was a gesture as aristocratic and as intensely civilized as the weapon that destroyed her. He would have known by that gesture alone, without her flame-thrower or the unmistakable fineness of her body and her face, that she was eons in advance of the beasts she fled.

In the brief second while the brute-men stood awed in the broken wall, staring at the charred heap upon the pavement and at the tall golden man who stood over it, Eric's mind was busy, turning over quick wonderings and speculations even as his hands reached for the switches at his belt.

Her race must have reared that immense, unearthly city, long ago. A forgotten race, wise in forgotten arts. Perhaps not born on earth. And the hordes of brutish things which would one day become men must have assailed them as time beat down their Cyclopean city and thinned their inbred ranks.

This girl, this unknown, unimaginably far-distant girl, perhaps starborn, certainly very alien—had died as all her race must be doomed to die, until the last flicker of that stupendous civilization was stamped out and earth forgot the very existence of the slim, long-legged human race which had once dwelt upon her surface when her own primordial man was still an apish beast.

But—they had not wholly died. He had seen her in other ages. Her smoky eyes has looked down upon him in the Roman pit; her own gay voice had called across the Elizabethan street. He was very sure of that. And the queer, stunning sense of loss which had swept over him as he saw her die lightened. She had died, but she was not gone. Her daughters lived through countless ages. He would find her again, somewhere, somehow, in some other age and land. He would comb the centuries until he found her. And he would ask her then what her last long stare had meant, so meltingly tender, so surely recognizing, as she turned the blue-hot blaze upon herself. He would—

A deep-throated bellow from the doorway in the wall startled him out of his thoughts even as he realized their absurdity. The foremost of the brute-men had overcome his awe. He lifted a rusty sword, forged by what strange hands for what unknown and forever forgotten purpose there was no way of knowing, and plunged forward.

Barely in time, Eric's hands closed on the switches and the stupendous, time-forgotten city swirled sidewise and melted forever into the abysses of the past.

In the mental and physical inertia that drowned him with its oblivion as the current closed he waited moveless, and once more the centuries rushed by. The inexorable machinery clicked on. After a timeless interval light broke again. He awoke into more than tropical sultriness, the stench of mud and musk and welter of prehistoric swamps. There was nothing here save great splashing monsters and the wriggling life of hot seas. He flicked the switches again.

† † †

The next time a broad plain surrounded him, featureless to the horizon, unrecognizable, and the next a horde of hairy, yelling men charged up a rocky hill upon whose height he had materialized. After that he visited and left in rapid succession a ruined temple in the midst of a jungle, a camp of ragged nomads with slant eyes and crooked legs, and an inexplicable foggy place through which reverberated the roar of staccato guns which sounded like no guns he had ever heard. Nowhere appeared the girl with the smoke-blue eyes.

He was beginning to despair, when, after so many flashing scenes that he had lost count of them, the darkness of rushing centuries faded into a dawning scene of noise and confusion. He stood upon the trampled earth of a courtyard, hot under the rays of a broiling, noon-high sun.

He heard shouts in an unknown tongue, the trample of horses' feet and the impatient jingle of harness, the creak of wheels. Through the shining dust that eddied, cloudlike, under the feet of the crowd that bustled about the inclosure, he made out a train of heavy wagons about which strange, short, bearded men swarmed in busy confusion, heaving crates and bales into the vehicles and calling in odd gutterals. Men on horseback galloped to and fro recklessly through the crowd, and the heavy-headed oxen stood in patient twos at each wagon.

Eric found himself in a corner of the low wall that circled the yard and, in the tumult, quite unnoticed so far. He stood there quietly, hand resting lightly on the butt of his revolver, watching the scene. He could not guess where he was, in what land or time, in the presence of what alien race. The men were all little and dark and hairy, and somehow crooked, like gnomes. He had never heard a tongue like the gutterals they mouthed.

Then at the far side of the courtyard a lane opened in the crowd, and through it a column of the crooked brown men with curly-pronged pikes across their shoulders came marching. They had a captive with them— a girl. A tall girl, slim and straight, high-headed. Eric leaned forward eagerly. Yes, it was she. No mistaking the poise of that high, dark head, the swing of her body as she walked. As she came nearer he saw her eyes, but he did not need the smoky blue darkness in them to convince him.

She wore manicals on her wrists, and chains clanked between her ankles as she walked. A leather tunic hung from one shoulder in tatters, belted at the waist by a twisted thong from which an empty scabbard swung. She walked very proudly among the gnarled soldiers, looking out over their heads in studied disdain. At a glance the highbred aristocracy of her was clear, and he could not mistake the fact that her own people must be centuries in advance of the squat, dark race which held her captive.

The clamor had quieted now in the courtyard. Dust was settling over the long wagon train, the low-headed oxen, the horsemen stationed at intervals along the line. In silence, the crowd fell back as the soldiers and their aloof captive paced slowly across the couryard. Tension was in the air.

†   †   †

Eric had the vague feeling that he should know what was to come. A haunting familiarity about this scene teased him. He racked a reluctant memory as he watched the procession near the center of the great yard. A stone block stood there, worn and stained. Not until the tall girl had actually reached that block, and the soldiers were forcing her to her knees, did Eric remember. Sacrifice—always before a caravan set forth in the very old days, when the gods were greedy and had to be bribed with human lives.

His gun was in his hand and he was plunging forward through the startled crowd before he quite realized what he was doing. They gave way before him in sheer amazement, falling back and staring with bulging eyes at this sudden apparition in their midst of a tall, yellow-headed Juggernaut yelling like a madman as he surged forward.

Not until he had reached the line of soldiers did he meet any resistance. They turned on him in gutterally shouting fury, and he shot them down as fast as his revolver would pump bullets. At that range he could not miss, and six of the squat gnomes crumpled to the dust in a haze of blue gun smoke.

They must have thought him a god, dealing death in a crash of thunder and the hot blaze of lightning. They shrieked in panic, terror, and the courtyard emptied like magic. Horses plunged and reared, squealing. Pandemonium streamed out of the inclosure, leaving behind only a haze of churned dust, slowly settling. Through the shimmer of it, across the huddle of bodies, Eric looked again into the smoky eyes of that girl he had last seen under the stupendous walls of the time-buried city. And again he thought he saw a puzzled and uncomprehending recognition on her face, shining even through her terror. She fronted him resolutely, standing up proudly in her chains and staring with frightened eyes that would not admit their fear.

"Don't be afraid," he said in as gentle a voice as he could command, for he knew the tone would convey a message, though the words did not. "We'd better get out of here before they come back."

He was reloading his gun as he spoke. She still did nothing but stare, wide-eyed, rigid in sternly suppressed terror. There was no time to waste now trying to quiet her fears. Already he saw dark, bearded faces peering around corners at him. He skirted the heap of fallen soldiers and swung the girl off her feet. She gasped as his arms closed, but no other sound escaped her as he hoisted her over one shoulder, holding her there with a clasp around her knees so that he might have his gun hand free. With long, unhurried strides he left the courtyard.

A mud-walled village ringed the big inclosure. Serenely, he went down the dusty street, wary eyes scanning the building, gun ready in one hand and the chained girl slung across his heavy shoulder. From behind shelter they watched him go, tall and golden under the noonday sun, a god out of nowhere. Legends were to grow up about that noon's events—a god come down to earth to claim his sacrifice in person.

When he reached the outskirts of the village he paused and set the girl on her feet, turning his attention to the shackles that bound her. The chains were apparently for ceremonial use rather than utilitarian, for in his powerful hands they snapped easily, and after a brief struggle with the metal links he had her free of chains, though the anklets and cuffs still gripped her limbs. These he could not loosen, but they were not heavy and she could, he thought, wear them without discomfort. He rose as the last chain gave in his hands, and stared round the wide circle of rolling hills that hemmed them in.

"What now?" he asked, looking down at her.

The uncertainty of his attitude and the query in his voice must have reassured her that he was at least human, for the look of terror faded a little from her eyes and she glanced back down the street as if searching for pursuers, and spoke to him—for the first time he heard her voice—in a low, lilting tongue that startled him by the hint of familiarity he caught in its cadences. He had a smattering of many languages, and he was sure that this was akin to one he knew, but for the moment he could not place it.

When he did not answer she laid an impatient hand on his arm and pulled him along a few steps, then paused and looked up inquiringly. Clearly she was anxious to leave the village. He shrugged and gestured helplessly. She nodded, as if in understanding, and set off at a rapid pace toward the hills. He followed her.

†   †   †

It was a tireless pace she set. The metal circles on wrists and ankles seemed not to hinder her, and she led the way over hill after hill, through clumps of woodland and past a swamp or two, without slackening her pace. For hours they traveled. The sun slid down the sky; the shadows lengthened across the hills. Not until darkness came did she pause. They had reached a little hollow ringed with trees. On one side of it a rocky outcropping formed a shelter, and a spring bubbled up among the stones. It was an ideal spot for a camp.

She turned and spoke for the second time, and he knew then why her language was familiar. Definitely it was akin to the Basque tongue. He had once had opportunity to pick up a little of that queer, ancient language, perhaps the oldest spoken in the world. It is thought to be the last remnant of the pre-Aryan tongues, and linked with vanished races and forgotten times. And the supposition must have been true, for this girl's speech echoed it in baff_ingly familiar phrases. Or—he paused here— was he in the future or the past from his own time? Well, no matter— she was saying something all but incomprehensible about fire, and looking about among the underbrush. Eric shrugged off his speculations on the subject of tongues and helped her gather firewood.

His matches caused her a few minutes of awe-struck terror when the fire was kindled under the overhanging rocks of the hillside. She quieted after a bit, though, and presently pressed him to a seat by the fire and vanished into the dark. He waited uneasily until she returned, stepping softly into the light with a kicking rabbit in her hands. He never understood, then or later, how it was that she could vanish into the hills and return with some small animal unhurt in her arms. He could scarcely believe her swift enough to run them down, and she had nothing with which to make snares. It was one of the many mysteries about her that he never fathomed.

They skinned and cleaned the little beast with his hunting knife, and she broiled it over the smoldering coals. It was larger and stronger than the rabbits of his own day, and its meat was tough and sharply tangy.

Afterward they sat by the carefully banked fire and tried to talk. Her name was Maia. Her people lived in a direction vaguely eastward and about one day's journey away, in a white-walled city. All his attempts to learn in what age he found himself were fruitless. He thought from her almost incomprehensible speech that she was telling him how ancient her race was, and how it had descended through countless generations from a race of gods who dwelt in a sky-high city in the world's beginning. It was all so vague and broken that he could not be sure.

She looked at him a great deal out of grave blue eyes as she talked, and there was in their depths a haunted remembrance. He was to recall that look of hers more clearly than anything else about her, afterward. So many times he caught the puzzled, brooding gaze searching his face in troubled incomprehension.

He sat there silently, scarcely heeding the occasional low cadences of her voice. He was learning the grave, sweet lines of her young face, the way her eyes tilted ever so faintly at the corners, the smooth plane of her cheek, the curved line on which her lips closed. And sometimes the wonder of their meeting, through so many ages, came down upon him breathlessly, the realization of something too vast and strange and wonderful to put into words, and he stared into the sweet, familiar face almost with awe, thinking of those other grave, dark eyes and serene faces, so like hers, that ranged through time. There was a tremendous purpose behind that patterning of faces through the centuries, too great for him to grasp.

He watched her talk, the firelight turning that dearly familiar face ruddy, and shining in the deep, troubled blueness of her eyes, and a strange and sudden tenderness came over him. He bent forward, a catch in his throat, laying his hands over hers, looking into the memory-haunted depths of her eyes.

He said not a word, but he stared deep and long, and he could have sworn that sudden answer lighted in her gaze, for one swift instant blotting out that puzzled straining after remembrance and turning her whole face serene and lovely with understanding. The moment held them enchanted, warm in the deeps of something so breathlessly lovely that he felt the sting of sudden hotness behind his eyes. In that instant all puzzlement and incomprehension was swept aside and the answer to the great purpose behind their meetings hovered almost within grasp.

† † †

Then, without warning, the girl's face crumpled into tears and she snatched her hands away, leaping to her feet with the long, startled bound of a wild thing and facing him in the firelight with clenched fists and swimming eyes. It was not rebellion against his clasp of her hands—surely she could see that he meant no violence—but a revolt against some inner enemy that dwelt behind the tear-bright blue eyes. She stood irresolutely there for a moment, then made a helpless little gesture and dropped to the ground once more, sitting there with bowed shoulders and bent head, staring into the embers.

Presently her voice began softly, speaking in little disconnected phrases that fell monotonously into the silence. He made out enough to understand her sudden revulsion against the strange and lovely oneness of understanding that had gripped them both. She was betrothed. She made him realize that it was more than the simple plighting of vows between lovers. He caught vague references to religious ceremonies, marriage of high priest and chosen virgin, temple rites and the anger of a jealous god. That much he understood.

She must fulfill the requisites of the priest god's bride. No man must touch her until she came into the holy embrace of the church. She must not even know love for another man. And that, perhaps, was why she had pulled away from him in the firelight and struggled through tears with an inner enemy that reached traitorously out to the golden stranger who held her hands.

She was unshakable in her devotion to that concept. Eric had known, from the moment he first looked into her smoke-filled eyes, that she would be faithful to any ideal that stirred her. A girl like this had destroyed the body from which her soul was slipping, that barbarians might not defile it. A girl like this, imperiously royal and inflexibly cruel, had watched torture in a sun-hot pit, refusing to doubt her civilization's concept of the divine right of emperors over their subjects' lives. She was stubborn, this girl. Stubborn in her beliefs whether they were kind or cruel. She was of the stuff from which martyrs are made.

They stood watch in turn over the fire that night, she insisting on her share of it with a grave certainty that brooked no opposition. What the dangers were which made it impossible for both to sleep at once he did not know. On those times when he dropped off into slumber the last thing his closing eyes saw was the girl Maia's figure, slim and round in her torn leather tunic, warm in the firelight, serene in her determination upon her life's ordered plan. Nothing could swerve her. She was so fine—

an ache came up in his throat as he closed his eyes.

When he awoke in the morning she had brought in a brace of small, fat birds like quail and was preparing them at the edge of the spring. She smiled gravely as he sat up, but she said nothing, and she did not look at him any more than she could help. She was taking no chances with that traitor within.

In silence, they shared the birds she cooked over the embers. Afterward he tried to make her understand that he would take her as far as the gates of her city. At first she demurred. She knew this country well. She was strong and young, wise in the lore of the hills. She needed no escort. But Eric could not bring himself to leave her until he must. That moment of crystal understanding, the warm, sweet unity they had shared even for so short a breath had forged a bond between them that he could not bear to break.

And at last she consented. They spoke very little after that. They put out the fire and set off again over the rolling hills toward the bright patch on the sky where the sun was rising. All day they traveled. In her mysterious, secret way she found another rabbit when hunger came on them around noontide, and they paused to eat. In the afternoon the pack on his back that held that time machine began to irk Eric's Viking strength. She eyed it curiously as he hitched his load forward to ease its burden, but she said nothing.

Twilight was darkening over the hills when Maia paused on the crest of a little rise and pointed ahead. Eric saw a pattern of white houses ringed by a broken wall a little way distant upon the crown of a higher hill than the rest. And here she made it clear that she must leave him. He was not to accompany her within sight of the city walls.

He stood on the hilltop, watching her go. She did not look back. She walked lightly, surely, the long grass breaking like green surf about her knees, her head high and resolute. He watched her until she passed, a little far-off figure, under the broken wall, and its gateway swallowed her up out of his sight forever. And in his heart was a mingling of pain and loss and high anticipation. For he was growing increasingly sure now that there was much more than chance behind these brief and seemingly so futile meetings with the one deathless, blue-eyed girl.

He laid his hands on the switches at his belt confidently as that proudly moving young figure vanished under the gate. He had lost her—but not for long. Somewhere in the veiled, remote future, somewhere in the unexplored past she waited him. His fingers closed over the switch.

† † †

Darkly the rush of centuries swept over him, blotting away the hills and the green meadows between, and the nameless white city that was crumbling into decay. He would never see Maia again, but there were other Maias, waiting. Oblivion swallowed him up and his impatience and his dawning conviction of a vast purpose behind his journeyings, in the great grayness of its peace.

Out of that blankness a blue day dawned, bright over a moated castle's battlements. From a hilltop perhaps a quarter of a mile away he saw the surge of armored men under the walls, heard shouts and the clang of metal on metal drifting to him on the gentleness of a little breeze. And it occurred to him how often it was upon scenes of strife and sudden death that he chanced in his haphazard journeying. He wondered if they had been so thick in the past that the odds were against his coming into peaceful places, or if his own life of danger and adventuring had any influence upon the points in time which he visited so briefly.

But it mattered little. He looked around searchingly, wondering if another blue-eyed Maia dwelt near him in this medieval world. But there was nothing here. Green forest closed in at the hill's foot. Save for the castle there was no sign of civilization, no sign of men but for the shouting besiegers. Perhaps she lived somewhere in this blue, primitive world, but he could not risk a search for her. She was elsewhere, too.

Suddenly he was awed by the certainty of that—the incomprehensible vastness of his certainty and of her presence. She was everywhere. From time's beginning to time's close—she was. No era had not known her; no spot on the world's surface had not felt the press of her feet. And though the infinite future and the infinite past held her, and the earth's farthest corners, yet in reality every incarnation of her was here and now, available to him with no greater interval between her countless daughters than the instant flash of the centuries that poured over him when the switches closed. She was omnipresent, eternal. He knew her presence in the oblivion that swallowed him as his hands gripped the switches again and the beleaguered castle melted into the past.

† † †

Two children were playing by a shallow river. Eric walked slowly toward them through the warm sand. A little girl, a little boy in brief tunics of soiled white. Perhaps ten years old they were, and absorbed in their play at the water's edge. Not until his shadow fell across their castle of rocks and sand did they look up. And the girl child's eyes were blue as smoke in her small, tanned face.

Those familiar eyes met his. For a long moment she stared. Then she smiled hesitantly, very sweetly, and rose to her bare feet, shaking the sand from her tunic and looking up at him still with that grave, sweet smile illuminating her small face and a queer hesitation checking her speech.

At last she said, *"Ou e'voo?"* in the softest, gentlest voice imaginable. It was remotely recognizable as a tongue that might one day be—or once had been—French. "Who are you?"

"*Je suis* Eric," he told her gravely.

She shook her head a little. "*Zh n'compren—*" she began doubtfully, in that strange, garbled tongue so like French. But she broke off in her denial, for though the name was strange to her yet he was sure he saw recognition begin to dawn in the smoke-blue eyes he knew so well. "*Zh voo z'ai vu?*"

"Have you?" he asked her very gently, trying to distort his French into the queer sounds of hers. "Have you really seen me before?"

"I thought so," she murmured shyly, bewilderment muting her speech until it sounded scarcely above a childish whisper. "I have seen your face before—somewhere, once—long ago. Have I? Have I—Eric? I do not know your name. I never heard it before. But your face—you—O, Eric dear—I do love you!"

Halfway through that speech she had changed her "*voo*" to the "*tu*" of intimacy, and the last of it came out in a little rush of childish affection, "*Eric, cher—zh t'aime!*"

Somewhere back among the willows that lined the shallow stream a woman's voice called sharply. The sound of feet among dead leaves approached. The little boy jumped to his feet, but the girl seemed not to hear. She was looking up at Eric with wide blue eyes, her small face rapt with a child's swift adoration. Ten years older and she might have questioned the possibility of that instant recognition, perhaps unconsciously checked the instant warmth that rose within her, but the child's mind accepted it without question.

The woman was very near now. He knew he must not frighten her. He stooped and kissed the little girl's cheek gently. Then he took her by the shoulders and turned her toward the woods into which the boy had already vanished.

"Go to your mother," he told her softly. And he laid his hands again on the switches. She was beginning to know him, he thought, as the river bank swirled sidewise into nothingness. Each time they met the recognition grew stronger. And though there was no continuity in their meetings, so that he seemed to be jumping back and forth through time and this child might be the remote ancestress or the far descendant of his resolute Maia, yet somehow—by no racial memory surely, for it was not down a direct line of women that he progressed, but haphazardly to and fro through their ranks—somehow they were beginning to know him. Oblivion blotted out his puzzling.

† † †

Out of the rushing dark a steel-walled city blazed into sudden, harsh life. He stood on one tower of its many heights, looking out and down over a dizzy vista of distances that swam with the reflections of sunlight on steel. He stood still for a moment, shading his eyes and staring. But he was impatient. Something instinctive in him, growing stronger now and surer of itself as this strange chain of circumstance and meeting drew on to its conclusion, told him that what he sought lay nowhere in this section out of time. Without a glance around the stupendous steel marvel of the city he gripped the switches once more, and in a shimmer and a dazzle the shining metropolis melted into oblivion.

A burst of wild yelling like the voices of wolves baying from savage human throats smote through the darkness at him even before the sight of what was coming. Then a plank flooring was under his feet and he looked out over a tossing surface of tousled heads and brandished fists and weapons, toward another platform, this of stone, the height of his across the thunderous sea of the mob. The crackle of flames was mounting even above that roaring. On the other platform bound to a tall, charred stake, ringed with fagots and rising flames, the blue-eyed girl stood proudly. She was very straight against the pillar, chin high, looking out in disdain over the tumult below.

For the breath of a second Eric glanced round him, snatching at straws in a frantic effort to find some way of saving her. On that platform behind him speechless amazement had striken dumb a little party of men and women in brightly colored garments of 16th century cut. They must have been nobles, viewing the burning from this favored seat. Eric wasted only one glance at their stupefied surprise. He swung round again, his desperate eyes raking the mob. No hope there. It clamored for the tall girl's life in one tremendous, wolf-savage baying that ripped from every throat there in a single blending roar.

"Witch!" they yelled. "Death to the witch!" in an archaic English that he understood without too much difficulty, a blood-hungry baying that brooked no denial. They had not seen him yet. But the girl had.

Over their heads, through the little shimmering heat waves that were rising about her already in veils of scorching breath, her smoke-blue eyes met his. It was a meeting as tangible almost as the meeting of hands. And like the grip of hands so that gaze held, steady and unswerving for a long moment—burning witch of old England and tall young adventurer of modern America gazing with sure recognition in the eyes of each. Eric's heart jumped into a quickened beating as he saw the sureness in those smoke-blue eyes he had gazed into so often. She knew him—without any question or doubt she recognized him.

Over the wolf-baying of the mob he heard her voice in one high, clear scream.

"You've come! I knew you'd come!"

At the sound of it silence dropped over the crowd. Almost in one motion they swung round to follow her ecstatic stare. And in the instant of their stricken surprise at the man they saw there, tall and golden against the sky, a figure out of no experience they had ever had before—the witch's voice rang clear.

"You've come! O, I knew you would, in the end. *They* always said you would. *They* knew! And I must die for the knowledge I got from *Them*—but by that knowledge I know this is not the end. Somewhere, someday, we will meet again. Good-by—good-by, my dearest!"

Her voice had not faltered, though the flames were licking up about her, and now, in a great burst of crimson, they caught in the fagots and blazed up in a gush that enveloped her in raving inferno. Choked with horror, Eric swung up his gun hand. The bark of the report sent half the crowd to its knees in terror, and he saw through the flames the girl's tall figure slump suddenly against her bonds. This much at least he could do.

Then, in the midst of a silence so deep that the creak of the planks under his feet was loud as he moved, he sheathed the gun and closed his hands over the switches. Impatience boiled up in him as the prostrate crowd and the flame-wrapped witch and the whole ugly scene before him reeled into nothingness.

He was coming near the goal now. Each successive step found recognition surer in her eyes. She knew him in this incarnation, and he was full of confidence now that the end and the solution was near. For though in all their meetings there had been barriers, so that they two could never wholly know one another or come into the unity of love and comprehension which each meeting promised, yet he knew very surely that in the end they must. All this had not been in vain.

In the oblivion that washed over him was so sure a consciousness of her omnipresence—in all the centuries that were sweeping past, in all the lands those centuries washed over, throughout time and space and life itself, her ever-present loveliness—that he welcomed the darkness as if he embraced the girl herself. It was full of her, one with her. He could not lose her or be far from her or even miss her now. She was everywhere, always. And the end was coming. Very soon—very soon he would know—

† † †

He woke out of the oblivion, blindly into darkness. Like the fold of wings it engulfed him. If he was standing on solid earth, he did not know it. He was straining every faculty to pierce that blinding dark, and he could not. It was living darkness, pulsing with anticipation. He waited in silence.

Presently she spoke.

"I have waited so long," she said out of the blackness in her sweet, clear voice that he knew so well he did not need the evidence of his eyes to tell him who spoke.

"Is this the end?" he asked her breathlessly. "Is this the goal we've been traveling toward so long?"

"The end?" she murmured with a little catch of mirth in her voice. "Or the beginning, perhaps. Where in a circle is end or beginning? It is enough that we are together at last."

"But what—why—"

"Something went wrong, somewhere," she told him softly. "It doesn't matter now. We have expiated the forgotten sins that kept us apart to the very end. Our troubled reflections upon the river of time sought each other and never wholly met. And we, who should have been time's masters, struggled in the changing currents and knew only that everything was wrong with us, who did not know each other.

"But all that is ended now. Our lives are lived out and we can escape time and space into our own place at last. Our love has been so great a thing that though it never fulfilled itself, yet it brimmed time and the void to overflowing, so that everywhere you adventured the knowledge of my presence tormented you—and I waited for you in vain. Forget it now. It's over. We have found ourselves at last."

"If I could only see you," he said fretfully, reaching out into the blackness. "It's so dark here. Where are we?"

"Dark?" the gentle voice laughed softly. "Dark? My dearest—this is not darkness! Wait a moment—here!"

Out of the night a hand clasped his. "Come with me."

Together they stepped forward.

Afterword

Perhaps the strongest source of occult beliefs is the human tendency to deny the fact of death. After all, only human beings, as far as we know, are aware of the inevitability of death. Worse yet, human beings are aware of the inevitability of death not only in general but in each individual case, including their own. In other words, each individual human being knows that he himself will someday die and that that portion of the future is at least fixed, irrevocable, and inevitable, even if the exact details are not known.

There must have been a time in prehistory when human beings first came to realize this, and the shock must have been enormous. The natural tendency would be to deny death; to insist that it does not take place but only seems to take place; that only the body dies, while the "I" it contains, the "personality," the "soul," lives on forever.

One might suppose that the soul has come from some realm of bliss, inhabits the body for a brief period, then returns to the realm of bliss. Or one might suppose that the soul, after death, goes to bliss or to torment, depending on whether the body it inhabited was virtuous or not, but that, in either case, it does not die.

Another general feeling is that the soul remains on Earth, but that after the death of its body it enters that of a newborn baby and lives another life—and so on indefinitely. This process of soul transfer from body to body is called "reincarnation" from Latin words meaning "into a body again." However, belief in reincarnation or in an afterlife is merely an invented device for denying death, and there is no evidence for either.—I.A.

Additional Reading

L. Adams Beck, "The Interpreter. A Romance of the East," in *The Ninth Vibration and Other Stories* (New York: Dodd, Mead, 1922).

Jane Roberts, "The Red Wagon," in *Ladies of Fantasy: Two Centuries of Sinister Stories by the Gentler Sex,* Seon Manley and Gogo Lewis, eds. (New York: Lothrop, Lee, and Shepard, 1975).

Saki (pseud. of H. H. Munro), "Laura," in *Beasts and Superbeasts* (London: John Lane, 1912).

Evelyn E. Smith, "Teragram," in *Young Witches and Warlocks,* Isaac Asimov, Martin H. Greenberg, & Charles G. Waugh, eds. (New York: Harper and Row, 1987).

Jay Williams, "The Beetle," in *The Magazine of Fantasy and Science Fiction,* March 1961.

18

Séances

John Hay
The Blood Seedling

In a bit of green pasture that rose, gradually narrowing, to the tableland that ended in prairie, and widened out descending to the wet and willowy sands that border the Great River, a broad-shouldered young man was planting an apple-tree one sunny spring morning when Tyler was President. The little valley was shut in on the south and east by rocky hills, patched with the immortal green of cedars and gay with clambering columbines. In front was the Mississippi, reposing from its plunge over the rapids, and idling down among the golden sandbars and the low, moist islands, which were looking their loveliest in their new spring dresses of delicate green.

The young man was digging with a certain vicious energy, forcing the spade into the black, crumbling loam with a movement full of vigor and malice. His straight, black brows were knitted till they formed one dark line over his deep-set eyes. His beard was not yet old enough to hide the massive outline of his firm, square jaw. In the set teeth, in the clouded face, in the half-articulate exclamations that shot from time to time from the compressed lips, it was easy to see that the thoughts of the young horticulturist were far from his work.

A bright young girl came down the path through the hazel-thicket that skirted the hillside, and putting a plump brown hand on the topmost rail of the fence vaulted lightly over, and lit on the soft, springy turf with a thud that announced a wholesome and liberal architecture. It is usually expected of poets and lovers that they shall describe the ladies of their love as so airy and delicate in structure that the flowers they tread on are greatly improved in health and spirits by the visitation. But not being a poet or in love, we must admit that there was no resurrection for the larkspurs and pansies upon which the little boots of Miss Susie Barringer landed.

Yet she was not of the coarse peasant type, though her cheeks were so rosy as to cause her great heaviness of heart on Sunday mornings, and her blue lawn dress was as full as it could afford from shoulders to waist. She was a neat, hearty, and very pretty country girl, with a slightly freckled face, and rippled brown hair, and astonished blue eyes, but perfectly self-possessed and graceful as a young quail.

A young man's ears are quick to catch the rustling of a woman's dress. The flight of this plump bird in its fluttering blue plumage over the fence-rail caused our young man to look up from his spading: the scowl was routed from his brow by a sudden incursion of blushes, and his mouth was attacked by an awkward smile.

The young lady nodded and was hurrying past. The scowl came back in force, and the smile was repulsed from the bearded mouth with great loss: "Miss Tudie, are you in a hurry?"

The lady thus addressed turned and said, in a voice that was half pert and half coaxing: "No particular hurry. Al, I've told you a dozen times not to call me that redicklis name."

"Why, Tudie, I hain't never called you nothing else sence you was a little one so high. You ort to know yer own name, and you give yourself that name when you was a yearling. Howsomever, ef you don't like it now, sence you've been to Jacksonville, I reckon I can call you Miss Susie—when I don't disremember."

The frank amende seemed to satisfy Miss Susie, for she at once interrupted in the kindest manner: "Never mind, Al Golyer: You can call me what you are a-mind to." Then, as if conscious of the feminine inconsistency, she changed the subject by asking, "What are you going to do with that great hole?—big enough to bury a fellow."

"I'm going to plant this here seedlin' that growed up in Colonel Blood's pastur', nobody knows how: belike somebody was eatin' an apple and throwed the core down-like. I'm going to plant a little orchard here next spring, but the Colonel and me, we reckoned this one 'ud be too old by that time for moving, so I thought I'd stick it in now, and see what come out'n it. It's a powerful thrifty chunk of a saplin'."

"Yes. I speak for the first peck of apples off'n it. Don't forget. Good-morning."

"Hold on a minute, Miss Susan, twell I git my coat. I'll walk down a piece with you. I have got something to say to you."

†   †   †

Miss Susie turned a little red and a little pale. These occasions were not entirely unknown in her short experience of life. When young men in the country in that primitive period had something to say, it was something very serious and earnest. Allen Golyer was a good-looking, stalwart young farmer, well-to-do, honest, able to provide for a family. There was nothing presumptuous in his aspiring to the hand of the prettiest girl in Chaney Creek. In childhood he had trotted her to Banbury Cross and back a hundred times, beguiling the tedium of the journey with kisses and the music of bells. When the little girl was old enough to go to school, the big boy carried her books and gave her the rosiest apple out of his dinner-basket. He fought all her battles and wrote all her compositions; which latter, by the way, never gained her any great credit. When she was fifteen and he twenty he had his great reward in taking her twice a week during one happy winter to singing-school. This was the bloom of life—nothing before or after could compare with it. The blacking of shoes and brushing of stiff, electric, bristling hair, all on end with frost and hope, the struggling into the plate-armor of his starched shirt, the tying of the portentous and uncontrollable cravat before the glass, which was hopelessly dimmed every moment by his eager breath—these trivial and vulgar details were made beautiful and unreal by the magic of youth and love. Then came the walk through the crisp, dry snow to the Widow Barringer's, the sheepish talk with the old lady while Susie "got on her things," and the long, enchanting tramp to the "deestrick school-house."

There is not a country-bred man or woman now living but will tell you that life can offer nothing comparable with the innocent zest of that old style of courting that was done at singing-school in the starlight and candlelight of the first half of our century. There are few hearts so withered and old but they beat quicker sometimes when they hear, in old-fashioned churches, the wailing, sobbing, or exulting strains of "Bradstreet" or "China" or "Coronation," and the mind floats down on the current of these old melodies to that fresh young day of hopes and illusions—of voices that were sweet, no matter how false they sang—of nights that were rosy with dreams, no matter what Fahrenheit said—of girls that blushed without cause, and of lovers who talked for hours about everything but love.

I know I shall excite the scorn of all the ingenuous youth of my time when I say that there was nothing that our superior civilization would call love-making in those long walks through the winter nights. The heart of Allen Golyer swelled under his satin waistcoat with love and joy and devotion as he walked over the crunching roads with his pretty enslaver. But he talked of apples and pigs and the heathen and the teacher's wig, and sometimes ventured an allusion to other people's flirtations in a jocose and distant way; but as to the state of his own heart his lips were sealed. It would move a blasé smile on the downy lips of juvenile Lovelaces, who count their conquests by their cotillions, and think nothing of making a declaration in an avant-deux, to be told of young people spending several evenings of each week in the year together, and speaking no word of love until they were ready to name their wedding-day. Yet such was the sober habit of the place and time.

So there was no troth plighted between Allen and Susie, though the youth loved the maiden with all the energy of his fresh, unused nature, and she knew it very well. He never dreamed of marrying any other woman than Susie Barringer, and she sometimes tried a new pen by writing and carefully erasing the initials S. M. G., which, as she was christened Susan Minerva, may be taken as showing the direction of her thoughts.

If Allen Golyer had been less bashful or more enterprising, this history would never have been written; for Susie would probably have said Yes for want of anything better to say, and when she went to visit her Aunt Abigail in Jacksonville she would have gone *engaged,* her finger bound with gold and her maiden meditations fettered by promises. But she went, as it was, fancy free, and there is no tinder so inflammable as the imagination of a pretty country girl of sixteen.

One day she went out with her easy-going Aunt Abigail to buy ribbons, the Chaney Creek invoices not supplying the requirements of Jacksonville society. As they traversed the court-house square on their way to Deacon Pettybone's place, and Miss Susie's vagrant glances rested on an iris of ribbons displayed in an opposition window, "Let's go in here," she said with the impetuous decision of her age and sex.

"We will go where you like, dear," said easy-going Aunt Abigail. "It makes no difference."

Aunt Abigail was wrong. It made the greatest difference to several persons whether Susie Barringer bought her ribbons at Simmon's or Pettybone's that day. If she had but known.

But, all unconscious of the Fate that beckoned invisibly on the threshold, Miss Susie tripped into "Simmon's Emporium" and asked for ribbons. Two young men stood at the long counter. One was Mr. Simmons, proprietor of the emporium, who advanced with his most conscientious smile: "Ribbons, Ma'am? Yes, Ma'am—all sorts, Ma'am. Cherry, Ma'am? Certingly, Ma'am. Jest got a splendid lot in from St. Louis this morning, Ma'am. This way, Ma'am."

The ladies were soon lost in the delight of the eyes. The voice of Mr. Simmons accompanied the feast of color, insinuating but unheeded.

The other young man approached: "Here is what you want, Miss— rich and elegant. Just suits your style. Sets off your hair and eyes beautiful."

The ladies looked up. A more decided voice than Mr. Simmon's; whiter hands than Mr. Simmon's handled the silken bands; bolder eyes than the weak, pink-bordered orbs of Mr. Simmons looked unabashed admiration into the pretty face of Susie Barringer.

"Look here, Simmons, old boy, introduce a fellow."

Mr. Simmons meekly obeyed: "Mrs. Barringer, let me intreduce you to Mr. Leon of St. Louis, of the house of Draper & Mercer."

"Bertie Leon, at your service," said the brisk young fellow, seizing Miss Susie's hand with energy. His hand was so much softer and whiter than hers that she felt quite hot and angry about it.

When they had made their purchases, Mr. Leon insisted on walking home with them, and was very witty and agreeable all the way. He had all the wit of the newspapers, of the concert-rooms, of the steamboat bars, at his fingers' ends. In his wandering life he had met all kinds of people: he had sold ribbons through a dozen States. He never had a moment's doubt of himself. He never hesitated to allow himself any indulgence which would not interfere with business. He had one ambition in life—to marry Miss Mercer and get a share in the house. Miss Mercer was as ugly as a millionaire's tombstone. Mr. Bertie Leon—who, when his mustache was not dyed nor his hair greased, was really quite a handsome fellow—considered that the sacrifice he proposed to make in the interests of trade must be made good to him in some way. So, "by way of getting even," he made violent love to all the pretty eyes he met in his commercial travels—"to have something to think about after he should have found favor in the strabismic optics of Miss Mercer," he observed disrespectfully.

Simple Susie, who had seen nothing of young men besides the awkward and blushing clodhoppers of Chaney Creek, was somewhat dazzled by the free-and-easy speech and manner of the hard-cheeked bagman. Yet there was something in his airy talk and point-blank compliments that aroused a faint feeling of resentment which she could scarcely account for. Aunt Abigail was delighted with him, and when he bowed his adieux at the gate in the most recent Planters'-House style she cordially invited him to call—"to drop in any time: he must be lonesome so fur from home."

He said he wouldn't neglect such a chance, with another Planters'-House bow.

"What a nice young man!" said Aunt Abigail.

"Awful conceited and not overly polite," said Susie as she took off her bonnet and went into a revel of bows and trimmings.

The oftener Albert Leon came to Mrs. Barringer's bowery cottage, the more the old lady was pleased with him and the more the young one criticised him, until it was plain to be seen that Aunt Abigail was growing tired of him and pretty Susan dangerously interested. But just at this point his inexorable carpet-bag dragged him off to a neighboring town, and Susie soon afterwards went back to Chaney Creek.

Her Jacksonville hat and ribbons made her what her pretty eyes never could have done—the belle of the neighborhood. *Non cuivis contingit adire Lutetiam,* but to a village where no one has been to Paris the country-town is a shrine of fashion. Allen Golyer felt a vague sense of distrust chilling his heart as he saw Mr. Simmons's ribbons decking the pretty head in the village choir the Sunday after her return, and, spurred on by a nascent jealousy of the unknown, resolved to learn his fate without loss of time. But the little lady received him with such cool and unconcerned friendliness, talked so much and so fast about her visit, that the honest fellow was quite bewildered, and had to go home to think the matter over and cudgel his dull wits to divine whether she was pleasanter than ever, or had drifted altogether out of his reach.

Allen Golyer was, after all, a man of nerve and decision. He wasted only a day or two in doubts and fears, and one Sunday afternoon, with a beating but resolute heart, he left his Sunday-school class to walk down to Crystal Glen and solve his questions and learn his doom. When he came in sight of the widow's modest house he saw a buggy hitched by the gate.

"Dow Padgett's chestnut sorrel, by jing! What is Dow after out here?"

It is natural, if not logical, that young men should regard the visits of all other persons of their age and sex in certain quarters as a serious impropriety.

But it was not his friend and crony, Dow Padgett, the liveryman, who came out of the widow's door, leading by the hand the blushing and bridling Susie. It was a startling apparition of the Southwestern dandy of the period— light hair drenched with bear's oil, blue eyes and jet-black mustache, an enormous paste brooch in his bosom, a waistcoat and trousers that shrieked in discordant tones, and very small and elegant varnished boots. The gamblers and bagmen of the Mississippi River are the best-shod men in the world.

Golyer's heart sank within him as this splendid being shone upon him. But with his rustic directness he walked to meet the laughing couple at the gate, and said, "Tudie, I come to see you. Shall I go in and talk to your mother twell you come back?"

"No, that won't pay," promptly replied the brisk stranger. "We will be gone the heft of the afternoon, I reckon. This hoss is awful slow," he added with a wink of preternatural mystery to Miss Susie.

"Mr. Golyer," said the young lady, "let me introduce you to my friend, Mr. Leon."

Golyer put out his hand mechanically after the cordial fashion of the West. But Leon nodded and said, "I hope to see you again." He lifted Miss Susie into the buggy, sprang lightly in, and went off with laughter and the cracking of his whip after Dow Padgett's chestnut sorrel.

The young farmer walked home desolate, comparing in his simple mind his own plain exterior with his rival's gorgeous toilet, his awkward address with the other's easy audacity, till his heart was full to the brim with that infernal compound of love and hate which is called jealousy, from which pray Heaven to guard you.

It was the next morning that Miss Susie vaulted over the fence where Allen Golyer was digging the hole for Colonel Blood's apple-tree.

† † †

"Something middlin' particular," continued Golyer resolutely.

"There is no use leaving your work," said Miss Barringer pluckily. "I will stay and listen."

Poor Allen began as badly as possible, "Who was that feller with you yesterday?"

"Thank you, Mr. Golyer—my friends ain't fellers! What's that to you who he was?"

"Susie Barringer, we have been keeping company now a matter of a year. I have loved you well and true: I would have give my life to save you any little care or trouble. I never dreamed of nobody but you—not that I was half good enough for you, but because I did not know any better man around here. Ef it ain't too late, Susie, I ask you to be my wife. I will love you and care for you, good and true."

Before this solemn little speech was finished Susie was crying and biting her bonnet-strings in a most undignified manner. "Hush, Al Golyer!" she burst out. "You mustn't talk so. You are too good for me. I am kind of promised to that fellow. I 'most wish I had never seen him."

Allen sprang to her and took her in his strong arms: she struggled free from him. In a moment the vibration which his passionate speech had produced in her passed away. She dried her eyes and said firmly enough: "It's no use, Al: we wouldn't be happy together. Good-by! I shouldn't wonder if I went away from Chaney Creek before long."

She walked rapidly down to the river-road. Allen stood fixed and motionless, gazing at the plump, graceful form until the blue dress vanished behind the hill, and leaned long on his spade, unconscious of the lapse of time.

When Susan reached her home she found Leon at the gate.

"Ah, my little rosebud! I came near missing you. I am going to Keokuk this morning, to be gone a few days. I stopped here a minute to give you something to keep for me till I come back."

"What is it?"

He took her chubby cheeks between his hands and laid on her cherry-ripe lips a keepsake which he never reclaimed.

She stood watching him from the gate until, as a clump of willows snatched him from her, she thought: "He will go right by where Al is at work. It would be jest like him to jump over the fence and have a talk with him. I'd like to hear it."

An hour or so later, as she sat and sewed in the airy little entry, a shadow fell upon her work, and as she looked up her startled eyes met the piercing glance of her discarded lover. A momentary ripple of remorse passed over her cheerful heart as she saw Allen's pale and agitated face. He was paler than she had ever seen him, with that ghastly pallor of weather-beaten faces. His black hair, wet with perspiration, clung clammily to his temples. He looked beaten, discouraged, utterly fatigued with the conflict of emotion. But one who looked closely in his eyes would have seen a curious stealthy, half-shaded light in them, as of one who, though working against hope, was still not without resolute will.

Dame Barringer, who had seen him coming up the walk, bustled in: "Good-morning, Allen. How beat out you do look! Now, I like a stiddy young man, but don't you think you run this thing of workin' into the ground?"

"Wall, maybe so," said Golyer with a weary smile—"leastways I've been a-runnin' this spade into the ground all the morning, and—"

"*You* want buttermilk—that's your idee: ain't it, now?"

"Well, Mizzes Barringer, I reckon you know my failin's."

The good woman trotted off to the dairy, and Susie served demurely, waiting with some trepidation for what was to come next.

"Susie Barringer," said a low, husky voice which she could scarcely recognize as Golyer's, "I've come to ask pardon—not for nothing I've done, for I never did and never could do you wrong—but for what I thought for a while arter you left me this morning. It's all over now, but I tell *you* the Bad Man had his claws into my heart for a spell. Now it's all over, and I wish you well. I wish your husband well. If ever you git into any trouble where I can help, send for me: it's my right. It's the last favor I ask of you."

Susceptible Susie cried a little again. Allen, watching her with his ambushed eyes, said: "Don't take it to heart, Tudie. Perhaps there is better days in store for me yet."

This did not appear to comfort Miss Barringer in the least. She was greatly grieved when she thought she had broken a young man's heart: she was still more dismal at the slightest intimation that she had not. If any explanation of this paradox is required, I would observe, quoting a phrase much in vogue among the witty writers of the present age, that Miss Susie Barringer was "a very female woman."

So pretty Susan's rising sob subsided into a coquettish pout by the time her mother came in with the foaming pitcher of subacidulous nectar, and plied young Golyer with brimming beakers of it with all the beneficent delight of a Lady Bountiful.

"There, Mizzes Barringer! there's about as much as I can tote. Temperance in all things."

"Very well, then, you work less and play more. We never get a sight of you lately. Come in neighborly and play checkers with Tudie."

It was the darling wish of Mother Barringer's heart to see her daughter married and settled with "a stiddy young man that you knowed all about, and his folks before him." She had observed with great disquietude the brilliant avatar of Mr. Bertie Leon and the evident pride of her daugher in the bright-plumaged captive she had brought to Chaney Creek, the spoil of her maiden snare. "I don't more'n half like that little feller." (It is a Western habit to call a well-dressed man a "little feller." The epithet would light on Hercules Farnese if he should go to Illinois dressed as a Cocodes.) "No honest folks wears beard onto their upper lips. I wouldn't be surprised if he wasn't a gamboller."

Allen Golyer, apparently unconscious in his fatigue of the cap which Dame Barringer was vicariously setting for him, walked away with his spade on his shoulder, and the good woman went systematically to work in making Susie miserable by sharp little country criticisms of her heart's idol.

Day after day wore on, and, to Dame Barringer's delight and Susie's dismay, Mr. Leon did not come.

"He is such a business-man," thought trusting Susan, "he can't get away from Keokuk. But he'll be sure to write." So Susie put on her sunbonnet and hurried up to the post-office: "Any letters for me, Mr. Whaler?" The artful and indefinite plural was not disguise enough for Miss Susie, so she added, "I was expecting a letter from my aunt."

"No letters here from your aunt, nor your uncle, nor none of the tribe," said old Whaler, who had gone over with Tyler to keep his place, and so had no further use for good-manners.

"I think old Tommy Whaler is an impident old wretch," said Susie that evening, "and I won't go near his old post-office again." But Susie forgot her threat of vengeance the next day, and she went again, lured by family affection, to inquire for that letter which Aunt Abbie must have written. The third time she went, rummy old Whaler roared very improperly: "Bother your aunt. You've got a beau somewheres—that's what's the matter."

Poor Susan was so dazzled by this flash of clairvoyance that she hurried from that dreadful post-office, scarcely hearing the terrible words that the old ginpig hurled after her: *"And he's forgotten you!—that's what's the matter."*

Susie Barringer walked home along the river-road, revolving many things in her mind. She went to her room and locked her door by sticking a penknife over the latch, and sat down to have a good cry. Her faculties being thus cleared for action, she thought seriously for an hour. If you can remember when you were a school-girl, you know a great deal of solid thinking can be done in an hour. But we can tell you in a moment what it footed up. You can walk through the Louvre in a minute, but you cannot see it in a week.

Susan Barringer (sola, loquitur): "Three weeks yesterday. Yes, I s'pose it's so. What a little fool I was! He goes everywhere—says the same things to everybody, like he was selling ribbons. Mean little scamp! Mother seen through him in a minute. I'm mighty glad I didn't tell her nothing about it." [Fie, Susan! your principles are worse than your grammer.] "He'll marry some rich girl—I don't envy her, but I hate her—and I am as good as she is. Maybe he will come back—no, and I hope he won't—and I wish I was dead!" *(Pocket-handkerchief.)*

Yet in the midst of her grief there was one comforting thought—nobody knew of it. She had no confidante—she had not even opened her heart to her mother: these Western maidens have a fine gift of reticence. A few of her countryside friends and rivals had seen with envy and admiration the pretty couple on the day of Leon's arrival. But all their poisonous little compliments and questions had never elicited from the prudent Susie more than the safe statement that the handsome stranger was a friend of Aunt Abbie's, whom she had met at Jacksonville. They could not laugh at her: they could not sneer at gay deceivers and lovelorn damsels when she went to the sewing-circle. The bitterness of her tears was greatly sweetened by the consideration that in any case no one could pity her. She took such consolation from this thought that she faced her mother unflinchingly at tea, and baffled the maternal inquest on her "redness of eyes" by the school-girl's invaluable and ever-ready headache.

It was positively not until a week later, when she met Allen Golyer at choir-meeting, that she remembered that this man knew the secret of her baffled hopes. She blushed scarlet as he approached her: "Have you got company home, Miss Susie?"

"Yes—that is, Sally Withers and me came together, and—"

"No, that's hardly fair to Tom Fleming: three ain't the pleasantest company. I will go home with you."

Susie took the strong arm that was held out to her, and leaned upon it with a mingled feeling of confidence and dread as they walked home through the balmy night under the clear, starry heaven of the early spring. The air was full of the quickening breath of May.

Susie Barringer waited in vain for some signal of battle from Allen Golyer. He talked more than usual, but in a grave, quiet, protecting style, very different from his former manner of worshipping bashfulness. His tone had in it an air of fatherly caressing which was inexpressibly soothing to his pretty companion, tired and lonely with her silent struggle of the past month. When they came to her gate and he said good-night, she held his hand a moment with a tremulous grasp, and spoke impulsively: "Al, I once told you something I never told anybody else. I'll tell you something else now, because I believe I can trust you."

"Be sure of that, Susie Barringer."

"Well, Al, my engagement is broken off."

"I am sorry for you, Susie, if you set much store by him."

Miss Susie answered with great and unnecessary impetuosity, "I don't, and I am glad of it," and then ran into the house and to bed, her cheeks all aflame at the thought of her indiscretion, and yet with a certain comfort in having a friend from whom she had no secrets.

I protest there was no thought of coquetry in the declaration which Susan Barringer blurted out to her old lover under the sympathetic starlight of the May heaven. But Allen Golyer would have been a dull boy not to have taken heart and hope from it. He became, as of old, a frequent and welcome visitor at Crystal Glen. Before long the game of checkers with Susie became so enthralling a passion that it was only adjourned from one evening to another. Allen's white shirts grew fringy at the edges with fatigue-duty, and his large hands were furry at the fingers with much soap. Susie's affectionate heart, which had been swayed a moment from its orbit by the irresistible attraction of Bertie Leon's diamond breastpin and city swagger, swung back to its ancient course under the mild influence of time and the weather and opportunity. So that Dame Barringer was not in the least surprised, on entering her little parlor one soft afternoon in that very May, to see the two young people economically occupying one chair, and Susie shouting the useless appeal, "Mother, make him behave!"

"I never interfere in young folks' matters, especially when they're going all right," said the motherly old soul, kissing "her son Allen" and trotting away to dry her happy tears.

I am almost ashamed to say how soon they were married—so soon that when Miss Susan went with her mother to Keokuk to buy a wedding-garment she half expected to find, in every shop she entered, the elegant figure of Mr. Leon leaning over the counter. But the dress was bought and made, and worn at wedding and *in-fair* and in a round of family visits among the Barringer and Golyer kin, and carefully laid away in lavender when the pair came back from their modest holiday and settled down to real life on Allen's prosperous farm; and no word of Bertie Leon ever came to Mrs. Golyer to trouble her joy. In her calm and busy life the very name faded from her tranquil mind. These wholesome country hearts do not bleed long. In that wide-awake country eyes are too useful to be wasted in weeping. My dear Lothario Urbanus, those peaches are very sound and delicious, but they will not keep for ever. If you do not secure them to-day, they will go to someone else, and in no case, as the Autocrat hath said with authority, can you stand there "mellering 'em with your thumb."

There was no happier home in the country and few finer farms. The good sense and industry of Golyer and the practical helpfulness of his wife found their full exercise in the care of his spreading fields and growing orchards. The Warsaw merchants fought for his wheat, and his apples were known in St. Louis. Mrs. Golyer, with that spice of romance which is hidden away in every woman's heart, had taken a special fancy to the seedling apple-tree at whose planting she had so intimately assisted. Allen shared in this, as in all her whims, and tended and nursed it like a child. In time he gave up the care of his orchard to other hands, but he reserved this seedling for his own especial coddling. He spaded and mulched and pruned it, and guarded it in the winter from rodent rabbits, and in summer from terebrant grubs. It was not ungrateful. It grew a noble tree, producing a rich and luscious fruit, with a deep scarlet satin coat, and a flesh tinged as delicately as a pink sea-shell. The first peck of apples was given to Susie with great ceremony, and the next year the first bushel was carried to Colonel Blood, the Congressman. He was loud in his admiration, as the autumn elections were coming on: "Great Scott, Golyer! I'd rather give my name a horticultooral triumph like that there than be Senator."

"You've got your wish, then, Colonel," said Golyer. "Me and my wife have called that tree The Blood Seedling sence the day it was transplanted from your pastur'."

It was the pride and envy of the neighborhood. Several neighbors asked for scions and grafts, but could do nothing with them.

"Fact is," said old Silas Withers, "those folks that expects to raise good fruit by begging graffs, and then layin' abed and readin' newspapers, will have a good time waitin'. Elbow-grease is the secret of the Blood Seedlin', ain't it, Al?"

"Well, I reckon, Squire Withers, a man never gits anything wuth havin' without a tussle for it; and as to secrets, I don't believe in them, nohow."

A square-browed, resolute, silent, middle-aged man, who loved his home better than any amusement, regular at church, at the polls, something richer every Christmas than he had been on the New Year's preceding—a man whom everybody liked and few loved much—such had Allen Golyer grown to be.

† † †

If I have lingered too long over this colorless and commonplace picture of rural Western life, it is because I have felt an instinctive reluctance to recount the startling and most improbable incident which fell one night upon this quiet neighborhood, like a thunderbolt out of the blue sky. The story I must tell will be flatly denied and easily refuted. It is absurd and fantastic, but, unless human evidence is to go for nothing when it testifies of things unusual, the story is true.

At the head of the rocky hollow through which Chaney Creek ran to the river lived the family who gave the stream its name. They were among the early pioneers of the county. In the squatty yellow stone house the present Chaney occupied, his grandfather had stood a siege from Blackhawk all one summer day and night, until relieved by the garrison of Fort Edward. The family had not grown with the growth of the land. Like many others of the pioneers, they had shown no talent for keeping abreast of the civilization whose guides and skirmishers they had been. In the progress of a half century they had sold, bit by bit, their section of land, which kept intact would have proved a fortune. They lived quietly, working enough to secure their own pork and hominy, and regarding with a sort of impatient scorn every scheme of public or private enterprise that passed under their eyes.

The elder Chaney had married, some years before, at the Mormon town of Nauvoo, the fair-haired daughter of a Swedish mystic, who had come across the sea beguiled by dreams of a perfect theocracy, and who on arriving at the city of the Latter-Day Saints had died, broken-hearted from his lost illusions.

The only dowry that Seraphita Neilsen brought her husband, besides her delicate beauty and her wide blue eyes, was a full set of Swedenborg's later writings in English. These became the daily food of the solitary household. Saul Chaney would read the exalted rhapsodies of the Northern seer for hours together, without the first glimmer of their meaning crossing his brain. But there was something in the majesty of their language and the solemn roll of their poetical development that irresistibly impressed and attracted him. Little Gershom, his only child, sitting at his feet, would listen in childish wonder to the strange things his silent, morose, and gloomy father found in the well-worn volumes, until his tired eyelids would fall at last over his pale, bulging eyes.

As he grew up his eyes bulged more and more: his head seemed too large for his rickety body. He pored over the marvellous volumes until he knew long passages by heart, and understood less of them than his father—which was unnecessary. He looked a little like his mother, but while she in her youth had something of the faint and flickering beauty of the Boreal Lights, poor Gershom never could have suggested anything more heavenly than a foggy moonlight. When he was fifteen he went to the neighboring town of Warsaw to school. He had rather heavy weather among the well-knit, grubby-knuckled urchins of the town, and would have been thoroughly disheartened but for one happy chance. At the house where he boarded an amusement called the "Sperrit Rappin's" was much in vogue. A group of young folks, surcharged with all sorts of animal magnetism, with some capacity for belief and much more for fun, used to gather about a light pine table every evening, and put it through a complicated course of mystical gymnastics. It was a very good-tempered table: it would dance, hop, or slam at the word of command, or, if the exercises took a more intellectual turn, it would answer any questions addressed to it in a manner not much below the average capacity of its tormentors.

Gershom Chaney took all this in solemn earnest. He was from the first moment deeply impressed. He lay awake whole nights, with his eyes fast closed, in the wildest dreams. His school-hours were passed in trance-like contemplation. He cared no more for punishment than the fakeer for his self-inflicted tortures. He longed for the coming of the day when he could commune in solitude with the unfleshed and immortal. This was the full flowering of those seeds of fantasy that had fallen into his infant mind as he lay baking his brains by the wide fire in the old stone house at the head of the hollow, while his father read haltingly of the wonders of the invisible world.

But, to his great mortification, he saw nothing, heard nothing, experienced nothing but in the company of others. He must brave the ridicule of the profane to taste the raptures which his soul loved. His simple, trusting faith made him inevitably the butt of the mischievous circle. They were not slow in discovering his extreme sensibility to external influences. One muscular, black-haired, heavy-browed youth took especial delight in practising upon him. The table, under Gershom's tremulous hands, would skip like a lamb at the command of this Thomas Fay.

One evening Tom Fay had a great truimph. They had been trying to get the "medium"—for Gershom had reached that dignity—to answer sealed questions, and had met with indifferent success. Fay suddenly approached the table, scribbled a phrase, folded it, and tossed it, doubled up, before Gershom; then leaned over the table, staring at his pale, unwholesome face with all the might of his black eyes.

Chaney seized the pencil convulsively and wrote, "Balaam!"

Fay burst into a loud laugh and said, "Read the question?"

It was, "Who rode on your grandfather's back?"

This is a specimen of the cheap wit and harmless malice by which poor Gershom suffered as long as he stayed at school. He was never offended, but was often sorely perplexed, at the apparent treachery of his unseen counsellors. He was dismissed at last from the academy for utter and incorrigible indolence. He accepted his disgrace as a crown of martyrdom, and went proudly home to his sympathizing parents.

Here, with less criticism and more perfect faith, he renewed the exercise of what he considered his mysterious powers. His fastings and vigils, and want of bodily movement and fresh air, had so injured his health as to make him tenfold more nervous and sensitive than ever. But his faintings and hysterics and epileptic paroxysms were taken more and more as evidences of his lofty mission. His father and mother regarded him as an oracle, for the simple reason that he always answered just as they expected. A curious or superstitious neighbor was added from to time to the circle, and their reports heightened the half-uncanny interest with which the Chaney house was regarded.

It was on a moist and steamy evening of spring that Allen Golyer, standing by his gate, saw Saul Chaney slouching along in the twilight and hailed him, "What news from the sperrits, Saul?"

"Nothing for you, Al Golyer," said Saul gloomily. "The god of this world takes care of the like o' you."

Golyer smiled, as a prosperous man always does when his poorer neighbors abuse him for his luck, and rejoined: "I ain't so fortunate as you think for, Saul Chaney. I lost a Barksher pig yesterday: I reckon I must come up and ask Gershom what's come of it."

"Come along, if you like. It's been a long while sence you've crossed my sill. But I'm gitting to be quite the style. Young Lawyer Marshall is a-coming up this evening to see my Gershom."

Before Mr. Golyer started he filled a basket, "to make himself welcome and pay for the show," with the reddest and finest fruit of his favorite apple-tree. His wife followed him to the gate and kissed him—a rather unusual attention among Western farmer-people. Her face, still rosy and comely, was flushed and smiling: "Al, do you know what day o' the year it is?"

"Nineteenth of April?"

"Yes; and twenty years ago to-day you planted the Blood Seedlin' and I give you the mitten!" She turned and went into the house, laughing comfortably.

Allen walked slowly up the hollow to the Chaney house, and gave the apples to Seraphita and told her their story. A little company was assembled—two or three Chaney Creek people, small market-gardeners, with eyes the color of their gooseberries and hands the color of their currants; Mr. Marshall, a briefless young barrister from Warsaw, with a tawny friend, who spoke like a Spaniard.

"Take seats, friends, and form a circle o' harmony," said Saul Chaney. "The me'jum is in fine condition: he had two fits this arternoon."

Gershom looked shockingly ill and weak. He reclined in a great hickory armchair, with his eyes half open, his lips moving noiselessly. All the persons present formed a circle and joined hands.

The moment the circle was completed by Saul and Seraphita, who were on either side of their son, touching his hands, an expression of pain and perplexity passed over his pale face, and he began to writhe and mutter.

"He's seein' visions," said Saul.

"Yes, too many of 'em," said Gershom querulously. "A boy in a boat, a man on a shelf, and a man with a spade—all at once: too many. Get me a pencil. One at a time, I tell you—one at a time!"

The circle broke up, and a table was brought, with writing materials. Gershom grasped a pencil and said, with imperious and feverish impatience, "Come on, now, and don't waste the time of the shining ones."

An old woman took his right hand. He wrote with his left very rapidly an instant and threw her the paper, always with his eyes shut close.

Old Mrs. Schritcher read with difficulty, "A boy in a boat—over he goes;" and burst out into a piteous wail: "Oh, my poor little Ephraim! I always knowed it."

"Silence, woman!" said the relentless medium.

"Mr. Marshall," said Saul, "would you like a test?"

"No, thank you," said the young gentleman. "I brought my friend, Mr. Baldassano, who, as a traveller, is interested in these things."

"Will you take the medium's hand, Mr. What's-your-name?"

The young foreigner took the lean and feverish hand of Gershom, and again the pencil flew rapidly over the paper. He pushed the manuscript from him and snatched his hand away from Baldassano. As the latter looked at what was written his tawny cheek grew deadly pale. "Dios mio!" he exclaimed to Marshall, "this is written in Castilian!"

The two young men retired to the other end of the room and read by the tallow candle the notes scrawled on the paper. Baldassano translated: "A man on a shelf—table covered with bottles beside him: man's face yellow as gold: bottles tumble over without being touched."

"What nonsense is that?" said Marshall.

"My brother died of yellow fever at sea last year."

Both the young men became suddenly very thoughtful and observed with great interest the result of Golyer's "test." He sat by Gershom, holding his hand tightly, but gazing absently into the dying blaze of the wide chimney. He seemed to have forgotten where he was: a train of serious thought appeared to hold him completely under its control. His brows were knit with an expression of severe, almost fierce, determination. At one moment his breathing was hard and thick—a moment after hurried and broken.

All this while the fingers of Gershom were flying rapidly over the paper, independently of his eyes, which were sometimes closed and sometimes rolling as if in trouble.

A wind which had been gathering all the evening now came moaning up the hollow, rattling the window-blinds and twisting into dull complaint the boughs of the leafless trees. Its voice came chill and cheerless into the dusky room, where the fire was now glimmering near its death, and the only sounds were those of Gershom's rushing pencil, the whispering of Marshall and his friend, and old Mother Schritcher feebly whimpering in her corner. The scene was sinister. Suddenly, a rushing gust blew the door wide open.

Golyer started to his feet, trembling in every limb and looking furtively over his shoulder out into the night. Quickly recovering himself, he turned to resume his place. But the moment he dropped Gershom's hand the medium had dropped his pencil, and had sunk back in his chair in a deep and deathlike slumber. Golyer seized the sheet of paper, and with the first line that he read a strange and horrible transformation was wrought in the man. His eyes protruded, his teeth chattered; he passed his hand over his head mechanically, and his hair stood up like the bristles on the back of a swine in rage. His face was blotched white and purple. He looked piteously about him for a moment, then, crumpling the paper in his hand, cried out in a hoarse, choking voice: "Yes, it's a fact: I done it. It's no use denying on't. Here it is, in black and white. Everybody knows it: ghosts come spooking around to tattle about it. What's the use of lying? I done it."

He paused, as if struck by a sudden recollection, then burst into tears and shook like a tree in a high wind. In a moment he dropped on his knees and in that posture crawled over to Marshall: "Here, Mr. Marshall—

here's the whole story. For God's sake, spare my wife and children all you can. Fix my little property all right for 'em, and God bless you for it!" Even while he was speaking, with a quick revulsion of feeling he rose to his feet, with a certain return of his natural dignity, and said: "But they sha'n't take me! None of my kin ever died that way: I've got too much sand in my gizzard to be took that way. Good-by, friends all!"

He walked deliberately out into the wild, windy night.

Marshall glanced hurriedly at the fatal paper in his hand. It was full of that capricious detail with which in reverie we review scenes that are past. But a line here and there clearly enough told the story—how he went out to plant the apple-tree; how Susie came by and rejected him; how he passed into the power of the devil for the time; how Bertie Leon came by and spoke to him, and patted him on the shoulder, and talked about city life; how he hated him and his pretty face and his good clothes; how they came to words and blows, and he struck him with his spade, and he fell into the trench, and he buried him there at the roots of the tree.

Marshall, following his first impulse, thrust the paper into the dull red coals. It flamed for an instant, and flew with a sound like a sob up the chimney.

They hunted for Golyer all night, but in the morning found him lying as if asleep, with the peace of expiation on his pale face, his pruning-knife in his heart, and the red current of his life tingeing the turf with crimson around the roots of the Blood Seedling.

Afterword

Still another way of denying death is to suppose that the personality that inhabits the body—the spirit—clings to life but does not go into another body, or into Heaven or Hell. Instead, it drifts into another plane of existence, a plane we ordinary living people cannot sense. There is thus a "spirit world," coexistent with our own material one. This belief is "spiritualism."

Of course it is possible that some people may be able to contact the spirit world and serve as a bridge over which messages may pass from one to the other. Temporarily, at least, such people exist, so to speak, halfway between the worlds. They occupy a middle position and are therefore called "mediums."

The contact usually occurs when the medium meets with a group of people who sit around a table and hold hands while the medium goes into a trance. Such a meeting or session is called a "séance," which is a French word meaning "session."

Spiritualism is particularly attractive to those who have lost a loved family member and who ache to believe not only that the essence of that family member is still alive and, possibly, happy, but that contact can be made with the spirit, its voice heard, and assurances received of that happiness.

For that reason, many rather notable people have in the past believed in spiritualism. However, since mediums are almost always revealed to be fakers, and no evidence has ever been educed for the reality of spirits, spirit worlds, or communication with the dead, it only means that many rather notable people have in the past been victims of this baseless belief.—I.A.

Additional Reading

Agatha Christie, "The Red Signal," in *The Hound of Death and Other Stories* (London: Odhams Press, 1933).

Katharine Fullerton Gerould, "Belshazzar's Letter," in *Valiant Dust* (New York: Scribners, 1922).

Joseph Hergesheimer, "The Meeker Ritual," in *Century Magazine,* 98, June 1919.

Alice Mary Schnirring, "The Dear Departed," in *Who Knocks? Twenty Masterpieces of the Spectral for the Connoisseur,* August Derleth, ed. (New York: Rinehart, 1946).

Jesse Stuart, "Red Jacket: the Knockin Sperit," in *Head o' W-Hollow* (Lexington, Kent.: Univ. of Kentucky Press, 1979).

19

Soul Travel

Robert W. Chambers
The Tracer of Lost Persons
and the Seal of Solomon Cypher

Chapter 1: The Case

Young Harren drew from his pocket a card. It was the business card of Keen & Co., and, glancing up at Mr. Keen, he read it aloud, carefully:

KEEN & CO.
TRACERS OF LOST PERSONS
Keen & Co. are prepared to locate the
whereabouts of anybody on earth.
No charges will be made unless
the person searched for
is found.
Blanks on Application.
WESTREL KEEN, Manager

Harren raised his clear, gray eyes. "I assume this statement to be correct, Mr. Keen?"

"You may safely assume so, " said Mr. Keen, smiling.

"Does this statement include *all* that you are prepared to undertake?"

The Tracer of Lost Persons inspected him coolly. "What more is there, Captain Harren? I undertake to find lost people. I even undertake to find the undiscovered ideals of young people who have failed to meet them. What further field would you suggest?" Harren glanced at the card which he held in his gloved hand; then, very slowly, he re-read "the whereabouts of anybody *on earth,*" accenting the last two words deliberately as he encountered Keen's piercing gaze again.

"Well?" asked Mr. Keen laughingly, "is not that sufficient? Our clients could scarcely expect us to invade heaven in our search for the vanished."

"There are other regions," said Harren.

"Exactly. Sit down, sir. There is a row of bookcases for your amusement. Please help yourself while I clear the decks for action."

Harren stood fingering the card, his gray eyes lost in retrospection; then he sauntered over to the bookcases, scanning the titles. The Searcher for Lost Persons studied him for a moment or two, turned, and began to pace the room. After a moment or two he touched a bell. A sweet-faced young girl entered; she was gowned in black and wore a white collar, and cuffs turned back over her hands.

"Take this memorandum," he said. The girl picked up a pencil and pad, and Mr. Keen, still pacing the room, dictated in a quiet voice as he walked to and fro:

"Mrs. Regan's Danny is doing six months in Butte, Montana. Break it to her as mercifully as possible. He is a bad one. We make no charge. The truck driver, Becker, can find his wife at her mother's house, Leonia, New Jersey. Tell him to be less pig-headed or she'll go for good some day. Ten dollars. Mrs. M., No. 36001, can find her missing butler in service at 79 Vine Street, Hartford, Connecticut. She may notify the police whenever she wishes. His portrait is No. 170529, Rogues' Gallery. Five hundred dollars. Miss K., No. 3679, may send her letter, care of Cisneros & Co., Rio, where the person she is seeking has gone into the coffee business. If she decides that she really does love him, he'll come back fast enough. Two hundred and fifty dollars. Mr. W., No. 3620, must go to the morgue for further information. His repentance is too late; but he can see that there is a decent burial. The charge: one thousand dollars to the Florence Mission. You may add that we possess his full record."

The Tracer paused and waited for the stenographer to finish. When she looked up: "Who else is waiting?" he asked.

The girl read over the initials and numbers.

"Tell that policeman that Kid Conroy sails on the *Carania* tomorrow. Fifty dollars. There is nothing definite in the other cases. Report progress and send out a general alarm for the cashier inquired for by No. 3608. You will find details in vol. 34 under B."

"Is that all, Mr. Keen?"

"Yes. I'm going to be very busy with"—turning slowly toward Harren —"with Captain Harren, of the Philippine Scouts, until tomorrow—a very complicated case, Miss Borrow, involving cipher codes and photography—"

Harren started, then walked slowly to the center of the room as the pretty stenographer passed out with a curious level glance at him.

"Why do you say that photography plays a part in my case?" he asked.

"Doesn't it?"

"Yes. But how—"

"Oh, I only guessed it," said Keen with a smile. "I made another guess that your case involved a cipher code. Does it?"

"Y-es," said the young man, astonished, "but I don't see—"

"It also involves the occult," observed Keen calmly. "We may need Miss Borrow to help us."

Almost staggered, Harren stared at the Tracer out of his astonished gray eyes until that gentleman laughed outright and seated himself, motioning Harren to do likewise.

"Don't be surprised, Captain Harren," he said. "I suppose you have no conception of our business, no realization of its scope—its network of information bureaus all over the civilized world, its myriad sources of information, the immensity of its delicate machinery, the endless data and the infinitesimal details we have at our command. You, of course, have no idea of the number of people of every sort and condition who are in our employ, of the ceaseless yet inoffensive surveillance we maintain. For example, when your letter came last week I called up the person who has charge of the army list. There you were, Kenneth Harren, Captain, Philippine Scouts, with the date of your graduation from West Point. Then I called up a certain department devoted to personal detail, and in five minutes I knew your entire history. I then touched another electric button, and in a minute I had before me the date of your arrival in New York, your present address, and"—he looked up quizzically at Harren—"and several items of general information, such as your peculiar use of your camera, and the list of books on Psychical Phenomena and Cryptograms which you have been buying—"

Harren flushed up. "Do you mean to say that I have been spied upon, Mr. Keen?"

"No more than anybody else who comes to us as a client. There was nothing offensive in the surveillance." He shrugged his shoulders and made a deprecating gesture. "Ours is a business, my dear sir, like any other. We, of course, are obliged to know about people who call on us. Last week you wrote me, and I immediately set every wheel in motion; in other words, I had you under observation from the day I received your letter to this very moment."

"You learned much concerning me?" asked Harren quietly.

"*Ex*actly, my dear sir."

"But," continued Harren with a touch of malice, "you didn't learn that my leave is up tomorrow, did you?"

"Yes, I learned that, too."

"Then why did you initially try to give me an appointment for the day after tomorrow?" demanded the young man bluntly.

The Tracer looked him squarely in the eye. "Your leave is to be extended," he said.

"What?"

"*Ex*actly. It has been extended one week."

"How do you know that?"

"You applied for extension, did you not?"

"Yes," said Harren, turning red, "but I don't see how you knew that I—"

"By cable?"

"Y-yes."

"There's a cablegram in your rooms at this very moment," said the Tracer carelessly. "You have the extension you desired. And now, Captain Harren," with a singularly pleasant smile, "what can I do to help you to a pursuit of that true happiness which is guaranteed for all good citizens under our Constitution?"

Captain Harren crossed his long legs, dropping one knee over the other, and deliberately surveyed his interrogator.

"I really have no right to come to you," he said slowly. "Your prospectus distinctly states that Keen & Co. undertake to find *live* people, and I don't know whether the person I am seeking is alive or—or—"

His steady voice faltered; the Tracer watched him curiously.

"Of course, that is important," he said. "If she *is* dead—"

"*She!*"

"Didn't you say 'she,' Captain?"

"No, I did not."

"I beg your pardon, then, for anticipating you," said the Tracer carelessly.

"Anticipating? *How* do you know it is not a man I am in search of?" demanded Harren.

"Captain Harren, you are unmarried and have no son; you have no father, no brother, no sister. Therefore I infer—several things—for example, that you are in love."

"I? In love?"

"Desperately, Captain."

"Your inferences seem to satisfy you, at least," said Harren almost sullenly, "but they don't satisfy me—clever as they appear to be."

"*Ex*actly. Then you are *not* in love?"

"I don't know whether I am or not."

"I do," said the Tracer of Lost Persons.

"Then you know more than I," retorted Harren sharply.

"But that is my business—to know more than you do," returned Mr. Keen patiently. "Else why are you here to consult me?" And as Harren made no reply: "I have seen thousands and thousands of people in love.

I have reduced the superficial muscular phenomena and facial symptomatic aspect of such people to an exact science founded upon a schedule approximating the Bertillon system of records. And," he added, smiling, "out of the twenty-seven known vocal variations your voice betrays twenty-five unmistakable symptoms; and out of the sixteen reflex muscular symptoms your face has furnished six, your hands three, your limbs and feet six. Then there are other superficial symptoms—"

"Good heavens!" broke in Harren; "how can you prove a man to be in love when he himself doesn't know whether he is or not? If a man isn't in love no Bertillon system can make him so; and if a man doesn't know whether or not he is in love, who can tell him the truth?"

"I can," said the Tracer calmly.

"What! When I tell you I myself don't know?"

"*That,*" said the Tracer, smiling, "is the final and convincing symptom. *You* don't know. *I* know because you *don't* know. That is the easiest way to be sure that you are in love, Captain Harren, because you always are when you are not sure. You'd know if you were *not* in love. Now, my dear sir, you may lay your case confidently before me."

Harren, unconvinced, sat frowning and biting his lip and twisting his short, crisp mustache which the tropical sun had turned straw color and curly.

"I feel like a fool to tell you," he said. "I'm not an imaginative man, Mr. Keen; I'm not fanciful, not sentimental. I'm perfectly healthy, perfectly normal—a very busy man in my profession, with no time and no inclination to fall in love."

"Just the sort of man who does it," commented Keen. "Continue."

Harren fidgeted about in his chair, looked out of the window, squinted at the ceiling, then straightened up, folding his arms with sudden determination.

"I'd rather be boloed than tell you," he said. "Perhaps, after all, I *am* a lunatic; perhaps I've had a touch of the Luzon sun and don't know it."

"I'll be the judge of that," said the Tracer, smiling.

"Very well, sir. Then I'll begin by telling you that I've seen a ghost."

"There are such things," observed Keen quietly.

"Oh, I don't mean one of those fabled sheeted creatures that float about at night; I mean a phantom—a real phantom—in the sunlight— standing before my very eyes in broad day! . . . Now do you feel inclined to go on with my case, Mr. Keen?"

"Certainly," replied the Tracer gravely. "Please continue, Captain Harren."

"All right, then. Here's the beginning of it: Three years ago, here in New York, drifting along Fifth Avenue with the crowd, I looked up to encounter the most wonderful pair of eyes that I ever beheld—that any living man ever beheld! The most—wonderfully—beautiful—"

He sat so long immersed in retrospection that the Tracer said: "I am listening, Captain," and the Captain woke up with a start.

"What was I saying? How far had I proceeded?"

"Only to the eyes."

"Oh, I see! The eyes were dark, sir, dark and lovely beyond any power of description. The hair was also dark—very soft and thick and—er—wavy and dark. The face was extremely youthful, and ornamental to the uttermost verges of a beauty so exquisite that, were I to attempt to formulate for you its individual attractions, I should, I fear, transgress the strictly rigid bounds of that reticence which becomes a gentleman in complete possession of his senses."

"*Ex*actly," mused the Tracer.

"Also," continued Captain Harren, with growing animation, "to attempt to describe her figure would be utterly useless, because I am a practical man and not a poet, nor do I read poetry or indulge in futile novels or romances of any description. Therefore I can only add that it was a figure, a poise, absolutely faultless, youthful, beautiful, erect, wholesome, gracious, graceful, charmingly buoyant and—well, I cannot describe her figure, and I shall not try."

"*Ex*actly; don't try."

"No," said Harren mournfully, "it is useless"; and he relapsed into enchanted retrospection.

"Who was she?" asked Mr. Keen softly.

"I don't know."

"You never again saw her?"

"Mr. Keen, I—I am not ill-bred, but I simply could not help following her. She was so b-b-beautiful that it hurt; and I only wanted to look at her; I didn't mind being hurt. So I walked on and on, and sometimes I'd pass her and sometimes I'd let her pass me, and when she wasn't looking I'd look—not offensively, but just because I *couldn't* help it. And all the time my senses were humming like a top and my heart kept jumping to get into my throat, and I hadn't a notion where I was going or what time it was or what day of the week. She didn't see me; she didn't dream that I was looking at her; she didn't know me from any of the thousand silk-hatted, frock-coated men who passed and repassed her on Fifth Avenue. And when she went into St. Berold's Church, I went, too, and I stood where I could see her and where she couldn't see me. It was like a touch of the Luzon sun, Mr. Keen. And then she came out and got into a Fifth Avenue stage, and I got in, too. And whenever she looked away I looked at her—without the slightest offense, Mr. Keen, until, once, she caught my eye—"

He passed an unsteady hand over his forehead.

"For a moment we looked full at one another," he continued. "I got red, sir; I felt it, and I couldn't look away. And when I turned color like a blooming beet, she began to turn pink like a rosebud, and she looked full into my eyes with such a wonderful purity, such exquisite innocence, that I—never felt so near—er—heaven in my life! No, sir, not even when they ambushed us at Manoa Wells—but that's another thing—only it is part of this business."

He tightened his clasped hands over his knee until the knuckles whitened.

"*That's* my story, Mr. Keen," he said crisply.

"All of it?"

Harren looked at the floor, then at Keen: "No, not all. You'll think me a lunatic if I tell you all."

"Oh, you saw her again?"

"N-never! That is—"

"Never?"

"Not in—in the flesh."

"Oh, in dreams?"

Harren stirred uneasily. "I don't know what you call them. I have seen her since—in the sunlight, in the open, in my quarters in Manila, standing there perfectly distinct, looking at me with such strange, beautiful eyes—"

"Go on," said the Tracer, nodding.

"What else is there to say?" muttered Harren.

"You saw her—or a phantom which resembled her. Did she speak?"

"No."

"Did you speak to her?"

"N-no. Once I held out my—my arms."

"What happened?"

"She wasn't there," said Harren simply.

"She vanished?"

"No—I don't know. I—I didn't see her any more."

"Didn't she fade?"

"No. I can't explain. She—there was only myself in the room."

"How many times has she appeared to you?"

"A great many times."

"In your room?"

"Yes. And in the road under a vertical sun; in the forest, in the paddy fields. I have seen her passing through the hallway of a friend's house— turning on the stair to look back at me! I saw her standing just back of the firing-line at Manoa Wells when we were preparing to rush the forts, and it scared me so that I jumped forward to draw her back. But— she wasn't there, Mr. Keen. . . .

"On the transport she stood facing me on deck one moonlit evening for five minutes. I saw her in 'Frisco; she sat in the Pullman twice between Denver and this city. Twice in my room at the Vice-Regent she has sat opposite me at midday, so clear, so beautiful, so real that—that I could ieve she was only a—a—" He hesitated.

pparition of her own subconscious self," said the Tracer quietly.
ˉˉˉˉ ˉˉˉ been forced to admit such things, and, as you know, we are
on the verge of understanding the alphabet of some of the unknown forces
which we must some day reckon with."

Harren, tense, a trifle pale, gazed at him earnestly.

"Do *you* believe in such things?"

"How can I avoid believing?" said the Tracer. "Every day, in my
profession, we have proof of the existence of forces for which we have
as yet no explanation—or, at best, a very crude one. I have had case after
case of premonition; case after case of dual and even multiple personality;
case after case where apparitions played a vital part in the plot which was
brought to me to investigate. I'll tell you this, Captain: I, personally, never
saw an apparition, never was obsessed by premonitions, never received
any communications from the outer void. But I have had to do with those
who undoubtedly did. Therefore I listen with all seriousness and respect
to what you tell me."

"Suppose," said Harren, growing suddenly red, "that I should tell you
I have succeeded in photographing this phantom."

The Tracer sat silent. He was astounded, but he did not betray it.

"You have that photograph, Captain Harren?"

"Yes."

"Where is it?"

"In my rooms."

"You wish me to see it?"

Harren hesitated. "I—there is—seems to be—something almost sacred
to me in that photograph. . . . You understand me, do you not? Yet, if
it will help you in finding her—"

"Oh," said the Tracer in guileless astonishment, "you desire to find
this young lady. Why?"

Harren stared. "Why? Why do I want to find her? Man, I—I can't
live without her!"

"I thought you were not certain whether you really could be in love."

The hot color in the Captain's bronzed cheeks mounted to his hair.

"*Ex*actly," purred the Tracer, looking out of the window. "Suppose
we walk around to your rooms after luncheon. Shall we?"

Harren picked up his hat and gloves, hesitating, lingering on the
threshold. "You *don't* think she is—a—dead?" he asked unsteadily.

"No," said Mr. Keen, "I don't."

"Because," said Harren wistfully, "her apparition is so superbly healthy
and—and glowing with youth and life—"

"That is probably what sent it half the world over to confront you,"
said the Tracer gravely; "youth and life aglow with spiritual health. I think,
Captain, that she had been seeing you, too, during these three years, but

probably only in her dreams—memories of your encounters with her subconscious self floating over continents and oceans in a quest of which her waking intelligence is innocently unaware."

The Captain colored like a schoolboy, lingering at the door, hat in hand. Then he straightened up to the full height of his slim but powerful figure.

"At three?" he inquired bluntly.

"At three o'clock in your room, Hotel Vice-Regent. Good morning, Captain."

"Good morning," said Harren dreamily, and walked away, head bent, gray eyes lost in retrospection, and on his lean, bronzed, attractive face an afterglow of color wholly becoming.

†   †   †

Chapter 2: The Cypher

When the Tracer of Lost Persons entered Captain Harren's room at the Hotel Vice-Regent that afternoon he found the young man standing at a center table, pencil in hand, studying a sheet of paper which was covered with letters and figures.

The two men eyed one another in silence for a moment, then Harren pointed grimly to the confusion of letters and figures covering dozens of scattered sheets lying on the table.

"That's part of my madness," he said with a short laugh. "Can you make anything of such lunatic work?"

The Tracer picked up a sheet of paper covered with letters of the alphabet and Roman and Arabic numerals. He dropped it presently and picked up another comparatively blank sheet, on which were the following figures:

He studied it for a while, then glanced interrogatively at Harren.

"It's nothing," said Harren. "I've been groping for three years—but it's no use. That's lunatics' work." He wheeled squarely on his heels, looking straight at the Tracer. *"Do* you think I've had a touch of the sun?"

"No," said Mr. Keen, drawing a chair to the table. "Saner men than you or I have spent a lifetime over this so-called Seal of Solomon." He laid his finger on the two symbols—

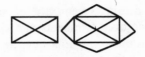

Then, looking across the table at Harren: "What," he asked, "has the Seal of Solomon to do with your case?"

"*She—*" muttered Harren, and fell silent.

The Tracer waited; Harren said nothing.

"Where is the photograph?"

Harren unlocked a drawer in the table, hesitated, looked strangely at the Tracer.

"Mr. Keen," he said, "there is nothing on earth I hold more sacred than this. There is only one thing in the world that could justify me in showing it to a living soul—my—my desire to find—her—"

"No," said Keen coolly, "that is not enough to justify you—the mere desire to find the living original of this apparition. Nothing could justify your showing it unless you love her."

Harren held the picture tightly, staring full at the Tracer. A dull flush mounted to his forehead, and very slowly he laid the picture before the Tracer of Lost Persons.

Minute after minute sped while the Tracer bent above the photograph, his finely modeled features absolutely devoid of expression. Harren had drawn his chair beside him, and now sat leaning forward, bronzed cheek resting in his hand, staring fixedly at the picture.

"When was this—this photograph taken?" asked the Tracer quietly.

"The day after I arrived in New York. I was here, alone, smoking my pipe and glancing over the evening paper just before dressing for dinner. It was growing rather dark in the room; I had not turned on the electric light. My camera lay on the table—there it is!—that Kodak. I had taken a few snapshots on shipboard; there was one film left."

He leaned more heavily on his elbow, eyes fixed upon the picture.

"It was almost dark," he repeated. "I laid aside the evening paper and stood up, thinking about dressing for dinner, when my eyes happened to fall on the camera. It occurred to me that I might as well unload it, let the unused film go, and send the roll to be developed and printed; and I picked up the camera—"

"Yes," said the Tracer softly.

"I picked it up and was starting toward the window where there remained enough daylight to see by—"

The Tracer nodded gently.

"Then I saw *her!*" said Harren under his breath.

"Where?"

"There—standing by that window. You can see the window and curtain in the photograph."

The Tracer gazed intently at the picture.

"She looked at me," said Harren, steadying his voice. "She was as real as you are, and she stood there, smiling faintly, her dark, lovely eyes meeting mine."

"Did you speak?"

"No."

"How long did she remain there?"

"I don't know—time seemed to stop—the world—everything grew still. . . . Then, little by little, something began to stir under my stunned senses—that germ of misgiving, that dreadful doubt of my own sanity. . . . I scarcely knew what I was doing when I took the photograph; besides, it had grown quite dark, and I could scarcely see her." He drew himself erect with a nervous movement. "How on earth could I have obtained that photograph of her in the darkness?" he demanded.

"N-rays," said the Tracer coolly. "It has been done in France."

"Yes, from living people, but—"

"What the N-ray is in living organisms, we must call, for lack of a better term, the subaura in the phantom."

They bent over the photograph together. Presently the Tracer said: "She is very, very beautiful?"

Harren's dry lips unclosed, but he uttered no sound.

"She is beautiful, is she not?" repeated the Tracer, turning to look at the young man.

"Can you not see she is?" he asked impatiently.

"No," said the Tracer.

Harren stared at him.

"Captain Harren," continued the Tracer, "I can see nothing upon this bit of paper that resembles in the remotest degree a human face or figure."

Harren turned white.

"Not that I doubt that *you* can see it," pursued the Tracer calmly. "I simply repeat that I see absolutely nothing on this paper except a part of a curtain, a window pane, and—and—"

"What! for God's sake!" cried Harren hoarsely.

"I don't know yet. Wait; let me study it."

"Can you not see her face, her eyes? *Don't* you see that exquisite slim figure standing there by the curtain?" demanded Harren, laying his shaking finger on the photograph. "Why, man, it is as clear, as clean cut, as distinct as though the picture had been taken in sunlight! Do you mean to say that there is nothing there—that I am crazy?"

"No. Wait."

"Wait! How can I wait when you sit staring at her picture and telling me that you can't see it, but that it is doubtless there? Are you deceiving me, Mr. Keen? Are you trying to humor me, trying to be kind to me, knowing all the while that I'm crazy—"

"Wait, man! You are no more crazy than I am. I tell you that I can see something on the window pane—"

He suddenly sprang up and walked to the window, leaning close and examining the glass. Harren followed and laid his hand lightly over the pane.

"Do you see any marks on the glass?" demanded Keen.

Harren shook his head.

"Have you a magnifying glass?" asked the Tracer.

Harren pointed back to the table, and they returned to the photograph, the Tracer bending over it and examining it through the glass.

"All I see," he said, still studying the photograph, "is a corner of a curtain and a window on which certain figures seem to have been cut. . . . Look, Captain Harren, can you see them?"

"I see some marks—some squares."

"You can't see anything written on that pane—as though cut by a diamond?"

"Nothing distinct."

"But you see *her?*"

"Perfectly."

"In minute detail?"

"Yes."

The Tracer thought a moment: "Does she wear a ring?"

"Yes; can't you see?"

"Draw it for me."

They seated themselves side by side, and Harren drew a rough sketch of the ring which he insisted was so plainly visible on her hand:

"Oh," observed the Tracer, "she wears the Seal of Solomon on her ring."

Harren looked up at him. "That symbol has haunted me persistently for three years," he said. "I have found it everywhere—on articles that I buy, on house furniture, on the belt of dead ladrones, on the hilts of creeses, on the funnels of steamers, on the headstalls of horses. If they put a laundry mark on my linen it's certain to be this!

If I buy a box of matches the sign is on it. Why, I've even seen it on the brilliant wings of tropical insects. It's got on my nerves. I dream about it."

"And you buy books about it and try to work out its mystical meaning?"

suggested the Tracer, smiling.

But Harren's gray eyes were serious. He said: *"She* never comes to me without that symbol somewhere about her. . . . I told you she never spoke to me. That is true; yet once, in a vivid dream of her, she did speak. I—I was almost ashamed to tell you of that."

"Tell me."

"A—a dream? Do you wish to know what I dreamed?"

"Yes—if it was a dream."

"It was. I was asleep on the deck of the *Mindinao,* dead tired after a fruitless hike. I dreamed she came toward me through a young woodland all lighted by the sun, and in her hands she held masses of that wild flower we call Solomon's Seal. And she said—in the voice I know must be like hers: 'If you could only read! If you would only understand the message I send you! It is everywhere on earth for you to read, if you only would!'

"I said: 'Is the message in the seal? Is that the key to it?'

"She nodded, laughing, burying her face in the flowers, and said:

" 'Perhaps I can write it more plainly for you some day; I will try very, very hard.'

"And after that she went away—not swiftly—for I saw her at moments far away in the woods; but I must have confused her with the glimmering shafts of sunlight, and in a little while the woodland grew dark and I woke with the racket of a Colt's automatic in my ears."

He passed his sun-bronzed hand over his face, hesitated, then leaned over the photograph once more, which the Tracer was studying intently through the magnifying glass.

"There is something on that window in the photograph which I'm going to copy," he said. "Please shove a pad and pencil toward me."

Still examining the photograph through the glass he held in his right hand, Mr. Keen picked up the pencil and, feeling for the pad, began very slowly to form the following series of symbols:

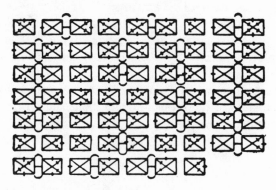

"What on earth are you doing?" muttered Captain Harren, twisting his short mustache in perplexity.

"I am copying what I see through this magnifying glass written on the window pane in the photograph," said the Tracer calmly. "Can't you see those marks?"

"I—I do now; I never noticed them before particularly—only that there were scratches there."

When at length the Tracer had finished his work he sat, chin on hand, examining it in silence. Presently he turned toward Harren, smiling.

"Well?" inquired the younger man impatiently; "do those scratches representing Solomon's Seal mean anything?"

"It's the strangest cipher I ever encountered," said Mr. Keen—"the strangest I ever heard of. I have seen hundreds of ciphers—hundreds— secret codes of the State Department, secret military codes, elaborate Oriental ciphers, symbols used in commercial transactions, symbols used by criminals and every species of malefactor. And every one of them can be solved with time and patience and a little knowledge of the subject. But this"—he sat looking at it with eyes half closed—"this is *too* simple."

"Simple!"

"Very. It's so simple that it's baffling."

"Do you mean to say you are going to be able to find a meaning in squares and crosses?"

"I—I don't believe it is going to be so very difficult to translate them."

"Great guns!" said the Captain. "Do you mean to say that you can ultimately translate that cipher?"

The Tracer smiled. "Let's examine it for repetitions first. Here we have this symbol

repeated five times. It's likely to be the letter E. I think—" His voice ceased; for a quarter of an hour he poured over the symbols, pencil in hand, checking off some, substituting a letter here and there.

"No," he said; "the usual doesn't work in this case. It's an absurdly simple cipher. I have a notion that numbers play a part in it—you see where these crossed squares are bracketed—those must be numbers requiring two figures—"

He fell silent again, and for another quarter of an hour he remained motionless, immersed in the problem before him, Harren frowning at the paper over his shoulder.

†   †   †

Chapter 3: The Solution

"Come!" said the Tracer suddenly; "this won't do. There are too few symbols to give us a key; too few repetitions to furnish us with any key basis. Come, Captain, let us use our intellects; let us talk it over with that paper lying there between us. It's a simple cipher—a childishly simple one if we use our wits. Now, sir, what I see repeated before us on this sheet of paper is merely one of the forms of a symbol known as Solomon's Seal. The symbol is, as we see, repeated a great many times. Every seal

has been dotted or crossed on some one of the line composing it; some seals are coupled with brackets and armatures."

"What of it?" inquired Harren vacantly.

"Well, sir, in the first place, that symbol

is supposed to represent the spiritual and material, as you know. What else do you know about it?"

"Nothing. I bought a book about it, but made nothing of it."

"Isn't it supposed," asked Mr. Keen, "to contain within itself the nine numerals, 1, 2, 3, 4, 5, 6, 7, 8, 9, and even the zero symbol?"

"I believe so."

"*Ex*actly. Here's the seal.

Now I'll mark the one, two, and three by crossing the lines, like this:

one, two, three,

Now, eliminating all lines not crossed there remains

the one, **1** the two, **Z** the three, **Ƨ**

And here is the entire series:

IZƷ⊲Ƽ⌐7Ȣ၇

and the zero— **▷**"

A sudden excitement stirred Harren; he leaned over the paper, gazing earnestly at the cipher; the Tracer rose and glanced around the room as though in search of something.

"Is there a telephone here?" he asked.

"For Heaven's sake, don't give this up just yet," exclaimed Harren. "These things mean numbers; don't you see? Look at that!" pointing to a linked pair of seals,

"That means the number nineteen! You can form it by using only the crossed lines of the seal.

Don't you see, Mr. Keen?"

"Yes, Captain Harren, the cipher is, as you say, very plain; quite as easy to read as so much handwriting. That is why I wish to use your telephone—at once, if you please."

"It's in my bedroom; you don't mind if I go on working out this cipher while you're telephoning?"

"Not in the least," said the Tracer blandly. He walked into the Captain's bedroom, closing the door behind him; then he stepped over to the telephone, unhooked the receiver, and called up his own headquarters.

"Hello. This is Mr. Keen. I want to speak to Miss Borrow."

In a few moments Miss Borrow answered: "I am here, Mr. Keen."

"Good. Look up the name Inwood. Try New York first—Edith Inwood is the name. Look sharp, please; I am holding the wire."

He held it for ten full minutes; then Miss Borrow's low voice called him over the wire.

"Go ahead," said the Tracer quietly.

"There is only one Edith Inwood in New York, Mr. Keen—Miss Edith Inwood, graduate of Barnard, 1902—left an orphan 1903 and obliged to support herself—became an assistant to Professor Boggs of the Museum of Inscriptions. Is considered an authority upon Arabian cryptograms. Has written a monograph on the Herati symbol—a short treatise on the Swastika. She is twenty-four years of age. Do you require further details?"

"No," said the Tracer; "please ring off."

Then he called up General Information. "I want the Museum of Inscriptions. Get me their number, please." After a moment: "Is this the Museum of Inscriptions?"

· · · · ·

"Is Professor Boggs there?"

.   .   .   .   .

"Is this Professor Boggs?"

.   .   .   .   .

"Could you find time to decipher an inscription for me at once?"

.   .   .   .   .

"Of course I know you are extremely busy, but have you no assistant who could do it?"

.   .   .   .   .

"What did you say her name is? Miss Inwood?"

.   .   .   .   .

"Oh! And will the young lady translate the inscription at once if I send a copy of it to her by messenger?"

.   .   .   .   .

"Thank you very much, Professor. I will send a messenger to Miss Inwood with a copy of the inscription. Good-by."

He hung up the receiver, turned thoughtfully, opened the door again, and walked into the sunlit living room.

"Look here!" cried the Captain in a high state of excitement. "I've got a lot of numbers out of it already."

"Wonderful!" murmured the Tracer, looking over the young man's broad shoulders at a sheet of paper bearing these numbers:

9—14—5—22—5—18—19—1—23—25—15—21—2—21—20—15—
14—3—5—9—12—15—22—5—25—15—21—5—4—9—20—8—9—14—
23—15—15—4.

"Marvelous!" repeated the Tracer, smiling. "Now what *do* you suppose those numbers can stand for?"

"Letters!" announced the Captain triumphantly. "Take the number nine, for example. The ninth letter in the alphabet is I! Mr. Keen, suppose we try writing down the letters according to that system!"

"Suppose we do," agreed the Tracer gravely.

So, counting under his breath, the young man set down the letters in the following order, not attempting to group them into words:

INEVERSAWYOUBUTONCEILOVEYOUEDITHINWOOD.

Then he leaned back, excited, triumphant.

"There you are!" he said; "only, of course, it makes no sense." He examined it in silence, and gradually a hopeless expression effaced the animation. "How the deuce am I going to separate that mass of letters into words?" he muttered.

"This way," said the Tracer, smilingly taking the pencil from his fingers, and he wrote: I—NEVER—SAW—YOU—BUT—ONCE. I—LOVE—YOU. EDITH INWOOD.

Then he laid the pencil on the table and walked to the window.

Once or twice he fancied that he heard incoherent sounds behind him. And after a while he turned, retracing his steps leisurely. Captain Harren, extremely pink, stood tugging at his short mustache and studying the papers on the desk.

"Well?" inquired the Tracer, amused.

The young man pointed to the translation with an unsteady finger. "W-what on earth does that mean?" he demanded shakily. "Who is Edith Inwood? W-what on earth does that cryptogram mean on the window pane in the photograph? How did it come there? It isn't on my window pane, you see!"

The Tracer said quietly: "That is not a photograph of your window."

"What!"

"No, Captain. Here! Look at it closely through this glass. There are sixteen small panes in that sash; now count the panes in your window—eight! Besides, look at that curtain. It is made of some figured stuff like chintz. Now, look at your own curtain yonder! It is of plain velour."

"But—but I took that photograph! She stood there—there by that very window!"

The Tracer leaned over the photograph, examining it through the glass. And, studying it, he said: "Do you still see *her* in this photograph, Captain Harren?"

"Certainly. Can you not see her?"

"No," murmured the Tracer, "but I see the window which she really stood by when her phantom came here seeking you. And that is sufficient. Come, Captain Harren, we are going out together."

The Captain looked at him earnestly; something in Mr. Keen's eyes seemed to fascinate him.

"You think that—that it's likely we are g-going to see—*her!*" he faltered.

"If I were you," mused the Tracer of Lost Persons, joining the tips of his lean fingers meditatively—"If I were you I should wear a silk hat and a frock coat. It's—it's afternoon, anyhow," he added deprecatingly, "and we are liable to make a call."

Captain Harren turned like a man in a dream and entered his bedroom. And when he emerged he was dressed and groomed with pathetic precision.

"Mr. Keen," he said, "I—I don't know why I am d-daring to hope for all s-sorts of things. Nothing you have said really warrants it. But somehow I'm venturing to cherish an absurd notion that I may s-see her."

"Perhaps," said the Tracer, smiling.

"Mr. Keen! You wouldn't say that if—if there was no chance, would you? You wouldn't dash a fellow's hopes—"

"No, I wouldn't," said Mr. Keen. "I tell you frankly that I expect to find her."

"To-day?"

"We'll see," said Mr. Keen guardedly. "Come, Captain, don't look that way! Courage, sir! We are about to execute a turning movement; but you look like a Russian general on his way to the south front."

Harren managed to laugh; they went out, side by side, descended the elevator, and found a cab at the *porte-cochère*. Mr. Keen gave the directions and followed the Captain into the cab.

"Now," he said, as they wheeled south, "we are first going to visit the Museum of Inscriptions and have this cipher translation verified. Here is the cipher as I copied it. Hold it tightly, Captain; we've only a few blocks."

Indeed they were already nearly there. The hansom drew up in front of a plain granite building wedged in between some rather elaborate private dwelling-houses. Over the door were letters of dull bronze:

AMERICAN MUSEUM OF INSCRIPTIONS

and the two men descended and entered a wide marble hall lined with glass-covered cabinets containing plaster casts of various ancient inscriptions and a few bronze and marble originals. Several female frumps were nosing the exhibits.

An attendant in livery stood in the middle distance. The Tracer walked over to him. "I have an appointment to consult Miss Inwood," he whispered.

"This way, sir," nodded the attendant, and the Tracer signaled the Captain to follow.

They climbed several marble stairways, crossed a rotunda, and entered a room—a sort of library. Beyond was a door which bore the inscription:

ASSISTANT CURATOR

"Now," said the Tracer of Lost Persons in a low voice to Captain Harren, "I am going to ask you to sit here for a few minutes while I interview the assistant curator. You don't mind, do you?"

"No, I don't mind," said Harren wearily, "only, when are we going to begin to search for—*her?*"

"Very soon—I may say extremely soon," said Mr. Keen gravely. "By the way, I think I'll take that sheet of paper on which I copied the cipher. Thank you. I won't be long."

The attendant had vanished. Captain Harren sat down by a window and gazed out into the late afternoon sunshine. The Tracer of Lost Persons, treading softly across the carpeted floor, approached the sanctuary, turned the handle, and walked in, carefully closing the door behind him.

There was a young girl seated at a desk by an open window; she looked up quietly as he entered, then rose leisurely.

"Miss Inwood?"

"Yes."

She was slender, dark-eyed, dark-haired—a lovely, wholesome young creature, gracious and graceful. And that was all—for the Tracer of Lost Persons could not see through the eyes of Captain Harren, and perhaps that is why he was not able to discern a miracle of beauty in the pretty girl who confronted him—no magic and matchless marvel of transcendent loveliness—only a quiet, sweet-faced, dark-eyed young girl whose features and figure were attractive in the manner that youth is always attractive. But then it is a gift of the gods to see through eyes anointed by the gods.

The Tracer touched his gray mustache and bowed; the girl bowed very sweetly.

"You are Mr. Keen," she said; "you have an inscription for me to translate."

"A mystery for young eyes to interpret," he said, smiling. "May I sit here—and tell my story before I show you my inscription?"

"Please do," she said, seating herself at her desk and facing him, one slender white hand supporting the oval of her face.

The Tracer drew his chair a little forward. "It is a curious matter," he said. "May I give you a brief outline of the details?"

"By all means, Mr. Keen."

"Then let me begin by saying that the inscription of which I have a copy was probably scratched upon a window pane by means of a diamond."

"Oh! Then—then it is not an ancient inscription, Mr. Keen."

"The theme is ancient—the oldest theme in the world—love! The cipher is old—as old as King Solomon." She looked up quickly. The Tracer, apparently engrossed in his own story, went on with it. "Three years ago the young girl who wrote this inscription up on the window pane of her—her bedroom, I think it was—fell in love. Do you follow me, Miss Inwood?"

Miss Inwood sat very still—wide, dark eyes fixed on him.

"Fell in love," repeated the Tracer musingly, "not in the ordinary way. That is the point, you see. No, she fell in love at first sight; fell in love with a young man whom she never before had seen, never again beheld— and never forgot. Do you still follow me, Miss Inwood?"

She made the slightest motion with her lips.

"No," mused the Tracer of Lost Persons, "she never forgot him. I am not sure, but I think she sometimes dreamed of him. She dreamed of him awake, too. Once she inscribed a message to him, cutting it with the diamond in her ring on the window pane—"

A slight sound escaped from Miss Inwood's lips. "I beg your pardon," said the Tracer, "did you say something?"

The girl had risen, pale, astounded, incredulous.

"Who are you? she faltered. "What has this—this story to do with me?"

"Child," said the Tracer of Lost Persons, "the Seal of Solomon is a splendid mystery. All of heaven and earth are included within its symbol.

And more, more than you dream of, more than I dare fathom; and I am an old man, my child—old, alone, with nobody to fear for, nothing to dread, not even the end of all—because I am ready for that, too. Yet I, having nothing on earth to dread, dare not fathom what that symbol may mean, nor what vast powers it may exert on life. God knows. It may be the very signet of Fate itself; the sign manual of Destiny."

He drew the paper from his pocket, unrolled it, and spread it out under her frightened eyes.

"*That!*" she whispered, steadying herself blindly against the arm he offered. She stood a moment so, then, shuddering, covered her eyes with both hands. The Tracer of Lost Persons looked at her, turned and opened the door.

"Captain Harren!" he called quietly. Harren, pacing the anteroom, turned and came forward. As he entered the door he caught sight of the girl crouching by the window, her face hidden in her hands, and at the same moment she dropped her hands and looked straight at him.

"*You!*" she gasped.

The Tracer of Lost Persons stepped out, closing the door. For a moment he stood there, tall, gaunt, gray, staring vacantly into space.

"She *was* beautiful—when she looked at him," he muttered.

For another minute he stood there, hesitating, glancing backward at the closed door. Then he went away, stooping slightly, his top hat held close against the breast of his tightly buttoned frock coat.

Afterword

Another consequence of belief in the separateness of the body and the "I" that occupies it is the feeling that it is possible for the incorporeal "I" (or astral body) to travel around while one's physical body stays home.

This lends itself to romantic complications, as the Chambers story shows, but of course there has never been any evidence for such personality-contacts, or for the separateness of body and personality.

Incidentally, in the midpoint of the story reference is made to a photograph taken in darkness. Puzzlement is expressed over the fact that such a photograph could be made. Whereupon the hero of the story says: "N-rays. It has been done in France."

This is an example of an error frozen in mid-air. At the time this story was written there was a tremendous furor in France over the discovery of a mysterious radiation called "N-rays."

It was not a hoax, but it was a case of self-delusion by French scientists who were patriotically overeager to match the discovery of X-rays by a German scientist. Unfortunately, N-rays lasted only about two years before they were shown to be nonexistent.

This demonstrates why one must be careful at snatching too whole-heartedly at scientific advances that have not yet been fully established, especially if they seem far-out. Not all advances prove to be valid.—I.A.

Additional Reading

L. Adams Beck, "The Ninth Vibration," in *The Ninth Vibration and Other Stories* (New York: Dodd, Mead, 1922).

Walter C. Everett, "The Lady in Gray," in *The Other Worlds,* Phil Stong, ed. (New York: W. Funk, 1941).

Davis Grubb, "The Horsehair Trunk," in *Twelve Tales of Suspense and the Supernatural* (New York: Scribners, 1964).

Kurt Vonnegut, "Unready to Wear," in *Welcome to the Monkey House* (New York: Delacorte Press, 1968).

H. G. Wells, "The Stolen Body," in *The Short Stories of H. G. Wells* (London: Ernest Benn, 1927).

20

Sympathetic Magic

August Derleth
Miss Esperson

I remembered Miss' Esperson quite by chance, when I came upon her family name in the obituary column of a metropolitan newspaper. I suppose it is always by such obscure means that the proper bridges are made to memories, particularly those of childhood, though there is no accounting for the subsequent train of thought which may come. In Miss Esperson's case, perhaps it was the difference between a more mature outlook and that of the small boy I had been. Certainly it was not likely that there existed any relationship between the newly-deceased gentleman named Esperson and the genteel old lady of that small Louisiana town where I spent so much of my childhood.

The fact is, I had forgotten all about Miss Esperson. For two decades I had not once had occasion to remember her, and sight of the name Esperson among the obituaries was the purest happenstance, for I caught it only in passing. But thereupon immediately the image of Miss Esperson rose out of that dark well of memory, and instantly I was once more a small boy in a forgotten Louisiana town. There was Miss Esperson— tall, with a strangely rectangular face, strong jaws—almost equine, I think in retrospect—and marvellously dark eyes set off by her greying hair; and there was her little "estate," enclosed by rows of trees and a shrub-grown garden, hedged away from the rest of the town, all the way from the shaded street in front back to the river which made the rear boundary of her land, the grounds that were such a paradise for those children who found their way there. And there was, once more, all that superstition of fear, so meaningless to a child.

For Miss Esperson, who was surely the soul of gentleness and troubled no one, going her way as serenely as might be expected of the spinsterly last of her line, was the victim of a curious conspiracy of fear on the part of the poorer elements of the town. It was strange very largely because it seemed so unfounded. Miss Esperson had never in all her life so much as uttered a word against anyone. Yet, many inevitably crossed the street at sight of her, or avoided her glance, or looked at her sideways, from the corners of their eyes. They believed that Miss Esperson was a fearful person who had certain "powers" because she had been born in the British West Indies when her father was a consul there, and she had learned many things from the voodoo priests of that country of her childhood.

The black children had a name for her, certainly gleaned from the mutterings of some parents; they called her "obiooman"; this, broken down, became "obi woman," which held no meaning whatsoever for us, though we sometimes spoke of her among ourselves like that. But there was seldom any fear of Miss Esperson among the children of her neighborhood; for we knew her house as a mecca, a place where we were sure to find all sorts of things which made for transports of joy—cakes and cookies, ice cream, strawberries and honey, watermelon and even games, which she played with us. Was she lonely, perhaps? She must have been, though she had her select circle of friends, and she went about paying her calls and accepting the calls of her friends, who liked her in direct proportion to the odd way in which others feared her.

I remembered all this; as I have said, it rose up out of the past without change, without blemish—but there was an indefinable aura of difference, not in the facts of that memory, but in the instant interpretation; the perspective was changed. Since that last time, in my teens, when I had looked upon Miss Esperson in the dignity of death, I had not once glanced back into those early years; but here, now, strangely, out of a newspaper which was alien to her and to all the culture for which she stood, there rose up a Miss Esperson who, though precisely the same woman I had known, offered suddenly a little more, vouchsafed a revelation, as it were, to an adult both less sure of the meaning of life and death, and more sure, than that boy he had been two decades ago.

I remembered Miss Esperson, and I remembered Jamie.

Jamie lived on one side of Miss Esperson's with his father and his stepmother, just as I lived on the other, and both of us looked to Miss Esperson's house as a sort of refuge. But it was never I who needed that refuge; it was Jamie, for his stepmother was unkind and cruel to him, and I can remember readily how furiously, blindly angry I sometimes got in my helplessness before the knowledge of what his stepmother did to him when his father had left the house, hating him as she did, an instinct of protection rising up within me in the face of his pain and suffering.

I should imagine that Jamie was about seven at this time; his mother had died two years before, and his father had married again, a striking, auburn-haired woman whose acquaintance he had made in New Orleans.

From the very first this woman had resented Jamie, perhaps initially because he persisted in clinging to his memories of his mother, which doubtless she interpreted as criticism of herself, and to which she responded not with the patience that the situation called for, but with an antagonism the boy was quick to feel; so that whatever chance there might have been for an ultimate rapproachement between the two was irrevocably lost. Moreover, she attacked him at his most vulnerable point, by seeking to deprive him of all those physical properties he owned which bore any link to his mother—the things his mother had given him, even the clothes which had been ordered or made or repaired by her, though he was in any event fast outgrowing them. Hers was a refined cruelty which was more than spiteful unkindness, and which presently degenerated into an almost beastly physical brutality, when his hatred of her showed openly and his devotion to his mother's memory would not be in any way lessened.

Whenever he could escape her, he fled to my home or to Miss Esperson, who had known his mother and was therefore another link to that dear past so free of cruelty and pain. And to us, as to no one else—not even to his father, for he had learned how his stepmother could twist his complaints into triumphs for her—he told everything that had happened, not with any eagerness, rather with a reluctance born of the dire necessity of lessening somehow the burden of his suffering by sharing it. And Miss Esperson in her gentle way would comfort him, drawing him out very skillfully.

"Nothing is ever as bad as you think it is," she would say.

"She wouldn't let me have anything to eat for breakfast except some spoiled milk," he would confess.

Always *She;* he would never call her anything else. Even a whip would not have driven him to call her by any word which might suggest a maternal relationship.

"Then you shall have what you like here."

And, while he ate the food she put out for him, he went on with a recital of his woes. He was not a complaining child. That is to say, there was nothing whining or pathetic about him, though he looked soft, with his great, mellow eyes, and a pale skin through which the veins showed a shadowy blue. No, he merely recited the tale of his hardships in a flat, monotonous voice with a note of dubiety in it, as if he felt that what he had to say was far too incredible to be believed even by people like us, whom he trusted.

Towards the end—for there was an end to Jamie's misery, though we did not foresee it then—he was persuaded from time to time to show Miss Esperson the welts he bore on his thin back, and, remembering her now from this vantage point, I can see quite clearly in my mind's eye the way in which initially she winced, and then the way in which her face seemed to pale and set, and a kind of hardness which shone in her eyes.

"Oh, you poor boy!" she would exclaim, and trot him off into the house where she laved his bruised back and salved it, and from which she brought him out again with perhaps something special to take his mind from his woes—chocolates or a kind of honey-cake she made now and then.

But Jamie's mind was never very far from his troubles, for all that he did not complain. You saw it in his eyes, whenever he looked toward the house where he lived, though little of that was to be seen for the trees and the hedge. His house, like mine and Miss Esperson's, had a beautiful back yard sweeping to the river, though there was less shrubbery and garden now that his mother had died, his stepmother finding little enough time to care for herself to spend any on the grounds either in person or in giving directions to the gardeners who were always to be recruited from among the black population. You knew, too, that he had long since been forbidden to visit Miss Esperson; doubtless his stepmother suspected that he had Miss Esperson's sympathy, for on one occasion even before she had begun to beat Jamie, she marched over into Miss Esperson's yard, took hold of Jamie, and literally dragged him home—though not before she had told Miss Esperson what she thought of her, which was neither kind nor pleasant—leaving Miss Esperson standing all a-tremble, with her lace handkerchief pressed to her lips, and her astonished eyes following the pair retreating among the trees, and Jamie's screams of angry protest rising and falling—and the sound, too, of Mrs. Fallon's blows falling upon the boy.

I said then what I had heard my mother say. "Mrs. Fallon's not a lady, is she, Miss Esperson?"

"I'm afraid not, Stephen," she said. "She doesn't act the way a lady should act, does she?"

But Jamie came all the same. He desperately needed the refuge Miss Esperson offered him. He needed it more than he feared the punishment he knew would be given him when his stepmother discovered where he had gone; so his seeking this place was a course forced upon him by something more vital than the normal revulsion he experienced at the certain knowledge of the punishment, corporal or otherwise, he inevitably incurred.

My mother always spoke of Mr. Fallon as a "fatuous man." Though no one knew what tales his second wife told him, certainly he should have known what was going on. Perhaps the second Mrs. Fallon went through a well-planned show of appealing for Jamie's affection whenever Mr. Fallon was at home, knowing she could count on being spurned proudly and angrily, as she naturally would have been after having abused Jamie all day long. Surely there were many devious ways in which she could have deceived her husband, many opportunities for concealing the truth of the matter and of subtly prejudicing him against his own son. Mr. Fallon was, in any case, "a fool about women," as my father put it.

I suppose the torture of Jamie went on for about a year. Now, twenty years later, I could not be sure; certain aspects of memory are perfect enough, but the consideration of time as a dimension alters with the years. Certainly it was a long time; it may have been more than a year, because it was apparent that Jamie's health had become affected finally, and it was manifest that his stepmother meant to rid herself of him by any means short of outright murder. And perhaps she might not have stopped even at that, if she believed that she could escape the consequences, though it was easy for a boy to become prejudiced against her, knowing of Jamie's misery, and an emotional small boy may not be the best of evidence.

One day Jamie had a tale to tell—a warm day following an unseasonably cold night. He had caught a bad cold. How had he come by it? asked Miss Esperson kindly, concerned about his hacking cough.

"I didn't have enough covers," he said.

"Oh, but you just had to unroll the patch-quilt, Jamie," said Miss Esperson, knowing that he slept with a little quilt rolled up at the foot of his bed—as so many of us did; so that, if the night grew cold, we could simply reach down and unroll it for the additional warmth it offered.

"She took it."

For a moment or two Miss Esperson did not know what to say; a kind of conflict showed in her face, a certain wonder. "When?" she asked at last.

"When she came in to open the windows."

The night had been too chill for open windows—much too chill.

"Were you asleep?" asked Miss Esperson gently.

"She thought I was."

What was not apparent to an eight-year-old like myself at that time must certainly have been evident to Miss Esperson. If Jamie's stepmother had come into his room while he slept to remove the quilt at the same time she opened the windows, then she must have meant him to catch cold—or worse. Worse, probably. To that degree, at least, he had thwarted her, and Miss Esperson helped by taking him into the house and rubbing his chest with goose-grease, and giving him something hot to drink, something she made out of what she took from some strange little cloth bags high up in one of her cupboards, something smelling very wonderful to a boy, spicy and sweet—herbs, doubtless, for she had been known to gather them on the edge of town along the river where the swamps were.

So Jamie's cold went away.

But the distress Miss Esperson felt was not so readily put down. And there was, too, an always evident apprehension, as if she could never be sure that some day Jamie would not come secretly through the hedge, as if he might never come to this haven again, as if she might fail him, or rather, she and I, for she had a faculty of making me feel that in this protection of Jamie we were at one. And so, I suppose, we were, for if ire and hatred could have slain Mrs. Fallon, I could have accomplished it with ease. I remember quite often weeping with helpless rage, weeping at the knowledge that I could do nothing to protect Jamie from his stepmother's viciousness. So it was distress and apprehension that we shared—not alone sweet-cakes and honey, not alone the little games we played.

On another day, Jamie crawled through the hedge violently ill. He was not able to walk upright. Miss Esperson saw him from her drawing-room and ran out to him; she carried him into her own bedroom and there he still lay when I came from my home later, still wretchedly ill, though Miss Esperson had given him something, and, when I came in, she was walking back and forth, white as one of the daisies in the vase at the window, and the moment she saw me, she poured some of Jamie's vomit from the dish beside the bed into a fruit jar, and sent me with that and a little note to Dr. Lefevre, who was old and retired, and belonged, like Miss Esperson, to the old families of Louisiana.

Afterward, when he felt somewhat better, Miss Esperson questioned him. What had he eaten?

Nothing but breakfast.

And that was what?

"Milk and toast. It tasted funny."

He had grown steadily more ill, and by noon he had begun to vomit. His stepmother had shut him up in the bathroom, literally. There she had left him. He had crawled out of the window in mortal terror, weak as he was. Doubtless Miss Esperson felt that his instinct was right.

After that she put on her bonnet, took her umbrellla, and started out of the house.

But she did not, after all, call on either Mrs. Fallon or Jamie's father. That she meant to do so was evident, for she walked directly over toward the Fallon house. But she turned at the hedge and came back to where I sat watching over Jamie at her instruction. She came back and without a word she took off her bonnet and put her umbrella away.

Jamie was terribly weak still, but feeling better.

I remember how she looked, coming back into that room. Her eyes were very strange; if I had not known her so well, she might have frightened me. She sat down beside Jamie and took one of his hands between hers, and she talked to him. She talked to him very strangely—not the way she was accustomed to talk, though she was as gentle as always.

"Jamie, your stepmother has beautiful hair," she said.

"I don't like red hair."

"And when she combs it, some of it comes out."

"I wish it would all fall out. I wish I could tear it out."

"Jamie, does your stepmother keep her hair?"

"Yes."

"Will you bring some of it to me?"

"Yes."

Then she smiled, and he smiled, and something went out of the air in that room. It was queer, though at that time perhaps it did not seem more than just a little unusual; children accept many things adults will not accept, since the world of a child is a constant revelation without any need for knowledge of cause and effect. Of course, Mrs. Fallon, like most of the white women of that town—and doubtless of all small towns in the country in those years—kept her combed-out hair to use later on in padding out her coiffures. What instinct Jamie possessed, I could not know, of course; certainly he must have imagined that he was entering into a conspiracy with Miss Esperson; undoubtedly he felt that his stepmother would not want him to take any of her combed-out hair, and this knowledge lent determination to his promise.

So one day he came with a fistful of hair and gave it to Miss Esperson, who held it up to the sun and said, "Oh, see how it shines red in the sun!" and, "And wouldn't she be angry if she knew you had given some of it to me!" at which we all laughed together, intoxicated by this secret. "But you didn't take all of it—you didn't empty it of hair?"

"Oh, no, Miss Esperson."

"Yes, then she would have known—this way, she will be annoyed and wonder," she said, and put the auburn hairs into her pocket.

Never a word after that about Mrs. Fallon's hair. But there was no lessening of interest in and apprehension about Jamie. He had been cautioned about his food; he must not eat anything at all which tasted funny, and if he did—or if he were forced to eat something he did not think he should eat, for Miss Esperson considered this possibility, too—he must take some of the little pills Dr. Lefevre had sent up to make him vomit anything bad from his stomach.

It was perhaps a fortnight or so after that that we began to play a new game under Miss Esperson's guidance. We were going to play at making a "pond" for her goldfish, and Miss Esperson laid out a little plan we were to follow. There would be, first of all, the hole in the lawn for the pool itself, with a few stones here and there, and sand. Then there would be the pipe which came from the house and brought the running water to the pool; and then the runway for the overflow water to escape to the river at the foot of Miss Esperson's lawn. In addition to all this, there would be a kind of miniature landscaping, to make the pond look like a big lake or a pool in a river, since the water flowed in and out.

Day after day we worked at it, and from time to time Miss Esperson would give advice; or she would change this or that, until the pond was finished, and the water filled in, and running out. Across the "pond" was a dwarf woods—just like that which rose across the river from Miss Esperson's garden; and on this side gardens sloped down, with a hedge separating them right in the middle of the pond's bank. But Miss Esperson did not bring down the goldfish, though each day she changed this or that about the pond, so that we never had time to wonder about the goldfish, and we guessed that probably she was afraid passing cats might paw them out and devour them. It did not matter about the goldfish, in any case; the pond was something new, and the three of us talked of more play of this kind—talked of building a full-sized brook, with dams and waterfalls, to which Miss Esperson said, yes, it could be done, perhaps we would do it, but not now—not yet.

On Thursdays every week Jamie took a music lesson. He would not have been permitted to take it if his stepmother had thought he enjoyed music; but he pretended to hate it; so she forced him to go, convinced that she was but adding to the discomfort of his small life. And usually I went along. But that Thursday was hot, and Miss Quentin's house, where Jamie went, was old and musty and damp, and in that hot afternoon waiting there and listening to Jamie would be very uncomfortable; it was too hot even to go outside and play on the corner lot with George Washington Osmond and the rest of the kids; so I did not go; I slept as long as I could in the heat, and then I got up, meaning to go to Miss Esperson's.

But she would not expect me, of course, since I customarily went with Jamie.

I walked over to the window of my room, which was on the second floor. Downstairs my mother was doing something with the dishes and talking to Libby, the black cook; out in the back swing my little sister, who had got up before me, was playing house with her dolls; the black boys and girls were screaming and hollering in the corner lot; the heat never bothered them. And over in her back yard, over beyond the hedge, Miss Esperson was playing at her pond. Perhaps she had brought the goldfish out at last.

I wanted to run right over.

But there was something about Miss Esperson's movements that prevented me, something about her attitude that was alien. She was on her knees, which was strange for Miss Esperson, who usually stood and gave directions or bent and changed things. And she was kneeling very straight and tall, except once in a while when she bent over; and all the time she made odd, jerky movements, as if she were imitating something mechanical. She seemed to be talking to herself, and it looked, after I had watched her for a while, as if she had something on the ground in front of her and pushed it from time to time toward the pond. I knelt at the window and looked out through the lace curtains, and I began to have a strange feeling, the way I felt when I saw a cat playing with a mouse, letting it go and then pawing it again just when the mouse thought it had got away, letting it go again, and catching it—over and over. It was horrible. I remember that horrible feeling even today, chiefly because it was so meaningless at that time.

But it was coming close to the time when Jamie would come home, and I knew he would come either here or to Miss Esperson, wondering where I had been. I got up and left the window. The moment I was out of sight of Miss Esperson, that horrible feeling was gone.

I went outside. Oh, it was hot that day! It was too hot even to tease Clara; so I went past. "There goes your Uncle Stephen, Children," said Clara to her dolls. It was too hot even for the dog to wag his tail; he lay in a shady spot and looked at me out of one drowsy eye.

I went through the hedge.

Miss Esperson was still kneeling there. I thought I would surprise her; perhaps I would scare her; it would be fun to see her jump.

I walked without a sound across the lawn, slipping from one bush to another. As I came closer to her, I could hear her voice. It sounded different. It sounded hoarse and throaty; it sounded like the way Libby sounded when she talked to herself while at work in the kitchen; or the way old Mose, who worked at the livery stable, talked to the horses— kind of low and intimate, but rough, guttural, muttered-like, a strange, queer way for Miss Esperson to talk. It made me feel odd, too, but not scared, though the language she spoke was not English; it was a kind of animal-like gibberish, and to hear it from Miss Esperson's lips was like hearing a holy person cursing and talking obscenities.

I walked up behind her and she heard me. Quick as a flash her hand came down to cover something there, and I saw her long index finger push something down under the water—for it had been lying there in the sunlight in the shallow water at the edge of the pond. But not before I saw it—a tiny little doll, dressed all in white, with a head of auburn hair— like Mrs. Fallon's.

"Oh," cried Miss Esperson in mock fright, "how you scared me! You're a rascal, Steve!"

"I'm not either," I said.

And at that moment Jamie came running through the hedge from the other side, crying out to me, "Where were you today?"

"It was too hot," I said.

"Does your mother know you came without changing your clothes?" asked Miss Esperson severely.

"No. She's not home," answered Jamie. "What have you been doing?" he asked, looking at the pond accusingly. "Why didn't you wait for me?"

"Nothing," I said. "I just came."

Miss Esperson smiled. "Don't be selfish Jamie. Today we're going to start making the brook, just as I promised."

She reached down and began to obliterate the landscape nearest her.

The imitation trees, the hedge on her right, which was toward Jamie's house, the place where she had pushed the doll down out of sight, into the water and perhaps the sand and mud beneath—in moments, all were gone. She reached across the pond, and down went the woods there. She raised the far end of the pond a little and a waterfall sprang into being. By that time we were both on our knees at her side, impatiently waiting for her directions. They came, calculatingly.

"Jamie will take the sand-shovel and make the bed of the brook to the river," she said. "And you, Stephen—you will dam up the water so that it cannot flow out. Let's just imagine that my goldfish are here, after all—we couldn't let them get away, could we?"

She laughed and we laughed and we began to play.

That was the way I remembered her well into my teens—a strange woman in many ways. But now I ask myself often—was there indeed something in that odd little pond she did not want to get away? And I remember that, after all, the landscape on the side of the pool nearest Miss Esperson's house was very much like the landscape there in reality—with the hedge and all, and that the doll which I never saw again had been pushed down into the water on what would have been Fallon's side of that hedge. I suppose that would never have occurred to me as a child; I suppose only an adult mind could be so devious.

That evening my father came home late, and he looked very grave.

My mother noticed it at once. "John—something's happened!" she cried.

"Haven't you heard?"

"No. What is it?"

"It's Mrs. Fallon. She drowned herself in the river this afternoon."

"Oh, how horrible!"

"We've just now found the body. It was down quite deep, with something holding it—roots or a stone or something. God knows why she should have wanted to take her own life—but she did."

I remember how glad I was for Jamie; I remember how happy he was, too, though he tried not to show it to anyone but Miss Esperson and me. But now, looking back, I remember what the blacks called Miss Esperson; I remember that strange, red-haired doll; and I recognize the quality of Miss Esperson's marvellously dark eyes—the deep, unfathomable inscrutability which hid something more than children were meant to see.

Afterword

It would seem natural, in a prescientific society, to assume that like brings about like. This is "sympathetic magic."

Thus, if you want to encourage crops to grow, you engage in orgies in the freshly turned furrows. Not only is this fun, but it will give the various nature gods and goddesses some good ideas.

Again, if you want it to rain, you may pour water onto the ground along with appropriate remarks of encouragement to the gods, or abject pleadings, if you think that will work.

And most of all (given the nasty nature of people), if you want to harm or kill an enemy, you can make a waxen image of the person you hate and allow it to melt slowly before a fire. As it loses shape and melts down, so your enemy will wither and fail. Or you can stick pins into the image and your enemy will feel pain where the pins enter. Naturally, it will help if the image is clearly that of the enemy and, since you are not likely to be artist enough to make the resemblance unmistakable, it would help if you could incorporate an actual part of the person you're aiming at—some hairs or fingernail clippings, for instance.

There's something to this in a backhanded way. If your enemy knows you are doing it, and thoroughly believes in the efficacy of sympathetic magic, he or she may indeed die, since mental suggestion can be powerful. If a doctor you trusted read the wrong X-rays and told you that you would die of incurable cancer in six months, I wouldn't be surprised if you really did.

(Incidentally, one who possesses ESP is sometimes referred to as an "esper"; hence, the title.)—I.A.

Additional Reading

Stuart Cloete, "The Second Nail," in *Ellery Queen Mystery Magazine,* Jan. 1968.

Stephen King, "I Know What You Need," in *Night Shift* (Garden City, N.Y.: Doubleday & Company, Inc., 1978).

R. H. LeNormand, "Moroccan Spring" in *Best French Stories, 1923-24 The Best French Short Stories of 1923-24,* Richard Eaton, ed. (Boston: Small, Maynard & Co. Publ., 1924).

Theodore Sturgeon, "A Way of Thinking," in *E Pluribus Unicorn* (New York: Abelard Press, 1953).

William Tenn, "Mistress Sary," in *Young Witches and Warlocks,* Isaac Asimov, Martin H. Greenberg, and Charles G. Waugh, eds. (New York: Harper & Row, 1987).

21

Telepathy

Judith Merril
Peeping Tom

Y ou take a boy like Tommy Bender—a nice American boy, well-brought-
up in a nice, average, middle-class family; chock-full of vitamins,
manners, and baseball statistics; clean-shaven, soft-spoken, and respectful
to women and his elders. You take a boy like that, fit him out with a
uniform, teach him to operate the most modern means of manslaughter,
reward him with a bright gold bar, and send him out to an exotic eastern
land to prove his manhood and his patriotism.

You take a kid like that. Send him into combat in a steaming jungle
inferno; teach him to sweat and swear with conviction; then wait till he
makes just one wrong move, pick him out of the pool of drying blood,
beat off the flies, and settle him safely on a hospital cot in an ill-equipped
base behind the lines, cut off from everyone and everywhere, except the
little native village nearby. Let him rest and rot there for a while. Then
bring him home, and pin a medal on him, and give him his civvies and
a pension to go with his limp. You take a boy like Tommy Bender, and
do all that to him, you won't expect him to be quite the same nice, apple-
cheeked youngster afterwards.

He wasn't.

When Tommy Bender came home, he was firmly disillusioned and
grimly determined. He knew what he wanted out of life, had practically
no hope of getting it, and didn't much care how he went about getting
the next-best things. And in a remarkably short time, he made it clear
to his erstwhile friends and neighbors that he was almost certain to get

anything he went after. He made money; he made love; he made enemies. Eventually, he made enough of a success so that the enemies could be as thoroughly ignored as yesterday's woman. The money, and the things it bought for him, he took good care of.

For almost five years after he came home, Tommy Bender continued to build a career and ruin reputations. People tried to understand what had happened to him; but they didn't really.

Then, abruptly, something happened to change Tommy. His business associates noticed it first; his family afterwards. The girls he was seeing at the time were the last to know, because he'd always been undependable with them, and not hearing from him for two or three weeks wasn't unusual.

What happened was a girl. Her name was Candace, and when she was married to Tommy, seven weeks after her arrival, the papers carried the whole romantic story. It was she who had nursed him back to health in that remote village on the edge of the jungle years ago. He'd been in love with her then, but she'd turned him down.

That last part wasn't in the news story, of course, but it got around town just as fast as the paper did. Tommy's bitterness, it seemed, was due to his long-frustrated love. And anyone could see how he'd changed since Candace came back to him. His employees, his debtors, his old friends and discarded women, his nervous mother and his angry brother all sighed with relief and decided ·everything was going to be all right now. At last they really understood.

But they didn't. They didn't, for instance, understand what happened to Tommy Bender in that God-forsaken little town where he'd spent two months on crutches, waiting for his leg to heal enough to travel home.

†   †   †

It was hot and sticky in the shack. The mattress was lumpy. His leg itched to the very fringes of madness, and the man on his right had an erratically syncopated snore that took him past the raveled edge straight to insanity. All he needed to make the torture complete was the guy on his left— and the nurse.

The nurse was young and round and lithe, and she wore battle fatigues: slacks, and a khaki shirt that was always draped against her high, full breast in the damp heat. Her hair, dark blonde or light brown, was just long enough to be pinned back in a tiny bun, and just short enough so wisps of it were always escaping to curl around her ears or over her forehead.

When she bent over him to do any of the small humiliating services he needed done for him, he could see tiny beads of sweat on her upper lip, and that somehow was always the one little touch too much.

So that after she moved on to the next bed, and beyond it, it would be torture to have Dake, the guy on the left, turn toward him and start describing, graphically, what he would do if he could just get his remaining arm out of the cast for fifteen minutes some day.

You see Tommy Bender was still a nice young man then—after the combat, and the wound, and the flies, and the rough hospitalization.

Dake was nothing of the sort. He'd been around, and he knew exactly what value he placed on a woman. And he enjoyed talking about it.

Tommy listened because there was no way not to, and he wriggled and sweated and suffered, and the itch in his leg got worse, and the stench from the garbage pile outside became unbearable. It went on that way, hour after hour and day after day, punctuated only by the morning visit from the medic, who would stop and look him over, and shake a weary, discouraged head, and then go on to the next man.

The leg was a long time healing. It was better after Dake left and was replaced with a quietly dying man who'd got it in the belly. After him, there was a nice young Negro soldier, somewhat embarrassed about being in sick bay with nothing more dramatic than appendicitis. But at least, now, Tommy could keep his thoughts and dreams about Candace to himself, untarnished.

Then one day, when it had begun to seem as if nothing would ever change again in his life, except the occupants of the beds on either side of him, something happened to break the monotony of discomfort and despair. The medic stopped a little longer than usual in front of Tommy's cot, studied the neat chart Candy was always filling in, and furrowed his brow with concern. Then he muttered something to Candace, and she looked worried too. After that, they both turned and looked at Tommy as if they were seeing him for the first time, and Candy smiled, and the doctor frowned a little deeper.

"Well, young man," he said, "We're going to let you get up."

"Thanks, doc," Tommy said, talking like a GI was supposed to. "What should I do with the leg? Leave it in bed?"

"Ha, ha," the doctor laughed. Just like that. "Good to see you haven't lost your spirit." Then he moved on to the next bed, and Tommy lay there wondering. What would he do with the leg?

That afternoon, they came for him with a stretcher, and took him to the surgery shack, and cut off the cast. They all stood around, five or six of them, looking at it and shaking their heads and agreeing it was pretty bad. Then they put a new cast on, a little less bulky than the first one, and handed him a pair of crutches, and said: "Okay, boy, you're on your own."

An orderly showed him how to use them, and helped him get back to his own bed. The next day he practiced up a little, and by the day after that, he could really get around.

It made a difference.

Tommy Bender was a nice normal American boy, with all the usual impulses. He had been weeks on end in the jungle, and further weeks on his back in the cot. It was not strange that he should show a distinct tendency to follow Candy about from place to place, now he was on his feet again.

The pursuit was not so much hopeful as it was instinctive. He never, quite, made any direct advance to her. He ran little errands, and helped in every way he could, as soon as he was sufficiently adept in the handling of his crutches. She was certainly not ill-pleased by his devotion, but neither, he knew, was she inclined to any sort of romantic attachment to him.

Once or twice, acting on private advice from the more experienced ambulant patients, he made tentative approaches to some of the other nurses, but met always the same kindly advice that they felt chasing nurses would not be good for his leg. He accepted his rebuffs in good part, as a nice boy will, and continued to trail around after Candy.

It was she, quite inadvertently, who led him to a piece of good fortune. He saw her leave the base one early evening, laden with packages, and traveling on foot. Alone. For a GI, these phenomena might not have been unusual. For a nurse to depart in this manner was extraordinary, and Candace slipped out so quietly that Tommy felt certain no one but himself was aware of it.

He hesitated about following at first; then he started worrying about her, threw social caution to the winds, and went swinging down the narrow road behind her, till she heard him coming and turned to look, then to wait.

She was irritated at first; then, abruptly, she seemed to change her mind.

"All right, come along," she said. "It's just a visit I'm going to pay. You can't come in with me, but you can wait if you want to, and walk me back again."

He couldn't have been more pleased. Or curious.

Their walk took them directly into the native village, where Candace seemed to become confused. She led Tommy and his crutches up and down a number of dirty streets and evil-looking alleys before she located the small earthen hut she was looking for, with a wide stripe of blue clay over its door.

While they searched for the place, she explained nervously to Tommy that she was fulfilling a mission for a dead soldier, who had, in a period of false recovery just before the end, made friends with an old man of this village. The dying GI had entrusted her with messages and gifts for his friend—most notably a sealed envelope and his last month's cigarette ration. That had been three weeks ago, and she'd spent the time since working up her courage to make the trip. Now, she confessed, she was more than glad Tommy had come along.

When they found the hut at last, they found a comparatively clean old man sitting cross-legged by the doorway, completely enveloped in a long gray robe with a hood thrown back off his shaven head. There was a begging bowl at his side, and Tommy suggested that Candace might do best just to leave her offerings in the bowl. But when she bent down to do so, the old man raised his head and smiled at her.

"You are a friend of my friend, Karl?" he asked in astonishing good English.

"Why . . . yes," she fumbled. "Yes. Karl Larsen. He said to bring you these. . . ."

"I thank you. You were most kind to come so soon." He stood up, and added, just to her, ignoring Tommy: "Will you come inside and drink tea with me, and speak with me of his death?"

"Why, I—" Suddenly she too smiled, apparently quite at ease once more. "Yes, I'd be glad to. Thank you. Tommy," she added, "would you mind waiting for me? I . . . I'd appreciate having someone to walk back with. It won't be long. Maybe—" She looked at the old man who was smiling, waiting. "Maybe half an hour," she finished.

"A little more or less perhaps," he said, in his startlingly clear American diction. "Perhaps your friend would enjoy looking about our small village meanwhile, and you two can meet again here in front of my door?"

"Why, sure," Tommy said, but he wasn't sure at all. Because as he started to say it, he had no intention of moving away from that door at all while Candy was inside. He'd stay right there, within earshot. But by the time the second word was forming in his mouth, he had a sudden clear image of what he'd be doing during that time.

And he was right.

No sooner had Candy passed under the blue-topped doorway than a small boy appeared at Tommy's other elbow. The youngster's English was in no way comparable to that of the old man. He knew just two words, but they were sufficient. The first was: "Youguhcigarreh?" The second: "Iguhsisseh."

Tommy dug in his pockets, came out with a half-full pack, registered the boy's look of approval, and swung his crutches into action. He followed his young friend up and down several of the twisty village alleys, and out along a footpath into the forest. Just about the time he was beginning to get worried, they came out into a small clearing, and a moment later "Sisseh" emerged from behind a tree at the far edge.

She was disconcertingly young, but also unexpectedly attractive: smooth-skinned, graceful, and roundly shaped. . . .

Somewhat later when he found his way back to the blue-topped door in the village, Candy was already waiting for him, looking thoughtful and a little sad. She seemed to be no more in the mood for conversation than was Tommy himself, and they walked back to the base in almost complete silence. Though he noted once or twice that her quiet mood was dictated by less-happy considerations than his own, Tommy's ease of mind and body was too great at that moment to encourage much concern for even so desirable a symbol of American womanhood as the beautiful nurse, Candace.

Not that his devotion to her lessened. He dreamed of her still, but the dreams were more pleasantly romantic, and less distressingly carnal. And on those occasions when he found his thoughts of her verging once more toward the improper, he would wander off to the little village and regain what he felt was a more natural and suitable attitude toward life and love in general.

Then, inevitably, there came one such day when his young procurer was nowhere to be found. Tommy went out to the clearing where Sisseh usually met them, but it was quiet, empty and deserted. Back in the village again, he wandered aimlessly up and down narrow twisting streets, till he found himself passing the blue-topped doorway of the old man whose friendship with a dead GI had started the whole chain of events in motion.

"Good morning, sir," the old man said, and Tommy stopped politely to return the greeting.

"You are looking for your young friend?"

Tommy nodded, and hoped the warmth he could feel on his face didn't show. Small-town gossip, apparently, was much the same in one part of the world as in another.

"I think he will be busy for some time yet," the old man volunteered. "Perhaps another hour. . . . His mother required his services for an errand to another village."

"Well, thanks," Tommy said. "Guess I'll come back this afternoon or something. Thanks a lot."

"You may wait here with me if you like. You are most welcome," the old man said hastily. "Perhaps you would care to come to my home and drink tea with me?"

Tommy's manners were good. He had been taught to be respectful to his elders, even to the old colored man who came to clip the hedges. And he knew that an invitation to tea can never be refused without excellent good reason. He had no such reason, and he did have a warm interest in seeing his dusky beauty just as soon as possible. He therefore overcame a natural reluctance to become a visitor in one of the (doubtless) vermin-infested native huts, thanked the old man politely, and accepted the invitation.

Those few steps, passing under the blue-topped doorway for the first time, into the earthen shack, were beyond doubt the most momentous of his young life. When he came out again, a full two hours later, there was nothing on the surface to show what had happened to him . . . except perhaps a more-than-usually-thoughtful look on his face. But when Sisseh's little brother pursued him down the village street, Tommy only shook his head. And when the boy persisted, the soldier said briefly: "No got cigarettes."

The statement did not in any way express the empty-handed regret one might have expected. It was rather an impatient dismissal by a man too deeply immersed in weighty affairs to regard either the cigarettes or their value in trade as having much importance.

Not that Tommy had lost any of his vigorous interest in the pleasures of the flesh. He had simply acquired a more far-sighted point of view. He had plans for the future now, and they did not concern a native girl whose affection was exchangeable for half a pack of Camels.

Swinging along the jungle path on his crutches, Tommy was approaching a dazzling new vista of hope and ambition. The goals he had once considered quite out of reach now seemed to be just barely beyond his grasp, and he had already embarked on a course of action calculated to remedy that situation. Tommy was apprenticed to a telepath.

The way it happened, the whole incredible notion seemed like a perfectly natural idea. Inside the one-room hut, the old man had introduced himself as Armod Something-or-other. (The last name was a confusion of clashing consonants and strangely inflected vowels that Tommy never quite got straight.) He then invited his young guest to make himself comfortable, and began the preparation of the tea by pouring water from a swan-necked glass bottle into a burnished copper kettle suspended by graceful chains from a wrought-iron tripod over a standard-brand hardware-store Sterno stove.

The arrangement was typical of everything in the room. East met West at every point with a surprising minimum of friction, once the first impact was absorbed and the psychological dislocation adjusted.

Tommy settled down at first on a low couch, really no more than a native mat covering some woven webbing, stretched across a frame that stood a few inches off the floor on carved ivory claws. But he discovered quickly enough that it did not provide much in the way of comfort for a long-legged young man equipped with a bulky cast. An awful lot of him seemed to be stretched out over the red-and-white-tile-pattern linoleum that covered the center of the dirt floor . . . and he noticed, too, that his crutches had left a trail of round dust-prints on the otherwise spotless surface.

He wiped off the padded bottoms of the crutches with his clean hand-kerchief, and struggled rather painfully back to his feet.

The whole place was astonishingly clean. Tommy wandered around, considerably relieved at the absence of any very noticeable insect life, examining the curious contents of the room, and politely refraining from asking the many questions that came to mind.

The furnishings consisted primarily of low stools and tables, with a few shelves somehow set into the clay wall. There was one large, magnificently carved mahogany chest, which might have contained Ali Baba's fortune; and on a teakwood table in the corner, with a pad on the floor for a seat, stood a large and shiny late-model American standard typewriter.

A bookshelf near the table caught Tommy's eye, and the old man, without turning around, invited his guest to inspect it. Here again was the curious mixture of East and West: new books on philosophy, psychology, semantics, cybernetics published in England and America. Several others, though fewer, on spiritualism, psychic phenomena, and radio-esthesia. And mixed in with them, apparently at random, short squat volumes and long thin ones, lettered in unfamiliar scripts and ideographs.

On the wall over the bookshelf hung two strips of parchment, such as may be seen in many Eastern homes, covered with ideograph characters brilliantly illuminated. Between them was a glass-faced black frame containing the certification of Armod's license to practice medicine in the state of Idaho, U.S.A.

It did not seem in any way unnatural that Armod should come over and answer explicitly the obvious questions that this collection of anomalies brought to mind. In fact, it took half an hour or more of conversation before Tommy began to realize that his host was consistently replying to his thoughts rather than to his words. It took even longer for him to agree to the simple experiment that started him on his course of study.

But not *much* longer. An hour after he first entered the hut, Tommy Bender sat staring at eight slips of white paper on which were written, one word to each, the names of eight different objects in the room. The handwriting was careful, precise and clear. Not so the thoughts in Tommy's mind. He had "guessed," accurately, five of the eight objects, holding the faded piece of paper in his hand. He tried to tell himself it was coincidence; that some form of trickery might be involved. *The hand is quicker than the eye.* . . . But it was his *own* hand that held the paper; he himself unfolded it after making his guess. And Armod's calm certainty was no help in the direction of skepticism.

"Well," Tommy asked uncertainly, "what made you think I could do it?"

"Anyone can do it," Armod said quietly. "For some it is easier than for others. To bring it under control, to learn to do it accurately, every time, is another matter altogether. But the sense is there, in all of us."

Tommy was a bit crestfallen; whether he *believed* in it or not, he preferred to think there was something a bit special about it.

Armod smiled, and answered his disappointment. "For you, it is easier I think than for many others. You are—ah, I despise your psychiatric jargon, but there is no other way to say it so you will understand—you are at ease with yourself. Relaxed. You have few basic conflicts in your personality, so you can reach more easily into the—no, it is *not* the 'subconscious.' It is a part of your mind you have simply not used before. You can use it. You can train it. You need only the awareness of it, and—practice."

Tommy thought that over, slowly, and one by one the implications of it dawned on him.

"You mean I can be a mind reader? Like the acts they do on the stage? I could do it professionally?"

"If you wished to. Few of those who pretend to read minds for the entertainment of others can really do so. Few who have the ability and training would use it in that way. You—ah, you are beginning to grasp some of the possibilities," the old man said, smiling.

"Go on," Tommy grinned. "Tell me what I'm thinking now."

"It would be most . . . indelicate. And . . . I *will* tell you; I do not believe you will have much chance of success, with *her*. She is an unusual young woman. Others . . . you will be startled, I think, to find how often a forbidding young lady is more hopeful even than willing."

"You're on," Tommy told him. "When do the lessons start, and how much?"

The price was easy; the practice was harder. Tommy gave up smoking entirely, suffered a bit, got over it, and turned his full attention to the procedures involved in gaining "awareness." He lay for hours on his cot, or sat by himself on a lonely hillside in the afternoon sun, learning to sense the presence of every part of himself as fully as that of the world around him.

He learned a dozen different ways of breathing, and discovered how each of them changed, to some slight degree, the way the rest of his body "felt" about things. He found out how to be completely receptive to impressions and sensations from outside himself; and after that, how to exclude them and be aware only of his own functioning organism. He discovered he could *feel* his heart beating and his food digesting, and later imagined he could feel the wound in his leg healing, and thought he was actually helping it along.

This last piece of news he took excitedly to Armod—along with his full ration of cigarettes—and was disappointed to have his mentor receive his excited outpourings with indifference.

"If you waste your substance on such side issues," Armod finally answered his insistence with downright disapproval, "you will be much longer in coming to the true understanding."

Tommy thought that over, swinging back along the jungle path on his crutches, and came to the conclusion that he could do without telepathy a little longer, if he could just walk on his own two feet again. Not that he really believed the progress was anything but illusory—until he heard the medics' exclamations of surprise the next time they changed the cast.

After that, he was convinced. The whole rigamarole was producing *some* kind of result; maybe it would even, incredibly, do what Armod said it would.

Two weeks later, Tommy got his first flash of *certainty*. He was, by then, readily proficient in picking thoughts out of Armod's mind; but he knew, too, that the old man was "helping" him . . . maintaining no barriers at all against invasion. Other people had habitual defenses that they didn't even know how to let down. Getting through the walls of verbalization, habitual reaction, hurt, fear and anger, to find out what was really happening inside the mind of a telepathically "inert" person took skill and determination.

That first flash could not in any way be described as "mind reading." Tommy did not *hear* or *see* any words or images. All he got was a wave of feeling; he was sure it was not his own feeling only because he was just then on his way back from a solitary hillside session in which he had, with considerable thoroughness, identified all the sensations his body then contained.

He was crossing what was laughably referred to as the "lawn"—an area of barren ground decorated with unrootable clumps of tropical weeds, extending from the mess hall to the surgery shack and surrounded by the barracks buildings—when the overwhelming wave of emotion hit him.

It contained elements of affection, interest, and—he checked again to be certain—desire. Desire for a *man.* He was quite sure now that the feeling was not his, but somebody else's.

He looked about, with sudden dismay, aware for the first time of a difficulty he had not anticipated. That he was "receiving" someone else's emotions he was certain; *whose,* he did not know.

In front of the surgery shack, a group of nurses stood together, talking. No one else was in sight. Tommy realized, unhappily, that the lady who was currently feeling amorous did not necessarily have to be in his line of vision. He had learned enough about the nature of telepathy by then to understand that it could penetrate physical barriers with relative ease. But he had a hunch. . . .

He had learned enough, too, to understand some part of the meaning of that word, "hunch." He deliberately stopped *thinking,* insofar as he could, and followed his hunch across the lawn to the group of nurses. As he approached them, he let instinct take over entirely. Instead of speaking to them, he made as if to walk by, into the shack.

"Hey there, Lieutenant," one of them called out, and Tommy strained his muscles not to smile with delight. He turned around, innocently, inquiring.

"Surgery's closed now," the little red-headed one said sharply. That wasn't the one who'd called to him. It was the big blonde; he was *almost* sure.

"Oh?" he said. "I was out back of the base, on the hill there, and some damn bug bit me. Thought I ought to get some junk put on it. You never know what's hit you with the kind of skeeters they grow out here." He addressed the remark to the group in general, and threw in a grin that he had been told made him look most appealing, like a little boy, meanwhile pulling up the trouser on his good leg to show a fortuitously placed two-day-old swelling. "One leg out of commission is enough for me," he added. "Thought maybe I ought to kind of keep a special eye on the one that still works." He looked up, and smiled straight at the big blonde.

She regarded the area of exposed skin with apparent lack of interest, hesitated, jangled a key in her pocket, and said abruptly, "All right, big boy."

Inside the shack, she locked the door behind them, without appearing to do anything the least bit unusual. Then she got a tube of something out of a cabinet on the wall, and told him to put his leg up on the table.

Right then, Tommy began to understand the real value of what he'd learned, and how to use it. There was nothing in her words or her brisk movements to show him how she felt. While she was smoothing the gooey disinfectant paste on his bite, and covering it with a bandage, she kept up a stream of light talk and banter that gave no clue at all to the way she was appraising him covertly. Tommy had nothing to do but make the proper responses—two sets of them.

Out loud, he described with appropriate humor the monstrous size and appearance of the bug that they both knew hadn't bitten him. But all the time he kept talking and kidding just as if he was still a nice American boy, he could feel her *wanting* him, until he began to get confused between what she wanted and what he did; and his eyes kept meeting hers, unrelated to the words either of them were saying, to let her know he knew.

Each time her hand touched his leg, it was a little more difficult to banter. When it got too difficult, he didn't.

Later, stretched out on his cot in the barracks, he reviewed the entire incident with approval, and made a mental note of one important item. The only overt act the girl made—locking the door—had been accompanied by a strong isolated thought surge of "Don't touch me!" Conversely, the more eager she felt, the more professional she acted. Without the aid of his special one-way window into her mind, he knew he would have made his play at precisely the wrong moment—assuming he'd had the courage to make it at all. As it was, he'd waited till there was no longer any reason for her to believe that he'd even noticed the locking of the door.

That was Lesson Number One about women: *Wait!* Wait till you're sure she's sure. Tommy repeated it happily to himself as he fell asleep that night; and only one small regret marred his contentment. It wasn't Candace. . . .

Lesson Number Two came more slowly, but Tommy was an apt pupil, and he learned it equally well: *Don't wait too long!* The same simple forthright maneuver, he found, that would sweep a normally cooperative young lady literally off her feet if the timing was right would, ten minutes later, earn him nothing more than an indignant slap in the face. By that time, the girl had already decided either that he wasn't interested (insulted); or that he wasn't experienced enough to do anything about it (contemptuous); or that he was entirely lacking in sensitivity, and couldn't possibly understand her at all (both).

These two lessons Tommy studied assiduously. Between them, they defined the limits of that most remarkable point in time, *the Precise Moment*. And the greatest practical value of his new skill, so far as Tommy could see, was in being able to locate that point with increasing accuracy. The most noticeable property of the human mind is its constant activity; it is a rare man—and notoriously an even rarer woman—who has only one point of view on a given subject, and can stick to it. Tommy discovered soon enough that whatever he was after, whether it was five bucks to get into a poker game, or a date with one of the nurses, the best way to get it was to wait for that particular moment when the other person really *wanted* to give it to him.

It should be noted that Tommy Bender retained some ethics during this period. After the first two games, he stopped playing poker. Possibly, he was affected by the fact that suspicious rumors about his "luck" were circulating too freely; but it is more likely that the game had lost its punch. He didn't really need the money out there anyhow. And the process of his embitterment was really just beginning.

Three weeks after the incident in the surgery shack, Tommy got his orders for transfer to a stateside hospital. During that short time, though still impeded by cast and crutches, he acquired a quantity and quality of experience with women that more than equaled the total of his previous successes. And along with it, he suffered a few shocks.

That Tommy had both manners and ethics has already been established. He also had morals. He thought he ought to go to church more often than he did; he took it for granted that all unmarried women were virgins till proved otherwise; he never (or hardly ever) used foul language in mixed company. That kind of thing.

It was, actually, one of the smaller shocks, discovering the kind of language some of those girls knew. Most of them were nurses, after all, he reminded himself; they heard a lot of guys talking when they were delirious or in pain, but—but that didn't explain how clearly they seemed to *understand* the words. Or that the ones who talked the most refined were almost always the worst offenders in their minds.

The men's faults he could take in stride; it was the women who dismayed him. Not that he didn't find some "pure" girls; he did, to his horror. But the kind of feminine innocence he'd grown up believing in just didn't seem to exist. The few remaining virgins fell into two categories: those who were so convinced of their own unattractiveness that they didn't even know it when a pass was being made at them; and those who were completely preoccupied with a sick kind of fear-and-loathing that Tommy couldn't even stand to peep at for very long.

Generally speaking, the girls who weren't actually *looking* for men (which they did with a gratifying but immoral enthusiasm), were either filled with terror and disgust, or were calculating wenches who made their choice for or against the primrose path entirely in terms of the possible profit involved, be it in fast cash or future wedded bliss.

Tommy did find one exception to this generally unpleasant picture. To his determined dismay, and secret pleasure, he discovered that Candace really lived up to his ideal of the American girl. Her mind was a lovely, orderly place, full of softness and a sort of generalized liking for almost everybody. Her thoughts on the subject of most interest to him were also in order: She was apparently well-informed in an impersonal sort of way, ignorant of any personal experience, and rather hazily, pleasurably, anticipating the acquisition of that experience in some dim future when she pictured herself as happily in love and married.

As soon as he was quite sure of this state of affairs, Tommy proposed. Candace as promptly declined, and that, for the time being, terminated their relationship. The nurse went about her duties, and whatever personal matters occupied her in her free time. The soldier returned to his pursuit of parapsychology, women, and disillusion.

Tommy had no intention of taking these troubles to his teacher. But neither did Armod have to wait for the young man to speak before he knew. This time he was neither stern nor impatient. He spoke once again of the necessity for continuing study till one arrived at the "true understanding," but now he was alternately pleading and encouraging. At one point he was even apologetic.

"I did not know that you would learn so quickly," he said. "If I had foreseen this—doubtless I would have done precisely what I did. One cannot withhold knowledge, and . . ."

He paused, smiling gently and with great sadness. "And the truth of the matter is, you did not *ask* for knowledge. I offered it. I *sold* it! Because I could not deny myself the petty pleasure of your cigarettes!"

"Well," Tommy put in uncomfortably, "you made good on it, didn't you? Seems to me you did what you said you would."

"Yes—no," he corrected himself. "I did nothing but show the way. What has been done you did for yourself, as all men must. I cannot see or smell or taste for you; no more could I open the way into men's hearts for you. I gave you a key, let us say, and with it you unlocked the door. Now you look at the other side, but you do not, you cannot, understand what you see. It is as though one were to show an infant, just learning to use his eyes, a vision of violent death and bloody birth. He sees, but he does not *know*. . . ."

Tommy stirred on the low couch, where he could now sit, as the old man did, cross-legged and at ease. But he was uneasy now. He picked up the cane that had replaced the crutches, toying with it, thinking hopefully of departure. Armod understood, and said quickly, "Listen now: I am an old man, and weak in my way. But I have shown you that I have knowledge of a sort. There is much you have yet to learn. If you are to perceive so clearly the depths of the human soul, then it is essential that you learn also to *understand.* . . . "

The old man spoke on; the young one barely listened. He knew he was going home in another week. There was no sense talking about continuing his studies with Armod. And there was no need to continue; certainly no wish to. What he had already learned, Tommy felt, was very likely more than enough. He sat as quietly as he could, being patient till the old man was done talking. Then he stood up, and muttered something about getting back in time for lunch.

Armod shook his head and smiled, still sadly. "You will not hear me. Perhaps you are right. How can I speak to you of the true understanding, when I am still the willing victim of my own body's cravings? I am not fit. I am not fit. . . . "

Tommy Bender was a very disturbed young man. He was getting what he'd wanted, and he didn't like it. He was grateful to Armod, and also angry at him. His whole life seemed to be a string of contradictions.

He drifted along in this unsettled state for the remaining week of his foreign service. Then, in a sudden flurry of affection and making amends, the day he got his orders, he decided to see the old man just once more. Most of the morning he spent racing around the base rounding up all the cigarettes he could get with what cash he had on hand, plus a liberal use of the new skills Armod had taught him. Then he got his gear together quickly. He was due at the air strip at 1400 hours, and at 1130 he left the base for a last walk to the village, the cane in one hand, two full cartons of butts in the other.

He found Armod waiting for him in a state of some agitation, apparently expecting him. There ensued a brief formal presentation of Tommy's gift, and acceptance of it; then for the last time, the old man invited him to drink tea, and ceremoniously set the water to simmer in the copper pot.

They both made an effort, and managed to get through the tea-drinking with no more than light polite talk. But when Tommy stood up to leave, Armod broke down.

"Come back," he begged. "When you are free of your service, and have funds to travel, come back to study again."

"Why, sure, Armod," Tommy said. "Just as soon as I can manage it."

"Yes, I see. This is what they call a social lie. It is meant not to convince me, but to terminate the discussion. But listen, I beg you, one moment more. You can see and hear in the mind now; but you cannot talk, nor can you keep silence. Your own mind is open to all who come and know how to look—"

"Armod, please, I—"

"You can learn to project thought as I do. To build a barrier against intrusion. You can—"

"Listen, Armod," Tommy broke in determinedly again. "I don't *have* to know any of that stuff. In my home town, there isn't anybody else who can do this stuff. And there's no reason for me to ever come back here. Look, I'll tell you what I can do. When I get back home, I can send you all the cigarettes you want—"

"*No!*"

The old man jumped up from his mat on the floor, and took two rapid strides to the shelf where Tommy's present lay. He picked up the two cartons, and tossed them contemptuously across the room, to land on the couch next to the soldier.

"No!" he said again, just a little less shrilly. "I do not want your cigarettes! I want nothing, do you understand? Nothing for myself! Only to regain the peace of mind I have lost through my weakness! Go to another teacher, then," he was struggling for calm. "There are many others. In India. In China. Perhaps even in your own country. Go to one who is better fitted than I. But do not stop now! You can learn more, much more!"

He was trembling with emotion as he spoke, his skinny frame shaking, his black eyes popping as though they would burst out of his head. "As for your cigarettes," he concluded, "I want none of them. I vow now, until the day I die, I shall never again give way to this weakness!"

He was a silly, excitable old man, who was going to regret these words. Tommy stood up feeling the foolish apologetic grin on his face and unable to erase it. He did not pick up the cigarettes.

"Good-bye, Armod," he said, and walked out for the last time through the blue-topped door.

† † †

But whatever either of them expected, and regardless of Tommy's own wishes, his education did not stop there. It had already gone too far to stop. The perception-awareness process seemed to be self-perpetuating, and though he practiced his exercises no more, his senses continued to become more acute—both the physical and the psychological.

At the stateside hospital, where his leg rapidly improved, Tommy had some opportunity to get out and investigate the situation with the nice old-fashioned girls who'd stayed at home and didn't go to war. By that time, he could "see" and "hear" pretty clearly.

He didn't like what he found.

That did it, really. All along, out at the base hospital, he'd clung to the notion that the women at home would be different—that girls so far from civilization were exposed to all sorts of indecencies a nice girl never had to face, and *shouldn't* have to. Small wonder they turned cynical and evil-minded.

The girls at home, he discovered, were less of the first and far more of the second.

When Tommy Bender got home again, he was grimly determined and firmly disillusioned. He knew what he wanted out of life, saw no hope at all of ever getting it, and had very few scruples about the methods he used to get the next-best things.

In a remarkably short time, he made it clear to his erstwhile friends and neighbors that he was almost certain to get anything he went after. He made money; he made love; and of course he made enemies. All the while, his friends and neighbors tried to understand. Indeed, they thought they did. A lot of things can happen to a man when he's been through hell in combat, and then had to spend months rotting and recuperating in a lonely Far Eastern field hospital.

But of course they couldn't even begin to understand what had happened to Tommy. They didn't know what it was like to live on a steadily plunging spiral of anger and disillusionment, all the time liking people less, and always aware of how little they liked you.

To sign a contract with a man, knowing he would defraud you if he could; he couldn't, of course, because you got there first. But when you met him afterward, you rocked with the blast of hate and envy he threw at you.

To make love to a woman, and know she was the wrong woman for you or you the wrong man for her. And then to meet *her* afterward. . . .

Tommy had, in the worst possible sense, got out of bed on the wrong side. When he first awoke to the knowledge of other peoples' minds, he had seen ugliness and fear wherever he looked, and that first impress of bitterness on his own mind had colored everything he had seen since.

For almost five years after he came home, Tommy Bender continued to build a career, and ruin reputations. People tried to understand what had happened to him . . . but how *could* they?

Then something happened. It started with an envelope in his morning mail. The envelope was marked "Personal," so it was unopened by his secretary and left on the side of his desk along with three or four other thin, squarish, obviously non-business, envelopes. As a result, Tommy didn't read it till late that afternoon, when he was trying to decide which girl to see that night.

The return address said "C. Harper, Hotel Albemarle, Topeka, Kansas." He didn't know anyone in Topeka, but the name Harper was vaguely reminiscent. He was intrigued enough to open that one first, and the others never were opened at all.

"Dear Tommy," it read. "First of all, I hope you still remember me. It's been quite a long time, hasn't it? I just heard, from Lee Potter (the little, dark girl who came just before you left . . . remember her?)"—Tommy did, with some pleasure—"that you were living in Hartsdale, and had some real estate connections there. Now I'd like to ask a favor. . . .

I've just had word that I've been accepted as Assistant Superintendent of the Public Health Service there—in Hartsdale—and I'm supposed to start work on the 22nd. The only thing is, I can't leave my job here till just the day before. So I wondered if you could help me find a place to stay beforehand? Sort of mail-order real-estate service?

"I feel I'm being a little presumptuous, asking this, when perhaps you don't even remember me—but I so hope you won't mind. And please don't go to any special trouble. From what Lee said, I got the idea this might be right in your line of business. If it's not, don't worry. I'm sure I can fine something when I get there.

"And thanks, ahead of time, for anything you can do.

"Cordially," it concluded, "Candace Harper."

Tommy answered the letter the same day, including a varied list of places and prices hurriedly worked up by his real-estate agent. That he owned real estate was true; that he dealt in it, not at all. His letter to Candy did not go into these details. Just told her how vividly he remembered her, and how good it would be to see her again, with some questions about the kind of furnishings and décor she'd prefer. "If you're going to get in early enough on the 21st," he wound up, "how about having dinner with me? Let me know when you're coming, anyhow. I'd like to meet you, and help you get settled."

For the next eleven days, Tommy lived in an almost happy whirl of preparation, memory, and anticipation. In all the years since he had proposed to Candace, he had never met another girl who filled so perfectly the mental image of the ideal woman with which he had first left home. He kept telling himself she wouldn't, couldn't, still be the same person. Even a non-telepath would get bitter and disillusioned in five years of the Wonderful Post-War World. She *couldn't* be the same. . . .

And she wasn't. She was older, more understanding, more tolerant, and, if possible, warmer and pleasanter than before. Tommy met her at the station, bought her some dinner, took her to the perfect small apartment where she was, unknown to herself, paying only half the rent. He stayed an hour, went down to run some errands for her, stayed another half-hour, and knew by then that in the most important respects she hadn't changed at all.

There wasn't going to be any "Precise Moment" with Candy; not that side of a wedding ceremony.

Tommy couldn't have been more pleased. Still, he was cautious. He didn't propose again till three weeks later, when he'd missed seeing her two days in a row due to business-social affairs. If they were married, he could have taken her along.

When he did propose, she lived up to all his qualifications again. She said she wanted to think it over. What she *thought* was: *Oh, yes! he's the one I want! But it's too quick! How do I know for sure? He never even thought of me all this time . . . all the time I was waiting and hoping to hear from him . . . How can he be sure so soon? He might be sorry. . . .*

"Let me think about it a few days, will you, Tommy?" she said, and he was afraid to take her in his arms for fear he'd crush her with his hunger.

Four weeks later they were married. And when Candy told him her answer, she also confessed what he already knew: that she'd regretted turning him down ever since he left the field hospital; that she'd been thinking of him, loving him, all the long years in between.

Candy was a perfect wife, just as she had been a perfect nurse, and an all-too-perfect dream girl. The Benders' wedding was talked about for years afterwards; it was one of those rare occasions when everything turned out just right. And the bride was so beautiful. . . .

The honeymoon was the same way. They took six weeks to complete a tour of the Caribbean, by plane, ship and car. They stayed where they liked as long as they liked, and did what they liked, all the time. And not once in those six weeks was there any serious difference in *what* they liked. Candy's greatest wish at every point was to please Tommy, and that made things very easy for both of them.

And all the while, Tommy was gently, ardently, instructing his lovely bride in the arts of matrimony. He was tender, patient, and understanding, as he had known beforehand he would have to be. A girl who gets to the age of twenty-six with her innocence intact is bound to require a little time for readjustment.

Still, by the time they came back, Tommy was beginning to feel a sense of failure. He knew that Candace had yet to experience the fulfillment she had hoped for, and that he had planned to give her.

Watching her across the breakfast table on the dining terrace of their new home, he was enthralled as ever. She was lovely in her negligee, her soft hair falling around her face, her eyes shining with true love as they met his.

It was a warm day, and he saw, as he watched her, the tiny beads of sweat form on her upper lip. It took him back . . . way back . . . and from the vividness of the hospital scene, he skipped to an equally clear memory of that last visit to Armod, the teacher.

He smiled, and reached for his wife's hand, wondering if ever he would be able to tell her what had come of that walk they took to the village together. And he pressed her hand tighter, smiling again, as he realized that now, for the first time, he had a use for the further talents the old man had promised him.

That would be one way to show Candace the true pleasure she did not yet know. If he could project his own thoughts and emotions . . .

He let go of her hand, and sat back, sipping his coffee, happy and content, with just the one small problem to think about. *Maybe I should have gone back for a while, after all,* he thought idly.

"Perhaps you should have, dear," said innocent Candace. "I did."

Afterword

Communication is, if you stop to think of it, quite astonishing. How is it possible to modulate sound-waves by rapid and precise movements of palate, tongue, and lips, producing sound-combinations that represent thousands of different words that, alone and in combination, in turn represent thousands of different objects, actions, qualities, and abstractions. If speech didn't exist, we wouldn't think it possible.

Then, writing involves a second layer of symbols. Handwritten markings, produced as fast as the hand can move, can convert speech into a curved line that can be reconverted into speech as fast as the eyes can move. If writing didn't exist, we wouldn't think it possible.

Speech is indirect and writing is even more indirect. What we're really doing is imaging, or feeling a flux of emotion, or, at the most, saying words silently to ourselves.

Why should it not be possible to cut out the middlemen, the endlessly curving markings of writing, or the endlessly modulated sound-waves of speech, and directly interpret the thoughts of another?

Might you not "hear" or "sense" another person's thoughts? In fact, is that totally nonscientific? Nerve actions, and particularly those within the brain, are accompanied by tiny rises and falls in voltage. These will set up varying magnetic fields that will impress similar rises and falls in voltage on another brain, and thus we can have "telepathy" (from Greek words meaning "to feel, or sense, at a distance"). However, that such a form of communication can exist has never been shown by anything but anecdotal evidence or by the naive experimentation of men like J. B. Rhine.—I.A.

Additional Reading

Edward Bellamy, "To Whom This May Come," in *Isaac Asimov Presents the Best Science Fiction of the 19th Century,* Isaac Asimov, Charles G. Waugh, and Martin H. Greenberg, eds. (New York: Beaufort Books, 1981).

Rebecca Harding Davis, "The Captain's Story," in *Little Classics, Volume Two: Intellect,* Rossiter Johnson, ed. (Boston: J. R. Osgood, 1875).

Katharine MacLean, "Defense Mechanism," in *The Diploids and Other Flights of Fancy* (New York: Avon, 1962).

Walter M. Miller, Jr., "Anyone Else Like Me?" (aka: "Command Performance"), in *The View from the Stars* (New York: Ballantine Books, 1965).

Irving Shaw, "Whispers in Bedlam," in *Arena: Sports SF,* Edward Ferman and Barry Malzberg, eds. (Garden City, N.Y.: Doubleday and Company, 1976).

22

Will Control

Edith Wharton
The Moving Finger

The news of Mrs. Grancy's death came to me with the shock of an immense blunder—one of fate's most irretrievable acts of vandalism. It was as though all sorts of renovating forces had been checked by the clogging of that one wheel. Not that Mrs. Grancy contributed any perceptible momentum to the social machine: her unique distinction was that of filling to perfection her special place in the world. So many people are like badly-composed statues, overlapping their niches at one point and leaving them vacant at another. Mrs. Grancy's niche was her husband's life; and if it be argued that the space was not large enough for its vacancy to leave a very big gap, I can only say that, at the last resort, such dimensions must be determined by finer instruments than any ready-made standard of utility. Ralph Grancy's was in short a kind of disembodied usefulness: one of those constructive influences that, instead of crystallizing into definite forms, remain as it were a medium for the development of clear thinking and fine feeling. He faithfully irrigated his own dusty patch of life, and the fruitful moisture stole far beyond his boundaries. If, to carry on the metaphor, Grancy's life was a sedulously-cultivated enclosure, his wife was the flower he had planted in its midst—the embowering tree, rather, which gave him rest and shade at its foot and the wind of dreams in its upper branches.

We had all—his small but devoted band of followers—known a moment when it seemed likely that Grancy would fail us. We had watched him pitted against one stupid obstacle after another—ill-health, poverty, misunderstanding and, worst of all for a man of his texture, his first wife's soft insidious egotism. We had seen him sinking under the leaden embrace of her affection like a swimmer in a drowning clutch; but just as we despaired he had always come to the surface again, blinded, panting, but striking out fiercely for the shore. When at last her death released him it became a question as to how much of the man she had carried with her. Left alone, he revealed numb withered patches, like a tree from which a parasite had been stripped. But gradually he began to put out new leaves; and when he met the lady who was to become his second wife—his one *real* wife, as his friends reckoned—the whole man burst into flower.

The second Mrs. Grancy was past thirty when he married her, and it was clear that she had harvested that crop of middle joy which is rooted in young despair. But if she had lost the surface of eighteen she had kept its inner light; if her cheek lacked the gloss of immaturity her eyes were young with the stored youth of half a lifetime. Grancy had first known her somewhere in the East—I believe she was the sister of one of our consuls out there—and when he brought her home to New York she came among us as a stranger. The idea of Grancy's remarriage had been a shock to us all. After one such calcining most men would have kept out of the fire; but we agreed that he was predestined to sentimental blunders, and we awaited with resignation the embodiment of his latest mistake. Then Mrs. Grancy came—and we understood. She was the most beautiful and the most complete of explanations. We shuffled our defeated omniscience out of sight and gave it hasty burial under a prodigality of welcome. For the first time in years we had Grancy off our minds. "He'll do something great now!" the least sanguine of us prophesied; and our sentimentalist amended: "He *has* done it—in marrying her!"

It was Claydon, the portrait painter, who risked this hyperbole; and who soon afterward, at the happy husband's request, prepared to defend it in a portrait of Mrs. Grancy. We were all—even Claydon—ready to concede that Mrs. Grancy's unwontedness was in some degree a matter of environment. Her graces were complementary and it needed the mate's call to reveal the flash of color beneath her neutral-tinted wings. But if she needed Grancy to interpret her, how much greater was the service she rendered him! Claydon professionally described her as the right frame for him; but if she defined she also enlarged, if she threw the whole into perspective she also cleared new ground, opened fresh vistas, reclaimed whole areas of activity that had run to waste under the harsh husbandry of privation. This interaction of sympathies was not without its visible expression. Claydon was not alone in maintaining that Grancy's presence— or indeed the mere mention of his name—had a perceptible effect on his wife's appearance. It was as though a light were shifted, a curtain drawn back, as though, to borrow another of Claydon's metaphors, Love the indefatigable artist were perpetually seeking a happier "pose" for his model. In this interpretative light Mrs. Grancy acquired the charm which makes some women's faces like a book of which the last page is never turned. There was always something new to read in her eyes. What Claydon read there—or at least such scattered hints of the ritual as reached him through the sanctuary doors—his portrait in due course declared to us. When the picture was exhibited it was at once acclaimed as his masterpiece; but the people who knew Mrs. Grancy smiled and said it was flattered. Claydon, however, had not set out to paint *their* Mrs. Grancy—or ours even—but Ralph's; and Ralph knew his own at a glance. At the first confrontation he saw that Claydon had understood. As for Mrs. Grancy, when the finished picture was shown to her she turned to the painter and said simply: "Ah, you've done me facing the east!"

The picture, then, for all its value, seemed a mere incident in the unfolding of their double destiny, a footnote to the illuminated text of their lives. It was not till afterward that it acquired the significance of last words spoken on a threshold never to be recrossed. Grancy, a year after his marriage, had given up his town house and carried his bliss an hour's journey away, to a little place among the hills. His various duties and interests brought him frequently to New York but we necessarily saw him less often than when his house had served as the rallying point of kindred enthusiasms. It seemed a pity that such an influence should be withdrawn, but we all felt that his long arrears of happiness should be paid in whatever coin he chose. The distance from which the fortunate couple radiated warmth on us was not too great for friendship to traverse; and our conception of a glorified leisure took the form of Sundays spent in the Grancys' library, with its sedative rural outlook, and the portrait of Mrs. Grancy illuminating its studious walls. The picture was at its best in that setting; and we used to accuse Claydon of visiting Mrs. Grancy in order to see her portrait. He met this by declaring that the portrait *was* Mrs. Grancy; and there were moments when the statement seemed unanswerable. One of us, indeed— I think it must have been the novelist—said that Claydon had been saved from falling in love with Mrs. Grancy only by falling in love with his picture of her; and it was noticeable that he, to whom his finished work was no more than the shed husk of future effort, showed a perennial tenderness for this one achievement. We smiled afterward to think how often, when Mrs. Grancy was in the room, her presence reflecting itself in our talk like a gleam of sky in a hurrying current, Claydon, averted from the real woman, would sit as it were listening to the picture. His attitude, at the time, seemed only a part of the unusualness of those picturesque afternoons, when the most familiar combinations of life underwent a magical change. Some human happiness is a landlocked lake; but the Grancys' was an open sea, stretching a buoyant and illimitable surface to the voyaging interests of life. There was room and to spare on those waters for all our separate ventures; and always, beyond the sunset, a mirage of the fortunate isles toward which our prows were bent.

II

It was in Rome that, three years later, I heard of her death. The notice said "suddenly"; I was glad of that. I was glad too—basely perhaps—to be away from Grancy at a time when silence must have seemed obtuse and speech derisive.

I was still in Rome when, a few months afterward, he suddenly arrived there. He had been appointed secretary of legation at Constantinople and was on the way to his post. He had taken the place, he said frankly, "to get away." Our relations with the Porte held out a prospect of hard work, and that, he explained, was what he needed. He could never be satisfied to sit down among the ruins. I saw that, like most of us in moments of extreme moral tension, he was playing a part, behaving as he thought it became a man to behave in the eye of disaster. The instinctive posture of grief is a shuffling compromise between defiance and prostration; and pride feels the need of striking a worthier attitude in face of such a foe. Grancy, by nature musing and retrospective, had chosen the role of the man of action, who answers blow for blow and opposes a mailed front to the thrusts of destiny; and the completeness of the equipment testified to his inner weakness. We talked only of what we were not thinking of, and parted, after a few days, with a sense of relief that proved the inadequacy of friendship to perform, in such cases, the office assigned to it by tradition.

Soon afterward my own work called me home, but Grancy remained several years in Europe. International diplomacy kept its promise of giving him work to do, and during the year in which he acted as *chargé d'affaires* he acquitted himself, under trying conditions, with conspicuous zeal and discretion. A political redistribution of matter removed him from office just as he had proved his usefulness to the government; and the following summer I heard that he had come home and was down at his place in the country.

On my return to town I wrote him and his reply came by the next post. He answered as it were in his natural voice, urging me to spend the following Sunday with him, and suggesting that I should bring down any of the old set who could be persuaded to join me. I thought this a good sign, and yet—shall I own it?—I was vaguely disappointed. Perhaps we are apt to feel that our friends' sorrows should be kept like those historic monuments from which the encroaching ivy is periodically removed.

That very evening at the club I ran across Claydon. I told him of Grancy's invitation and proposed that we should go down together; but he pleaded an engagement. I was sorry, for I had always felt that he and I stood nearer Ralph than the others, and if the old Sundays were to be renewed I should have preferred that we two should spend the first alone with him. I said as much to Claydon and offered to fit my time to his; but he met this by a general refusal.

"I don't want to go to Grancy's," he said bluntly. I waited a moment, but he appended no qualifying clause.

"You've seen him since he came back?" I finally ventured.

Claydon nodded.

"And is he so awfully bad?"

"Bad? No, he's all right."

"All right? How can he be, unless he's changed beyond all recognition?"

"Oh, you'll recognize *him*," said Claydon, with a puzzling deflection of emphasis.

His ambiguity was beginning to exasperate me, and I felt myself shut out from some knowledge to which I had as good a right as he.

"You've been down there already, I suppose?"

"Yes; I've been down there."

"And you've done with each other—the partnership is dissolved?"

"Done with each other? I wish to God we had!" He rose nervously and tossed aside the review from which my approach had diverted him. "Look here," he said, standing before me, "Ralph's the best fellow going and there's nothing under heaven I wouldn't do for him—short of going down there again." And with that he walked out of the room.

Claydon was incalculable enough for me to read a dozen different meanings into his words; but none of my interpretations satisfied me. I determined, at any rate, to seek no farther for a companion; and the next Sunday I traveled down to Grancy's alone. He met me at the station and I saw at once that he had changed since our last meeting. Then he had been in fighting array, but now if he and grief still housed together it was no longer as enemies. Physically the transformation was as marked but less reassuring. If the spirit triumphed the body showed its scars. At five-and-forty he was gray and stooping, with the tired gate of an old man. His serenity, however, was not the resignation of age. I saw that he did not mean to drop out of the game. Almost immediately he began to speak of our old interests; not with an effort, as at our former meeting, but simply and naturally, in the tone of a man whose life has flowed back into its normal channels. I remembered, with a touch of self-reproach, how I had distrusted his reconstructive powers; but my admiration for his reserved force was now tinged by the sense that, after all, such happiness as his ought to have been paid with his last coin. The feeling grew as we neared the house and I found how inextricably his wife was interwoven with my remembrance of the place: how the whole scene was but an extension of that vivid presence.

Within doors nothing was changed, and my hand would have dropped without surprise into her welcoming clasp. It was luncheon time, and Grancy led me at once to the dining room, where the walls, the furniture, the very plate and porcelain, seemed a mirror in which a moment since her face had been reflected. I wondered whether Grancy, under the recovered tranquillity of his smile, concealed the same sense of her nearness, saw perpetually between himself and the actual her bright unappeasable ghost. He spoke of her once or twice, in an easy incidental way, and her name seemed to hang in the air after he had uttered it, like a chord that continues to vibrate. If he felt her presence it was evidently as an enveloping medium, the moral atmosphere in which he breathed. I had never before known how completely the dead may survive.

After luncheon we went for a long walk through the autumnal fields and woods, and dusk was falling when we re-entered the house. Grancy led the way to the library, where, at this hour, his wife had always welcomed us back to a bright fire and a cup of tea. The room faced the west, and held a clear light of its own after the rest of the house had grown dark. I remembered how young she had looked in this pale gold light, which irradiated her eyes and hair, or silhouetted her girlish outline as she passed before the windows. Of all the rooms the library was most peculiarly hers; and here I felt that her nearness might take visible shape. Then, all in a moment, as Grancy opened the door, the feeling vanished and a kind of resistance met me on the threshold. I looked about me. Was the room changed? Had some desecrating hand effaced the traces of her presence? No; here too the setting was undisturbed. My feet sank into the same deep-piled Daghestan; the bookshelves took the firelight on the same rows of rich subdued bindings, her armchair stood in its old place near the tea table; and from the opposite wall her face confronted me.

Her face—but *was* it hers? I moved nearer and stood looking up at the portrait. Grancy's glance had followed mine and I heard him move to my side.

"You see a change in it?" he said.

"What does it mean?" I asked.

"It means—that five years have passed."

"Over *her?*"

"Why not?—Look at me!" He pointed to his gray hair and furrowed temples. "What do you think kept *her* so young? It was happiness! But now—" he looked up at her with infinite tenderness. "I like her better so," he said. "It's what she would have wished."

"Have wished?"

"That we should grow old together. Do you think she would have wanted to be left behind?"

I stood speechless, my gaze traveling from his worn grief-beaten features to the painted face above. It was not furrowed like his; but a veil of years seemed to have descended on it. The bright hair had lost its elasticity, the cheek its clearness, the brow its light: the whole woman had waned.

Grancy laid his hand on my arm. "You don't like it?" he said sadly.

"Like it?—I've lost her!" I burst out.

"And I've found her," he answered.

"In *that?*" I cried with a reproachful gesture.

"Yes, in that." He swung round on me almost defiantly. "The other had become a sham, a lie! This is the way she would have looked—does look, I mean. Claydon ought to know, oughtn't he?"

I turned suddenly. "Did Claydon do this for you?"

Grancy nodded.

"Since your return?"

"Yes. I sent for him after I'd been back a week—" He turned away and gave a thrust to the smoldering fire. I followed, glad to leave the picture behind me. Grancy threw himself into a chair near the hearth, so that the light fell on his sensitive variable face. He leaned his head back, shading his eyes with his hand, and began to speak.

III

"You fellows knew enough of my early history to guess what my second marriage meant to me. I say guess, because no one could understand—really. I've always had a feminine streak in me, I suppose: the need of a pair of eyes that should see with me, of a pulse that should keep time with mine. Life is a big thing, of course; a magnificent spectacle; but I got so tired of looking at it alone! Still, it's always good to live, and I had plenty of happiness—of the evolved kind. What I'd never had a taste of was the simple inconscient sort that one breathes in like the air.

"Well—I met her. It was like finding the climate in which I was meant to live. You know what she was—how indefinitely she multiplied one's points of contact with life, how she lit up the caverns and bridged the abysses! Well, I swear to you (though I suppose the sense of all that was latent in me) that what I used to think of on my way home at the end of the day, was simply that when I opened this door she'd be sitting over there, with the lamplight falling in a particular way on one little curl in her neck. When Claydon painted her he caught just the look she used to lift to mine when I came in—I've wondered, sometimes, at his knowing how she looked when she and I were alone. How I rejoiced in that picture! I used to say to her, 'You're my prisoner now—I shall never lose you. If you grew tired of me and left me you'd leave your real self there on the wall!' It was always one of our jokes that she was going to grow tired of me.

"Three years of it—and then she died. It was so sudden that there was no change, no diminution. It was as if she had suddenly become fixed, immovable, like her own portrait: as if Time had ceased at its happiest hour, just as Claydon had thrown down his brush one day and said, 'I can't do better than that.'

"I went away, as you know, and stayed over there five years. I worked as hard as I knew how, and after the first black months a little light stole in on me. From thinking that she would have been interested in what I was doing I came to feel that she *was* interested—that she was there and that she knew. I'm not talking any psychical jargon—I'm simply trying to express the sense I had that an influence so full, so abounding as hers couldn't pass like a spring shower. We had so lived into each other's hearts and minds that the consciousness of what she would have thought and felt illuminated all I did. At first she used to come back shyly, tentatively, as though not sure of finding me; then she stayed longer and longer, till at last she became again the very air I breathed. There were bad moments, of course, when her nearness mocked me with the loss of the real woman; but gradually the distinction between the two was effaced and the mere thought of her grew warm as flesh and blood.

"Then I came home. I landed in the morning and came straight down here. The thought of seeing her portrait possessed me and my heart beat like a lover's as I opened the library door. It was in the afternoon and the room was full of light. It fell on her picture—the picture of a young and radiant woman. She smiled at me coldly across the distance that divided us. I had the feeling that she didn't even recognize me. And then I caught sight of myself in the mirror over there—a gray-haired broken man whom she had never known!

"For a week we two lived together—the strange woman and the strange man. I used to sit night after night and question her smiling face; but no answer ever came. What did she know of me, after all? We were irrevocably separated by the five years of life that lay between us. At times, as I sat here, I almost grew to hate her; for her presence had driven away my gentle ghost, the real wife who had wept, aged, struggled with me during those awful years. It was the worst loneliness I've ever known. Then, gradually, I began to notice a look of sadness in the picture's eyes; a look that seemed to say: 'Don't you see that *I* am lonely too?' And all at once it came over me how she would have hated to be left behind! I remembered her comparing life to a heavy book that could not be read with ease unless two people held it together; and I thought how impatiently her hand would have turned the pages that divided us! So the idea came to me: 'It's the picture that stands between us; the picture that is dead, and not my wife. To sit in this room is to keep watch beside a corpse.' As this feeling grew on me the portrait became like a beautiful mausoleum in which she had been buried alive: I could hear her beating against the painted walls and crying to me faintly for help.

"One day I found I couldn't stand it any longer and I sent for Claydon. He came down and I told him what I'd been through and what I wanted him to do. At first he refused point-blank to touch the picture. The next morning I went off for a long tramp, and when I came home I found him sitting here alone. He looked at me sharply for a moment and then he said: 'I've changed my mind; I'll do it.' I arranged one of the north rooms as a studio and he shut himself up there for a day; then he sent for me. The picture stood there as you see it now—it was as though she'd met me on the threshold and taken me in her arms! I tried to thank him, to tell him what it meant to me, but he cut me short.

" 'There's an up train at five, isn't there?' he asked. 'I'm booked for a dinner tonight. I shall just have time to make a bolt for the station and you can send my traps after me.' I haven't seen him since.

"I can guess what it cost him to lay hands on his masterpiece; but, after all, to him it was only a picture lost, to me it was my wife regained!"

IV

After that, for ten years or more, I watched the strange spectacle of a life of hopeful and productive effort based on the structure of a dream. There could be no doubt to those who saw Grancy during this period that he drew his strength and courage from the sense of his wife's mystic participation in his task. When I went back to see him a few months later I found the portrait had been removed from the library and placed in a small study upstairs, to which he had transferred his desk and a few books. He told me he always sat there when he was alone, keeping the library for his Sunday visitors. Those who missed the portrait of course made no comment on its absence, and the few who were in his secret respected it. Gradually all his old friends had gathered about him and our Sunday afternoons regained something of their former character; but Claydon never reappeared among us.

As I look back now I see that Grancy must have been failing from the time of his return home. His invincible spirit belied and disguised the signs of weakness that afterward asserted themselves in my remembrance of him. He seemed to have an inexhaustible fund of life to draw on, and more than one of us was a pensioner on his superfluity.

Nevertheless, when I came back one summer from my European holiday and heard that he had been at the point of death, I understood at once that we had believed him well only because he wished us to.

I hastened down to the country and found him midway in a slow convalescence. I felt then that he was lost to us and he read my thought at a glance.

"Ah," he said, "I'm an old man now and no mistake. I suppose we shall have to go half-speed after this; but we shan't need towing just yet!"

The plural pronoun struck me, and involuntarily I looked up at Mrs. Grancy's portrait. Line by line I saw my fear reflected in it. It was the face of a woman *who knows her husband is dying*. My heart stood still at the thought of what Claydon had done.

Grancy had followed my glance. "Yes, it's changed her," he said quietly. "For months, you know, it was touch and go with me—we had a long fight of it, and it was worse for her than for me." After a pause he added: "Claydon has been very kind; he's so busy nowadays that I seldom see him, but when I sent for him the other day he came down at once."

I was silent and we spoke no more of Grancy's illness; but when I took leave it seemed like shutting him in alone with his death warrant.

The next time I went down to see him he looked much better. It was a Sunday and he received me in the library, so that I did not see the portrait again. He continued to improve and toward spring we began to feel that, as he had said, he might yet travel a long way without being towed.

One evening, on returning to town after a visit which had confirmed my sense of reassurance, I found Claydon dining alone at the club. He asked me to join him and over the coffee our talk turned to his work.

"If you're not too busy," I said at length, "you ought to make time to go down to Grancy's again."

He looked up quickly. "Why?" he asked.

"Because he's quite well again," I returned with a touch of cruelty. "His wife's prognostications were mistaken."

Claydon stared at me a moment. "Oh, *she* knows," he affirmed with a smile that chilled me.

"You mean to leave the portrait as it is then?" I persisted.

He shrugged his shoulders. "He hasn't sent for me yet!"

A waiter came up with the cigars and Claydon rose and joined another group.

It was just a fortnight later that Grancy's housekeeper telegraphed for me. She met me at the station with the news that he had been "taken bad" and that the doctors were with him. I had to wait for some time in the deserted library before the medical men appeared. They had the baffled manner of empirics who have been superseded by the Great Healer; and I lingered only long enough to hear that Grancy was not suffering and that my presence could do him no harm.

I found him seated in his armchair in the little study. He held out his hand with a smile.

"You see she was right after all," he said.

"She?" I repeated, perplexed for the moment.

"My wife." He indicated the picture. "Of course I knew she had no hope from the first. I saw that"—he lowered his voice—"after Claydon had been here. But I wouldn't believe it at first!"

I caught his hands in mine. "For God's sake don't believe it now!" I adjured him.

He shook his head gently. "It's too late," he said. "I might have known that she knew."

"But, Grancy, listen to me," I began; and then I stopped. What could I say that would convince him? There was no common ground of argument on which we could meet; and after all it would be easier for him to die feeling that she *had* known. Strangely enough, I saw that Claydon had missed his mark.

V

Grancy's will named me as one of his executors; and my associate, having other duties on his hands, begged me to assume the task of carrying out our friend's wishes. This placed me under the necessity of informing Claydon that the portrait of Mrs. Grancy had been bequeathed to him; and he replied by the next post that he would send for the picture at once. I was staying in the deserted house when the portrait was taken away; and as the door closed on it I felt that Grancy's presence had vanished too. Was it his turn to follow her now, and could one ghost haunt another?

After that, for a year or two, I heard nothing more of the picture, and though I met Claydon from time to time we had little to say to each other. I had no definable grievance against the man and I tried to remember that he had done a fine thing in sacrificing his best picture to a friend; but my resentment had all the tenacity of unreason.

One day, however, a lady whose portrait he had just finished begged me to go with her to see it. To refuse was impossible, and I went with the less reluctance that I knew I was not the only friend she had invited. The others were all grouped around the easel when I entered, and after contributing my share to the chorus of approval I turned away and began to stroll about the studio. Claydon was something of a collector and his things were generally worth looking at. The studio was a long tapestried room with a curtained archway at one end. The curtains were looped back, showing a smaller apartment, with books and flowers and a few fine bits of bronze and porcelain. The tea table standing in this inner room proclaimed that it was open to inspection, and I wandered in. A *bleu poudré* vase first attracted me; then I turned to examine a slender bronze Ganymede, and in so doing found myself face to face with Mrs. Grancy's portrait. I stared up at her blankly and she smiled back at me in all the recovered radiance of youth. The artist had effaced every trace of his later touches and the original picture had reappeared. It throned alone on the paneled wall, asserting a brilliant supremacy over its carefully chosen surroundings. I felt in an instant that the whole room was tributary to it: that Claydon had heaped his treasures at the feet of the woman he loved. Yes—it was the woman he had loved and not the picture; and my instinctive resentment was explained.

Suddenly I felt a hand on my shoulder.

"Ah, how could you?" I cried, turning on him.

"How could I?" he retorted. "How could I *not?* Doesn't she belong to me now?"

I moved away impatiently.

"Wait a moment," he said with a detaining gesture. "The others have gone and I want to say a word to you. Oh, I know what you've thought of me—I can guess! You think I killed Grancy, I suppose?"

I was startled by his sudden vehemence. "I think you tried to do a cruel thing," I said.

"Ah—what a little way you others see into life!" he murmured. "Sit down a moment—here, where we can look at her—and I'll tell you."

He threw himself on the ottoman beside me and sat gazing up at the picture, with his hands clasped about his knee.

"Pygmalion," he began slowly, "turned his statue into a real woman; *I* turned my real woman into a picture. Small compensation, you think—but you don't know how much of a woman belongs to you after you've painted her! Well, I made the best of it, at any rate—I gave her the best I had in me; and she gave me in return what such a woman gives by merely being. And after all she rewarded me enough by making me paint as I shall never paint again! There was one side of her, though, that was mine alone, and that was her beauty; for no one else understood it. To Grancy even it was the mere expression of herself—what language is to thought. Even when he saw the picture he didn't guess my secret—he was so sure she was all his! As though a man should think he owned the moon because it was reflected in the pool at his door.

"Well—when he came home and sent for me to change the picture it was like asking me to commit murder. He wanted me to make an old woman of her—of her who been so divinely, unchangeably young! As if any man who really loved a woman would ask her to sacrifice her youth and beauty for his sake! At first I told him I couldn't do it—but afterward, when he left me alone with the picture, something queer happened. I suppose it was because I was always so confoundedly fond of Grancy that it went against me to refuse what he asked. Anyhow, as I sat looking up at her, she seemed to say, 'I'm not yours but his, and I want you to make me what he wishes.' And so I did it. I could have cut my hand off when the work was done—I dare say he told you I never would go back and look at it. He thought I was too busy—he never understood.

"Well—and then last year he sent for me again—you remember. It was after his illness, and he told me he'd grown twenty years older and that he wanted her to grow older too—he didn't want her to be left behind. The doctors all thought he was going to get well at that time, and he thought so too; and so did I when I first looked at him. But when I turned to the picture—ah, now I don't ask you to believe me; but I swear it was *her* face that told me he was dying, and that she wanted him to know it! She had a message for him and she made me deliver it."

He rose abruptly and walked toward the portrait; then he sat down beside me again.

"Cruel! Yes, it seemed so to me at first; and this time, if I resisted, it was for *his* sake and not for mine. But all the while I felt her eyes drawing me, and gradually she made me understand. If she'd been there in the flesh (she seemed to say) wouldn't she have seen before any of us that he was dying? Wouldn't he have read the news first in her face? And wouldn't it be horrible if now he should discover it instead in strange eyes?— Well—that was what she wanted of me and I did it—I kept them together to the last!" He looked up at the picture again. "But now she belongs to me," he repeated. . . .

Afterword

An image of one's self, a real, lifelike image that is so like one's self that it cannot be mistaken, has been a rare thing through much of history. A sheet of water will reflect a face, but it is usually in motion and distorts the reflection. Polished metal will reflect, but some metals will quickly tarnish and lose the power of reflection or, if immune from tarnishing, are usually too expensive to be owned by any but the very rich.

True mirrors (a mercury film on glass) were so unusual when they came along, that there was almost something magical about them. (Remember the mirror in Snow White?) And they were so expensive and rare that breaking one meant seven years bad luck while you tried to scrape the money together to replace it.

Images, when accurate, were therefore representative of something weird. Whether painted or photographed, the existence of an image that is unmistakably you is equivalent to the existence of an actual piece of you.

Primitive tribes fear being photographed, for it is as though some of their life-force is abstracted from them and frozen on paper. If someone else owns your photograph, he owns part of you. (Before images came to exist, such power resided in names. That is why we are reluctant to use God's name, and speak of "the Lord" or "the Almighty" instead.)

The power of a painting to take on a life of its own, or to compete with the real person for the attributes of life, was most memorably used in Oscar Wilde's "The Portrait of Dorian Gray," but Edith Wharton does her bit in "The Moving Finger."—I.A.

Additional Reading

Algernon Blackwood, "The Wendigo," in *Best Ghost Stories of Algernon Blackwood,* E. F. Bleiler, ed. (New York: Dover Publications, 1973).

Mary Wilkins Freeman, "Luella Miller," in *Vamps,* Martin H. Greenberg and Charles G. Waugh, eds. (New York: DAW Books, Inc., 1987).

Richard Marsh, "Strange Occurrences in Canterstone Jail," in *Amusement Only* (London: Hurst and Blackett, 1901).

Richard Matheson, "The Likeness of Julie," in *Shock II* (New York: Dell Books, 1984).

Mack Reynolds, "Optical Illusion," in *Young Monsters,* Isaac Asimov, Martin H. Greenberg, and Charles G. Waugh, eds. (New York: Harper & Row, Publishers, 1985).

Acknowledgments

"The Occult," by Isaac Asimov. © 1989 by Nightfall, Inc.

"The Girl Who Found Things," by Henry Slesar. © 1973 by H.S.D. Publications. Reprinted by permission of the author.

"Through a Glass, Darkly," by Helen McCloy. © 1948 by Helen McCloy; renewed © 1976 by Helen McCloy. Reprinted by permission of Richard Curtis Associates, Inc.

"Dumb Supper," by Kris Neville. © 1950 by Fantasy House, Inc.; renewed © 1978; reprinted by permission of the Agent, Forrest J. Ackerman, 2495 Glendower Ave., Hollywood, Calif. 90027, on behalf of the author's widow, Mrs. Lil Neville.

"The Dead Man's Hand," by Manly Wade Wellman. © 1944 by Weird Tales, Inc. for *Weird Tales,* November 1944. Reprinted by permission of Karl Edward Wagner, Literary Executor for Manly Wade Wellman.

"The Scythe," by Ray Bradbury. © 1943 by Weird Tales, Inc.; renewed © 1970 by Ray Bradbury. Reprinted by permission of Don Congdon Associates, Inc.

"Do You Know Dave Wenzel?" by Fritz Leiber. © 1974 by Fritz Leiber. Reprinted by permission of Richard Curtis Associates, Inc.

"Speak to Me of Death," by Cornell Woolrich. © 1937 by Cornell Woolrich; renewed © 1965. Reprinted by permission of the agents for the author's estate, the Scott Meredith Literary Agency, Inc., 845 Third Avenue, New York, N.Y. 10022.

"The Woman Who Thought She Could Read," by Avram Davidson. © 1958 by Mercury Press, Inc.; renewed © 1986 by Avram Davidson. From *The Magazine of Fantasy and Science Fiction,* January 1959. Reprinted by permission of the author and his agent, Richard D. Grant.

"Tryst in Time," by C. L. Moore. © 1936 by Street & Smith Publications, Inc.; renewed © 1964 by C. L. Moore. Reprinted by permission of Don Congdon Associates, Inc.

"Miss Esperson," by August Derleth. © 1962 by August Derleth. Reprinted by permission of the agents for the author's estate, the Scott Meredith

Literary Agency, Inc., 845 Third Avenue, New York, N.Y. 10022.
"Peeping Tom," by Judith Merril. © 1954; renewed © 1973 by Judith Merril; reprinted by permission of the author and the author's agent, Virginia Kidd.